THEY ONLY COME OUT AT NIGHT

F. M. Kearney

They Only Come Out at Night

By F. M. Kearney

Copyright @ 2013 by F. M. Kearney

Starlite Press

New York, NY

ISBN 13: 978-0-9888418-1-9

Printed in the United States of America

Cover art: Manuel Guzman
www.LolosArt.com

Dedicated to my lovely wife,
Marian

CHAPTER 1

November 30, 1996 – 10:14 p.m. Saturday Evening

Janet watched with great curiosity as a convoy of six or seven waiters and waitresses snaked their way through the maze of tables in the restaurant. The head waiter, the one leading the pack, carried a large, ornately decorated silver dessert tray. It was oval-shaped and covered with a highly polished dome lid that reflected the brilliance of the Waterford crystal chandeliers adorning the hand-carved plaster ceiling. Atop the dome was a similarly decorated handle. It was the largest tray of its kind she had ever seen. Actually, she had never *really* seen one in person. It was the kind of tray she usually saw on TV or in a movie about the super rich – the kind of tray that's ceremoniously ushered into the room, by a white-gloved, tuxedo-clad butler.

She continued to watch as the tray and its accompanying entourage seemed to be cutting a path straight toward her and her husband Matthew's table.

"They're not coming over *here*, are they?" she asked. "Please, tell me this isn't for us."

Matthew just looked at her and smiled.

"Matt, honey, I'm stuffed. I really couldn't eat another thing. I didn't even know you ordered dessert."

"I think you'll be able to find room for one more thing."

"One more thing!? You can't be serious! I feel like I just had a seven course meal. I'm telling you, I can't even move."

The group was only a few feet away from their table, and attracting the attention of almost every patron in the large room. It was now clearly obvious that they were headed for their table.

1

"Matt… sweetie, please… send it back. I'm really not hungry."

"But I ordered it just for you. Won't you try just a little of it?"

"Look at the size of that tray! What the heck did you order… a whole cake?"

"I really think you'll be able to find room for one more thing."

"But… I---"

The group finally reached their table and completely encircled it, as if rehearsed. A couple of the waitresses moved aside several plates and glasses from the center of the table, and the head waiter placed the tray in the newly cleared spot.

Realizing she wasn't going to be able to change her husband's mind, Janet decided to plead her case directly to the group.

"Look, I'm really sorry… I know you all must have gone through a lot of trouble, but I really don't want any dessert. Could you please just wrap up whatever this is in a doggie bag and---"

Before she could finish, the headwaiter lifted the top and revealed a stunning silver necklace. It glistened with even more brilliance than the tray. Janet recognized it immediately as an eighteen-karat gold Paloma Picasso Loving Heart sterling silver necklace. It was exquisitely detailed and finely crafted with tiny linked silver hearts, interspersed at every fourth link with a gold heart. Although she definitely had her fair share of fine jewelry, she had dreamed of owning that particular necklace for years. But, not being the type of wife to nag her husband into buying it for her, she had only vaguely hinted from time to time about her latent desire. Unfortunately, when it came to hints, Matthew wasn't exactly quick in picking up on them. She certainly didn't hold out much hope that he would detect her little clues. Also, she really didn't want him spending so much money on her anyway. She knew the necklace retailed for almost $4,000 – a luxury that was simply out of reach on his auto mechanic's salary. Today, however, he more than made up for all those years of missed hints. As it turned out, he didn't miss

2

anything at all. Apparently, he was just saving up his money to be able to surprise her someday... a day that had finally arrived.

She sat motionlessly – her gaze transfixed upon the magnificent piece of jewelry before her – totally unaware of everything going on around her.

She was suddenly roused out of her stupor when Matthew and the assembled staff shouted out in unison, "HAPPY ANNIVERSARY!"

As if on cue, the entire room, patrons and staff alike, erupted into thunderous applause.

"Oh... my God, honey... it's so beautiful!" she choked, with tears welling up in her eyes.

"You see, I told you you'd find room for one more thing. I think I see a spot right there around your neck."

Matthew and Janet Manning were in the final stages of their 23rd wedding anniversary celebration. Matthew, an incurable romantic by nature, had planned a day filled with many wonderful surprises. The first one was delivered early that morning to their Co-Op City apartment in the Bronx, in the form of 30 long stem roses. The note attached simply read: *To My Love... My Life... My Wife. Thank You for a Wonderful 23 Years.*

Everyone had always considered them to be the perfect couple. At 41, Janet could have easily passed for a woman 10 years her junior. Born and raised in the city, she was a statuesque, African-American woman with thick, luscious dark brown hair that fell just below her shoulders. Her impeccable caramel-colored complexion, and naturally slender eyebrows, gave her an exotic appearance – somewhat resembling a celebrity. Despite the fact she already had one child, and was five months pregnant with her second, she was still capable of turning many heads. On more than one occasion – especially when wearing a pair of her form fitting red stretch jeans she was even the cause of a couple of near traffic accidents. Although Matthew loved his wife's sexy, curvaceous figure, he was quite the jealous type, and wasn't always thrilled with her frequent choice of slightly revealing attire.

Unfortunately, when it came to age, he wasn't as blessed as his wife. Also African-American, and approximately the same complexion as Janet, he was a handsome man with a powerful physique and rugged features in an imposing 6'2" frame. When he started growing his goatee, everyone told him it made him look very distinguished. Unfortunately, it did little to mask his 48 years of age. Actually, aging was one of his biggest fears… specifically, aging at a faster rate than Janet. He often kidded her about having some sort of "Dick Clark" gene – allowing her to maintain her youthful appearance far longer than most other women her age.

"When we go out, people are going to think I'm your father," he would half jokingly say to her.

In fact, for most of his life, he was cursed with looking much older than he actually was. He attributed it to the fact that much of his youth was spent overseas, witnessing the horrors and atrocities of war. As a child, he grew up and lived a carefree – almost idyllic – life in Beaufort, South Carolina, but at 18, he enlisted in the army, and spent the next five years serving active duty in Vietnam. A decorated soldier, he received a Battlefield Commission, and was awarded two Bronze Stars and a Purple Heart. By the end of his final tour, he had achieved the rank of 2nd Lieutenant. Despite the massive negative public opinion of the war, he never wavered in his belief that their cause was just. Although, at times, he was forced to do things he wasn't exactly proud of, overall, he considered it a very positive experience. He was always quick to clarify that it wasn't the *war* he liked, but more so, the strong bonds and friendships he developed. But there was something else he liked even more. Ironically, it was the one thing that most people would probably say they liked *least* about the military – its strict, regimented lifestyle. He was always a very organized and detail-oriented individual. Also, atypical of most teenagers, he had a deep respect for authority. The military practically made him feel at home. It got even better when he became an officer. He was downright fascinated with the respect and obedience he received from the men under his command – a type of discipline which he felt was sorely lacking in the civilian world.

In 1971, he received an honorable discharge. He found it a little difficult readjusting to a relatively lax and carefree lifestyle. However, there was one old military habit he happily carried over into his new civilian life. The military intensified his fastidiousness. He became extremely meticulous – some would even say anal – when it came to making any type of plan. Whether he was going across town to do a little shopping, or leaving town on a big trip, he would always write out an in-depth schedule – complete with estimated arrival and departure times – which he adhered to religiously. His friends thought he was nuts to put so much time and energy into some of the minutest aspects of his life, but he felt it was the perfect way to ease back into "normal" society.

Another great transitional aid was the Veterans' Action Association – an organization that not only provided a number of opportunities and benefits for vets of past wars, but also a place where they could get together and socialize amongst others with shared experiences. The VAA became like a second home to him. He attended regular meetings on a weekly basis for many years.

Despite the age-factor, Matthew and Janet still made a handsome couple. Their looks complimented each other so well, people often asked if they were professional models. Janet had actually considered modeling at one point in her life. But the cut-throat nature of the business – not to mention the extremely short-lived careers and Madison Avenue's penchant for women with flat, featureless bodies resembling 13-year-old boys – steered her into the more stable, although less lucrative field of accounting.

Throughout their relationship, Matthew had always considered "30" to be their lucky number. They met on November 30, 1972 – one year after his final tour in Vietnam – while waiting for the Q30 bus on Utopia Parkway in Queens. Their initial conversation revealed not only a mutual attraction to each other, but also an uncanny number of coincidences involving this number. Both were born on a Friday – he on January 30, 1948, and she on September 30, 1955. At the time they met, he was 24 and living on his own on the second floor of a modest 4-storey walk-up on 30th Street on the West side of Manhattan. She was only 17 and still living at home with her parents in a two-bedroom apartment on 30th Avenue in Astoria, Queens. They later discovered that even the digits in their phone numbers equaled "30" when added together.

This was more than enough to convince an extremely superstitious person like Matthew that they were soul mates, and destined to be together. Janet, on the other hand, often scoffed at his beliefs. It was one thing to be a *little* superstitious, but she felt he took it to an entirely different level – bordering on obsession. She tended to see things more in "black and white." When Matthew would admonish her for doing things that would *supposedly* bring about bad luck, she would often resort to simple scientific logic.

"What connection could there possibly be between something as innocent as opening up an umbrella indoors, and bad luck?" she'd usually ask.

By that logic, she reasoned, umbrella factories should be on the top of the list as one of the most dangerous places to work. She also believed that superstitions were far too vague to be taken seriously. She would often ask him his definition of "bad luck." She figured that without specific guidelines, a superstitious person could claim just about anything from losing a pen to losing a limb – and everything in between – as "bad luck." That being the case, it would be very easy for a diehard believer to single out any one of the many common occurrences that take place *every day* in *everyone's* life as "proof" of their ridiculous beliefs.

They soon fell deeply in love and set their wedding date for November 30, 1973 – exactly one year after the date they met. This didn't sit well with either set of their parents. Both very old-school, they questioned their hasty decision to wed after such a "brief" courtship. Additionally, since the date fell on a Friday, it was going to be difficult for most people attending.

Matthew, nevertheless, steadfastly maintained that there was definitely something to all of these numerical coincidences – eventually referring to them as *The Lucky Thirty* – and insisted on keeping the date set for the 30th.

They moved into a Co-Op City high-rise apartment in The Bronx, and enjoyed a married life that was about as close to a fairy tale as one could get. Janet kept anticipating him to "change" – to turn into the quintessential jerk many of her friends' husbands eventually did. But it never happened. Years into their marriage, he remained as loving and devoted to her as the day they met. Ironically, it was this nurturing side of him that caused the rare conflicts in their relationship. For some reason, he always felt obliged to champion the cause of the underdog. He often found it difficult to simply walk by a vagrant on the street without tossing a few coins (or bills) their way – whether they asked for it or not. Sometimes, much to Janet's chagrin, he would even stop and engage them in conversation.

"Why do you have to do that!?" she'd angrily ask. "Can't you just give 'em the money and go!?"

All he would tell her was that it takes so little to make such a big difference in their lives. Over time, he befriended many of the disadvantaged in their neighborhood. Once, he even went so far as to invite one of them home for Thanksgiving dinner – a decision which sparked one of the biggest fights they ever had. Eventually, however, she came to accept, and even admire, this aspect of his personality. She knew he had a good heart, and was proud to be married to such a selfless humanitarian.

Throughout their marriage, *The Lucky Thirty* continued to show up in various ways. Although Janet never considered it anything more than a bunch of weird coincidences, she started having second thoughts after the birth of their first child, Melissa, on May 30, 1978. As Matthew fully expected, *The Lucky Thirty* turned out to be just as prolific in her life as it had been in theirs.

As far as the Manning's were concerned, this anniversary couldn't have fallen on a better day. Since it was a Saturday, they both had the day off and – for the first time in months – could plan an entire day to spend together. It was also the first real night out Janet had since learning of her unexpected, but welcomed, second pregnancy. At 41, she was a little nervous about all the possible medical problems she might encounter. Fortunately, her doctor assured her that both she and little Susan – as they affectionately named her – were in perfect health.

Even though Matthew thought their diaper changing days were long over, he was also looking forward to the birth with much anticipation. Despite their advancing years, and the obvious concerns as to whether or not either of them would be physically able to keep up with a toddler; he had an even bigger concern on his mind… *The Lucky Thirty*. Aside from being born healthy, his biggest hope was for Susan to be born on March 30, 1997.

After the floral delivery that morning, Matthew treated his wife to a romantic day and night on the town. This included a romantic horse-drawn carriage ride, and a Broadway show, culminating with a limo ride to dinner at Tavern On The Green in Central Park – one of the most elegant restaurants in the city. The necklace, of course, was the highlight of the entire day.

Having only given Matthew a watch for his anniversary gift – albeit, a $150 Citizen watch that he proudly wore throughout the day – Janet felt a little embarrassed at the lavishness of his gifts, and the obvious time and effort it must have taken to plan such a wonderful day. He had always gone a little overboard when it came to gift giving. After every surprise, he could see her getting more and more uncomfortable. He constantly assured her that she had absolutely nothing to feel bad about. Still, the sight of the gleaming, multi-thousand dollar Paloma Picasso necklace on the dessert tray was making it very hard for her to believe that.

More or less a private and somewhat shy person; Janet was never particularly fond of the spotlight. She was overjoyed, but also a little embarrassed after the restaurant staff's surprise – and quite public – anniversary salutation. The fact that they were the only black couple in the room made her feel even more on display. Nevertheless, she appreciated every minute of it, and aside from their wedding day, never felt more in love with her husband than at that moment.

Matthew was a little nervous as well. He fumbled for a few seconds as he stood behind her and placed the necklace around her neck. When he finally got the clasp fastened, he bent down and gave her a passionate kiss on the lips. Once again, everyone in the room burst into a second round of applause.

"I can't believe you did all this," gushed Janet, with tears of joy trickling down her face.

"Did you have a good time today?" he asked.

"Are you kidding? I think this is the best anniversary we've ever had. Every year I wonder how you're going to top yourself, and you never cease to amaze me."

After a round of congratulatory handshakes, the restaurant staff returned to their regular duties, but many of the patrons were still smiling and looking in their direction. In some strange way, he kind of felt obligated to do something more. But at the same time, he was hoping their attention would eventually shift to other matters. After all, what was once a public presentation was now a private moment between himself and his wife.

"If you think this year was good, just wait 'till you see what I have planned for our *30th*!"

"What!? You're planning that *already*? What makes you think we'll even still be together seven years from now?" she joked.

"Well, then… I guess I'll just have to celebrate it with one of my mistresses."

They both laughed.

"You know, I kind of feel guilty about not bringing Melissa with us today," she remarked.

"Jan, this is supposed to be *our* day, not a *family* day. Besides, I hardly think an 18-year-old teenage girl is going to want to spend an entire Saturday shackled to her parents."

"I know, but still… I think she would have enjoyed it."

Janet's relationship with her daughter was exceptional. Usually, daughters tend to bond more with their fathers, but that wasn't the case with Melissa. Although she would always contend she loved both her parents equally, it was clear there was a special connection between her and her mother. People often said they acted more like sisters, than like mother and daughter. Melissa felt the connection was even deeper – almost like that of twins. It wasn't uncommon for them to finish each other's sentences; or even to feel the pain the other was experiencing.

Matthew also felt a strong bond with Melissa. She, on the other hand, sometimes perceived it as a totalitarian rule over her life. He had always been an over-protective father, but as soon as she hit puberty, and started to develop – not just a womanly body, but also an interest in boys – his over-protectiveness increased tenfold, and was the cause of many heated arguments. He saw her as his little baby girl – regardless of how old she got – and vowed to always protect her… no matter what.

"Do you think today was a little too much excitement for little Suzie?" Matthew asked, as he patted her stomach.

"Oh, no… I'm sure she had fun, too. I could feel her happily dancing around all day. But, are you *sure* this dress looks O.K. on me?"

"You look fine, honey… you can barely see the bulge."

"You're just saying that because you're my husband, and required by law to shower me with compliments."

"Sweetie, you're one of the best-looking women in the room."

Ever since she started showing, she was a little self-conscious about her looks. Looking pregnant is fine when you're in your twenties, she reasoned, but as an older woman, she wasn't sure if she was going to look ravishing… or simply ridiculous. She was wearing a silk chiffon ruffled top and skirt set in a gentle shade of aqua. The top was adorned with soft, pastel floral prints, designed in a flattering wrap-style to show a tasteful amount of cleavage. It wasn't exactly maternity-wear, but she knew this was probably going to be her last chance to show off her still voluptuous figure before it was transformed by motherhood.

Throughout the remainder of the evening, Janet was like a child on Christmas morning. Hardly a minute went by when she wasn't fiddling with her necklace. In fact, since her pregnancy, this was the first thing she touched more often than her stomach.

"How about this, is it straight now?" she asked Matthew, as she adjusted it to hang just above her cleavage.

"That looks perfect. It really compliments your outfit."

Although she trusted her husband's opinion, she just had to see for herself. She grabbed her purse and hastily rummaged through it for her compact. When she opened it and saw her reflection, she let out an audible gasp. "Beautiful" could not even describe the image she saw staring back at her in the mirror. The necklace shined with such intensity, it appeared to be glowing.

"I'm gorgeous!" she said aloud – not realizing just *how* loud until a few nearby patrons looked at her and smiled.

Too exuberant to be embarrassed, she continued her self-praise.

"I always knew this was a beautiful piece, but I had no idea how *good* it would look on me."

"You deserve it sweetie. I'm just sorry it took 23 years."

"Oh, don't worry about that, this is one helleva expensive piece. Just how much *did* you spend on it anyway?"

"Now, now… you know it's rude to ask the price of a gift."

"Yeah, I know, but can we really afford it? I mean, on top of everything else you did today, not to mention the money we'll need when the baby's born. It's just so much!"

"Sweetheart, don't worry about it. The look in your eyes made it worth every penny."

"I'd still like to know just how *many* pennies you spent."

"Let's just say, I made some salesman very happy."

"I'll bet you did. Now, I'm really glad I had you send the limo away."

Earlier, she had convinced Matthew not to have the limo wait until they finished dinner. She saw no reason why he should have to continue to pay an hourly rate for an idling limo.

"So how do you propose we get home? Should we take a cab?" he asked

"I don't know, I was kinda thinking we could take the subway."

"The *subway*!? It'll take forever to get up to the Bronx from here by subway! Besides, don't you think we're a little overdressed?"

11

"It'll be fun! It's been years since we've been on the subway together."

They had both become accustomed, and perhaps even a little spoiled, by the express bus service that shuttled them back and forth between Co-Op City, and their respective jobs in Midtown Manhattan.

"Jan, sweetie, there's a reason why we haven't taken the subway in so long. In fact, I can think of several right now."

"Name one."

"For starters, it hasn't been the safest mode of transportation lately. Every night, you hear something on the news about another assault or mugging. Also, like I said, we're not exactly dressed for the subway… we'd stand out like sore thumbs."

"Oh, come on honey, it'll be like it was when we first started dating. Remember all those romantic, late-night rides home on the "N" train?"

"Yeah, but, things are different now, Jan. There's a lot of craziness going on down there."

"Look, it's not even eleven o'clock yet. I promise I'll protect you from all the nasty little boogie men."

After a few more minutes of futile protesting, he finally relented. It was against his better judgment, but deep down, he too, thought it might be kind of romantic. Even though it could never match the comfort of an express bus, it would probably bring back a lot of fond memories of days gone by. After all, what better time to reminisce, than on your anniversary?

He helped her with her coat when they were ready to leave. She deliberately left it open so everyone could see her exquisite necklace. The path to the exit was a long, meandering trek through a maze of tables. Along the way, they were met with admiring glances from women and congratulatory, outstretched hands of men. Much like the earlier entourage of restaurant staffers, their slow progression through the room began to attract the attention of other patrons. What began as a smattering of individual claps, gradually blossomed into another roaring round of applause, followed by a standing ovation. This puzzled many of the newly-arrived patrons who missed the initial celebration. As the couple continued to make their way toward the exit, they could overhear a barrage of questions being asked around the room.

"Who are they?"

"Are they famous?"

"What show are they on?"

Janet was used to looking like a celebrity, but this was the first time she actually *felt* like one. She finally stopped obsessing about her slightly bulging belly. The applause was just the confirmation she needed to allay her concerns about her figure. Of course, they weren't applauding her figure; they were applauding *them* as a couple. But, no matter... applause was applause. Not many people could say they'd ever received a standing ovation at any time in their lives. She always wondered what it was like for the stars on Oscar Night as they made their way down the red carpet. She figured this was as close as any average person would ever get to the jubilation of that experience, and she wanted to savor it. It was the perfect ending to the perfect day.

After a short cross-town bus ride through Central Park, they entered the 68th Street/Hunter College subway station on Lexington Avenue. They were going to take the uptown # 6 train to the last stop – running through the Upper East Side of Manhattan, then, into The Bronx to Pelham Bay Park. From there, they planned to catch a connecting bus to take them the rest of the way home.

It had been quite some time since Janet had been on the subway. Although the cars were newer, and virtually graffiti free, it still wasn't exactly what she had anticipated. She had envisioned a time of days gone by, a time of innocence and wonder. One of her favorite memories from the early days of their relationship involved Coney Island. The boredom of many long, hot summer days was always remedied at the famous Brooklyn amusement park. However, as far as she was concerned, the best – or at least, most memorable – part of the day, was often the ride home on the "F" train. Waiting on the platform of the elevated station – just down the block from the world-renowned, Nathan's Famous eatery – she recalled the irrepressible aroma of hot dogs and cotton candy. The mouth-watering scent would hang in the air – seemingly to taunt departing subway riders. Matthew would usually be loaded down with a couple of giant stuffed bears or elephants – the fruits of his efforts to win the top prize in a ring-toss or a precision water-gun game. If space permitted, they would place them on the seats next to them as though they were their kids. This cute little "family" drew many smiles, a few chuckles and even an occasional photo request. Long stretches of the trip would be spent in silence, but not an awkward silence. No words needed to be spoken as Matthew lovingly cradled her in his arms. The muffled rumbling and gentle swaying of the train would practically lull them to sleep as they gazed out the windows at the last vestiges of a fun-filled day. As the train neared the city, it was always a breathtaking sight to see downtown Brooklyn, and the majestic skyline of lower Manhattan bathed in the beautiful golden light of a late summer sunset. It always amazed them that such a spectacular sight could be seen while riding the New York City subway. Janet would try to capture a mental photograph of this scene before it was eventually blotted out as the train slowly descended into its more familiar, darkened subterranean world a few stops before entering Manhattan. The warm, natural golden sunlight would be instantly replaced by the harsh, artificial fluorescent glare of the car's interior lights. If there were any romantic thoughts of far-away, exotic places dancing in her head, they were shut off as abruptly as the sunlight. Although that exact moment of the day had been always somewhat of a letdown, overall, it still contributed to the wonderful subway riding memories she shared with Matthew.

Of course, this was how she remembered the subway. What it had actually become was totally different. From the moment they descended the stairs into the transportation labyrinth, she detected a very unpleasant change in the atmosphere. She was immediately accosted by the distinct stench of urine and extremely bad body odor. Although Matthew seemed unfazed by it, it was all she could do to keep from gagging.

After paying their fare, they went through the turnstiles, and descended another flight of stairs to reach the platform level.

Being a typical Saturday night, the station was quite crowded with couples on dates, groups of rowdy teenagers, people going to and from work, and even a few tourists. When the train finally arrived, it was even more crowded than the station. Janet and Matthew got on near the rear where it was somewhat less crowded, but even there it was standing room only and they had to push their way on. Many others weren't as lucky and were forced to wait on the platform for the next train. Despite temperatures hovering in the upper 30's outside, the crush of people in such a confined space made it uncomfortably warm within the car. When Janet opened her coat for relief, she inadvertently put her necklace on display. This drew considerable attention from everyone – the women looked upon her jewelry with envy, but the men seemed to be more attracted to her natural attributes.

They were finally able to get two seats together when the train reached 86th Street. By the time it reached the Bronx, the crowd had considerably thinned out even more. Janet started to feel a bit uneasy and attempted to discreetly hide her necklace under the lapel of her coat. The large crowd gave her a feeling of "safety in numbers." Indeed, a sense of camaraderie seemed to permeate throughout the car. But now, the once boisterous crowd was reduced to a handful of seedy-looking, randomly scattered about passengers. She and Matthew were sitting approximately in the center of the car. Directly across the aisle was a young, light-skinned man of either black or Spanish descent. Next to him was a middle-aged, Puerto Rican couple.

At the far end of the car were a couple of foreign-looking men in work clothes. They appeared to be some type of painters or contractors who had just gotten off work.

But, none of the remaining passengers made Janet as uncomfortable as the trio of men sitting at the far end of the car. They ranged in ages from their late teens to early twenties. All were African-American and wearing, pretty much, the "uniform of the streets" – "bubble" jackets and jeans about three or four sizes too big.

One wore a gray jacket and a do-rag under a black wool-knit cap that came to a peak at the top. He was tall with a medium-build, and boldly displayed a large, garish-looking gold medallion around his neck. It was supported by a thick gold chain and swayed conspicuously back and forth with his every move. His jeans were so baggy he had to keep one hand on them whenever he stood up to prevent them from falling completely off. Despite his best efforts just about everyone in the car, at one time or another, was "treated" to a glimpse of his blue and white boxers. On his feet, he wore a pair of partially laced black Nikes. His most noticeable feature was a hideous scar that ran from the corner of his mouth almost all the way up to his right ear.

Although somewhat shorter, his friend sitting next to him had a similar build and outfit. He wore a black jacket, and a pair of equally baggy jeans. On his feet, he wore an imposing-looking pair of heavy, steel-tipped, light brown Timberland boots – also laced only half way up. He had a chipped front tooth and sleepy eyes. His most unusual and extremely dated feature was his large Afro – complete with a plastic Afro pick sticking out the top.

The third member of the group looked the most menacing. He was about 300 lbs. and incredibly tall – easily towering over everyone else in the car, including Matthew. Janet placed him somewhere around 6'4" or 6'5". He had an unusual physique, seemingly composed of an equal amount of fat and muscle. Although he had a large stomach, it was apparent that he worked out considerably with weights. He too wore a black "bubble" jacket and slightly baggy jeans. They were probably intended to be much baggier than they were, but his immense girth filled them out to the point where they were almost form fitting. He wore a wool knit cap under a hooded, gray sweatshirt, and a several inch wide, two-finger rectangular gold ring on his right hand. Its surface was elaborately decorated, but basically flat, except for the slightly raised "DT" in the center. The edges were sharply beveled. The piece was so large it almost completely obscured the entire upper portion of his fingers.

Janet had felt a little uneasy ever since the trio entered the car somewhere in uptown Manhattan. At that time, it had been very crowded, and both she and Matthew were still standing in the aisle. As the group passed by, the largest one brushed against her. She felt what seemed like his hand deliberately cupping her behind. When she looked back, he was totally engrossed in conversation with his buddies, and seemed completely oblivious to her. She purposely didn't say anything to Matthew because she didn't want him to make a scene, or worse, get in a fight. He had always had somewhat of a short fuse whenever he saw (or thought he saw) men staring at her a little too long. If any were so bold as to actually make a comment, he was ready to fight. Even though he was a large man and could easily take care of himself, in this particular case, it would have been three against one, and she knew he wouldn't have stood much of a chance. Besides, considering the thickness of her coat, she wasn't 100% positive that what she felt was his hand at all, or if it was even done deliberately. Frankly, it would have been very difficult, if not impossible, for a man of that size to maneuver through a crowded subway car and *not* touch anyone.

All through Manhattan the train traveled swiftly and smoothly. For some reason, once it entered The Bronx, it began to move noticeably slower. At Cypress Ave., just three stops into the borough, it sat in the station for several minutes.

"You see, this is just why I didn't want to take the train," complained Matthew.

"Oh, come on Matt… this is the first time we've stopped like this since we got on."

"Yeah, but we've got almost twenty more stops to go. At this rate, we'll be lucky to get home by daybreak."

"Don't be such a drama-queen," she laughed, while stroking her belly. "Let's not have little Suzie see this side of you. Anyway, by my count, we've only got *fifteen* more to go!"

"Oh, well… now, that makes me feel a *lot* better," he said, sarcastically.

The silence of the idle train was disrupted by a barely decipherable announcement from the conductor that suddenly boomed over the PA system:

"Ladies and gentlemen, we're being delayed. Please be patient."

"Oh, great! That's just great!" complained Matthew.

"I'm sure we'll be moving soon, honey."

After a few more minutes the train started moving, but once it reached the next stop, it again sat idle in the station for several minutes.

The conductor repeated his previous announcement.

Matthew was trying hard to contain his impatience, which was slowly brewing into anger. The last thing he wanted to do was to put a damper on an otherwise perfect day by getting upset over something so menial.

The delays seemed to lengthen as the train traveled from station to station. Also, more and more people were getting off at each stop. For some, it most likely *was* their stop; others may have decided that walking the rest of the way would have been infinitely quicker than remaining on the sluggish train. With over ten more stops still to go, *that*, unfortunately, wasn't an option for Janet and Matthew.

The situation was starting to take its toll on Janet as well. Her cheerful optimism was gradually giving way to the uneasiness she felt earlier. At the Longwood Ave. Station, just six stops into The Bronx, only a handful of people remained in the car. The two foreign-looking men at one end and the trio of young men on the other flanked her and Matthew. There was just something about that group that made her increasingly uncomfortable, but she wasn't sure why. She had been in her share of bad neighborhoods around the city. She had walked dangerous streets *alone* and rubbed shoulders with people who looked even more intimidating than the trio. Yet, for some reason, despite being with Matthew, these three gave her the creeps. Ever since they got on, she would often catch one or more of them staring at her from time to time. They weren't the usual stares of flirtation or even lust. There was something dark behind their looks that made her flesh crawl.

At the next stop, Hunts Point Ave., there was another delay, and the usual announcement was repeated yet again.

"Jan, this is ridiculous. Why don't we just get off here and try to get a cab?"

"It's almost midnight. Do you think we'll be able to find one at this hour?"

"I don't know, but anything's gotta be better than this."

Before she could answer him, the conductor came back on the PA in a much louder and more commanding voice.

"Passengers, this is your conductor speaking, may I have your attention, please? Due to a mechanical problem we've been having with the doors, this train is now out of service. I repeat… this train is out of service. Hunts Point Ave. will be the last stop on this train. No passengers please… all passengers off. Please wait on the platform for the next train. We apologize for this inconvenience, and we thank you for your cooperation."

Matthew was trying hard to make the best of the situation, even though he was now highly upset.

"Well, I guess that settles it," he said, "so much for *rapid* transportation."

"I'm sorry, I had no idea something like this would happen."

"Oh… it's not your fault. I suppose, up to this point, it *was* sort of nostalgic."

The conductor repeated his message, this time following it up by flashing the interior lights off and on several times.

"I guess they mean business," chuckled Janet.

As they stepped off the train and onto the platform, she was surprised at how well he was dealing with the situation.

"You know," she said, "I would have thought you'd be fuming by now."

"What's the point? I mean… you just have to learn to accept certain things when living in this city."

"I'm sorry I had you send the limo away. I just didn't want you to spend an arm and a leg for no reason."

"Oh, don't worry about that, sweetie. No one could have predicted this."

She looked into his eyes and smiled. It was one of those times when she felt really close to him. A time that brought back memories of how she felt when they first met and fell in love 24 years ago. She grabbed his arm with one hand, then, reached around his neck and pulled him near and kissed him with the other. It wasn't an overly passionate kiss, but just enough to make it clear the magic was still there.

"I couldn't have asked for a better husband," she whispered.

"I love you, too."

Not wanting to get *too* caught up in the moment, she quickly shifted gears and forced herself to deal with the more pressing matters at hand.

"Hey, we better give Melissa a call and let her know we're gonna be late," she said.

"Yeah, I guess we should. Did you bring your cell phone?"

"No, did you?"

"No, I didn't want anything interrupting us today."

"It doesn't matter; we'd never get a signal down here anyway."

"Let's just go upstairs and get a cab. We can call her from a pay phone on the street. I really don't feel like waiting around here for another train."

He checked his watch.

"It's already after twelve-thirty. There's no telling when the next train's coming at this time of night," he said.

"Alright, I guess you've suffered enough. Let's get you home."

As they prepared to leave, the crippled train closed its doors and pulled out of the station. The loud hum of its powerful motors gradually faded, leaving a surprisingly thick shroud of silence in the station. For the first time, they took a good look around at their surroundings. They were standing just past the center of the platform, closer to the rear. At the extreme rear was a staircase leading directly up to the street. Closer to them were two other staircases, facing back to back, which led upstairs to the station agent booth. It was a mid-sized station serviced by only one express track that separated the uptown and downtown platforms. At peak times of travel the station was used quite heavily, and was often very crowded. Even during off-peak hours, a handful of passengers would usually be present. At this particular time, since their train had just "dumped its load," there were even more passengers than normal. Most of them had already exited via one of the two center staircases. The rest were congregating at the front of the platform, apparently choosing to stick it out and wait for the next train. The two foreign-looking men in work clothes had gone up the rear stairway, leaving Matthew and Janet the only remaining passengers at the back of the platform.

Just before they were about to ascend the first staircase, Matthew slowed his stride.

"Hey, wait a minute... when we got off the train, I think I saw some pay phones up here," he said, pointing towards the front of the station. "Why don't we just call Melissa from here? I mean, who knows... we might have to walk for blocks before we find a working phone on the street. Since we're already here, we might as well try these to see if they work."

"Yeah, I guess so," she agreed, "let's give it a shot."

He led the way as they headed toward the front. The platform narrowed to just a few feet on either side of the staircases, forcing them to walk single-file. Before they could squeeze pass the second staircase, a large figure suddenly loomed in front of them, blocking their path.

In all the confusion, Janet had completely forgotten about the trio of young men that made her feel so uncomfortable just moments ago. Only now, it was just one... the largest one... the 300-lb. one. His immense girth completely blocked their path on the narrow section of the platform. The sudden appearance of such an imposing figure sent cold chills down her spine. Even though Matthew was standing in front, offering somewhat of a buffer, it wasn't enough to alleviate her mounting fear. She could feel every hair on her body standing on end. Her stomach felt as though she had just come to an abrupt stop in a rapidly rising elevator.

"Yo, you gots the time?" the man asked, as he slowly advanced toward them.

Matthew also recognized him as one of three men on the train earlier. Since Janet hadn't mentioned anything about how uncomfortable they made her feel – or even about the possible groping – he really hadn't paid much attention to them.

Janet clutched Matthew's arm with one hand, and held her stomach with the other.

"It's about ten to one," said Matthew, without even checking his watch.

"It's that late!? I don't believe you, lemme see yo watch," he demanded, pointing at Matthew's Citizen.

Janet tightly clutched his arm with both hands. Her fingernails were starting to dig into his flesh.

"Matt, let's go around the other way," she said nervously.

Now, clearly angry, Matthew challenged the man.

"What are you talkin' about? Get the hell outta our way!" he shouted, taking a step forward.

"Matt, please… let's just go back!" she pleaded, as she held him and prevented him from taking another step.

Reluctantly, Matthew relented, and began a slow retreat. He was never one to back down from a fight, but in this particular case, he figured it was probably the wisest decision. He just wanted to get home as quickly as possible, and didn't want to spoil their day by getting into an altercation with the man. The main reason he decided to back down was the sheer size of the man. Not that he feared his size, but only because it would have been very stupid and very dangerous to get into a physical confrontation on such a narrow platform with *anyone*, much less, a 300-lb. behemoth. He didn't want to risk tripping and falling to the tracks – possibly onto the 600 deadly volts of electricity coursing through the third rail.

As they turned around to go back to the first staircase, the sight of another man slowly walking along the edge of the platform in their direction startled Janet. At almost the same time, another man appeared on the opposite side of the staircase.

The trio was complete!

The couple was trapped within a small, twenty-foot area in between the back ends of the two staircases. Much of the area was effectively hidden from view from the rest of the platform, making it the perfect spot for an ambush. Realizing they were in a very bad spot, Matthew tried reasoning with the men.

"Look… guys… all we want to do is get upstairs and go home."

"This punk-ass bitch be tryin' to make nice now," said the shortest of the three with the larger Afro. "Before, he be like all big and bad!"

Janet maintained a vice-like grip onto her husband's arm. She could feel her legs beginning to tremble.

"Please… this is our anniversary… we don't want any trouble," she pleaded, haltingly. Her heart was pounding so hard; she thought it might be the beginning stages of a heart attack.

"There ain't gonna be no trouble, sweetheart, we just wanna talk to you," said the taller man wearing the gold medallion.

The trio closed in tighter around the couple – almost completely encircling them. The 300-lb. man was standing directly in front of them, blocking their path. The shorter man stood behind Janet, and the taller one was behind Matthew. Only a few feet of distance separated the hunters from their prey.

Flick!

Janet screamed.

Matthew whirled around and saw that the shorter man had just ejected a several inch long switchblade and was advancing towards Janet.

After pushing her to the side, he lunged at the man. But, before he could lay a hand on him, a white flash blinded him. A sharp pain shot through his head, causing his knees to buckle, sending him down to the ground. The 300-lb. man had sucker-punched him in the back of the head. The blow was delivered with such force; he was almost knocked unconscious. To make matters worse, the man had thrown the punch using the hand sporting the large, two-finger ring. Its sharp beveled edge sliced open an ugly, three-inch wide wound in the back of his head.

"Oh my God… MATTHEW!!" Janet shrieked.

Instinctively, she rushed to her husband's aid. Before she could reach him, she was stopped dead in her tracks. The taller man grabbed her by her hair, thrusting her sharply upward. The 300-pounder delivered a powerful slap across her face; producing a loud *"crack"* that resonated throughout the station. Since it was an open-hand blow, her face did not come into contact with the dangerous ring. The blow did; however, open up a cut on her lip. It was also strong enough to jar her loose from her other attacker's grip – leaving him holding nothing but a large clump of hair.

"Oh shit… the bitch be wearin' a wig!" laughed the shorter man; not realizing it was her own hair.

The blow sent her sprawling on her back to the ground on the other side of the platform. Her coat flung open, revealing her necklace.

"Yo, get dat chain, dog!" one of the attackers yelled.

Dazed and bleeding from the wounds on her lip and head, she tried to scramble to her feet and run for help.

She had only gotten a few feet before being stopped by an unseen, wire-like device around her neck. The 300-lb. man had grabbed her necklace from behind. Not content to simply stop her, he proceeded to use the necklace as a type of garrote to choke her. Grabbing both ends of the chain with his beefy hands, he pulled in opposite directions, driving the metal deeply into the soft flesh of her neck.

No longer able to scream, she started to gag and drool. As the metal was driven in deeper, it began to break the skin, gradually producing a ring of blood around her neck. This, combined with the blood from her other wounds, trickled down onto her chest and the ruffled lapels of her once elegant green chiffon top. He applied so much pressure that she was lifted off her feet a couple of inches.

Only a few feet away, but still unable to help his wife, Matthew desperately tried to regain his composure. The blow had left him with a mild concussion, but he never completely lost consciousness.

"Let… her… go!" he managed to utter in a raspy voice, as he staggered to his feet.

"Make sure he don't get back up!" the 300-lb. man commanded.

Before he had much of a chance to do anything, the other two men quickly set upon him – delivering a vicious assault of kicks and punches to his face, stomach and groin. Once again, he was knocked off his feet and sent face down onto the platform into a puddle of filthy water. As he lay there, he could feel a strange itching sensation all over his body. At the same time, he felt a warm, sticky liquid accumulating under his clothes. He looked down and noticed that the puddle he had fallen into was turning a dark shade of crimson. The shorter attacker had managed to inflict a series of stab wounds all over his body. Fortunately, his heavy coat rendered most of them superficial. Still, he had undergone a tremendous beating, and was left virtually paralyzed and helpless on the ground.

By this time, the sounds of the assault were starting to attract the attention of the people at the front of the platform, as well as those on the downtown side, directly across the way. Although bleeding and badly beaten, Matthew was aware of the growing crowd of onlookers slowly forming around them. He saw more and more heads peeking around the front staircase, trying to get a glimpse of what was happening. He also noticed the activity on the downtown platform. The once randomly scattered about individuals had now congealed into a tight ball of spectators.

What the hell are they doing! Why won't they help us! He wondered.

Whether it was a staircase or the short span separating the two platforms, everyone seemed intent on keeping a safety buffer between themselves and the scene of the attack. The only response to the couple's pleas for help was an occasional shout of *"HEY!"* or *"LEAVE THEM ALONE!"* But as far as anyone physically coming to their aid – they were completely on their own.

The man continued to apply pressure to Janet's neck. Her eyes began to roll to the back of her head, and she could feel herself slipping in and out of consciousness. Just when she was about to black-out, the pressure was suddenly released, and she fell to the ground in a heap. The necklace broke. Tiny gold and silver hearts came showering down around her. What was once a magnificent, multi-thousand dollar piece of jewelry was now reduced to little more than shiny confetti – loosely strewn all over the filthy platform.

With Matthew basically out of commission, all three attackers turned their attention to Janet.

"Damn! Look at all dis shit, yo!" the taller man said as he bent down to gather a handful of the glistening links.

"You think it be real, dog?" asked the shorter one.

"Probably… look how fine dis bitch be dressed."

Janet's coat had come undone in the fall, and hung loosely off her right shoulder. Dazed and disoriented, she frantically struggled to get to her feet. It was a difficult task because she didn't use her hands for support. One hand was pressed tightly against her throat. Not knowing how severe her neck wounds were, she was afraid to remove it for fear of bleeding to death. Her other hand firmly cupped her stomach. At this point, she really didn't care what happened to her. Her maternal instincts had kicked in and her only concern was to protect her baby.

Oh, God… please don't let anything happen to my baby… please God… PLEEEEASE! She prayed.

Her wobbly, jerky movements caused her coat to fall off her other shoulder. Although bloodstained, her silk chiffon top still looked elegant and completely out of place amongst the grimy surroundings.

"Where you think you going!?" the taller man yelled, as he grabbed her by the hair again and brutally yanked her to her feet.

"Please, stop… let me go… please!" she pleaded.

Matthew was still in no condition to do much of anything. Every time he heard his wife cry for help his body would somehow become infused with a sudden burst of untapped energy, bringing him halfway to his feet. But, each time he'd receive a savage punch or kick to the face or stomach – sending him back down to the ground thwarting his valiant efforts.

"MATTHEEEEW!!!" screamed Janet.

She had never seen him in such a vulnerable state, and was more concerned for his safety than her own.

"I'm sick and tired of hearin' yo' fuckin' mouth!" the 300-pounder said as he approached Janet.

Before she could scream again, he punched her in the face – this time, with a closed fist. The sharp edge of his two-finger ring sliced open an ugly, several inch long gash on the left side of her face – permanently disfiguring the flawless flesh just below her eye and above the corner of her mouth. He jammed his other hand in between her cleavage and ripped open her top – ejecting her right breast from her bra.

"Damn, yo… she gots some big-ass titties!" the shorter man exclaimed.

"Yeah, I'll bet she likes 'em sucked real hard, too… don't you, bitch?" said the taller one.

While still holding her hair with one hand, he savagely grabbed her exposed breast with the other.

Matthew felt emasculated. For the first time in his life he was literally powerless. Not only was he unable to help himself, but his wife… his best friend… his partner in life for the past 23 years, was being brutally violated right before his eyes – and there was nothing he could do to stop it. Worse yet, was the growing numbers of spectators, still standing idly by – at a safe distance – doing absolutely nothing.

What the fuck are those assholes doing!!??

He knew if the situation was reversed, and *he* was watching a savage assault take place, he sure as hell wouldn't be just watching for long. He would certainly do something… *anything* to intervene and help the helpless. With each passing moment, his anger intensified.

"MATTHEEEEW!!" Janet screamed, still trying to free herself from her attacker's grip.

The sight of his wife being publicly debased was more than he could stand. He searched through his pockets for a weapon – any weapon he could find. When his fingers ran across a ballpoint pen, he discretely pulled it out. Fighting through the pain and summoning every ounce of remaining strength, he was somehow energized with a tremendous surge of adrenaline. He managed to get to his feet

27

surprisingly fast, catching all the men off guard. In fact, with most of their attention now focused on his half-naked wife, none of them actually saw him until he was already on his feet, charging toward the 300-lb. man.

The shorter man was the first to see him, and yelled, "YO, LOOK OUT!!"

As the large man turned to Matthew, he was met with a vicious stab in the face. He clutched his face and immediately dropped to his knees – screaming in agony, and spewing a barrage of profanities.

Matthew aimed for his eye, but missed. He plunged the pen deep into his cheek, about an inch below his right eye – actually imbedding it several inches into his face.

"MY EYE... HE STABBED ME IN MY FUCKIN' EYE!!!" he screamed, hysterical.

He was in shock and hadn't yet realized that his eye had actually been spared.

The surreal image of their injured partner thrashing about in pain with a pen sticking out of his face caused the shorter man to lose focus. Before he could process what was happening, Matthew was already upon him. With his adrenaline still pumping, he landed a crippling punch to the man's face. A stream of blood flew out his mouth – along with one of his teeth – producing a straight, diagonal red streak on the wall behind the staircase. His head snapped to the side with such force, you could actually hear the cracking of the bones in his neck. Before he could regain his composure, Matthew grabbed him by his Afro with both hands, and rammed him face-first into the wall. The knife was knocked out of his hand as he slumped to the ground, dazed and bleeding from a melon-size abrasion on his forehead.

Matthew emitted a series of grunts that sounded half human and half animal.

There was no stopping him now. Against all odds, he was quickly gaining the upper hand. The rush of adrenaline had awakened his dark side. He was now the empowered hunter, and the trio was his prey. He began advancing on the final attacker... the one

28

most responsible for fueling his rage… the one who had defiled what was most sacred to him.

"Yo, stay back, man… STAY BACK!!" the man shouted in desperation, as he slowly retreated – cowardly using Janet as a shield.

"Matthew...be careful!!" she pleaded.

"Look, man… I ain't did nuthin'… I ain't hurt her!!"

Matthew was too filled with rage to stop. Rapidly regaining his strength, he continued to advance.

"MATTHEW!!" screamed Janet. "BEHIND YOU… LOOK OUT!!!"

In all the frenzy, the large man had managed to retrieve the switchblade off the ground. Before Matthew could respond to her warning, he felt a sharp, searing pain in his upper right thigh.

He cried out in agony, as he dropped to the ground.

Janet screamed again.

Still on his knees, the large man had plunged the blade deep into Matthew's thigh. The entire length of the unforgiving steel penetrated his flesh, leaving only the wooden handle visible.

Had he been able to get to his feet faster, he most certainly would have chosen a more vital area. As it was, it effectively put the brakes on Matthew's counter-attack long enough to allow the trio to regroup.

"Get up, man...we gotta teach dis fool a lesson!!" the large man shouted to his shorter partner – still on the ground holding his head and looking for his tooth.

"What you wanna do with dis bitch?" asked the man holding onto Janet.

"Just keep her still! I wanna take care of him first!!"

"MATTHEEEEEW!!!" Janet screamed, again.

"SHUT UP!!" her captor commanded, as he covered her mouth with his hand.

"Get on your goddamn feet already!!" the large man yelled, as he grabbed his shorter accomplice by the arm and forcibly lifted him off the ground.

"Da muthafucka' done knocked out my tooth, dog!" he said.

"Stop being such a little bitch! You see what he done to my face, don't you!?"

"Yo, man… let's just off him!"

"Nah, nah...I'm gonna make his ass suffer!!"

"Yeah, but we ain't gots the time, dog!" he said, looking around at the growing crowd in the distance. "Let's just snuff him and dis bitch and get the hell outta here!"

"NAH, FUCK DAT! But he gonna *wish* he be dead!!"

The most brutal assault thus far on Matthew commenced. The large man unleashed a savage fury of solid punches to his face and body. Each time his ring came into contact with bare skin, more and more of Matthew's flesh was ripped and shredded.

Janet could hardly stand to see her husband being beaten to a bloody pulp. She fought as hard as she could to get free, but it was futile. With her mouth still covered, all she could utter were a few muffled grunts and groans.

Matthew screamed in agony as the beating continued.

The shorter man was concentrating his assault on Matthew's injured leg. With the knife still impaled, and the blade completely imbedded, he delivered a series of vicious kicks in a deliberate attempt to drive it in even further. Using the steel tips of his boots, he succeeded in jamming several inches of the wooden handle into his leg. He landed one final, well-placed kick, driving almost the *entire* knife into his leg – only about an inch of the handle still remained visible.

Matthew's cries began sounding more like a wounded animal than a man. He was beyond pain. His body was taking more abuse than it ever had in his life. The beating was tantamount to a shark feeding frenzy. His attackers were intent on inflicting major bodily harm. Nothing was going to deter them from their heinous mission. Not the growing numbers of curious onlookers or even the arrival of a downtown train on the opposite side of the station – spitting out a handful of more onlookers.

Janet managed to momentarily pry her captor's hand away from her mouth.

"STOP IT… YOU'RE KILLING HIM… STOP IT!!!" she screamed, hysterical.

"We just be gettin' started wit yo' man, bitch!" the large man snarled.

He pulled Matthew to his feet, but he immediately crumpled back down to the ground. The injury to his leg made it impossible for him to stand under his own power.

He grabbed Matthew by his coat with his left hand, and pulled him halfway up. With his right fist, he unfurled a merciless punch to his bloody and shattered face. His beefy arm produced a whooshing sound as it sliced through the air. Matthew fell backwards – his head making a resounding *clump* as it smacked onto the platform.

Janet screamed again.

The large man's two-finger ring was an incredibly effective and lethal weapon. It opened up numerous deep gashes on Matthew's face – rendering it swollen, bloodied and almost unrecognizable. After a while, his skin started to resemble the texture of a blood-soaked sponge. Each blow produced such a significant splatter; both Matthew and the attackers were soon coated in a thick shade of red. He saw bright flashes of white light after each punch, quickly followed by random glimpses of faces of gawking spectators.

FLASH!

A young Hispanic man – peering over the banister of the first staircase.

FLASH!

A middle-aged black woman – standing on the downtown platform, covering her nose and mouth with her hands and wincing at every blow.

FLASH!

A young black girl – standing directly across the way on the downtown platform looking like "a deer caught in the headlights."

FLASH!

A white man in his thirties – surveying the carnage from several *safe* feet away at the front of the platform.

31

FLASH!

A white train conductor – staring emotionlessly out the cab window of his downtown train as it exited the station.

FLASH!

A young black man – sitting on a bench on the downtown platform, staring over the top of his newspaper.

FLASH!

A middle-aged white or Hispanic man – leaning over the banister of the other staircase.

There were, of course, other people around, but those were the faces that made the biggest impression on his subconscious. Perhaps they stood out purely by chance, or because they were in Matthew's direct line of sight.

Only when the large man ran out of steam, did the vicious, one-sided beating stop. Matthew was left in a crumpled, bloodied heap on the platform. Incredibly, he was still conscious.

"Oh, God...Matthew...MATTHEEEEEW!!!" Janet screamed.

With her husband now completely incapacitated, she became the primary focus of the large man. Splattered with Matthew's blood, he approached to within inches of her face – the pen, still hideously lodged in his cheek.

"Look like yo man ain't nothin' but a pussy-ass, punk bitch!" he said, as he ran his blood-coated hands through her dark brown hair. "Why don't you let me show you what it be like to be wit a *real* man?"

"FUCK YOU!!!" she screamed – spitting a huge wad of bloody phlegm in his face.

He recoiled, shocked and angered by her unexpected display of defiance.

"You dirty little fuck!"

His retaliation was swift and violent. He released a vicious, backhanded slap to the right side of her face. Once again, his lethal ring found its mark. Blood began oozing out of a long, straight – almost surgical – slit in her cheek. Within seconds, she was bleeding profusely from the wounds on both sides of her face. The only thing keeping her from collapsing was the vice-like restraint the taller man still had on her.

"Please… please let me go… please," she pleaded – her voice almost a whisper.

"You ain't goin' nowhere!" he retorted. "Nasty bitches like you deserve *special* treatment!"

He then roughly pinched the nipple of her exposed breast, causing her to wince in pain.

"Yo, man… let's run a train on dis bitch!" the taller man excitedly said.

Janet gasped. She knew that was street-lingo for a sexual assault, where each attacker takes turns raping one woman.

"No… please, no… I'm pregnant… I'M PREGNANT!!" she cried, as she struggled to break free of her captor's grip.

The large man felt the tender bulge of her belly.

"Pregnant, huh? I thought you was just a fat bitch! Is dis the baby, right… HERE!?"

Without warning, he punched her directly in her womb. The brutality of the act caught everyone by surprise, including the man holding her. He momentarily lost his grip. She slumped to her knees and grabbed her stomach. With the wind knocked out of her, she was temporarily unable to speak or yell. Deep, protracted inhales and exhales were the only sounds she could make. Her only concern was her baby.

The taller man grabbed her by her coat to pull her back up to her feet. He succeeded in only pulling it completely off – leaving her on her knees, in excruciating pain. The shorter man came over and ripped off her blood stained top. Humiliated, and shred of dignity, she was left wearing only her skirt and half a bra.

Matthew was still conscious, but unable to help his wife – or himself – in any way. He had always been her protector, but tonight, he had been reduced to little more than a twitching invalid – writhing in pain, face down on the ground in a puddle of filth. The worst part was being forced to witness the assault through his teary, blood-soaked eyes.

He, of course, wasn't the only witness to this debauchery. The sounds of the attack, and the spectacle of Janet's bloody, half-naked body, was beginning to attract the attention of more and more curious and horrified onlookers. Realizing the scene was becoming too public, the large man ordered his accomplices to move her to a slightly more hidden area.

"Bring her over here… against the wall!" he shouted.

They each grabbed her by her arms and pulled her to her feet. Unable to stand under her own power, they dragged her to the designated spot. One of her shoes came off as her feet scraped along the ground. They propped her up against the back wall of the second staircase. Although by no means a private area, they were, at least, partially hidden from view from the onlookers at the front of the platform, but the scene was still within full view of everyone else on the downtown platform.

With Janet restrained by his two partners, the large man took advantage of the situation.

"Nobody spits in my face, bitch!"

He then administered a series of brutal kicks and punches to her stomach.

Being backed up against the wall, she absorbed the full impact of the blows. Each one felt like a knife driving deep into her womb.

"I'm … pregnant… I'm…" she whimpered, as blood began oozing out of her mouth.

A few gasps and screams could be heard coming from the onlookers.

"STOP THEM!" someone shouted.

"CALL THE POLICE!" another person screamed.

Oblivious to the increased attention, the large man continued his sadistic assault. He intentionally aimed directly at the bulge in her stomach.

Racked with pain and crippling cramps, Janet could no longer cry out or even lift up her head. All she could think about was her unborn child. But any hopes or dreams she may have had for little Suzie were being ripped away with each jarring blow.

I'm sorry, Suzie... Oh, God... I'm so sorry!

She knew her baby was gone.

When he finally ceased his heartless pounding, he ordered his accomplices to release her. She was thrown to the ground with a thud. Her face landed just a few feet away from Matthew's. For the first time since the attack had begun, they were able to look each other directly in the eyes.

"I love you," mouthed Matthew, too weak to utter the words.

Janet was also unable to speak. All she could do was gaze into what was once the handsome face of her husband. A flood of precious memories flashed before her eyes. The day they met... when they fell in love... the trips they took together... the birth of Melissa... the day she learned of her pregnancy with Suzie... their silly fights and arguments – indeed, visions of their entire fairy tale life all came rushing back. She knew things would never be the same again, and started to cry.

Matthew was in no condition to offer her much comfort. The beating he sustained left him virtually paralyzed. He was unable to stand due to the knife would in his leg, and the amount of blood building up in his eyes was making it more and more difficult to see. But he desperately wanted to let Janet know that she wasn't alone... that he was still there for her, in spirit, if nothing else. He raised his right arm in her direction. If only he could touch her – a simple gesture of love to help both of them through their ordeal. She too extended her hand. Only a few inches remained before their bond was complete.

FLASH!

The large man planted a boot directly in Matthew's face, breaking his nose.

He then grabbed Janet by the back of her bra strap, and crudely began pulling her to her feet. She got only halfway up when the strap broke, sending her plunging face-first back to the ground. Her nose was shattered in the fall – spewing blood everywhere. Wearing only a skirt, she writhed in pain on the ground in a small pool of her own blood.

"Get over here, bitch!" he said, as he grabbed her by her hair and brutally threw her up against the back wall of the second staircase.

She landed on her butt in a sitting position, with her arms hanging lifelessly by her sides – profusely bleeding from her nose and mouth. Knowing her baby was gone put her in a different state of mind. She no longer had the power or the will to fight – nothing seemed to matter much anymore. She just sat there staring blankly into space – completely vulnerable.

She was then stripped naked and despite the growing crowd of onlookers, subjected to a sexual assault of unimaginable savagery by the trio.

This was the moment Matthew had been dreading ever since the attack began. Deep down, he kind of wished that they had continued beating her. He cursed himself for even thinking such a thought, but he considered the beating would have been the lesser of two evils. Her physical wounds would eventually heal, but she would have to live with the memory of this for the rest of her life. It was killing him to see his wife lying bloody and naked on a cold, filthy subway platform. Watching her being raped for the world to see was shredding away the very fabric of his soul. Having had all of this happen on their anniversary, and not being able to do a single thing to stop it, was pushing him closer to the edge of insanity.

The sexual shift of the attack was having a noticeable effect on the spectators as well. Audible gasps and several *"Oh my God's"* could be heard all over the station. The shock value had definitely increased, but it still wasn't enough to persuade anyone to intervene.

During the attack, the large man reached up to his face and extracted the imbedded pen. Blood began spurting out of the small, circular hole directly onto Janet's face. But it was hardly noticeable, due to the amount of blood still gushing out of her own, numerous facial wounds.

She tried to close her eyes and detach herself from the horrific scene… to travel to a better place.

This isn't really happening.

Matthew and I are still at Tavern On the Green, enjoying our anniversary dinner.

Little Suzie is still dancing around excitedly inside me.

The attack concluded with the large man forcing Janet to perform fellatio on him. It was at that moment when she suddenly became filled with more rage than fear. She hated them for what they had done to her and her family… their hopes… their dreams… their future. Seconds before he was able to completely withdraw, she mustered all of her available strength and bit down hard on him.

He let out a high-pitched, womanlike scream and dropped to the ground as though he'd been shot – desperately clutched his crotch. Writhing in pain in a fetal position, he continued to cry out – completely losing his intimidating persona.

She had bitten off a small piece of the tip of his penis and spat it out on the ground next to him.

The bold move shocked the other two men. They simply stood there looking on speechlessly, in a state of shock.

Although still in tremendous pain, the large man managed to drag himself back to his feet.

Without saying a word, he reached into his inside jacket pocket and pulled out another switchblade. He ejected a blade that was even longer than the one he buried in Matthew's leg. Driven by rage and pure evil, he let forth a prolonged, guttural shout, and charged at her. He plunged the knife directly into her belly button, using all of his force to drive it in as far as he possibly could. Her eyes glazed over as blood and other bodily fluids gushed out of the wound.

Screams echoed all throughout the station from the shocked crowd of spectators.

"OH, SHIT!! OH, SHIT!!" screamed his accomplices, also shocked by the brutality of the act.

No longer wishing to be part of a crime this vile, they turned and bolted towards the back of the platform and disappeared up the rear staircase into the streets above.

Unfazed by the departure of his partners, the large man continued his savage butchery. Even after Janet had collapsed into a heap on the platform, he continued to manically plunge the knife in and out of her stomach. Individual stab wounds became indistinguishable – gradually merging into one large, gaping hole.

The injuries she had suffered thus far, paled in comparison to the unspeakable mutilation she was now enduring. Fortunately, her body was in a complete state of shock – nature's merciful way of blocking out the excruciating agony. But she was still conscious – if just barely – and able to see and hear everything that was happening to her. Staring down at the steadily enlarging wound in her belly, she knew she was witnessing her own death.

For better leverage, the man knelt down between the couple, temporarily blocking Matthew's view of the atrocity. Hunching over her, he continued his attack like a crazed surgeon. Rivers of blood flowed from her body, as did her last breaths of life. Bone-chilling screams of horror from women *and* men erupted all over the station. Far off in the distance, the wails of approaching sirens could be heard. Only then did the man's manic momentum begin to slow. He lingered a few seconds over her body, then, stood up and made a hasty retreat from the station.

Matthew was finally able to make physical contact with his wife. He reached over and cradled her lifeless hand within his own. Barely above a whisper, he began uttering an expressionless, mantra-like chant.

"… you're gonna be okay, baby… you're gonna be okay, baby… you're gonna be okay, baby---"

His mind had suffered more trauma than it could handle.

With the attackers now gone, many of the spectators started venturing into the crime scene – tentatively at first, then, with increasing urgency. The sight before them provoked a variety of extreme reactions. Some screamed. Some quickly turned away in disgust. Some threw up. Most just stood there, staring in shock – unable to move or speak.

Matthew continued to chant. Having never lost consciousness, he witnessed the entire attack. He had seen things no one should ever have to see. Matters that seemed important to him just an hour ago meant absolutely nothing now. In the space of about twenty-five minutes, his whole life had been completely destroyed. His wife and unborn child were viciously taken away from him, and all he could do was watch.

The sirens in the distance grew louder, then finally stopped. The sounds of squawking walkie-talkies and several pairs of footsteps purposefully descending down the steps, filled the station. Six cops with guns drawn, simultaneously rounded the corners of both staircases.

"GET BACK! GET BACK!" they shouted at the assembled spectators.

The crowd dispersed, revealing a scene of horror to the officers that none were prepared to see. They slowly lowered their guns, and stood transfixed in front of the nightmare. Most of them – some seasoned veterans – had similar reactions to those of the spectators.

The small area between the two staircases looked as though it had been painted dark red. Sheets of blood were rolling off the walls. The platform was so saturated, it was hard to find a spot where they weren't standing in an almost inch-deep puddle. Most of the puddles had combined to form a fairly large pool. It extended all the way to the edges and was beginning to overflow onto the track bed. Incredibly, a few drops even dripped from the ceiling. Lying in the middle of it all were two people – a man and a woman – whom they first perceived to be dead. The man was African-American and bleeding from a puncture wound in his upper right thigh. Some type of unidentified wooden object was slightly protruding from the wound. Most of the blood came from his face. Covered with so many cuts and lesions, it looked like one big open wound – making him completely unrecognizable. He would have most likely needed to be identified through dental records, had it not been for one small sign of life – he was incessantly mumbling something unintelligible and staring blankly ahead with a weird, "detached from reality" look in his eyes. He was clutching the hand of the woman lying next to him. Except for a pair of ripped panties wrapped around her right thigh, she was completely naked. She was coated in blood almost from head to toe, making it difficult to immediately determine her

39

nationality. She too suffered many facial and head wounds, although not quite as severe as her male counterpart. Her most shocking injury – the thing that stopped everyone in their tracks – was a large, open wound extending from her groin to just below her breasts. Her eyes were wide open – staring straight ahead at the man lying next to her.

More sirens could be heard approaching in the distance. All of the frenzied activity inside the station had momentarily ceased. Time seemed to stand still as a thick shroud of silence suddenly befell the surreal scene. Aside from the random chatter occasionally spurting out of the police radios, the only other sound was the constant, incoherent mumbling coming from the man on the ground.

CHAPTER 2

October 11, 2003 – 1:12 p.m. Saturday Afternoon

Dark gray storm clouds hovered ominously over the city for most of the day. A light rain pelted the living room window next to the couch where Melissa sat after watering her plants. She took pride in them, and it showed. Flowerpots lined the entire length of the windowsill, with most of their inhabitants reaching a height of almost three feet. From a distance, they looked like a decorative green tapestry covering the bottom half of the window. Maintaining her little indoor garden was a task that usually lifted her spirits, but today, it didn't seem to be working.

It had been seven years since the horrible attack on her parents in the subway. She used to wonder if things might have gone differently had she been with them that night. *Maybe* she could have gotten away and run for help. *Maybe* her father wouldn't have been so severely beaten. *Maybe* her mother wouldn't have been so viciously raped, murdered and mutilated. Then again, *maybe* she would have suffered a similar fate. These thoughts consumed her life for months after the attack – sending her into a profoundly deep depression. Things got a little better as the years went by, but a considerable amount of pain and heartache remained – usually resurfacing on dreary days like this. Dealing with it had become a way of life. She had resigned herself to the fact that she would never again be the happy, carefree person she was before the attack. Of course, after going through such a traumatic experience, that was pretty much to be expected. But lately, she was feeling a different

41

type of discomfort – an anxious, ominous feeling for which she had no explanation.

The rain outside intensified. A solitary raindrop broke free on the glass and trickled down the center of the windowpane.

By all accounts, Melissa was a pretty girl – most would even say beautiful. She had long, naturally curly, reddish hair which she liked to wear up high – a style that gave her the appearance of being taller than her actual 5'8" stature. A few strands of her locks cascaded over her forehead, and along the sides of her slender face. Although her eyes were light brown, they seemed to perfectly match the color of her hair. She had a small, button nose, and a tiny, expressive mouth giving her a sultry and sexy appearance. Her perfect skin-tone and light-tan complexion drew plenty of compliments. Her eye-catching physique was the only thing needed to attract the attention of the opposite gender. Overall, she was very thin, but surprisingly well endowed. Her hourglass figure prompted countless looks and comments on a daily basis.

The media coverage after the crime was unprecedented. Of course, crime in the subway was nothing new, but the sheer savagery and utter disregard for life involved in this particular incident was quite rare. *"Subway Savages," "Slaughterhouse (on the) 6," "Mother and Unborn Child Slain," "Wife Slain While Husband Watches," "Murder Underground,"* were just a few of the sensational headlines splashed across the front pages of newspapers all over the city. For almost two full weeks, it was *the* top story covered on every local TV news station. The case also received national coverage, and even caught the attention of a few foreign news agencies.

Since her father was in the hospital, and in no condition to speak, the bulk of the media attention fell on Melissa. For days after the attack, she was besieged by the press for statements. A few reporters and photographers even camped out in front of her Co-Op City apartment building for a chance at grabbing a quick interview, or even just a glimpse of her coming or going. Every newspaper article and television report about the crime was like a stab to her heart. All she wanted to do was to put it all behind her as quickly as possible. But, no matter how hard she tried to avoid it, she became the face of what was eventually pinned, *"The Baby Butchers"* case.

The media reconstructed the crime minute-by-minute. It became a regular topic of discussion on *Nightline*, and was even featured on *20/20* and *America's Most Wanted*. One aspect of the case that generated the most debate, was the fact that it was witnessed by so many people – police estimated the number of spectators to vary from as few as 10, to as many as 25 during the 27-minute attack – without anyone coming to their aid.

It was later discovered that quite a few people did, in fact, go upstairs and report what was happening to the station agent, who eventually called the police. Even the conductor of the downtown train radioed for help. But, these things didn't happen until several minutes after the attack had begun. It was compared to the Kitty Genovese case – an incident that occurred in Queens, NY in 1964. In full view of 38 of her neighbors, the victim had been murdered in an attack that lasted 32 minutes – long enough for her attacker to leave and come back *twice* in order to finish the job. Nevertheless, no one ever came to her aid, or called the police. Each person assumed "someone else" was already doing something about it.

"Bystander apathy" became the catch phrase among experts when discussing the similar cases. They explained that this is a problem endemic in urban areas, where large numbers of onlookers are present at the scene of an attack. If only one person is present, any possible help *must* come from that person, thus, mounting pressure on them to intervene. However, in a crowd of people, the responsibility of helping the victim may be diffused among the spectators, limiting the potential blame that can be placed on any single individual. Also, the likelihood that *someone* is already doing *something* about it lessens the individual's feeling of responsibility. There are also certain personality traits common among people unwilling to take action. One is *egoism* – the exclusive concern for one's own welfare. Spectators often weigh the dangers of intervening.

Will I be hurt?

43

Will I be killed?

Another trait is *hedonism* – the desire to maximize their morbid voyeuristic pleasures. Additionally, failure to respond to a situation after three minutes greatly decreases the likelihood of any kind of intervention, including reporting the incident or calling for help. The attack in the subway lasted almost half an hour. Thus, all of the conditions for "bystander apathy" were ripe that night.

Fortunately, the three perpetrators were caught almost immediately. Although the witnesses may not have done much to stop the attack, they did provide the police with very detailed descriptions of the three attackers. The high-profile nature of the case – not to mention the fact that the trio stuck out like sore thumbs – made it all but impossible for them to hide anywhere. Within weeks, all three were apprehended and charged with the crime. The sea of DNA evidence left at the scene made for very swift and easy convictions. Because of their lesser role in the crime, the accomplices just served a few years. The large man, who had actually committed the murder, could have been charged with a double homicide for Janet and her unborn child. Unfortunately, New York State laws only recognize it as murder if the fetus is twenty four weeks or older. Janet's baby was only twenty weeks old. In any event, he still *should* have served a minimum of 12 years to life. However, he decided it was in his best interest to cut a deal and turn state's evidence against a large New York drug kingpin. Because of these deals and technicalities, all three were released from prison within five years after the murder.

Melissa's father was never the same after the attack. Losing his wife and unborn child literally turned him into another person. He was left both emotionally and physically scarred. Even after hours of painful, reconstructive surgery, his face was still considerably disfigured – almost resembling a burn victim. After his release from the hospital, he and Melissa continued to live in their apartment in the Bronx. He tried hard to carry on "life as usual," but it soon became an impossible task. The severe knife wound in his right leg left him partially crippled. He required the aid of a cane in order to walk properly. This made him look much older than his fifty-five years of age. As such, his vanity would often compel him to leave it behind – forcing Melissa to chastise him for not following doctor's orders. Unable to cope with the pressures and demands of everyday life, he eventually lost his job – leaving Melissa to shoulder most of the financial burden.

His emotional state was even worse. In essence, he was an angry man. He was angry that half his family was so savagely ripped away from him, and that his life was now in complete shambles. Of course, he was angry at the three thugs directly responsible, but he was absolutely incensed with the scores of onlookers that stood by and did nothing. It didn't help matters much that the incident was still receiving copious amounts of media attention. Whenever the term "bystander apathy" was mentioned, it was like rubbing salt in a wound – sending him into an uncontrollable and frightening rage. It got to the point where he became obsessed with it, and would sit for hours in front of the television – soaking up every news report and special he could find about the attack. Unaware of her presence, she would sometimes catch him slowly rocking back and forth – staring blankly at the screen. The day she found a sheet of loose-leaf paper in his room, which he had completely scribbled with gibberish, she knew it was time for action. After weeks of begging, she finally convinced him to place himself under the care of a psychiatrist. He went through hours of consultation and a medicine cabinet full of anti-depressants. Unfortunately, nothing worked; in fact, he seemed to get worse. Whenever she talked to him, he would have a far-away look in his eyes, and appear to be looking right through her. Eventually, he could no longer handle the pain of being around anything that reminded him of Janet. Every semblance of their happy life together was like a stab to his broken heart. Sadly, this also included Melissa. Instead of taking solace in the fact that he still, at least, had a daughter, it only exacerbated his heart ache. Although he loved her deeply, all he could see when he looked at her was the product of a blessed union he knew he would never experience again. He felt the only way he could truly heal was to leave New York. In February 1997, three months after the attack, he decided to move back to his hometown of Beaufort, South Carolina.

Life was extremely difficult for Melissa, now 25, in the six years after her father left. Facing tremendous financial hardships, she was forced to give up the spacious, Co-Op City apartment in 1999. For the past four years, her home was a small, one-bedroom apartment on the ground floor of a two-family on Bradford Street, in a dilapidated section of East New York, Brooklyn.

Unlike the secure, manicured environment she had known all her life, East New York was an economically depressed neighborhood – basically, a slum. She was required to install security bars on her windows – a necessity for all street-level dwellers in the city, and *especially* for anyone living in her neighborhood. For the first time in her life, she knew what it felt like to be a prisoner in one's own home.

The neighborhood was also socially repressed – replete with as many broken homes as broken sidewalks. It wasn't unusual to see kids as young as eight or nine years old hanging out all hours of the night, completely unsupervised. In most cases, their "parents" – sometimes just a few years older themselves – either didn't care, or were too busy hanging with their own circle of friends just a few blocks away. What made Melissa the most uncomfortable was the general lack of security. It was a dangerous area, fraught with drugs and vicious gangs that owned the streets at night and didn't discriminate when it came to choosing their victims. Just last week, even a nun wearing her white habit was mugged. She was knocked to the ground, and robbed of $60 and her rosary beads. Luckily, she only suffered a few cuts and bruises, but the incident – which happened just a block away from Melissa's house – left her feeling extremely vulnerable and frightened. Although she had never been assaulted herself, she feared it was only a matter of time. She figured, if they would target a nun, they would target anyone.

Probably the only upside to living in that neighborhood was that it was located very close to the Cypress Hills Cemetery – the spot where her mother was buried. She would go there whenever she felt as though the world was closing in on her. The long "conversations" she would have at her mother's grave were a tremendous calming influence, and gave her a lot of comfort and strength. She no longer felt so alone.

Ever since she had been living in East New York, she never felt comfortable enough to actually call it "home." She lived almost four blocks away from the Van Siclen Avenue subway station on the "A" and "C" line. She hated having to weave her way through several pockets of unsavory-looking characters, all the while dodging an obstacle course of dog feces, liquor bottles, old newspapers, used condoms and a host of other discarded items littering the cracked pavement. When coming home late at night, safety was her primary concern. After exiting the station, she would walk on the north side of Pitkin Avenue – the side that provided slightly better lighting – for two blocks, until she reached Bradford Street. She would then make a left and cross the avenue and walk down Bradford another block and a half to her home. Friends would advise her to vary her route, so as not to become too predictable. That may have been true, but any deviation would take her down darker, less traveled paths, so she insisted on sticking with her familiar routine.

She grew to somewhat resent her father for moving away, but hated harboring such feelings towards a man who had gone through so much heartache and agony. Seeing your family destroyed right before your eyes would be more than most people could take. She knew this, but she also knew he wasn't the only person affected by the tragedy. She had also lost her mother. She understood that he was physically and mentally incapable of giving her the love and support she so desperately needed at the time. But leaving her behind and "running" away, as she perceived it, just seemed like sheer cowardice. Because of this, she was forced to grow up a lot faster than most kids her age. Coping with the tragedy while working *and* going to school was difficult enough… having to do it alone was next to impossible. But, against all odds, she managed to graduate Brooklyn College with honors.

For the first year or so after her father's departure, they kept in touch through phone calls. When his phone got disconnected, they continued corresponding through letters. As time went on, his writing became more and more unfocused – almost deteriorating into nonsensical gibberish. Eventually, he stopped writing all together. She continued to write until her letters were returned stamped, "No Forwarding Address." All ties with her father were severed. She couldn't even turn to her grandparents for support. The ones on her father's side passed away years ago, and her mother's parents had moved out of the city and were now living in an assisted care facility in Chicago. She felt abandoned and alone.

Ever since the attack, Melissa always wanted to be involved with law enforcement in some way. With hopes of one day becoming a crime scene investigator, she took evening classes in forensic science at The John Jay College of Criminal Justice on the west side of Manhattan. During the day, she worked as a legal secretary for a law firm, located just across town on East 57th Street. The non-stop hustle and bustle of the area did wonders to boost her spirits. So drastically different from East New York, she couldn't imagine how such dissimilar areas could be part of the same city. Here, she felt safe. She could walk around freely and not have to worry about looking over her shoulder. Even the looks and comments she got from the men on the streets were different. Instead of making her feel like a cheap piece of meat, she felt more like a lady – admired for her inner beauty. She also truly enjoyed her job, not only because she was in a field she loved, but because her boss, Richard Lordan, was *someone* she loved.

She had been working at the firm for a little over a year. There was a mutual attraction between them that blossomed almost immediately. At first, she was a little cautious, and unwilling to get into a full-fledged relationship. Since the firm had no rule against dating co-workers, Richard initially felt her hesitation was because he was white. She assured him that she had no problem dating interracial. Although she had never dated outside of her race before, she found the idea somewhat intriguing. Basically, her problem was that she wasn't sure if he really liked her for herself or if he just felt sorry for her because of the tragedy in her past. He eventually convinced her that his feelings for her were genuine, and not based on sympathy. Of course, he *did* feel sorry for what she had gone through – anyone would – but he assured her it had absolutely no bearing on his desire to be with her romantically. For the past nine months or so, she saw him as not only her boyfriend, but as one of the few bright spots in her overall dreary world.

He was a handsome man with presence. At six feet, with deep-set, hazel eyes and curly, jet black hair, he was the recipient of many admiring glances from women of all races. He wasn't exactly a health-nut, but he took pride in his appearance – working out in the gym an average of two to three times a week. He was 34, but looked like he was in his late twenties.

Although the dress code in the office was formal, he absolutely hated wearing suits and ties. At the end of the day, he couldn't wait to get into something a little more casual. Before leaving the office, he would sometimes go in the bathroom and change into a sporty Polo shirt and jeans – a *very* form-fitting pair of jeans. Many of the women in the office would swear that they were custom-made. In fact, some would even hang around five or ten minutes after work just to witness his sexy transformation.

Having a boyfriend who was the object of so many women's fantasies used to bother Melissa at first. In time, she grew to accept it, and even secretly reveled in their frustrations. After all… he was with her, and not them.

Richard would always tell her how lucky he was to be with a girl like her. But, in all actuality, she was the one who felt truly lucky.

Like most women, she too, was initially attracted to his looks. When out in public, they would get more than their fair share of attention. Individually, they were both extremely attractive people – as a couple, they were absolutely stunning.

Occasionally, she detected a few angry stares from black men, and could almost read their thoughts.

What's a fine sista like you doin' with this white guy?

After a while, she simply learned to ignore it – realizing that society still had quite a way to go in its acceptance of interracial couples.

Physical attractiveness was secondary when it came to her feelings for Richard. She also greatly appreciated his patience. Her mother's murder affected her much more deeply than she ever could have imagined. To lose a parent through natural causes due to old age is bad enough, but to lose one through such a senseless, violent act is completely unthinkable. She and her mother were *extremely* close. Their relationship was more like best friends than mother and daughter. After the murder, aside from unfathomable grief, she also experienced a strange feeling of disconnectedness. Many have attributed this to the unique umbilical connection a mother shares with a child – a connection that not even death can sever. A loss such as this will affect one in many different ways. Melissa was affected by a loss of interest (more like a fear) of sexual activity. Ever since the tragedy, she had not engaged in any type of sexual intimacy with anyone. She wasn't a virgin, but the horrible rape and murder of her mother so traumatized her that she was turned off by anything remotely associated with sex. In fact, the mere thought of it sent her into a panic. She considered these feelings normal right after the attack, but when they persisted for months, then eventually years… she knew she had a serious problem. It concerned her that she might not ever enjoy a normal sex life again. She remembered how she hounded her father to see a psychiatrist, but when it came to seeking help for herself, she had trouble practicing what she preached. She had dated on and off before she met Richard, but it never amounted to anything serious. She could always avoid getting romantic by telling the guy that she "just wanted to be friends." But now, she was in a committed relationship, and no longer able to hide behind such an excuse. Unfortunately, no matter how hard she tried, she just wasn't able to handle much more than some hugs and a few light kisses. It really bothered her that she couldn't give more of herself to Richard. He always told her that he understood what she was going through *and* was willing to wait for as long as it took. His patience and understanding touched her deeply. But, she also knew everyone had their limits, and still feared she might one day lose him if she didn't get over her problem soon.

On the outside, Richard may have seemed like the perfect man, but, like Melissa, he too had dealt with a personal struggle. His demon was alcohol. At his worst, he would drink until he actually started hallucinating, or simply passed out. Before he met Melissa, his world was filled with a string of broken relationships and dreams, and missed opportunities. It was a lifestyle he knew he had to change. Through sheer willpower and determination, he eventually got his life back on track. By the time Melissa came around, he had been clean and sober for at least a couple of years. It was a notable accomplishment of which he was truly proud, but also something that frequently worried him. Because he had done it completely on his own – without the aid of any organized support groups – he often worried that it wouldn't take much for him to slip back into the deep, dark coffers of what was once his life. But Melissa has been always there for him whenever he felt weak. She admired him even more for his courage, and knew in her heart that they were soul mates – destined to meet in order to help each other through their dark periods. For the first time in her life, she knew she was experiencing true love.

Although she enjoyed her job, the fact that she was dating the boss made things a bit awkward at times between her and some of her female co-workers. Most were older women, and nowhere near as attractive as she. Many of them had a crush on Richard, and weren't shy about making their feelings known. Some had even taken the initiative to ask him out. But he always politely turned down their advances – explaining how he thought it would best to keep things on a "professional" level. However, when Melissa joined the team, this policy was quickly abandoned. At first, they tried to keep their relationship quiet, but, as in most office environments, word soon got out. Many of these women felt slighted, and unfairly took out their jealous frustrations on her by excluding her from their clique. As much as Melissa would have appreciated being more warmly accepted, deep down it didn't really bother her that much. She viewed them as a childish, pathetic lot – wholly unworthy of her time or attention.

School was the one place where she could go and not have to deal with any controversy. Her night classes at John Jay gave her the opportunity to be around people more her own age. Although her classmates were young, she found them to be much more mature than most of her co-workers at the firm. Here, there was no drama, and the environment was a lot more relaxed. When her last class ended at 11 p.m., she would walk a couple of blocks to the Columbus Circle subway station to catch the "C" train to Brooklyn. She didn't mind the walk; in fact, she even looked forward to it. The vast majority of students went this way, so she would always be with a large group of her friends. But, once there, many of them would dissipate throughout the maze of stairways, hallways and platforms to seek out their respective trains among the six subway lines that converged at the huge station. A few people went her way, but they got off the train long before it reached her stop – leaving her by herself for the remainder of her journey. On most nights, the trip would take almost an hour. It was typical for her not to get home until well past midnight.

She has never been completely comfortable in the subway since the tragedy. After the attack, the police department flooded the system with cops. One could hardly get on a train without seeing a uniformed officer stroll through their car at some point during the ride. Some stations even set up permanent police booths on the platforms. But as the shock of the crime began to fade, so did the police presence. Crime underground slowly increased until it reached levels as high, or even higher, than they were at the time of her parents' attack.

Naturally, this would be on Melissa's mind every time she traveled underground. She often thought about the three thugs who attacked her parents. The fact that they were now all out of jail was very unsettling. The fact that she couldn't even remember what they looked like after so many years was even worse. She might be standing right next to one of them on the platform one day and never even know it.

These were certainly stressful thoughts and cause for *some* concern, but lately she had been worried about something far worse than ordinary subway thugs. For the past several weeks, she had been experiencing an eerie feeling whenever she was on the subway. Whether she was waiting on a platform for a train or riding one, she felt that something just wasn't quite right. Unlike some people who have the ability to sense an evil presence, she had never been able to detect such a thing herself – until now. At first, she tried to shrug it off as just her imagination. But constantly feeling the tiny hairs on the back of her neck stand on end and seeing goose bumps form on her arms was physical proof that it wasn't just in her mind. Many times she'd have the distinct impression that someone was watching her… following her. Late at night, when the station was quiet, she would sometimes hear a strange scraping sound far off in the distance. It was a subtle noise, but just enough to let her know that she wasn't alone.

So far, she had shared this with no one. She wanted to tell Richard, but was afraid of what he might think. He was more than understanding about her problems with intimacy. To divulge her latest fears about "things that go bump in the night," might be more than even *he* would be willing to deal with.

The phone rang – startling her.

It was Richard.

"Hey, sweetie, what's goin' on?" he asked.

Just hearing his voice put her in better spirits.

"Hi, Richie… I was just thinking about you."

"All good thoughts, I hope?"

"Of course, what other kind of thoughts are there when it comes to you?" she said, smiling to herself.

"So, what are you doin'? Are you busy?"

"No, I'm just watering my plants. Sometimes I forget, but the rain always helps to remind me."

"I don't know how you could possibly forget about that botanical garden you've got growing in your living room. You've really got one helleva green thumb!"

"Sometimes, I get a little distracted."

"What's wrong?" he asked, sensing a sudden change in her tone. "Thinking about your mother?"

"Yeah," she sighed, "I guess I think about her more on days like this."

"Yeah, I know. What about your father? Have you heard anything from him lately?"

"No… nothing at all," she answered.

Realizing he had just reopened old wounds, he quickly changed the subject.

"Hey, listen, since you're not doing anything, why don't I come over?"

Richard lived pretty far out on Long Island. Although he had a car, she hated for him to drive in the rain.

"No… don't come by now, it's pouring outside."

"You think I'm gonna let a little water stop me from seeing my baby?"

"I know how fast you like to drive. The last thing I want is for you to go hydroplaning off the Long Island Expressway."

"It's supposed to clear up later this evening. Why don't I come by then, and we can go into the city for dinner and maybe catch a movie?"

"That sounds great! About what time do you want to meet?"

"How 'bout I swing by around six?"

"Perfect. Now, I just need to figure out what I'm going to wear."

"Why don't you wear those tight stretch jeans I love so much?" he eagerly suggested.

She laughed.

"You just want to see me squeeze my big butt in those pants, don't you?"

"Look… on the job, you're forced to wear business suits; covering up that beautiful body of yours. When we go out, I really like seeing you in something a lot more revealing… especially if it reveals that plump little ass of yours."

"I thought only black men were into that sort of thing?"

"Well, you know… they say we're all supposed to be descendants from Africa. Maybe I just got a little more black in me than the average white guy!"

They both laughed.

Considering the attention she normally received on the street, she wasn't too keen on wearing a lot of sexy clothes. But she didn't mind doing it for Richard. Since he was willing to put up with a celibate relationship, she thought it was a small price to pay.

"Alright, alright… I'll wear the stretch jeans. Are you happy now?"

"Actually, I'm drooling right now, but that's beside the point."

They laughed again.

"So, I'll see you at six?" she asked.

"Six it is."

"Love you," she said.

"Love you, too, sweetie. Bye-bye."

She hung up the phone and smiled. She felt the crowds and bright lights of Manhattan would be just what she needed to get her out of the dumps. She wasn't sure exactly where things were headed with Richard, but if they continued the way they were, there just might be wedding bells in their near future.

She looked down when something furry brushed against her leg.

"Why, Mr. Snuggles… where have you been hiding all day?" she reached down and picked up her cat.

She felt very isolated and alone after her father moved away. To alleviate her loneliness, she decided to get a pet. She went to the local ASPCA and immediately fell in love with the sweetest little ball of orange fur in the room. As a kitten, he was extremely playful and friendly. He was now a slightly overweight, six-year-old tabby. Although unable to run and jump around as friskily as he did in his younger years, his friendly disposition remained the same. Whenever a visitor would stop by, he'd go to the door to greet them, then proceed to stick by their side for the duration of their stay. She always thought he acted more like a dog, than a characteristically aloof feline. Next to Richard, Mr. Snuggles was the only other bright spot in her life.

"You don't like rainy days too much either, do you?" she asked, as she picked him up and cradled him in her lap.

"Mommy's got a date tonight, are you going to be O.K. on your own?"

He looked up at her with his big green, expressive eyes.

"Don't look at me like that, sweetie. I'll only be gone a few hours."

She stroked his beautiful coat, as he settled back down in her lap. She gazed out the window through the irregular spaces between the leaves of her plants. The weather was already starting to clear up. The rain had slowed to a drizzle. Patches of blue sky were beginning to peek through the retreating gray clouds. A few stray rays of sunlight were falling in random areas of the neighborhood like spotlights. Although her depression was slowly starting to subside, she still couldn't shake her nagging fear about the subway. Not only did she sense some type of evil presence… she could actually *feel* it getting stronger.

CHAPTER 3

October 14th – Early Tuesday Morning

He opened his eyes when he heard the sound. It was an unseen, distant tremble that broke the silence, approaching from above and from the left. As it came closer, it slowly increased in volume to a near deafening rumble. When directly overhead, it sounded and *felt* like an earthquake – causing vibrations in the wall he was leaning against and in the concrete floor below his feet. He even felt it in his chest. Suddenly, it all came to a stop. There was a momentary pause, but within seconds, the rumble started again – rapidly reaching an intensity of even greater than before. Once more, the very core of the foundation violently shook. He glanced at the ceiling, and for a split-second, wondered if a cave-in was possible. Just as the rumble was reaching an almost frightening crescendo, it, as well as the vibrations, began to subside. Gradually, the sound faded, slowly retreating to the right. In less than a minute, it had diminished to a soft murmur and was eventually completely consumed by the silence.

Hector Maldonado shifted his weight to his right leg, yawned, and checked the time on his watch.

3:19 a.m.

The noise from the downtown local train entering and leaving the upstairs platform jolted him from his drowsiness. It was the first indicator that *any* trains were running at all. The infrequency of subway service at that time of the morning was always a major source of annoyance to him, as well as anyone else who happened to be traveling at such a late hour. This morning, however, he seemed to be the *only* one traveling. He passed just one man on the stairs who was exiting the station as he descended toward the deserted, Manhattan-bound platform. He had been waiting for his train for over half an hour – during which time, not a single other passenger entered the station.

Hector had just left his girlfriend's Crown Heights apartment in Brooklyn, and was on his way home. He was in the cold, Kingston Avenue Station, trying hard to stay awake while waiting for the uptown #3 train. His destination was the 238th Street Station in the South Riverdale section of the Bronx – virtually, at the opposite end of the city. To get there, he would have to take the #3 through much of Brooklyn and into Manhattan. At some point in Manhattan, he would have to transfer to another train, which would continue on into the northernmost reaches of the Bronx. It was a grueling, 20-mile odyssey that would take close to two hours.

Tomorrow was a big day and he was anxious to get home. He was interviewing for a job at a large, public relations firm in Manhattan. At 25, it was the most important job he had ever applied for, and he wanted to make a good first impression. For the past three years, he had been working in the stockroom of a Duane Reade drug-store in lower Manhattan – a dead end job that was slowly killing him inside. Landing this new job would practically more than triple his present salary. So, he wanted to get at least a *few* hours of sleep, change his clothes, and look fresh for tomorrow. Right now, the only thing standing in his way was a train that refused to come.

He checked the time on his watch again.

3:24 a.m.

Dammit! He thought. *For a city that's never supposed to sleep, its subway system seems to have come down with a severe case of narcolepsy!*

He then heard the beginnings of another rumble coming from upstairs. It grew louder and the vibrations increased as it got closer, but unlike before, there was no pause. The rumblings continued until they faded out altogether. It was the downtown #4 express train.

Oh, that's just great! Isn't anything running uptown?!

Growing impatient, he walked to the edge of the platform and looked to the right into the tunnel for *some* sign of an approaching train. Seeing nothing but darkness, he went back and leaned against the wall – sighing in exasperation.

Besides the noticeable chill in the air, his frustration was the only other thing keeping him awake. The atmosphere of the station could hardly be described as "lively." Aside from the occasional rumblings from above, the only other sounds he heard were from a pack of subway rats squeaking and scampering around deep inside the tunnel.

There wasn't much to look at, either. With the downtown platform upstairs, there was just a dark, gray tunnel wall on the other side of the uptown local and express tracks. There were no posters on the wall or even any benches on which to sit. Actually, he considered that a good thing. As tired as he was, he knew that if he were to get the least bit comfortable he would fall soundly asleep – so soundly, that he might not even wake up when his train arrived.

He began to hear the rumble of another incoming train – this time, it was coming from the opposite direction.

"Yes!" he said, aloud, "Finally, an uptown train!"

He rushed to the edge of the platform with great expectations. Looking into the tunnel, he could hear it getting closer, but he couldn't see anything. His hope started to fade.

Oh, no… don't tell me!

An expanding row of bright reflections suddenly came into view from the express tunnel – flickering rapidly as they progressed between the pillars separating the two tracks. Within seconds, an uptown #4 train came into view and roared through the station. As it echoed its departure, a powerful wind trail was created in its wake.

Every goddamn train but mine!

He was now more than a little perturbed. He began pacing back and forth. Stopping at the platform edge, he defiantly stared into the tunnel – practically willing the train to appear. He then noticed something different about the tunnel, but wasn't exactly sure what. He had been in that station numerous times and knew it like the back of his hand. But something was different tonight. It then came to him. The tunnel was dark. Of course, *all* subway tunnels are dark, but it was eerily dark. In fact, it was pitch black. The fluorescent lights that ordinarily lined its walls were off – transforming the usual semi-darkness into a virtual Black Hole. His first assumption was that they were broken. But how could they all break at the same time? It surprised him that he hadn't noticed such a drastic change in lighting earlier, but dismissed it due to fatigue.

Suddenly, the squeaking and scampering of the rats in the tunnel increased. He felt a cool breeze – the first sign of an approaching train. He looked into the darkness once again. Instead of blackness, he saw a small red light.

"Finally, a light at the end of the tunnel!" he laughed to himself.

He checked his watch one more time.
3:31 a.m.

Now, in better spirits, he started walking in a circular pattern, briskly swinging his arms back and forth – something that not only helped to wake him up, but to warm him up as well. He looked again into the darkness to check the progress of the oncoming train.

Wait a minute… something's not right. He thought.

The red light he saw hadn't changed much in size or position. Initially, he assumed it was the large, red number "3" light at the top of the train. Sometimes, if a train is coming up over a hill, that light is the first thing visible, eventually followed by two bright headlights. But, this light didn't seem to be moving at all.

What the hell is that?

The light was much too small and faint to be coming from a train. As he stared at it, he could see that it was, in fact, moving, but slowly… *very* slowly. Also, his preoccupation with its appearance caused him to temporarily overlook another one of its oddities… its sound, or more specifically, its lack of sound. Aside from the rats – which were now squealing at an unusually high, fever pitch – there were no other sounds whatsoever coming from the tunnel. The New York City subway is known for a lot of things, but being quiet isn't one of them. In most cases, a train can be heard long before it's seen. Whatever it was, it definitely wasn't a train, but nevertheless, steadily advancing towards him. It was then when he realized that the cool breeze he *thought* he felt just prior to its appearance wasn't a breeze at all, but rather a sudden chill in the already cold air.

The exuberance he felt at the sight of what he believed was his ride home, was giving way to an uneasy nervousness. It was strange because he never felt afraid in the subways. He had been riding it ever since he came to New York from Puerto Rico, at the age of six. He rode it at all hours of the day and night, and in every borough of the city. Although he had seen crimes committed in the subway, he, at least, was fortunate never to have fallen victim to one himself. Besides, he was confident he could handle himself in any given situation. But this was different. This was weird. This was something he had never experienced before.

As the seconds ticked by, he had forgotten about his exhaustion. He had even stopped worrying about the time. He was now completely enthralled with the mysterious light silently cutting its way through the darkness towards him. All of a sudden, the single red light seemed to twinkle slightly, then, become two!

The lights had now almost completely progressed through the blackened tunnel. Only a few more feet of darkness remained. For the first time, he could finally begin to make out the shape of a figure – a *human* figure. His first thought was that this was simply a track worker. But, almost as soon as he entertained that idea, he dismissed it as nothing more than a wishful thought. First of all, the light was traveling too smoothly. The natural up and down rhythmic motions of a worker walking along the tracks were not present, nor were the lights of their ever-present, hand held safety lanterns. At this distance, and at this deathly quiet time in the morning, even a solitary track worker, he reasoned, would make *some* noise. Probably the most disturbing of all was the fact that these lights were traveling about four or five feet higher than the height of any normal-sized person. Additionally, they appeared to be coming from the figure's head, specifically… the eyes.

His nervousness was now turning to fear. But, he still maintained a healthy dose of curiosity – enough curiosity to find out what was coming through the tunnel, but not quite enough fear to make him flee the station into the relative safety of the streets above. He looked down the long stretch of platform to his left, vainly searching for someone else… anyone else. Unfortunately, he was completely alone. He would have to bear sole witness to whomever, or *whatever* was headed his way.

The figure finally emerged from its cloak of darkness into the light of the station. Only about 15 feet now separated him from what was undoubtedly the most gruesome and ungodly sight he had ever seen in his life. Levitating in mid air, about five feet above the tracks – slowly being propelled forward by some invisible force – was what appeared to be an extremely grotesque-looking homeless man. He had intensely glowing red eyes that blankly stared straight ahead. Clad in a tattered overcoat and a pair of jeans so dirty – aside from the eyes – he was almost perfectly camouflaged with the grayish filth coating the track bed. He appeared to be a middle-aged white man with dark brown, shoulder-length matted hair. His feet pointed downward towards the tracks, and his arms hung limply by his sides. Probably the most hideous feature of all was his face. With a corpse-like, deathly pale complexion, it was covered with numerous open wounds, oozing some type of disgusting yellowish pus. Thick, greenish mucus also oozed from his nose into the cracks of his severely chapped and abnormally enlarged lips. A substantial and steady stream of blood drooled out of his partially opened mouth, which emitted small, intermitted puffs of vapor – the only visible indication that he was actually alive.

Hector was paralyzed with heart-stopping fear. Unable to move or speak, all he could do was stare in horrific disbelief at the unimaginable sight before him.

This isn't happening. It can't be happening!

The man stopped when he was directly in front of Hector – no more than a few feet away. Still hovering in midair, he slowly began turning his head – *just* his head – towards Hector. As his head moved, it produced a stomach churning, crackling sound that permeated throughout the quietness of the station. It continued to turn until his piercing red eyes were solidly fixed on Hector. With his body now completely motionless, the man started to grin…revealing an obscene set of extremely rotted and bloodstained teeth. The expression could only be described as…demonic. He then rotated his entire body to match the angle of his head.

A type of terror Hector had never thought possible was sweeping through every inch of his body. All of his previous concerns were now permanently erased from his mind. Gone was his preoccupation with the time. Gone was his annoyance with the train that never arrived. Gone was his desire to get home as quickly as possible. All that remained was an all-encompassing terror, interrupted only by the sound of his heartbeat. Since the man appeared, the temperature in the station seemed to drop at least 10 degrees. But, even this bitter cold didn't faze him – partly because his adrenaline was working overtime, but mainly because his lower body was gradually being warmed by a small trickle of liquid cascading down his legs.

As the two faced eye to eye, the man began to glide in his direction – slowly at first, then, with increasing speed. Before Hector could comprehend what was happening, the man was fully upon him. He was trapped in a vise-like grip, looking directly into the face of pure evil. With each breath, the man released an odor so foul that Hector became instantly, and violently ill.

The man lowered his head to Hector's chest. Using superhuman strength, he plunged his head through his rib cage, and into his body cavity. When he pulled it out, it was completely covered in blood. Hanging out of his mouth was a red mass dripping with blood. Hector's eyes began to close – gradually shutting out his last few seconds of consciousness. The man released his grip – allowing him to fall lifelessly to the platform. He then spat out the bloody mass. It landed just inches from his head – splattering his face with blood. Mortally wounded from his basketball-sized chest wound, he futilely gasped for his last precious breaths of air. As his eyes slowly closed for the last time, he could barely make out the fuzzy outline of the blood mass lying next to his face – slightly steaming... and still pulsating.

No longer levitating, and saturated with blood, mucus and human tissue, the man turned and ambled back toward the tunnel opening. In a trance-like state, he lumbered through a small, swinging red gate, emblazoned with the warning: DO NOT ENTER OR CROSS TRACKS. He shuffled along the tunnel's catwalk and disappeared into the darkness.

It had begun.

CHAPTER 4

October 15th – 12:22 a.m. Wednesday Morning

It had been building for quite some time. She had seen dozens of people who had only been on the job for a few months get promoted to managerial positions. Most were fresh out of college with hardly a fraction of the experience she had accumulated in her many years at the agency. Was it a coincidence that most of these people were young, white and male? She had never been the type to play the "race card," but the situation was becoming a joke – a very unfunny one. She was the only black woman in the office, and was consistently – and downright blatantly – passed over for promotions. Whenever she complained to her superiors, she was told that the applicants possessed a certain qualification crucial for that position. As far as she was concerned, their explanation amounted to nothing more than bullshit. At 58, she had never been a computer person, but made a serious effort to keep up with all the latest technologies of the day. Nevertheless, she never rose above the level of "assistant."

Mary Garrison worked at an advertising agency in lower Manhattan. It was a good job that paid well. During her eleven years of service she had received small salary increases, and even a few bonuses. As the years went by, she began to view the meager pay raises as little more than "hush money" – the agency's way of keeping her happy, while scores of others passed over her into higher paying positions. As if that weren't bad enough, her workload had been increasing to the point where it could no longer be done in a normal 8-hour day. She worked a lot of overtime hours – getting home later and later each night. Tonight was no exception. Just a half hour before quitting time, her boss handed her a large stack of reports that had to be completed by tomorrow.

Why the hell didn't he give these to me earlier in the day?! She fumed.

Even after working past 11 p.m., she was still only halfway through. To finish, she decided to take the reports home, and work on them into the night. The stack was too large to fit in her shoulder bag, so she had to carry them by hand. Even though she placed them in a folder, a few pages would sometimes slip out – adding to her aggravation. In the past, any employee who had to work late could call the car service provided by the agency. But, due to recent budgetary cuts, that service was no longer available. She had no money for a cab, and a bus would have taken forever. Her only other alternative was to take the subway home.

She was deep in thought as the train made its way along the route. Aside from a few homeless people walking through the car asking for spare change, the ride had been fairly uneventful. She was on the "B" train, traveling north along Central Park West. The car was half full when she first got on, but only she and an older black man remained by the time it reached uptown. Throughout the ride, she noticed him periodically staring at her, but was too consumed with her own problems to give him much thought. She didn't like traveling so late at night, but felt fairly safe since her walk home from the subway only took about one minute. She lived on 97th Street, just off of Central Park West on the Upper West Side of Manhattan. Her stop was 96th Street, but there was an exit to 97th Street at the front of the station – putting her just half a block away from her apartment building.

As the train pulled into the 96th Street Station, she made no attempt to get up. The situation on her job had gotten her so upset; she wasn't even aware she was approaching her stop. She simply sat there stewing in anger, thinking about how long it was going to take to finish all her work. She remained motionless even when the train had come to a full stop and the doors opened.

Bing... Bong.

Not until she heard the bell-tone indicating that the doors were about to close, did she look up and realize she was about to pass her stop.

"Oh, shit!" she said aloud.

She quickly gathered the pile of papers she had placed on the seat next to her; stood up, and ran to the nearest door. It had already begun to close, so she was only able to get a portion of her shoulder bag through. Her right hand, holding the folder, was on the outside of the train – the rest of her body was still inside. She was stuck. Not only was she in danger of losing her papers, she might even lose her hand if the train were to pull off and head into the tunnel. She had heard many stories of people being dragged to their deaths when pieces of their clothing got caught in the doors. Unlike elevator doors, subway doors have no internal sensors and do not automatically reopen when blocked. They are controlled solely by the conductor. She hoped that he would see her and free her from her trap. Thankfully, she was released after just a few embarrassing seconds. The sudden opening caused her to drop the folder, spilling her papers all over the platform.

"God, dammit!" she cried.

She bent down to pick them up, and wondered what else could go wrong. She didn't have to wonder too long. After the train closed its doors and began moving out of the station, it generated a lot of wind – sending the papers into a swirling whirlpool.

She chased them down, frantically grabbing at the wayward pieces. As the train left the station it created a back draft – sending the papers into an even wilder frenzy. When she finally got everything corralled back into the folder, she smiled and quietly chuckled at her impromptu, comedy of error performance – slightly embarrassed at how ridiculous it must have looked to anyone watching. Fortunately, the only other passengers getting off were at the middle and rear of the platform.

She began walking towards the 97th Street exit at the front end of the station. She had gotten to within a few feet of it and realized why she was the only person in the area – the exit was closed.

"Oh, damn!" she uttered aloud.

So preoccupied with her thoughts, she had completely forgotten that this lesser-used exit closes at midnight. She made an about-face and began heading toward the main exit in the opposite direction.

She had traveled through that station every day and never felt threatened or uneasy. This was mainly because most of her traveling was done during peak, rush-hour periods, when the station was full of activity. After her train cleared the station and roared into the tunnel, the usual familiar surroundings took on a slightly more ominous appearance. She was surprised at just how quiet it got. The only sounds were from the footsteps and muted voices of the other passengers – the ones who sat at the *correct* end of the train – as they disappeared from the platform through the main exit. Although not visible to her, she could also hear the clanking sounds of them passing through the turnstiles, as they made their way up a flight of stairs to the street.

The station was also quite cold. She didn't remember it being this chilly when she was outside. Mid-October is supposed to be Indian summer, yet she was almost able to see her breath in the nippy air. She clumsily tried to pull her light jacket closed, while at the same time, making sure she didn't drop her papers again.

She turned and looked behind her at the closed exit – sort of hoping that she had only mistaken it for being closed. No such luck. It was definitely closed. When she looked forward again, she noticed something strange. Most of the people were moving at a brisk pace, hastily making their way to the exit. As the crowd thinned, she could barely make out a solitary dark figure in the rear of the group that didn't seem to be in much of a hurry. In fact, the figure didn't seem to be moving at all. The passengers continued to exit until only a few stragglers remained. As the strange figure came more clearly into view, it began to stand out like a sore thumb.

Mary's heart raced. She was mugged years ago in the subway, and had never gotten completely over it. Even though it was just a simple purse snatching, she avoided riding the subway for quite some time. When she finally worked up the nerve to venture underground again, her anxiety level would rise every time she saw a young person who might be up to no good. But this situation was different. This didn't look like a purse-snatcher. Besides, there were many other much closer and easier targets. She knew it was crazy, but it almost seemed as though this person was focused only on her.

The last passenger exited the platform. One final pass through a turnstile was heard. As if a switch had just been flipped, all sounds and activity in the station abruptly ceased. She and the lone, mysterious figure were now the only two individuals remaining on the platform. The only footsteps she heard were her own. A chill ran through her entire body.

As the distance between the two decreased, details of the figure's appearance became more evident. The person was wearing a black, "Dick Tracey"-type hat, with a wide rim. The head was cast slightly downward, with the rim blocking the face. The figure was clad in a long black coat that reached the ground. The arms hung limply from the sides.

Why the hell is he just standing there like that? She wondered. *Could he be asleep?*

Although she was thinking it was a "he," she really couldn't tell if the person was a man or a woman. Her eyes stayed transfixed on the creepy figure as she continued to make her way towards the exit – the exit which seemed to be moving further and further away with each step.

As she came closer, she could see that the clothes the figure was wearing were quite tattered – filthy even. But the closer she came; she noticed one tiny, but frightening detail. From afar, the long coat looked as though it touched the ground; but at her present distance, she could see several inches of clear space between the bottom of the coat and the platform. The figure didn't appear to have any feet!

Raw fear swept through her body. She had seen magic tricks like this before on TV, but this wasn't a TV studio. It was a subway station… *her* subway station. All of the little things she found only slightly ominous just seconds ago were now downright frightening.

Maybe… I'm not seeing this right. She thought.

If what she was seeing *was* correct, then, she had somehow just stepped into a real-life horror movie.

Could it be…a ghost!?

She had never personally seen a ghost, but knew of several people who did. From their accounts, she knew it was rarely the vague, shadowy figure that's often portrayed in movies. In most cases, a ghost could look just as solid as a real person. She didn't know what she was looking at, but for some reason, she didn't believe it was an apparition.

The sight of the startling spectacle caused her to slow her stride until – without realizing it – she had come to a complete stop. She gazed for several seconds – partly in disbelief, but mostly in terror – at the chilling sight before her. At this distance, there was no mistake in what she was seeing – the figure was inexplicably hovering or levitating in midair!

Her heart pounded so hard, it hurt. She clutched her chest to ease the pain.

Suddenly, the figure showed the first sign of movement. Slowly and methodically, it began to raise its head. Like a curtain rising on a macabre play, the wide hat rim gradually started to unveil a face.

Oh, God… no!

Her body began trembling uncontrollably. Despite the increasingly cold temperature in the station, she started to sweat. She knew whatever she was about to see was something that she really didn't *want* to see. But she couldn't turn away. She simply stood there like a deer frozen in headlights – a captive audience to the unfolding terror.

The figure's head continued to rise until the entire face was revealed. It appeared to be a young black man in his twenties. He had a very dark complexion – probably of African descent. His face was thin, and as far as she could tell, expressionless. The rim of the hat cast a shadow over the upper portion of the face, completely obscuring his eyes.

She started to panic.

She wasn't a religious person, but knew what she was witnessing was unholy and unearthly. She had a sick feeling that if she didn't start making her way toward the exit immediately, something unthinkable was about to happen. But the exit was still several feet in front of her. To get out, she would have to keep walking straight ahead... directly toward the mysterious levitating man. No matter how badly she wanted to get away, she just couldn't bring herself to move another inch in that direction.

Suddenly, the man's mouth began to open.

She gasped.

A set of yellow-stained teeth were revealed. As it opened further, she could see that they looked less like teeth, and more like... fangs. At first, they sort of reminded her of the fake Dracula fangs sold in novelty shops around Halloween. But, as the mouth continued to open wider it became obvious they definitely weren't some cheap, plastic child's toy. Each tooth was sharpened to a point and almost equal in length.

"Oh, my... God!" she whispered to herself, as she began to inch backwards.

Her adrenaline was racing. She was experiencing a degree of terror she never thought possible. The last thing she wanted to do was to face this alone. She turned around again and surveyed the long platform behind her. With the exit at the far end closed, she knew no other passengers would be back there – but she had to check just to be sure. As she fully expected, she and this... *thing*, were still the only two souls present in the deserted station. The sight she saw when she looked back at the man made her scream out in horror.

His mouth had opened even wider. It had stretched to more than twice the size any *normal* person's mouth should have been able. It had also increased in width. The needle-sharp teeth, already frightening-looking, were now terrifying since they too had increased in size. Each one was over an inch long. The expression resembled the menacing "grin" of a Great White shark. Only this was definitely not a grin – it was more like an angry growl.

Tears welled up in her eyes from fright. She continued her clumsy, backward retreat – almost tripping over her own feet with every step.

A white, lumpy substance began flowing out of the man's grotesquely enlarged mouth – a little at first, then, with increasing velocity. It was thick, and fell heavily to the platform surface in resounding "plops," that echoed throughout the silence. As she watched, strange wounds appeared to inexplicably form all over the man's face. As if been sliced by an unseen knife, the flesh of his cheeks and chin simultaneously began to part into numerous one to two-inch long slits. Seconds later, instead of blood, a disgusting type of yellowish pus began oozing out of the wounds.

"OH, NO… OH, NO!!" she cried, as she continued her slow retreat.

She could no longer think straight. Raw terror had caused her mind to blur the division between fantasy and reality.

Things like this only happen in the movies!

I'm not really here right now – I'm home, safe and sound, working on my reports!

That's it! I must have fallen asleep while working, and this is all just a dream… yes, just a dream!

As much as she wished for that to be the case, she knew it wasn't. Although defying all the laws of science and physics, she had no doubt that what she was seeing was very real.

Suddenly, two bright red lights pierced through the dark shadow on the upper portion of the man's face. He had opened his eyes and they were beet red. The light cut through the dim lighting in the station like a laser, and deliberately fixed itself upon her. Before she could fully comprehend what was happening, the man started to move towards her. Still levitating several inches above the ground, he began smoothly gliding down the platform in her direction.

She screamed and started to frantically pant. Her breaths rapidly increased, almost to the point of hyperventilation. She wanted to scream again, but was partially in shock, and temporarily robbed of her voice. All she could manage was a childlike whimper. The man was picking up speed – as if propelled forward by an invisible motor. She knew she would never be able to make it to the main exit in time. With no other option, she whirled around and bolted toward the front of the platform. So distracted by what was happening; she didn't realize how closely she had backed up to a heavy wooden bench directly behind her. She slammed her left leg into the side of it so hard the force completely doubled her over – sending her crashing face-first into the blunt edge of the backrest. Searing pain shot through her entire body. Any lingering thoughts that this was all just a dream were completely – and painfully – erased. She rolled off of the bench and landed on her back on the platform. The impact dislodged the folder from her hand and, once again, spilled all her papers. Her shoulder bag got turned upside down, and many of her personal items – including her purse and house keys – fell out onto the bench.

She cried out in pain. She had severely banged up her knee and bloodied her nose. Normally, after an injury like that she would have laid there for several minutes nursing her wounds – but, right now, that was a luxury she couldn't afford. When she looked up, she screamed again in terror. The man was now moving much faster and was alarmingly close. At this distance, his mouth looked even more menacing. It seemed to have opened even wider, and the teeth looked like sharpened daggers. The cold temperature produced a steady stream of cloud-like vapor from his mouth. The white, lumpy vomit flowed like diarrhea down the entire front of his long black coat. Yellowish pus continued to ooze out of his horrible facial wounds. His arms were now outstretched away from his sides in a bear-hug-like position. Each hand was wide open with all ten fingers splayed out as far as possible. Each fingernail was a freakish three to four inches long – looking more like the sharp claws of a grizzly bear.

The man was now past the main exit at 96th Street. With the 97th Street exit closed, her only other means of escape was the tunnel. She was going to have to run along its precariously narrow catwalk – all the way to the next station at 103rd Street. Only specially trained track workers, vandals or people with serious mental problems would dare enter this "forbidden zone." But, it was now her *only* means of escape.

She continued to scream as loud as she possibly could – hoping to attract the attention of the station agent at the main exit. She struggled to get to her feet, but kept slipping on the loose papers. Just seconds ago, they were of the utmost importance. Now, they were nothing more than annoying little pieces of debris, preventing her from getting away. She couldn't have cared any less about them, or about all of her personal items she was about to leave behind on the bench. When she finally got to her feet, she took off in earnest, running and screaming down the platform – too scared to look back. With only a few more feet of platform remaining, she suddenly felt as though she had been raked across her back with hot coals.

She screamed as she clutched her back and fell to the ground in pain.

The man had caught up with her. Using his sharpened, claw-like fingernails, he easily penetrated her light jacket, and cut into her flesh. With one blow, he sliced her back open, creating a diagonal wound starting just below her right shoulder and traveling all the way down to the left side of her lower back.

"Oh, God… no… please don't hurt me!!" she pleaded. "I don't have any money… my purse and everything's down there!!!"

Somehow, she knew that money wasn't what he was after. He loomed over her like a tower – his inhuman-like red eyes solidly locked onto hers. His height began to diminish. He gradually descended to the platform until he was no longer levitating and took a few steps closer to her.

"No… no… please, no," she whimpered, as she shook her head from side to side and cried. She got into a sitting position and used her feet and hands to push herself up against the wall.

The man continued to approach until he was standing directly over her. His hellishly large mouth opened and closed in a rhythmic motion like a monstrous grinder. Each time it opened thick clumps of vomit and saliva dripped out onto her face and chest. She quietly began mouthing the words to the Lord's Prayer.

The man bent down and grabbed her by her head, and brutally pulled her to her feet. The long nails dug deeply into the sides of her head. Before she could react to the pain, he opened his cavernous mouth one final time and bit into her face.

She screamed and frantically clutched her face. When she removed her hands, everything looked strange and she was having trouble focusing. She looked down and saw that she was saturated with blood. It looked as though someone had doused her with a bucket of red paint. There was even a steadily growing puddle of blood at her feet.

He bit me… he must have bitten me!!! She thought.

But how could there be so much blood from a single bite?!

She clutched her face again, but this time to *really* feel it.

She pulled her hands away in stunned disbelief. The initial shock of the attack caused her not to notice certain things the first time. What should have felt soft was hard. What should have been dry was wet. And where she should have felt resistance… there was none. Everything below her left eyebrow to the corner of her mouth – essentially, the entire left side of her face – was gone. The razor-like fangs ripped through her skin leaving nothing but a bloody reservoir of dangling tendons, ripped flesh and exposed bone.

The reality of what had just happened was slowly sinking in. She now understood why she was having so much difficulty with her vision. When she tried to touch her left eye, her fingers fell into a deep, empty cavity. She flew into an uncontrollable fit of hysterics and desperately pawed at what was left of her face – uttering a series of short, manic screams.

She struggled to break free, but her efforts were in vain. The man maintained a death-grip on her head – trapping her like a vise. With one, lightening-fast jerk of his hands, he violently twisted her head to the side – almost turning it completely backwards. Her screams were immediately halted, and followed by a loud crackling sound. All the bones in her neck were instantly snapped. Other than a few residual twitches, she had ceased struggling. There was silence.

The rumble of an approaching train began to fill the void.

The man released his grip and slammed her lifeless body to the platform. He stood over her for a few seconds, as if to confirm – or admire – his gruesome handiwork. When satisfied, he gradually closed his monstrous mouth. Showing no emotion or haste to escape, he turned, and slowly walked down the platform toward the front end. A train roared into the station on the express track – its breeze stirring Mary's papers into frenzy, once again. It continued its non-stop journey through the station and disappeared into the tunnel. Silence returned to the station – a silence punctuated only by the soft rustling of the loose papers fluttering aimlessly in the air.

The sound of a rotating turnstile echoed through the emptiness.

A male passenger entered the station. As he stepped onto the platform, he inadvertently stepped into a pile of the white, slimy substance.

"What the *hell*!?" he muttered to himself.

He looked down and saw that there was actually a trail of the white stuff on the platform as far as he could see in both directions. There was also an unusual amount of debris scattered about. Loose papers were everywhere. Most of the pieces were on the platform and in the trackbed, but a few were still airborne – gently wafting about. He then noticed what appeared to be a dark figure disappearing into the blackness of the tunnel. He only got a quick glimpse, and wasn't absolutely sure he had seen anything at all. While looking in that direction, he noticed a large mass lying near the wall. From where he stood, it appeared to be a large bag of some sort. Since the trail of white slime seemed to stop there, he concluded that someone must have dragged a leaky garbage bag along the platform, and simply left it where it lay.

"Only in New York!" he said, shaking his head in disgust.

He turned around and began making his way toward the rear of the platform – angrily trying to scrap the white substance off his shoe.

CHAPTER 5

October 16th – 9:34 a.m. Thursday Morning

The elevator door couldn't open fast enough for her. When it finally did, she bolted out onto the floor – accidentally banging her shoulder against the slowly opening door. She didn't have time to think about the pain. Her only concern was getting to her desk.

Melissa was late for work – over a half hour late. Normally, she prided herself on her punctuality. Since she'd been on the job, she had been late just a couple of times, and it was only by one or two minutes at the most. Being *this* late really upset her. The fact that she had simply overslept upset her even more. But it wasn't totally her fault. Due to a mechanical problem on her train the night before, she got home much later than usual. This threw her normal routine off-schedule, and ignited a chain reaction of delayed personal chores – culminating in her failure to hear her morning alarm clock.

She passed a sea of faces as she briskly made her way through the office to her desk. On any other day, this would have been a leisurely stroll, with a cup of coffee in one hand and a newspaper in the other – frequently stopping to chat with a few of her colleagues about the latest topics of the day. Today, she didn't have time for any of that. A few people attempted to approach her, but she wasn't about to stop for conversation. All she gave them was a quick but polite nod of acknowledgement and continued on her journey.

That's strange. She thought.

Some people looked worried. Some actually looked a little

surprised, and downright shocked to see her.

Although it wasn't commonplace for her to be late, she didn't think it should elicit such a widespread, stunned reaction, either. After all, it wasn't as though she committed some serious...

Wait!

What if they know something that I don't!?

She imagined the worst-case scenario.

What if I've been fired for being late!?

Lately, the firm had begun cracking down on employee lateness. Two people had already been written up, and another was given a verbal warning...and *none* of them were as late as she was today.

It was a horrible thought. With no one to support her *and* with her high tuition cost, she absolutely could not afford to lose her job. Her frustration was turning into a heart-pounding anxiety. Even though her boss was also her boyfriend, he still had to answer to higher powers. If the "suits" at the top wanted her gone, there really wasn't much he could do to save her.

She continued the journey to her desk. The walk seemed much longer than ever. She felt terrible, and the gauntlet of sorrowful faces she passed along the way made her feel even worse. For the rest of the way, she kept her head down and avoided any direct eye contact. When she got to her desk, she tossed her shoulder bag on top of it and quickly took off her jacket. Out the corner of her eye, she saw someone approaching. It was Richard. He was moving fast – almost running – and had an anguished look on his face.

"Oh, thank God, you're here!" he practically shouted.

She immediately started to defend her tardiness.

"Look, Rich, I'm sorry," she said, almost in tears. "The train I was on last night broke down and sat in the tunnel for thirty minutes. I didn't get home until after 1a.m. I know it's no excuse, but I overslept this morning, and I---"

"Melissa, I don't care about that... I only care that you're okay!"

"That I'm *okay*? Why wouldn't I be okay?"

"You don't know?"

"Know *what*? Richard, what are you *talking* about?"

They stared at each other for a few seconds in silence.

"Come with me," he said, taking her by the arm. He escorted her into his office.

Although relieved to know that she wasn't in trouble for being late, she was clueless as to what had gotten him so upset. When she walked into his office, he pointed to his wall-mounted television. A special news bulletin was being broadcast.

Again... she was found with her skull literally crushed, and her body stuffed behind a dumpster at the rear of the southbound platform of the Van Siclen Station in Brooklyn, shortly after 4 a.m. this morning. The victim is described as an African-American female in her early twenties. Police estimate the murder to have occurred sometime around midnight. This is the third, in a string of grisly murders committed in the subway system in as many days, in what police are now describing as one of the bloodiest weeks in the history of the subway. As you'll recall, Tuesday, a man was killed in the Kingston Avenue Station on the #2 line in Brooklyn – his heart ripped completely out of his chest. Yesterday, a woman was found murdered with her face mutilated and neck broken on the "A" and "C" line at the 96th Street Station, on the Upper West side of Manhattan. And now, just last night, this woman, who, so far, remains unidentified, was discovered here at the Van Siclen Station, also on the "A" and "C" line. At this point, police aren't sure if the murders are related, but do see a similarity in the extremely vicious way in which they were committed. Any witnesses to this, or the other two murders, are urged to contact the police immediately. All calls will, of course, be kept confidential. Reporting live from the East New York section of Brooklyn, I'm Barry Anthony Ramsay... New York One.

Even when they had moved on to another story, Melissa just stood there for several seconds, staring at the screen. That was *her* subway line they were talking about. That was *her* station they were standing in front of. The two prior murders already had her on edge – mainly because of her feelings of an evil presence in the subway. But at least, they were committed far away from home, in stations

79

she's never even passed through. But *this*… this was too close.

"You okay?" Richard asked, as he put his arm around her shoulder. "Here, sit down."

"That… that could've been me," she said, staring blankly into space.

"I know! That's why I was so worried… we all were!"

"*All?*"

"The office," he replied. "You're hardly ever late. When you didn't show up at nine o'clock, I asked around to see if, maybe, you had called in. When no one had heard from you… and when I turned on the TV and saw *that*… Well, I just started thinking the worst."

He pulled up a chair and sat down next to her. He put his arm around her shoulder, and pulled her closer to him. Although he wanted to comfort her more, the lack of privacy in his glass-walled office – the "fish bowl," as she often referred to it – discouraged him from going any further.

"I don't know what I'd do if I ever lost you," he whispered, as he gently rubbed her upper arm.

She smiled meekly, but said nothing.

"I can't believe you didn't know anything about the murder until now," he said. "Didn't you see the camera crews outside your station when you got on the subway this morning?"

"Yeah, I did, but I just assumed they were doing another story on the lousy service."

"Speaking of which… didn't you say something about your train breaking down last night?" he asked.

"Yeah, I didn't get home until late last night; or early this morning, to be exact. That's why I overslept and got in late."

He looked a bit perplexed.

"Wait a minute," he said, "You *normally* get home around midnight, right?"

"Yeah."

"And what time did you get home *last* night?"

"Around 1 a.m."

"My God, Melissa… they said that girl was probably killed around midnight. Had it not been for that little delay of yours…"

80

He didn't have to finish his sentence – the look on her face said it all. For the first time, she realized just how lucky she was at avoiding becoming another statistic. Her whole body started to shake. If she weren't already sitting down, she probably would have collapsed.

He worried about her ever since she had started taking night classes at John Jay. He hated the idea of her going home so late at night, especially in such a dangerous neighborhood. On many occasions, he had offered to drive her home, but she always declined – basically out of her concern for him as well. Since he had to drive all the way back to Long Island, she didn't want him getting home so late. Reluctantly, he always gave in to her. Since her parents' tragedy, she was forced to become a completely independent person practically overnight. For the most part, he felt it was a good thing. Instead of withering into an emotionally handicapped individual, she had developed into a very strong young woman. But, in light of the recent events, he felt it necessary to press the issue of safety and common sense.

"Sweetie, look," he said, as he held her tighter, "I think it's time you start letting me drive you home at night after class."

"Rich… we've been through this before. I just don't feel comfortable imposing on you like that."

"Imposing!? Melissa… you're my girlfriend; I don't mind doing things like that for you. That's what being in a relationship is all about. We're supposed to help each other out… it's in the contract, didn't you read it?"

She laughed.

"I know, but you'll be getting home so late."

"No I won't – not the way *I* drive."

"That's *exactly* one of the things I'm worried about!"

"Look… I may drive fast, but I'm careful."

"That's what they all say, until they wake up with their car wrapped around a tree… that is, *if,* they wake up at all!"

He sighed.

"I know you're not the type of person who likes to ask for help. I also know that riding the subway makes you uncomfortable enough as it is. But *now*, with all of this going on, *nobody* should be riding alone… especially that late at night."

"But I'm not alone. I'm with a bunch of my friends from class."

"Yeah, but they don't ride with you all the way to your stop in Brooklyn. And they certainly don't walk home with you, either."

"Richard, sweetie," she stroked his face with her hand. "Stop worrying about me. I'll be fine, honest."

"You know," he said, "things would be a lot simpler if we just took that next step."

She knew exactly where he was headed. For the past several months, he'd been suggesting they move in together. He reasoned that with their combined incomes, they'd be able to afford a decent place much closer to the city – perhaps even within the city. It would be a much easier commute, and they'd be together all the time. Ironically, that was precisely the reason why she was reluctant to do so. It was hard enough avoiding intimate situations once or twice a week. If they moved in together, it would be a daily struggle. This was not a battle she was ready to face just yet, nor was she willing to put Richard through all the frustrations he would undoubtedly endure. Until she was ready to deal with her sexual problems, she felt it was best if they just left things the way they were for now.

She sighed, and looked up at him with sad eyes. Without having to say a word, he knew what was wrong.

"Please, don't worry about that, sweetie. I love you, and I want to be with you… no matter what," he said softly.

"I love you too, honey… I just---"

"I know, I know," he cut her off, not wanting to make her any more uncomfortable than she already was, "you're not ready yet, but when the time is right… we'll know."

She smiled, appreciative of his understanding.

"I better get to work," she said, gesturing to her desk out in the bullpen.

"Alright, we'll talk later, okay?"

"Okay."

After a quick peck on the lips, she got up, and headed back to her desk. Even though the entire office was aware of their relationship, she still wanted to maintain a certain level of discretion and professionalism. Besides, the "fish bowl" wasn't exactly conducive to any higher levels of intimacy.

Back at her desk, she started thinking about how fortunate she was to have Richard in her life. Having someone like him for a boyfriend was something she always dreamed of, but never believed it would actually happen. Many of her friends were trapped – financially or psychologically – in dysfunctional relationships filled with infidelity, abuse or an addiction to any number of vices. Those who weren't – the "lucky" ones – found themselves settling for a partner whose feelings towards them could probably be described as "indifferent" at best. Melissa had definitely struck gold with Richard, and she knew it. Theirs was a relationship based on trust and mutual respect – a perfect combination that slowly matured into a deep, fulfilling love.

The phone rang loudly on the desk next to hers – rudely halting her blissful thoughts.

When she looked up, she caught the eye of Agnes Covington, sitting on the opposite side of the large room. Unlike the other women in the office, who seemed to exist just to make her life miserable, Agnes was different. Originally from the south, she was an older black woman who mainly kept to herself. Although no one knew exactly how old she was, best estimates placed her in her late fifties – making her one of the oldest workers in the office. As such, she tended to steer clear of all of the petty office drama. Aside from her quiet demeanor, she had a reputation of being somewhat odd – scary even. Maybe it was the slow, methodical way in which she spoke, or perhaps the dowdy, old-fashioned outfits she wore. Whatever it was, it was enough to give most people the willies whenever they were in her presence. But, Melissa was one of the few people who felt comfortable carrying on a conversation with her. In fact, she seemed to be the only person in the office Agnes connected with, and whose company she actually enjoyed.

After acknowledging each other with a smile and a nod, Melissa looked away into space – allowing her thoughts drift back to the weird goings-on in the subway. No matter how hard she tried, she just couldn't get it out of her mind. She *knew* something strange was going on and these murders finally confirmed her fears. Also, the fact that the police had absolutely no leads, made it even stranger.

She started thinking about the latest victim. She wondered what thoughts might have gone through her mind in the final seconds of her life.

Was she somebody's girlfriend, wife or mother?
Where was she headed?
What agony are her parents going through right now?
Her eyes began to water.
Suddenly, an unimaginable thought came to her.
What if the latest victim was supposed to be me!?
What if I was the intended target all along!?

Based on the news report, she matched the victim's physical description fairly well. What if the killer (or killers) actually *thought* that other girl was her!?

It petrified her to even consider such a notion...but it made sense.

The weird vibes...the strange sounds, and now, the murder of a girl who closely resembled her – at a time and place she normally would have been!

She felt sick. Her heart started beating wildly and she began sweating as though she was outside on a hot, summer day. Her hands and legs started to tremble uncontrollably. Everything began a blur.

"You sure you're okay?"

Startled, she jumped, and let out a short, but a quite audible cry of shock and surprise. So distracted by her thoughts, she didn't even notice that Richard had come out of his office, and was walking toward her desk.

"Oh, yeah...I'm fine," she said, still a bit disoriented. She tried to hide her trembling hands by sitting on them.

"My God, you look awful!" he said, as he got closer. "This has obviously affected you more than you thought. Why not take the rest of the day off?"

She thought about telling him the truth about what she had been experiencing for the past several weeks, but knew it wasn't the appropriate time or place.

"Oh, no, I'll...I'll be alright...really," she stammered, forcing a little smile. "I just need to sit here for a minute."

"You're sweating like crazy! Let me get you a cup of water."

"No, that's alright, I---"

Before she could stop him, he had gone to the water cooler and was returning with a cup filled almost to the brim.

"Here," he said, as he carefully handed it to her, "have some of this."

"Thanks."

Even though she grasped the cup with both hands, she was no longer able to downplay her anxiety. Still shaking, she spilled nearly half of it on her desk and herself.

"Jesus Christ, Melissa," he said, as he helped steady her hands, "I've never seen you like this. Are you *sure* you don't wanna take the day off?"

"I'm fine, Rich, honest. I guess I'm still trying to get over the shock of it happening so close to home, you know?"

"Yeah, I guess that can be one helleva shock."

Although he wasn't totally convinced there wasn't more to it than that, he decided to let it go.

"Alright, I gotta go downstairs for a little while. You sure you're going to be okay?"

"Yeah, I'll be fine," she smiled again, but with a little more sincerity this time.

As he walked away, she realized that she truly did feel much better. Her heart rate had slowed to near normal, and her trembling had almost completely subsided. She took a few more sips of water and started thinking about the situation more rationally. The other two murders took place in stations far away from hers, and the victims didn't resemble her in the slightest.

Could all of the similarities between me and the third victim really be just uncanny coincidences after all?

She wanted more than anything to believe that, but she

couldn't. There was still no explanation for her creepy feeling that she was being watched, and, of course...*that scraping sound*!

She would never be able to rest easy until she got some real answers. Hopefully, by that time...it wouldn't be too late.

CHAPTER 6

October 17th – 11:12 p.m. Friday Evening

Melissa had been in a daze ever since yesterday. She tried to go about her everyday routines as normally as possible, but it was only a charade – and not a very good one at that. She knew everyone at work and at school could clearly see that she wasn't herself, but she didn't care. Aside from the murders, she really didn't care much about anything else. She had become obsessed with the topic. She absorbed as much information about the crimes as she could from newspapers and television. She was still trying to convince herself that the strange murders were nothing more than random acts of violence – violence that she was in no way connected. Unfortunately, the more she learned, the less secure she felt.

After her last class, she said goodbye to her friends and slipped into the quietness of the student lounge to read yet another newspaper article. With all of the gory angles of the story exhausted, the media were now focusing on analyzing the murders. This particular story suggested that robbery probably wasn't a motivating factor in any of the three cases, since none of the victims' money or other valuables seemed to have been taken. Police theorized it was the work of a satanic cult, carrying out some type of ritualistic sacrifices. Cult experts, however, disagreed – pointing out that no satanic markings were found at the crime scenes. They went on to state that sacrificial ceremonies are usually performed outdoors in designated areas. Since ceremonies tend to go on for quite some time, these areas are often very isolated to avoid risk of detection. Also, animals are the usual sacrificial objects of choice.

Additionally, and most disturbingly, it would have taken super-human strength to inflict the type of wounds these victims exhibited.

Goosebumps formed on Melissa's arms. It was bad enough believing that she might be the target of some unknown killer. Now, there was speculation that this killer might not even be human!

She heard a rustling sound.

Already on edge, she was about to jump up and bolt from the large, empty room, when she noticed the newspaper she was holding was flapping like a flag in the breeze. She was totally unaware that her hands were trembling. Relieved, but somewhat embarrassed by her overreaction, she rested the paper on the table. Before she had a chance to fully calm her nerves, they were rattled again by an unexpected voice from behind.

"You're still *here*? I thought you'd be gone by now."

She gasped and quickly whirled around – almost knocking the newspaper to the floor. Steven Kippers, one of her classmates, was standing in the doorway.

"Oh, hi Steve."

"Sorry, I didn't mean to scare you."

"Oh, that's okay… I was just catching up on a little reading before I went home."

"Are you about done, or are you going to hang around here for a little while longer?"

"No, I'm done." She folded up the newspaper and stuffed it in her bag.

Steven went the same way home on the train after class. Usually, Melissa would ride with a group of five or six of her friends – a tight clique which not only served as great company, but as of late, an immeasurable degree of security. But tonight, she had lost track of time while reading the newspaper and they all left without her.

Steven wasn't exactly her first choice as a traveling companion. He was a lanky, dark-complexioned black man. He wore thick bifocals and wasn't a very attractive person, but perhaps, more so than his appearance, it was his personality that tended to put people off. He was a quiet man who always kept to himself.

Although he took the same train and even rode in the same car as Melissa and her friends, he wasn't exactly *with* the group. Usually, sitting a few feet away or across the aisle, he rarely joined in their conversation. If he said anything at all, it was often an off-topic, out-of-left-field remark that would bring the conversation to a screeching halt. After a few seconds of awkward silence, their banter would resume with everyone making a concerted effort to exclude him from the dialogue.

At first, Melissa felt bad for him. Thanks to most of the women on her job, she knew all too well what it felt like to be the outsider. She didn't think it was right to ostracize someone simply because they were a little *odd*. But as time went by, she started to get an uneasy vibe from him – a vibe that suggested his behavior was fueled by something more than mere shyness, or even a lack of social graces. For more than a couple of occasions, whether they were in class or on the train, she would suddenly look up and catch him staring directly at her. He would then immediately look away, or slightly avert his gaze to pretend he was looking at something else. For a woman with her looks, she was used to receiving a lot of attention from men. But, for some reason, it seemed different with Steven. There was just something about him that made her feel uncomfortable. This uneasiness was quelled by the presence of her friends – a security blanket which she would not be able to rely on tonight.

"I can't believe this week is finally over," he said, as they exited the building, and began their two-block trek to the Columbus Circle subway station. "I thought it would never end."

"Yeah, I know, it was a rough one."

"It must be especially rough for you... having to go to school *and* work."

"It can be a strain sometimes, but I've gotten used to it."

The next several seconds were spent in silence – an uneasy silence, emphasized by the sound of their footsteps echoing on the sidewalk. She could tell he wanted to say something, but seemed to be searching for just the right words. When he finally *did* speak, it only made the situation more awkward.

"Would you… like to go out with me sometime?" he timidly asked.

She smiled, and was momentarily speechless. She wasn't expecting such a direct question. In a group setting, he could barely look her in the eye. But tonight was the first time they were completely alone. Apparently, their one-on-one interaction gave him a new-found courage to ask what had probably been on his mind for quite some time.

"Steven, I'm flattered that you would ask, but I have a boyfriend."

"Oh… you do?"

"Yeah, I thought you knew."

"No, I didn't."

"Well, thanks for asking, anyway."

She realized just how little she had spoken to him in the past, and wondered how much, if *anything*, he knew about her at all.

"Would you go out with me if you didn't have a boyfriend?" he quickly blurted out.

"I… I don't know, Steven," she said, somewhat taken aback by the question, "I really don't know you that well."

"But if we went out, you could get to know me… *right*?"

She smiled nervously, but said nothing. She had absolutely no idea how to respond to such a question.

"I'm sorry," he apologized, "I shouldn't have said---"

"That's okay."

Actually, it wasn't okay. Their strange conversation was making her feel very uncomfortable. They walked in silence for the next several seconds. Once again, the lull was broken by another one of his off-putting remarks.

"I like the way you look in your pants."

Stunned, she turned to him, and asked, "You *what*?"

"NO, NO, NO!" he said, nervously, "I didn't mean anything sexual by that… not at all!"

"Ah, huh."

"No, believe me; I'm not tryin' to hit on you or anything. I… I'm just sayin' you have a very nice, healthy-looking body."

"*Healthy*-looking?"

"Yeah, you know, like… very fit."

"Oh, well… thank you," she said, still somewhat shocked by his comments.

After a slight pause, he asked, "I'll bet your boyfriend likes your body too, right?"

"*Steven*, that's really none of---"

"I know… I know! That's none of my business! I shouldn't have said that! I'm sorry… I'm really sorry!"

Despite his profuse apologies, she was upset and growing more nervous by the second. His conversation had taken a definite turn toward "creepy." Whether it was due to his inexperience with talking to women, or something more ominous… she really didn't care anymore. They were the only ones on the street, and she didn't feel safe. When he started to breathe a little heavy, she had just about all she could take. Thinking fast, she came up with an excuse to remove herself from the situation.

"Oh, damn!" she said, stopping abruptly.

"What… what's wrong?"

"I just remembered that there's a book I need for a test on Monday, and I left it at school. I gotta go back!"

"Oh, okay, I'll come with you."

"NO!" She practically shouted, throwing up her hand to stop him. Fearing she may have overreacted, she tried to soften her response by quickly adding, "I… I mean, it might take me a while to find it… I don't want to hold you up."

"Oh, that's okay… I'm not in any hurry to get home."

She realized subtlety wasn't going to work. At the risk of losing some of her dignity, she said, "Look, Steven, the truth of the matter is that I've had a bad case of diarrhea all day, and I really gotta go to the bathroom… RIGHT NOW!"

"But I---"

"I would have a problem, you know… *going*, if I knew you were waiting for me," she held her stomach, feigning discomfort. "Besides, I think I'm gonna be a while."

"But---"

"No Steven, really… you go on ahead without me," she began backing away from him, "I'll see you in class on Monday, okay?"

"Well…okay," he said, confused by the sudden turn of events.

She then turned around and began quickly walking back to the school. Halfway down the block, she looked back and saw that he was pretty much in the same location where she left him; still watching her. Hoping he wasn't actually going to wait *there* for her, she gave him a quick wave and continued on her way. At the corner, she turned around once more, and was relieved to see that he was now slowly walking toward the subway. To be on the safe side, she crossed the street and ducked behind a parked van. She waited there for a few seconds, then, cautiously peeked around it. He was gone. She felt silly for going to such lengths just to avoid him, but she couldn't ignore her gut instinct. She never felt comfortable around him, and after their first "real" conversation – which, hopefully, would also be their last – she finally understood why.

She checked her watch.

11:29 p.m.

She knew the trains ran much less frequently at that time of night. If she left now, there was a good chance she would run into him in the station. To kill time, she decided she might as well go back to the school. But before she could get there, she saw the custodian come out and lock up the building for the night.

Damn it! Now what!?

With no shops or restaurants in the immediate area, her choices of activity were limited. Even though it was late and the streets were somewhat deserted, she felt relatively safe in the neighborhood; so, she leaned against the building and took out her newspaper. She read the comics for several minutes, then, decided that enough was enough. She refused to allow Steven's "weirdness" to inconvenience her anymore. She put the paper back in her bag and began walking to the subway.

92

When she arrived at the station, she hesitated at the top of the stairs.

Usually a din of activity, filled with exuberant students loudly chatting – the stairway was now quiet and empty. She felt a little uneasy, and for a brief moment, wondered if she had done the right thing in ditching Steven. She also wished she had agreed to let Richard drive her home.

Oh, well. She thought. *What's done is done.*

She adjusted her shoulder bag and descended the steps into the station. Since no express service was available late at night, she mentally prepared herself for an almost hour-long, grueling journey through twenty-four stops to the Van Siclen Avenue Station.

She was relieved to find no sign of Steven anywhere on the platform. After waiting several minutes by herself for the train, she realized just how much she missed the usual companionship of her friends. If nothing else, it certainly passed the time.

It was almost midnight when her train finally ambled into the station. There were only three other passengers in her car. She remembered reading something in the paper about how ridership was down due to the *Subway Slayings*. As the train passed through the 42nd Street Port Authority and 34th Street Penn Station stops – usually the "hot spots" of tourist activity, and where it would pick up the bulk of its riders – only a smattering of new passengers got on. By the time it reached the Broadway-Nassau Station – the last stop in Manhattan before entering Brooklyn – only she and one other passenger remained in the car. Normally, she would have enjoyed the spaciousness, but she truly missed the crowds that night.

She hated this part of the ride. Unlike other Brooklyn-bound lines that traveled across the Manhattan or Williamsburg bridges – providing spectacular views of the skyline – the trains on this line made the trip under the East River through a tunnel which took about three minutes to traverse. It was the longest span between stations on the line.

Once in Brooklyn, the train seemed to move at a much slower pace. She wondered if it was always this slow, or if she had simply been so engrossed in conversation on other nights that she failed to notice. Each station it passed along the way seemed more deserted than the other. This was something she always found a bit unsettling. Most of the stations in the other boroughs of the city were much more populated, even during the off-peak hours. But, no matter what time of the day it was, there always seemed to be an eerie desolation about the stations along this line in much of Brooklyn. She used to feel uneasy about that even under normal circumstances… but now, she was extremely on edge. This feeling intensified as the train traveled deeper into Brooklyn. Instead of feeling relieved that she was almost home, and her long, arduous journey was nearing an end, she found herself feeling more panicky the closer she got to her stop.

The other passenger in the car got off at Liberty Avenue, one stop before hers. She looked at her watch as the train finally got to her stop.
12:21 a.m.

When the doors opened, she stepped out onto a completely deserted platform. After the train cleared the station, she could see that not only was her side of the platform empty, the opposite side was as well. At this time of night, it wasn't unusual for her to be the only person getting off at this stop. Like most of the stations along that route, it was extremely long, dimly lit and often deserted. Most people didn't even feel comfortable there in the daytime; and would often wait upstairs in the "Designated Waiting Area" near the station agent's booth – only venturing down to the platform when the train arrived.

Everything fell silent after the train left the station and disappeared into the tunnel. Only the sound of her footsteps shattered the hush. Accustomed to being the sole passenger exiting the station, it was a sound she was well familiar with… a sound she even considered soothing. But there was something different about them that night. She slowed her pace, then, abruptly came to a complete stop. There… somewhere buried deep within the recesses of the station, came the strange scraping sound! It wasn't a continuous sound, but rather intermittent – broken every few seconds by an equal amount of silence.

Her heart started to pound – her thoughts naturally turning to the woman who was killed in that very station just the other day. She could feel the tension inside her increasing as she tightly clutched the straps of her shoulder bag with both hands for some modicum of support. She looked around and confirmed that she was still the only person present. Attempting to suppress her mounting fear, she tried to think logically.

Maybe it's a sound that's always present, but I just don't hear it all the time.

Maybe it's something mechanical, operating automatically somewhere.

Maybe…

The sound stopped. Once again, the station was cloaked in thick silence. She began walking again, but tried to be as quiet as she possibly could – listening intently, albeit, reluctantly, for it to return. She had only gone a few feet when her footsteps were, once again, underscored by the weird sound. She quickened her pace, and to her dismay, so too did the sound!

She could feel every one of the tiny little hairs all over her body standing on end. She began to sweat. Convinced that the sound was definitely trailing her, she began running as fast as she could towards the exit in the center of the platform. Although she could no longer hear it over the noise she was making, she knew the sound was still there… somewhere. She reached the exit and quickly rounded the corner, almost slipping on the smooth surface. She regained her footing, and bounded up the stairs, taking them two at a time. Only when she was in the upstairs waiting area did she stop to catch her breath. She felt safer there because it was a much more confined area, and she was in full view of the agent sitting in the booth, reading a newspaper. She turned around and looked down the stairs at the platform level below, but saw nothing. The only sound she could hear was her own, near hysterical, panting. As she was about to look away, a dark shadow slowly began looming into view. It cast itself on the platform, growing larger and larger by the second.

She gasped, and stumbled backwards. She didn't see anyone else on the platform, but, obviously, someone – or *something* – was hiding and was now about to come up the stairs.

She wasn't going to wait to see what was behind the shadow. She cursed herself for even momentarily stopping; giving… whatever it was… a chance to catch up to her. She started running again – bursting through the turnstile so fast that she caught the attention of the agent. He briefly looked up from his newspaper, but didn't seem too concerned – most likely having seen more than his share of craziness working the night shift. As she passed the booth, she thought of screaming for help, but didn't see how much good it would do her. Although he had the capability of calling the police, they certainly wouldn't have arrived in time; and there was almost no chance she would be able to convince him to let her inside the safety of the bulletproof compartment. Besides, she couldn't afford to waste anymore time. She bolted up a final flight of stairs leading to the street, and exited the station. Without slowing down, she continued running through the darkened streets – trying to put as much distance between herself and the nightmare behind her.

She never viewed her gritty neighborhood as a "safe haven," but considering what she had just experienced in the subway… it seemed like heaven. Although only a few people were on the street at that time of night, it was still a more populated environment than the subway. She continued running until her body began to ache, and her lungs could no longer sustain the exertion, mainly due to the extra weight of her large shoulder bag. Feeling a little safer, she began to slow down. About a block away from the station, she finally stopped running, and tried to catch her breath. She had just run harder and faster than she ever had in years, and was panting wildly. She was doubled over with pain, and had to rest her hands on her knees for support. Her legs began to shake, and she feared she might collapse. She made her way over to a nearby short fence running adjacent to a deserted parking lot and grabbed onto it with both hands. Lacking the strength to pull herself out of her doubled-over position, she just leaned on it with her head resting on top of her hands. Still panting uncontrollably, she tried to make sense of what had just happened. She then looked back at the station, and gasped.

A large figure was ascending the stairs, and practically at street level. Silhouetted by a street lamp behind the stairway, it appeared even more sinister – like a featureless, black demon rising from the unholy sanctums of Hell.

She released the fence and began backing down the street. The most she could muster was a pathetic whimper, as she turned and ran as fast as she could. Her adrenaline made her impervious to the pain and shortness of breath plaguing her just seconds ago. Parked cars, shuttered storefronts and small pockets of loitering teenagers, all melded together as a blur in her peripheral vision as she blazed down the streets. This time, she didn't slow down or attempt to turn around. Each time she had done so, she was met with an even more startling sight. She was too petrified to imagine what she might see if she were to turn back again. She continued running for two blocks until she reached Bradford Street. Still too scared to look back or even to check for oncoming traffic – she made a sharp left, and blindly darted across the darkened avenue against the light. Luckily, traffic was light and she made it safely across. A street lamp on the other side of the avenue was out – hiding a broken piece of the curb that was protruding slightly upward. As she was about to run onto the sidewalk, her foot rammed against the raised piece of concrete. Before she knew what was happening, she was airborne – knocked completely off her feet, and falling headfirst toward the pavement. She violently slammed onto the ground – her momentum propelling her several feet along the unforgiving concrete, peppered with loose gravel and tiny shards of broken glass. She managed to hold onto her bag with her left hand, but her knuckles and the tops of her fingers were scraped raw. A few small pieces of flesh were left loosely dangling. Her right hand was outstretched and most vulnerable. As it slid along the razor sharp debris, a large, nasty wound was opened – leaving a bloody skid mark in its wake. Her hands weren't the only casualties in the fall. The thin fabric of her slacks was easily shredded and offered no protection to her knees. They too were rendered raw and bloody, but not quite as badly as her hands. Even her face wasn't left unscathed in the violent tumble. She received a few minor cuts and scratches on her right cheek, but was able to use her hands to raise herself slightly upward – preventing a lot of serious and permanent scarring. However, she was unable to avoid swallowing trace amounts of dust and debris. Already short of breath, she began coughing violently.

A fall this severe would have left most people temporarily incapacitated. But her adrenaline level was pumped so high she immediately picked herself up and continued running as if nothing had happened. She knew the few seconds she wasted on the ground probably gave her pursuer a huge opportunity to close the gap between them, but she was still too afraid to turn around to check. Pushing through the pain, she thundered down the dark and deserted street even *faster* – fearing at any second to be grabbed from behind.

She ran for another two blocks until finally reaching her house. Unable to completely stop her momentum, she slammed against her front door with considerable force. She started going into minor convulsions as her entire upper body heaved from exhaustion. She fought to regain her breath, but the dust and debris she took in from the fall was lodged firmly in her throat. She began to gag and drool as her coughing became more severe. Feeling as though she might pass out at any moment, she held onto the door for support.

God, please... please don't let me die out here like this... please!!

She reached in her bag for her keys... but they weren't there!
Oh, no... NOOO!!!

The little inner pocket she usually kept them in was empty. She frantically rummaged through every inch of the bag, but was unable to feel them, or even hear them jingling. She began to fear the worst.

What if they fell out in the fall!?

At the time, she didn't *think* anything fell out. But considering how fast it all happened – not to mention her terrified state of mind – she really couldn't be too sure about anything.

Using both hands to search, she madly flung things from side to side. She felt as though her heart was about to explode out of her chest. She had no idea how close her pursuer was, or if, in fact, she was even still being pursued. But she dared not turn around. She was already on the verge of hysteria. If she looked back and saw a large black figure slowly carving its way through the darkness toward her… it would have surely pushed her over the edge, and she'd never find her keys in that condition.

She knew she had to keep her head together and stay focused. But anger and frustration steadily mounted.

WHERE ARE THOSE FUCKING KEYS!!!???

She was about to dump the entire contents of her bag on the ground, when one of her hands brushed against something small and metallic. She reached down deeper and heard a familiar jingle.

YES!!!

She looped her finger through a ring and pulled out a large cluster of keys. She felt a momentary surge of exuberance, followed by even more anxiety. In her panicked state, she was going to have to find two keys – in a cluster of six or seven similarly shaped other keys – to unlock two locks in dim lighting conditions. Unable to fully catch her breath, she continued heaving, coughing and gagging. Her knees began to wobble – almost buckling under her weight. Her whole body, and especially her hands, began to tremble. After some initial fumbling, she managed to find the correct key to unlock the upper lock. Using her right hand, she tried to guide it into the hole. But she may as well have been trying to thread a needle in a hurricane. Her hand shook so violently, she felt there was no way she'd be able to unlock the door. She tried to steady herself by grabbing her wrist with her other hand, but it made little difference. Making matters worse, was the fact that it was becoming more and more difficult to simply even *hold* onto the keys. She was coated from head to toe in sweat. Because of her injury, her right hand was also badly bleeding. The keys kept sliding around in her slippery hands, and at one point she almost dropped them. She couldn't believe she had come this far and was so close to safety, only to be stopped now by a few keys and a door.

Just when it seemed the situation was hopeless, she felt the key slide into the door.

Oh, thank you, God… THANK YOU… THANK YOU!!!

Without a moment of hesitation, she turned the key and unlocked the lock. The sound of the tumblers turning was sweet, but there was no time to celebrate. She now had to unlock the second lock. Once again, she clumsily searched in the darkness for the right key, then, manically tried to insert it into the hole.

Still too terrified to turn around, she realized that each second she stood there fumbling with her keys could very well be her last. But how would it happen? Would it be a quick bullet piercing her skull, or a cold knife plunged into her back? Perhaps she'd be given a false sense of security, and actually be allowed to unlock and open the door… only to be pushed in and raped and mutilated like her mother.

These horrible thoughts crippled her with fear and tied her stomach in knots. Desperate frustration set in as she feverishly continued trying to open the second lock.

"Damn it! Come on! COME OOOOON!!!" she shouted to herself.

Her hands were shaking even worse than before – foiling all of her attempts. She started to cry.

"Oh, God… please… pleeease!!!" she sobbed.

Moments before she was about to give up, and succumb to whatever fate may lie in store, she finally managed to insert and turn the key. After hearing the familiar click, she pushed open the door. Fearing a push-in at any moment, she only opened it a few feet – just wide enough for her to barely squeeze through, then, immediately slammed it shut behind her. She relocked both locks, and threw her shoulder bag on the floor. Although safe in the sanctuary of her living room, her emotions continued to run high. Her heart still pounded like a drum, and her breathing was still rapid. In the hopes that her pursuer *didn't* see her, she didn't want to announce her presence by suddenly turning on any lights. Even though the room was pitch black, she closed the curtain at the window next to the front door – accidentally knocking over one of her plants in her haste. She then ran to the opposite side of the room and dove to the floor with her back against the wall. She sat in an upright fetal position – tightly clutching her knees to her chest, with her chin resting on her forearms. Petrified, and trembling with fear, she rocked back and forth – intently staring at the window straight ahead. Her eyes slowly acclimatized to the dim light filtering in from a lone street lamp down the block. The plant she had knocked over left an open space of about a foot wide. Peering through the opening, she surveyed the area in front of her house. The thick fabric of the drawn curtain reduced everything to a fuzzy blur, but she could clearly see the outline of trees, parked cars and the houses across the street. She could also see that no one else was there. She continued staring for several more seconds to see if anything out of the ordinary appeared, but it never did. A flood of thoughts bombarded her.

Maybe I outran him.

Maybe what I saw was just another passenger exiting the station.

Maybe… I wasn't really being chased at all!

She began to calm down. Her heart rate and breathing slowly returned to normal. As her eyes continued to adjust to the darkness, she detected some movement on the left side of the room. Hiding in the shadows was a pair of green eyes staring directly at her from just a few feet away! She was about to scream, when a familiar shape slowly came forth.

"Mr. Snuggles!" she shouted, gleefully.

She stretched out her arms, and the feline obediently pranced out of the darkness and climbed into her lap.

"Oh, Snuggles, I'm so happy to see you," she said, as she hugged him tightly, and kissed him on his head, "Mommy didn't scare you, did she?"

Normally, he would have met her at the door, but her entrance that night was far from normal – causing him to run and hide from all the commotion.

"I'm so sorry, sweetie… I'm so sorry."

She lovingly nuzzled him, and stroked his fur – providing just as much comfort to him as he was to her. She could feel the fear gradually draining from her body. Mr. Snuggles had the ability to make everything right with the world, and she deeply treasured him for that gift.

As she was about to pick herself up off the floor, she glanced out the window one final time. Her entire body went rigid, and she let out a short, but piercing scream – sending a startled Mr. Snuggles scurrying, once again, for cover. Standing on the sidewalk in front of her house – positioned dead center through the opening in the window – was the black figure! Like a tall, silhouetted statue, it stood motionlessly – not watching, but staring at the house… no… *through* the house… *through* the darkness… directly into her soul.

All of her fears came rushing back. She sprang to her feet and charged down the hallway into her bedroom. Although there were bars on all her windows, she still wanted to make sure the windows were closed and locked, and the curtains were drawn. Once satisfied the house was secure, she inched her way down the darkened hallway back to the living room. She tried to listen for any sounds of a break-in, but couldn't hear much above her own rapid panting and pounding heart. As she re-entered the room, she kept her eyes focused on the front window. Without looking away for a second, she continued moving slowly along the back wall of the room until she was *almost* able to get a clear angle of view through the open space. She then stopped. The fear of what might be lurking outside prevented her from looking any further. She didn't think she could handle much more stress. Her pounding heart was causing severe chest pains, but she couldn't stop now. For her own piece of mind, she *had* to know what was out there. Trembling and scared beyond belief, she carefully leaned over and peeked through the opening. As more and more of the sidewalk came into view, her heart pounded even faster. When the entire view was revealed she saw that the black figure was gone. Slowly, she walked across the room toward the couch under the window. She sat down and peeked through the opening again – getting a wider view of the area. She still saw nothing. Garnering up every ounce of her courage, she raised her trembling hand and gingerly lifted up the curtain. With great trepidation, she took one final look outside. She now had a perfectly clear view of the entire area in front of her house.

She saw nothing.

She looked up and down the street in both directions… again… nothing.

The bedroom! She thought.

She jumped up and ran back down the hall to her bedroom. A thorough check outside that window also revealed nothing lurking along the side of the house. Feeling somewhat relieved, she returned to the living room. She again checked the front window and saw nothing.

It was over. Whoever, or *whatever* it was had vanished back into the night.

The stress of what she had just gone through had taken a terrible toll on her beaten, bloodied and exhausted body. Her legs began to wobble again, and she started to feel light-headed. She felt as though she might faint, but she didn't have the energy to walk back over to the couch. She slumped to her knees and sat on the floor in the middle of the darkened living room. A few seconds later, she was again joined by Mr. Snuggles. Without saying a word, she picked him up and cradled him in her arms. Saturated with sweat, her clothes clung tightly to her body. She then noticed a very foul odor. Her first thought was that Mr. Snuggles had had an accident. But something told her to reach down and feel the crotch of her pants. They were wet… extremely wet, and not just from sweat. At *some* point during her ordeal, she had lost complete control of her bodily functions, and severely soiled herself – in the front *and* in the rear. But that was the least of her concerns.

She was then hit with a horrific realization and began to sob.

She had almost come face to face with whatever had been haunting her for the past several weeks. With her own eyes, she had just seen concrete proof that something evil *did* exist in the subway. Making matters worse was the fact it obviously wasn't *confined* to the subway, and as of now, knew exactly where she lived.

CHAPTER 7

October 18th – 10:14 p.m. Saturday Night

The first sentence was the hardest. But once she started speaking, it was surprisingly much easier than she thought. Her unbridled emotions gushed forth, and the words flowed freely and unabashedly out of her mouth. The more she talked, the more comfortable she felt. It was a tremendous relief to finally be able to share the burden of the terror she had secretly been dealing with for the past several weeks.

For the better part of an hour, Melissa had been telling Richard about her fears of an evil presence in the subway, and her strong belief that she was a target. They had just spent the entire day together, and were now relaxing on the couch at his home on Long Island. She had been putting this conversation off for quite some time. But, after recounting the events of her harrowing experience last night, she doubted he, or *anyone*, would think she was crazy, or merely jumping to conclusions.

Throughout it all, he listened intently with his mouth slightly agape – barely uttering a word. Their bond was such, that words really weren't necessary. She could easily read – more like *feel* – each of his varied emotions. Sometimes he seemed shocked and other times scared. But the biggest vibe she picked up on was empathy. This gave her the courage to tell him the *whole* story, sparing no details – no matter how extreme. When she was finished, he put his arm around her, and drew her closer.

"I can't believe you kept all of this bottled up for so long," he said, shaking his head. "It's all coming together now. How could I have been so *blind*?"

"What do you mean?" she asked.

"You know… your unusual interest in these murders, and how for the past couple of weeks you really haven't been yourself. I had no idea of the torment you were secretly going through."

"I'm glad I finally told you," she said, resting her head on his shoulder.

"But sweetie, how could you possibly think I wouldn't understand? We're supposed to be in a relationship, where we can tell each other anything."

"I know, but I just didn't think---"

"Yeah, I know… you didn't think I could handle hearing about *another* problem you were going through… that I would just take off, running for the hills, or worse… try to have you committed."

"Something like that, I guess."

"I thought you knew me better than that."

"I don't know what I was thinking. I guess I was just scared."

"Well, you don't have to be scared anymore," he said, hugging her tighter. "More importantly, you don't have to face this alone."

She felt as though a huge weight had been lifted off her shoulders. Although she cherished her independence, it was nice to know she now had someone she could lean on… someone who believed her.

"Why didn't you call me last night?" he asked.

"It was late, and I---"

"Melissa, I've told you a thousand times to stop worrying about how late it is! You can call me anytime, especially if something like *that* happens."

"But there's nothing you could have done about it from out here. I mean… you don't exactly live down the block from me."

"No, but at least I could have given you some moral support. It helps sometimes just to hear a friendly voice on the phone. Did you even call the police?"

"No, whatever it was it left real fast. By the time the police would have gotten there, they couldn't have done anything."

"They could have kept a closer eye on you. Maybe they could have done some extra patrols around your house."

She laughed.

"I don't live in the suburbs, Rich. Maybe out *here* the police do that, but not in East New York. They're not going to act as my personal bodyguards."

"So, what *did* you do?" he asked.

"Nothing really... I was too scared to do anything. I don't even remember going to bed last night."

"You said, 'whatever *it* was.' Do you really think it was some type of demon or something?"

"I don't know how else to describe it. It just wasn't normal. I mean... there were a few other people on the street, but it ignored them, and came right after me... just me!"

"Yeah, and that's what I don't understand. Don't get me wrong... I believe what you're saying. But if it really was a *demon*, or something supernatural... wouldn't the other people on the street see that? Wouldn't they scream or run for cover as well?"

"To tell you the truth, I really don't know what they did. I was running so fast that everything was just a blur."

"Were you able to get a look at the face?"

"No, every time I looked it was in the shadows."

"Couldn't it have just been some weirdo following you home from the subway?"

"I don't think so. It just didn't seem like a *normal* type of situation."

"Earlier today, when you told me you fell, I had no idea you were running for your life at the time," he said, as he gently picked up her injured hand, which she had since bandaged. He softly cradled it, and asked, "Why didn't you tell me about this before now?"

"I didn't want to put a damper on things. Besides, I don't think I was ready to talk about it then."

"I could tell something was on your mind all day. You were so quiet. I thought maybe you were upset at me for something."

"Oh, no," she smiled, "believe me, if I was mad at you…you'd know it."

He returned her smile and repositioned himself to the edge of the couch. He sat sideways so that he could face her more directly. When he put his hand on her knee, she winced.

"Oh, I'm sorry, sweetie!" he said, as he removed his hand. "It must still be really sore from last night."

"Yeah, it's still a bit tender. That sidewalk really did a number on me."

"Thank God you didn't break any bones, or fall flat on your beautiful face," he said, while stroking the injured side of her face. "These scratches could have been so much worse – you could've been horribly scarred for life.

She held his hand tighter to her face and kissed it. She was touched by his compassion and concern.

"Would you have left me if I was?" she joked.

He laughed.

"Sweetheart, it would take a helleva lot more than a few scratches on your face to drive me away. Now, if you had damaged that sweet ass of yours---"

"You bum!" she said, as she playfully punched him in the chest.

"Seriously, you should probably get that hand looked at," he warned, "You might still have some pieces of glass in there."

"Yeah, I guess you're right."

"Tell me the truth, sweetie, do you *honestly* believe that whoever's behind the subway murders is really after you?"

"I know it sounds crazy, Rich, but for the past several weeks, I've just had this uneasy feeling that something wasn't right down there."

"And you said you had these feelings even before the killings started, right?"

"Right, and don't forget… I also felt that someone was following me… and now, after last night---"

Before she could finish, he moved closer to her on the couch, and they hugged each other. She buried her face in his chest, and he rubbed the back of her neck.

"I don't care what you say. Until this guy, or *whatever* the hell you believe it is, is caught, I'm meeting you every night after school, and driving you straight home," he said, forcefully.

After last night, she eagerly agreed to the new arrangement without a word of protest. In fact, if he *hadn't* offered, she was already planning to request the escort.

"You know, now you should really think about moving out of that neighborhood," he said, "especially since he knows where you live. If you lived here with me you'd be safe, *and*… you wouldn't have to worry about me going out of my way to drive you home."

Usually, she'd have a ready-made comeback. But this time, she just sat there pondering his words. He had suggested this many times before, but this was the first time she was seriously considering it. She never felt completely safe in East New York, and now, there was a valid reason for her fears.

"I never thought about living out on the Island," she said.

"I'm not that far out. It's only about a forty-five minute drive from the city. This is a much better area, and the best part… you can kiss the subway goodbye."

She looked up at him, but said nothing.

"You don't have to make a decision right now," he said, "just tell me you'll think about it, okay?"

She nodded her head and gave a sigh of resignation.

He looked at his watch.

"Hey, it's almost eleven-thirty… wanna watch *Saturday Night Live*?" he asked, in a much more chipper tone.

"Nah, I'm kinda tired. I think I'll just go take a shower and get ready for bed."

Knowing her issues with intimacy were the main reason she often avoided sleeping over in the past, he asked, "Are you *sure* you're gonna be okay with this?"

"Oh, yeah… after last night, I really don't want to be alone."

"It can be like this every night, if you want," he hinted.

"I told you, sweetie," she said, as she smiled and kissed him lightly on the lips, "I'll think about it."

He smiled and watched her as she got up from the couch and went upstairs. All the while, he couldn't stop thinking about the story she just told him. He knew it took a lot of courage for her to share that with him, and it made him feel much closer to her than ever before. Her trust in him meant a lot. He had been knocking around the idea of taking their relationship to the next level for a while. He never pictured himself as the marrying-type, but then again, he had never met a woman quite like Melissa. Although he loved her, he wasn't sure if he was ready to take that step. He sat there for a long time in deep thought – pondering what might be in store for their future. The soothing sound of the upstairs shower almost lulled him to sleep.

Suddenly, a horrible crash came from the bedroom upstairs.

Startled, he jumped up from the couch and ran out of the living room.

"MELISSA!!!" he shouted, as he raced up the stairs. There was no response.

"MELISSA, ARE YOU O.K.?!!!"

Again… no response.

His heart pounded as he ran down the hall toward the bedroom. All sorts of sickening thoughts were running through his head. He stumbled into the bedroom, almost falling. The sight before him left him speechless. Melissa was standing on her tiptoes, struggling with a bunch of king-size comforters on the top shelf of the closet. She had removed the one on the very bottom of the pile when the others began to fall out. In the process, they knocked over a big, metal tool chest and spilled its contents all over the floor. She was holding the comforter in one hand and trying to hold back an avalanche of blankets with the other.

He stood in the doorway and started to laugh.

"A little help here… PLEEEESE!" she cried, somewhat annoyed that he would find her predicament so amusing.

Although it was a funny sight, his laughter was more out of relief than amusement. Having conjured up all kinds of terrible scenarios just seconds ago, he was almost giddy with joy to see that she was okay. He was also giddy with another sensation, brought on by her attire...or lack of one. She had donned one of his old white dress shirts, and not much else. Normally, the tail of the shirt would have hung just below her rear end, but with both her arms raised, it rode up and exposed her panty-clad bottom. Her struggle with the blankets had caused her tight yellow panties to wedge themselves deep into the crack of her butt, exposing a good portion of her plump cheeks. With each tiny movement, they rode up even higher. She had just gotten out of the shower and her body was still quite damp. Her moist, caramel-colored legs seductively glistened in the soft bedroom lighting.

He had never seen her naked in the entire nine months they had been going together – only catching a few glimpses of her in her underwear, before she quickly covered herself up. Seeing her in such a state of undress was a rare and unexpected treat. He lingered in the doorway – perhaps a little longer than he should have – admiring the sweet view.

"TODAY!!!" she shouted, rousing him out of his daze.

He snapped back to reality – somewhat embarrassed for gawking at her like an adolescent schoolboy. He rushed across the room to her aid – carefully stepping through the obstacle course of scattered tools on the floor. He positioned himself directly behind her and reached up to help push the falling blankets back on the shelf. Even though he was a few inches taller, it still took several attempts to secure the heavy quilts.

Throughout it all, he was firmly, but unavoidably, pressing himself against her rear. The sensation of feeling his manhood sinking deeply into the crevice between her soft, ample cheeks was heavenly – and instantly excited him. The more he wrestled with the blankets, the deeper it sank, and the more excited he became. He knew she *had* to feel his hardness pressing into her, but she never let on. When they finally got the blankets back on the shelf, he slowly – and somewhat reluctantly – stepped back.

"Why didn't you just take the one that was on top?" he snickered.

"This one was prettier," she replied, smiling sheepishly.

As she turned around and carried the comforter to the bed, he noticed that the shirt she was wearing had ridden up even further and was stuck to the small of her moist back – leaving her behind completely exposed. He followed closely behind her, totally enraptured by her half-naked, jiggling cheeks.

"There!" she exclaimed, as she tossed the comforter on the bed – somewhat winded after her ordeal.

She quickly turned around, but stopped abruptly – a little surprised at just how close he was behind her. The sudden movement caused her breasts to teasingly bounce beneath the light cotton fabric of her shirt.

"I'm sorry about the mess," she said, pointing to the tools on the floor.

"The what? Oh, yeah… the tools. It's okay, don't worry about it," he said, still noticeably distracted.

The tools were the last things on his mind. With the comforter now out of the way, he was able to get a *really* good look at her. The sizeable – and steadily growing – "pup-tent" in his sweatpants announced to the world that he liked what he saw. Her damp hair stuck to the sides of her face, partially covering her left eye. The wet shirt clung tightly to her body, leaving nothing to the imagination. Her large, C-cup breasts seemed to laughingly defy gravity. Dark, silver-dollar-sized areolas were clearly visible, punctuated by two succulent nipples, standing bold and erect and pressing tightly against the thin fabric.

Simply put, she oozed sexuality. But, this wasn't what excited him the most. The fact that she didn't even *realize* just how sexy she was is what really turned him on. Her issues with intimacy had gradually shifted all aspects of sex to the back burner throughout their relationship. She had become accustomed to their platonic arrangement. With the pressure gone, she almost began to perceive him as one of her "girlfriends" – viewing herself as more of a buddy, and less as a sexually stimulating, young woman. This was never

111

more obvious to him than at that moment as she stood almost naked before him. Had she been deliberately *trying* to turn him on, it wouldn't have been anywhere near as arousing. Instead, she had a childlike innocence about her and was completely oblivious to the effect she was having on him.

"I hope you don't mind me wearing your shirt," she said. "It was the first thing I saw when I got out of the shower."

"Oh, no… that's not a problem. It looks *much* better on you than it ever did on me," he said, making no attempt to hide his excitement.

She looked down and suddenly became aware of her near nakedness. She coyly smiled and bit her bottom lip. Slightly embarrassed, she discretely tried to pull the wet fabric away from her skin, but only succeeded in smoothing out the wrinkles – making her breasts even more visible.

This was more than he could handle. Without saying a word, he put his hands on her waist, and slowly pulled her close to him. She could tell by the look in his eyes that he wanted more than just a kiss. Her heart started to beat faster, but she offered no resistance. He continued pulling her closer until there was no longer any space between them. Her body had the fetching scent of cocoa butter. Looking into her eyes, he wrapped his arms completely around her waist and pulled her even closer – tightly pressing her body against his. Her hard nipples felt like marbles, and her soft, perky breasts melted into his chest. He closed his eyes and cocked his head slightly to the side, then, kissed her on the mouth – gently at first, then, with increasingly more passion. Their tongues feverishly intertwined in the union. He raised one hand to the back of her head to pull her in tighter and to kiss her more deeply. He wanted to taste every drop of her sweet juices.

She moaned with pleasure, and continued to offer no resistance – giving him the incentive to go even further.

He kissed her neck. A few wet strands of her hair tickled the side of his face, as he gently nibbled her tender flesh. He then lowered his hands and firmly gripped her hips. Slowly, he ran his hands down over the bulbous swell of her buttocks. It was the first time he had ever gone this far with her and he wanted to savor the moment. Firmly grabbing both of her cheeks, he pulled her in tighter still, and began grinding his hardness into her.

Again, she moaned, but still showed no signs of resistance.

He then started to massage her butt. With every squeeze, his fingers sunk deeply into her soft, pliable flesh. Her panties were now almost fully wedged between her cheeks. Taking advantage of the opportunity, he slid the fingers of his right hand into her warm, moist crevice – surprised at the depth at which they sank. He then slowly ran them up and down the entire length of her crack. Frustrated by the barrier of her wedgie, he used his other hand to dislodge it and to pull her panties to the side. Using both hands, he gripped the lower portion of her cheeks and spread them apart. Trembling with ecstasy, he used the index finger of his right hand, and teasingly ran it around the edge of her tight, puckered hole.

His hand wasn't the only thing trembling. Along with her pounding heart, he could feel her entire body starting to twitch. Her moans were becoming more frequent and steady. In fact, they were beginning to sound less like moans, and more like sobs. He stopped what he was doing and tentatively grabbed her shoulders – slowly pushing her away from him. He then cupped her downcast face in his hands and raised it until they were looking eye-to-eye. She was crying – apparently, for quite some time. Tears were running down both sides of her face, and she was literally shaking with fear.

"Oh, my God, honey, I'm sorry," he said. "Please forgive me. I'm so sorry!"

"You… can do it… if you want to," she said, between sobs.

"No, sweetheart, not like this… not with you feeling this way."

"But, I want to make you happy," she said, barely above a whisper.

"Sweetheart, you do make me happy. But you're just not ready for this right now, that's all."

"I'm so fucking useless!" she blurted out in disgust.

113

"Don't say that! Don't you ever say that!" he said, sharply. "You're the best thing that's ever happened to me, and together, we're going to get through this, okay?"

"But I can't even do what a woman's supposed to do."

"Honey, sex isn't the only thing that makes you a woman."

"I know, but I just want to have a normal relationship. When am I going to get over this?"

She began to cry in earnest.

He hugged her and lovingly caressed her back.

"It'll happen, sweetheart," he whispered, as he too, started to cry.

"I love you so much," she sobbed, as she rested her head on his shoulder.

"I love you too, sweetheart."

He felt horrible. He had pushed her too far… too fast. How could he have been so blind, he wondered, as to not notice – or worse, *choose* not to notice – the signs? Had he been so intent on satisfying his own selfish, carnal pleasures that he couldn't tell the difference between moans of ecstasy and cries of fear? Was his mind so clouded with lust that he couldn't distinguish between the sensation of wet hair and tears dripping on his face? Melissa wasn't some cheap, one-night-stand to be tossed away and forgotten the next day. She was the love of his life – the woman he would do absolutely anything in the world for. He had always vowed that he would never pressure her, or ask her to do anything she felt uncomfortable doing. Yet, here she stood, half naked, completely vulnerable and crying like an innocent schoolgirl – all because he couldn't control his hormonal urges. The fact that she was still willing to go through with it, despite her obvious inner turmoil, made him feel even worse. But there was one thing he *was* happy about. Her extreme selflessness proved, without a doubt, that she was definitely the girl for him. It was now no longer *if,* but *when* he was going to propose.

CHAPTER 8

The following week saw an escalation in gruesome and bizarre killings in the subway. An incident occurred on almost a nightly basis.

October 21st – Early Tuesday Morning

Shortly after 4 a.m., the body of a middle-aged man of Russian descent was found in a passageway at the 14th Street Station on the west side of Manhattan. Viciously attacked from behind, the back of his head had been caved in by a tremendous blunt force, and both of his eyes were crudely ripped out of their sockets – the right one was left hanging by a single tendon.

October 22nd – Wednesday Evening

At approximately 11 p.m., the headless body of a train conductor was discovered inside the locked conductor's cab of a downtown #6 train, shortly after it pulled into the Canal Street Station in lower Manhattan. Passengers reported that the train sat in the station for several minutes with its doors closed. The motorman made several unsuccessful attempts to contact the conductor over the PA system, inquiring about the delay. The true nature of the problem wasn't realized until passengers seated near the conductor's cab began to notice a pool of blood seeping from underneath the door. When the door was finally forced open by the motorman, he found the body slumped against the wall in a kneeling position, but the head was nowhere to be found. It was later discovered on the platform of the Spring Street Station – the stop right before Canal Street. Apparently, the conductor was peering out of his window to make sure all the passengers were clear of the train as it exited the station. Bloody claw marks on both sides of the head suggest that someone on the platform – someone possessing superhuman strength – ripped it off as the train zoomed by.

October 24ᵗʰ – Early Friday Morning

The mangled body of a young black man was found below the elevated tracks of the "F" train on Smith Street, in the Gowanus section of Brooklyn. The discovery was made by a dog walker, just after 1 a.m. At first, it was believed to be a hit-and-run, and not connected to the subway killings. But, after further investigation, and interviews with several eyewitnesses, police determined that the man had actually been thrown out the window of a passing southbound "F" train, just before it pulled into the Smith & 9ᵗʰ Street Station – the highest elevated station in the city, rising about 80 feet above street level.

The media had firmly sunken its teeth into these stories, and promptly labeled the crimes as *The Subway Slayings*. Throughout the week, increasing amounts of airtime on all local TV stations were devoted to it – making it the top story in the city. A few of the major networks even jumped into the fray, with CBS and ABC giving it national exposure on their evening newscasts. Not to be outdone, the print media wasted no time in sensationalizing the story with eye-catching headlines, and detailed accounts of each crime. Some Spanish-language papers took an even more "in-your-face" approach and went so far as to print full-color photos of the victims on their front pages.

It wasn't long before this type of media saturation had the city in a complete frenzy. A wave of fear surged through New York, unlike anything seen before. Tourism had fallen to its lowest levels since the week after "9/11." A byproduct of that date was the creation of the Color-Coded Threat Level System by the Department of Homeland Security. At that time, the city was on "yellow alert" – considered to be at an "Elevated" risk for a terrorist attack. Every so often, it would be raised to "High," an "orange alert" – only to be dropped back down to "Elevated" a few weeks later. Random polls showed that the public had a much greater fear of being murdered in

116

the subway than being attacked by terrorists. In fact, most people said that even if the level were raised to "Severe" – the highest level for "red alert" – it still wouldn't frighten them as much as the mutilations that were currently taking place underground. The main reason given was that…*they were currently taking place.* There hadn't been another terrorist attack in the city in over two years. The constant fluctuation between threat levels, without ever actually seeing the threat, had a way of diluting the effectiveness of the entire advisory system. People began to view it as "the system that cried wolf." But, waking up every other morning to news of yet another atrocity committed in the subway was all very real and much more frightening.

Commuters avoided the subway in droves. Although the murders were, *so far*, only occurring at night, or in the pre-dawn hours of the morning, it didn't seem to make much difference on the morning commute. Ridership dropped from a daily average of 4.5 million passengers to just a little over 3 million – with totals steadily dropping more and more each day. Those who could afford to take cabs to work did so, while others rode their bikes. Some even broke the ultimate taboo, and began driving their own cars into the city. However, the vast majority of people turned to city buses, which were woefully ill prepared to take up the slack – creating delays and overcrowding of monumental proportions.

This sudden increase in aboveground travel gridlocked the city to the point of paralysis. Manhattan was virtually transformed into one giant parking lot. Mayor Bloomberg formed a special task force, and flooded the subway with cops. He made several public appeals urging people to remain calm and to continue riding rapid transportation – vowing that the system was now safer than ever. The increased police presence did, in fact, reduce all "regular" crimes to practically non-existent levels, but the bizarre murders were still being committed.

As opposed to the first two murders committed a week earlier, there was something markedly different about these latest crimes… there were witnesses or at least, people in the general vicinity shortly after the murders occurred. They may not have been actual *eyewitnesses*, but were close enough to provide police with some pretty strange accounts of what they saw.

A rather chilling statement was taken from a man at the scene of the murder in the 14th Street Station. He was one of the first individuals to discover the body. Identifying himself only as "Raphael," he told police that he had just gotten off the L train, and was on his way upstairs to make a connection to the #1. As he rounded the corner on the landing at the top of the stairs, he said he came face-to-face with some "weird dude."

"He scared the hell out of me," he recalled, "I mean, he had this kind of strange, far-away look on his face. He was walking real slow… like one of those zombies in a *"Dawn of the Dead"*-type movie. His eyes were so bloodshot; I thought he was wearing some type of red contacts."

He went on to describe him as a somewhat older white man – probably in his sixties, with an unkempt, graying beard. He said he was about 5'8", and had a rather stocky build. He wore a black leather bomber jacket that looked relatively new, but his pants and sneakers had seen better days. He also noticed that his pants had no belt, and the cuffs were extremely frayed. Lastly, he said his sneakers were filthy and full of holes.

What he described next was truly unsettling.

"I didn't want to look at him too hard because he looked, you know… kind of crazy. But as we passed each other, I noticed that his face was covered with a lot of open sores, but they weren't bleeding. They looked like they were healing. I mean, like, right in front of my eyes… they actually looked like they were slowly closing up!"

Thinking he *must* have been seeing things, Raphael tried to put it out of his mind. He continued on his way, and turned another corner to go down a long hallway toward the #1 line. Normally, this area is packed with passengers, but at that time in the morning, it was nearly deserted. He only saw a couple of people standing over something at the opposite end of the span. It wasn't until he got closer that he made the horrible discovery. Still shaken up over the sight of the strange man with the strange wounds, *this* was almost too much to take. After he composed himself, he started thinking about a possible connection.

"Me and a few other people were just standing there, lookin' at this God-awful sight," he said, "and I remembered the freak that just passed me. I knew there was no way in hell that guy could've come down this hallway and *not* have seen this! First of all, if he did see it, he sure was calm about it; and if he was the one who *killed* him… he sure as hell wasn't in any hurry to get away!"

Police searched the area, but no suspect matching that description was ever found.

A witness to the murder of the train conductor didn't even know he was a witness until the crime was reported in the news the next day. Only then did he realize that the strange incident he saw in the Spring Street station the night before was most likely the actual murder. Wishing to remain anonymous, he called 911 and related his account of the event.

"I had just closed up my gallery in Soho, and was on my way home," he recalled. "I was waiting for the uptown #6 at Spring Street. While I was waiting, I noticed this disheveled-looking, black woman, standing across the way on the downtown side. What made me notice her was that she was just standing there, like a statue – sort of in a trance and looking straight ahead."

He said he didn't really have a clear view of her, because she was standing more towards the front of the downtown platform, and he was approximately in the middle on the uptown side – placing them at a diagonal angle from each other. Additionally, two express tracks separated them by about 100 feet. He simply wrote her off as another "mental-case." When the downtown train came in, his view was temporarily blocked, and he put her out of his mind. But, when the train pulled out of the station, something else caught his attention.

"I looked up, and there she was again. She didn't get on the train, and she was the only person left on the platform. Only now, she was holding something in her hands," he said. "I couldn't tell exactly what it was because of the distance, but it looked like some kind of ball – probably a basketball. I thought it was odd, because I

119

didn't see her holding anything before. I watched as she took a few steps back, and threw the object down on the ground. That's when I *knew* it wasn't a basketball because it didn't bounce, or anything, and it landed with a dull thud – like a lump of clay."

He said the woman then slowly walked further towards the front of the platform. Since the exit was in the opposite direction, he couldn't figure out where – other than the tunnel – she could possibly be going. But it wasn't the woman as much as it was the object she threw on the ground that piqued his interest. He described himself as a person who normally minds his own business, but curiosity got the better of him, and he simply *had* to get a closer look.

"I started walking towards the rear of the platform. I was almost directly across from it, when the downtown express came in – completely blocking my view. I was hoping it would hurry up and pass, but then my train came, and I got on. By the time the express cleared the station, my train was already pulling out, and I wasn't able to see it anymore. Good heavens! Now that I know it was a *head*… I'm glad I didn't see it. Until this maniac is caught, I guess I'll have to find another way home. I'm sure not going back to *that* station!"

After each murder was reported in the news, the police received more and more "tips" through anonymous phone calls. Most of the calls provided very little useful information. Some people reported seeing suspicious looking characters that they felt *might* have committed the murder, while a few "kooks" claimed to actually *be* the murderer. There was no shortage of these types of calls after the murder in Brooklyn was reported; but after sifting through a sea of frivolous nonsense, the police received a couple of credible reports from two men who happened to be on the "F" train early that Friday morning when the murder occurred. Although neither of them actually saw the murder, or were even in the same car where it took place – one was riding in the car in front, and the other was in the car behind – they both witnessed similar snippets of events through the windows in the doors separating the cars.

Each remembers seeing a strange looking guy "acting kind of crazy." They both described him as a short, bald, elderly black man.

"He kept pacing back and forth," reported the first witness. "It was weird because every time I saw him, it looked like he was, kinda gliding... like on roller skates or something. I couldn't see his feet, but that's what it looked like. But the guy had to be well into his sixties, I mean... how many sixty-year-olds have you ever seen on skates... on a moving train!?"

The second witness reported a similar type of movement, in addition to a strange red light.

"I see these two guys moving around a lot in the car behind me," he recalled. "It looked like the old guy was chasing this other guy. At first, I thought they were fighting, but I kept seeing these bright flashes of red light. I figured they were just fooling around with some kind of laser."

As the train was turning into the Smith & 9th Street Station, the witness in the front car got up and prepared to exit.

"I'm standing by the door to get off, and I looked back into the other car. The old guy is standing in the middle of the car, staring straight ahead. The weird thing was that he wasn't holding on to anything. When this train comes around that curve, it rocks like crazy. I've seen many people almost fall, if they're not holding on. I'm only 27, and even I have to hold on. But as old as this guy was, he was able to stand there completely still, even though the train's movin' all over the place. Also, from the angle of the train because of the turn, I could see that the car was empty. The other guy was gone. I figured he just went into the other car. It wasn't until I got off when it dawned on me that the doors between the cars on that train are locked... you *can't* move between cars. When I heard the news the next day, I couldn't believe it. That could've been me!"

The police were baffled. All of the witnesses seemed quite credible, but from their varied descriptions of the killer, it was obvious there was more than one. In fact, it seemed as though there was a small army of killers running loose in the subway. Even more baffling was the utter randomness of the murders. So far, the crimes were occurring in almost every borough and on several different subway lines. The only commonality was that they all took place late at night, or very early in the morning –the *only* times when one could commit such a gruesome crime, and get away without being seen by scores of eyewitnesses.

As far as the five victims were concerned – other than the fact that they all used the subway – no other unifying characteristic could be found. They all came from different walks of life, and were comprised of all different ethnic backgrounds, ages and sexes. Authorities found absolutely no connection between them… their families… their jobs… or anything else. They just simply seemed to be in the wrong place at the wrong time.

Although the witnesses' descriptions varied as much as night and day, they all seemed to agree on one aspect. They all classified the killers as being homeless. This was the one common denominator that seemed to tie all of the cases together. It was the only clue police had to go on, but it certainly didn't make their job any easier. According to the Coalition for the Homeless, well over 30,000 people lay their heads down in a New York City shelter each night. This, of course, didn't account for the untold number of other individuals, whom, for whatever reason, choose to make the city streets, park benches and subway stations their homes. For some, this choice is a matter of safety – citing that the streets and subways are a far better alternative to the crime-ridden shelters. But the vast majorities of street homeless individuals suffer from chronic mental illness, and simply refuse help. In any event, getting an accurate count of this elusive segment of the population is all but impossible. By their best guesstimate, experts place the amount anywhere between several thousand to tens of thousands.

If homeless people were committing these murders, it could be the beginning of what might be considered a "perfect" crime wave. With the exception of homeless families in shelters, for the most part, homeless adults are transitory individuals with little or no social ties to friends or family, or connections to organizations. Also, with the entire New York City subway system – encompassing 443 miles of underground track, and 468 stations, as well as scores of abandoned stations and tunnels at their disposal – they could virtually make themselves invisible at will.

After thoroughly questioning the relatives of the victims, the police found no connections between the deceased or anyone matching the descriptions of their killers. So far, an absence of motive was the prevailing factor in each case.

But, the main question was… *Why?*

Why would a bunch of apparently random homeless people suddenly go on a violent killing spree… simultaneously? Are they all working together?

From what little the authorities could piece together, they found no cohesive thread tying the killers to one another.

The next question was… *How?*

How could a woman (or anybody for that matter) rip off a man's head with her bare hands?

How could an old man subdue and throw a much younger man out a pane of high strength safety glass on a moving subway?

This was perhaps the most puzzling and frightening aspect of all the cases. None of the witnesses saw the killers – or alleged killers – using or carrying a weapon of any kind. No weapons were found at the scenes; nor was there any physical evidence that weapons had been used. In addition to strange facial features and unusual mannerisms, these witnesses were describing things that simply could *not* have been done by a normal human. Assuming the murder in the 14th Street station and the other two prior murders were also committed without using weapons, more questions about unexplained, super-human feats of strength would have to be addressed.

How could someone shatter a man's skull?

How could someone yank a woman's head almost completely backwards, and tear away most of her face?

How could someone crack open a man's chest and rip out his heart?

The authorities didn't have any answers. But, they knew the homeless were definitely involved, and in *some* way, were single-handedly, inflicting these massive injuries. Behavioral analysts and criminologists became the panel "experts" for many TV news stations. Each night, they touted their beliefs and theories as to the causes of the crisis to an increasingly nervous and frightened viewing public. According to them, 65-80 percent of all homeless people have some form of alcohol or drug addiction. If one of these drugs happens to be phencyclidine – more commonly referred to as PCP – it could explain some of the bizarre behavior reported by the witnesses.

They also pointed out that PCP, a.k.a., angel dust, ozone, wack or rocket fuel, is considered to be the most dangerous drug on the market. Its colorful street names reflect the strange and volatile effects users' experience while under its influence. It's an anesthetic, which deadens feelings – making users impervious to pain. Muscles contract so intensely, they cause jerky, uncoordinated movements and bizarre postures. It also produces strange, mask-like facial appearances, which causes blank stares and drooling. Users appear to be drunk or in a catatonic state. Probably the most dangerous thing about the drug is that it's a hallucinogen. It releases hidden or existing mental problems, causing a non-stop barrage of wild and unreal hallucinations. This causes users to feel threatened and behave violently. Feelings of strength, power and invulnerability take over. In the past, several cases have been reported where as many as four or five 200+ pound cops were needed to restrain a single 150 lb. person under the influence. In more extreme cases, some users had been driven to suicide. Also, if the drug is laced with an impurity, users may become infected with a type of virus causing them to commit senseless, violent murders.

Reports were coming in from all over the city about scores of "strange acting" homeless individuals. Officials tried to downplay it as nothing more than nervous people merely describing the "usual" behavior of a typical homeless person. But, it quickly became apparent that it was much more than that. A rogue band of "infected" homeless people became the most plausible and official explanation for the crimes.

But why *now*?

If tainted drugs were, in fact, to blame, it certainly wasn't the first time something like that had happened. There had been several instances in the past when deadly strains of a particular drug had found their way onto the streets of New York to infect scores of people. The end result is usually death for the user. Never before had it turned them into a violent bunch of deranged murderers.

It didn't make any sense.

Whether they've been called transients, vagrants, hobos, bums or the present, politically correct, "homeless," these people have always been a part of society. But contrary to popular belief, studies have shown that homeless people actually commit *less* violent crimes than housed people. While there is evidence that homeless individuals are more likely to commit crimes than the domiciled population, these crimes are relatively trivial and victimless crimes – arising more from their homeless condition than from deliberate criminal intent. Basically, these crimes are "quality of life" offenses, such as panhandling, rummaging through garbage, loitering or sleeping or relieving oneself in public. Other offenses may include drunkenness, drug possession, trafficking and prostitution – minor infractions that amount to little more than misdemeanors. Of course, this isn't to say that the homeless are mostly comprised of "gentle lambs." There have been several cases in the past where they've been convicted of rape and murder, but on a whole, serious crime has not been attributed to the homeless at any higher rate than the general population. In fact, the homeless are among the *least* threatening group in society, and are more likely to be the *victims* of crime.

Over the past several years, advocates and homeless shelter workers in New York, and around the country, have received several reports of homeless men, women and even children being harassed, kicked, set on fire, beaten to death, and also decapitated. From 1999 through 2002 alone, there were 212 hate crimes and violent acts committed against the homeless – all perpetrated by non-homeless individuals. Of these 212 attacks, 123 resulted in death.

Most hate crimes are not committed by organized hate groups, but by sick individuals who harbor a strong resentment against a certain group of people. These individuals tend to fall into three distinct categories. "Mission offenders," or vigilantes, are those who believe they are on a mission to cleanse the world of a particular evil. "Scapegoat offenders" are those who violently act out their resentment toward a perceived growing economic power of a certain racial or ethnic group. But the most common perpetrators of violence against the homeless are "thrill seekers" – primarily teenagers, who take advantage of the most vulnerable and disadvantaged group in society in order to satisfy their own warped pleasures.

Compounding the problem are city officials across the country, which pass ordinances, practically making it illegal to be homeless. In Milwaukee, a church was declared a public nuisance for feeding homeless people and allowing them to sleep there. In Gainesville, police threatened University of Florida students with arrest if they didn't stop serving meals to the homeless in a public park. In Santa Barbara, it's illegal to lean against the front of a building or store, and no one can park a motor home on the street in one place for more than two hours.

According to the National Coalition for the Homeless, in a survey of the top 20 "meanest" cities toward the homeless, Las Vegas was #1, followed by San Francisco, with New York City falling into the #3 position.

Many homeless people in New York are arrested for violating rules, not laws, but nevertheless, it leads to a criminal record. For instance, the fact that Central Park officially closes at 1 a.m. is a rule, not a law. Yet, individuals caught sleeping in the park after hours, are charged with "misuse of park property." Falling asleep on the subway and taking up more than one seat is ticketed as "stealing a fare."

Homeless advocates often stated that it would be one thing if these rules and laws were applied equally, but homeless activists have charged that the general public is not arrested or ticketed for the same conduct as the homeless, constituting an illegal police practice – selective enforcement. In Central Park, homeless people are arrested for drinking or camping, while concertgoers on blankets drinking wine in the same area are excused. This double standard also exists in Penn Station. While the homeless may be harassed or ticketed for drinking in public, commuters can buy a beer at one of the restaurants in the station, and drink it on the platform of the Long Island Railroad while waiting for their train. Adding insult to injury is the fact that many homeless arrests are the result of warrants which were issued for their inability to pay the fines for their "quality of life" tickets.

All of this, of course, makes New York City a very inhospitable environment for anyone unfortunate enough to find them self without a place to call home. Besieged daily by endless verbal and physical assaults, and arbitrarily singled out and unfairly punished under petty laws – a system which many believe was only exasperated by the heavy-handed tactics of recent administrations – many homeless individuals are caught in a vicious cycle of despair.

Analysts suggested that extreme desperation brought on by long-term homelessness could certainly push one to the brink of insanity. Also, many viewed the crimes as a sort of homeless retribution, or a "payback," if you will, of the unconscionable ways in which society has treated them. Some even went so far as to question why something like this hasn't happened sooner. Coupled with being infected with a tainted dose of PCP – you practically have the makings for a "super criminal," and a more than plausible motive for *The Subway Slayings*.

The effect of this news coverage stirred up an unprecedented amount of fervor throughout the city about the homeless. Having always been looked upon with considerable disdain, they were now viewed as an extremely dangerous pariah in society. *Every* homeless person was assumed "infected" and a potential maniacal murderer – a ticking time bomb, just waiting to go off. Attacks on the homeless were now at an all-time high. "Thrill-seekers," who usually preyed on them simply for sport, did so with renewed vigor – taking on the role of "mission offenders," in a warped belief that they were now on a legitimate crusade to rid the city of a "deadly scourge." In just the past week, hundreds of attacks on the homeless were reported all over the city.

In the Bronx, a man was shot at point-blank range as he approached a motorist who was stopped at a red light to ask for change.

In Port Authority, a man was severely beaten by a group of teens.

On a footbridge to Ward's Island – a small island in the East River between Manhattan and Queens – a group of youths jumped a man and slashed his throat.

These attacks were just the tip of the iceberg. Almost hourly, police in every borough were receiving similar reports. In most cases, the preferred weapon of choice was fire. An untold number of charred bodies were being discovered on park benches, in cardboard boxes and, of course, in the subway.

New York City was a city on the edge – a city out of control with fear and senseless violence. Given the randomness of the murders *and* the alleged murderers – not to mention the failure of authorities to produce a single suspect – New Yorkers were living under a climate of sheer terror. The fact that the murders were only taking place in the subway, gave people little comfort. No one knew when the next murder would take place, or if the violence would soon start to spread beyond the confines of the underground and into the city at large.

CHAPTER 9

October 28th – 11:00 p.m. Tuesday Evening

The shrill ringing of a bell echoed throughout the building. It was a joyous sound – heralding the end of another hectic day, and a chance to finally go home and relax.

Melissa used to feel that way, but there was no joy in it for her tonight. Her last class at John Jay had just ended, and she was slowly packing up to leave...*very* slowly. Every night last week, Richard met her after class and drove her straight home – sparing her the trauma of taking the subway. Unfortunately, he was unexpectedly called out of town on business yesterday, and wasn't going to be back until the end of the week. Since none of her traveling partners at school had come to class that night, she would have no choice but to take the train all by herself. Even the socially inept Steven Kippers was absent.

With *The Subway Slayings* weighing heavily on her mind, she wanted to stay in the safe and secure environment of her classroom as long as possible.

Lately, she was finding it hard to concentrate on much else. She didn't believe the city's explanation about "drug-infected" homeless people. In fact, she actually *wished* that it could all be blamed on a mere drug problem. As far as she was concerned, the killers may have been homeless, but drugs had nothing to do with their actions. Since last week, her belief of an evil presence had grown stronger than ever. The harrowing incident she had experienced a couple of weeks ago on her way home was all the proof she needed to know that she was still the primary focus of this "evil," and still in imminent danger.

With her bag finally packed, she was the last to leave the room. As she walked down the hallway on her way out, she was surprised at just how fast all the other students had exited the building. She then realized that her stalling tactics only delayed the inevitable and had actually made the situation worse. Instead of being nestled within the security of a vibrant throng of students, she was departing alone, and vulnerable.

As she opened the door and stepped outside, the cold air stung her face and hands. The temperature was in the low forties, but it felt more like the teens. But she was prepared. For the past several weeks, it had been unseasonably cool for autumn; so she wore a heavy leather jacket, and also brought along a pair of gloves. After pausing a minute to bundle up, she crossed the street and headed toward the station.

The two-block walk seemed longer than usual. In the year that she had been taking night courses, tonight was the first time she had ever made the walk completely by herself. Even though it was late and the streets were almost completely deserted, surprisingly, she wasn't afraid. The school was situated between Columbus Circle and Lincoln Center. It was a well lit area and most of the buildings were impeccably maintained. The eclectic mix of economic cultures gave the neighborhood a unique cosmopolitan flare.

When she finally reached the station, she hesitated for a moment. Like swallowing a bitter pill, she figured it best not to dwell on an unpleasant situation, but to get it over with as quickly as possible. She then trudged down the steps into the system.

After making her way down a couple of flights, she arrived at the platform for the Brooklyn-bound trains. She noticed the emptiness immediately, and could practically count the number of people in the normally hectic station on one hand.

She walked a few feet down the platform, then stopped, and leaned against a steel pillar. The mournful wail of an unseen saxophonist echoed throughout the empty silence. The music provided by subway musicians was usually uplifting – a pleasant diversion from the bleak surroundings. But tonight, it only served to underscore her apprehension about traveling alone.

She looked towards the rear of the station.

A cop was strolling nonchalantly along the platform in her direction.

She breathed a deep sigh of relief. The sight of a uniformed patrolman was a very welcomed sight indeed. As he passed by, he glanced at her, nodded and smiled. She returned the pleasantries – adding a small, timid wave. Had he slowed his pace, she might even have said something to him. She didn't know *what* she would have said, but most likely, it would have had something to do with the deserted conditions in the subway, or maybe, the boredom and loneliness of his patrol. She wasn't the type to initiate conversations with strangers, but was more than willing to step out of her comfort zone in this case. Basically, she would have said *anything* to keep him in her vicinity. But, before she knew it, the moment had passed and he disappeared up a flight of stairs at the front of the platform. Once again, she was on her own. The phantom saxophonist had also stopped playing.

Minutes later, an uptown "A" train rumbled into the station on the opposite side. When it came to a stop, the doors opened, and dozens of passengers spilled out – instantly filling the station with the sounds of footsteps and voices. The crackling sound of the conductor's voice could also be heard over the PA as he announced the next stop, and warned of the closing doors. Along with the noise from the train's motors, the station was now flooded with customary, and unusually soothing sounds and activity. She could feel herself starting to relax.

She watched the train as it exited the station.

"Excuse me, miss?"

She jumped with fright and quickly spun around. Standing just a couple of feet away from her was a homeless black man dressed in what could only be described as rags. He wore a pair of lace-less sneakers with large holes in the toes, exposing several hideously rotted and diseased toenails. His pants also had holes in the knees, and were about two or three sizes too big – held together only by a thin rope tied around his waist. The overcoat he was wearing had no zipper and was covered with countless rips and tears.

131

His face showed evidence of an extremely hard life and years of neglect – making him look like he was in his sixties, although he was probably much younger. He was coated from head to toe in a thick layer of dirt and grime and emanated a pungent, foul odor.

Up until now, she had been very conscious of her surroundings – constantly scanning the platform in both directions for signs of anything out of the ordinary. But, she was momentarily distracted by the departing train – its noise drowning out the sound of the man's approaching footsteps. Even under normal circumstances, this type of sudden and unexpected appearance would have given her quite a start. Now, it was all she could do to keep from screaming out loud. She clutched her chest to calm her palpitating heart.

"I'm sorry… I'm sorry, miss!" the man said, as he took several steps back. "I didn't mean to scare you."

"Oh, no… that's okay," she said, trying to downplay her fright – somewhat embarrassed by her over-reaction.

"I don't mean to bother you, miss, but… could you please spare some change?" he asked, apologetically. "I haven't eaten in two days."

"Yeah, sure."

She reached into her jacket pocket and felt a couple of loose bills. She knew one was a ten, and the other a single. To get rid of him as soon as possible, she quickly pulled one of the bills out and handed it to him without even looking at it.

"Thank you, miss… thank you very much," he said gratefully. "You have a good night."

"You too," she responded.

She watched him as he walked away, shuffling aimlessly towards the front of the platform. Usually, she would have ignored such a plea. She couldn't even remember the last time she gave anything to a panhandler, but fear pretty much got the better of her this time. Despite his seemingly harmless and somewhat pathetic appearance, no one really knew what was causing the homeless to kill. To avoid upsetting him in any way, she probably would have given him anything he asked for. When he was far enough away, she pulled out the remaining bill in her pocket and was relieved to see that she had only given him the dollar.

She checked the time on her watch. It was about a quarter to twelve.

She had been waiting about fifteen minutes. During that time, more and more people had gradually filtered into the station, but it was still far less populated than normal. Nevertheless, their presence made her feel *somewhat* safer.

As the noise level began to diminish, she heard something in the distance that sent ice water through her veins.

That sound... that infernal scraping sound!

The presence of other people made her feel unusually empowered. She moved out into the center of the platform to see if she could see exactly where it was coming from.

The front of the station! It's definitely coming from somewhere on the platform at the front of the station!

Boldly, she slowly started walking in that direction. Since the station wasn't deserted, she was now more curious than scared. She made her way for several feet along the platform. Suddenly, a low rumble coming from deep within the tunnel began to drown out the sound out.

She walked to the edge of the platform and looked back towards the rear. The tracks and tunnel walls were beginning to glow brightly from the lights of an approaching train. A Brooklyn-bound "A" train surged into the station – erasing all traces of the errant sound. When it came to a stop, she got on and stepped into an almost empty car. Only she and two other passengers – a young black man and a middle-aged black woman – were present. She took a seat at the front end of the car and tried to put the strange sound out of her mind.

The ride was agonizingly slow. Each time the train stopped at a station, it held its doors open for what seemed like an eternity. She was frustrated – mainly because she was anxious to get home, but also because she could see no apparent reason for the delay. As far as she could tell, hardly anybody was getting on. Even the usually bustling 42nd Street and 34th Street stops only netted about two or three additional passengers. Yet, the train would sit with its doors open for several excruciating seconds – as if pleading for more people to board. By the time it reached West 4ᵗʰ Street, the two passengers who were in her car had gotten off, leaving her completely alone. When the doors closed, she could feel her anxiety – laced with a twinge of fear – starting to return.

The train slowly made its way down Sixth Avenue, traveling beneath the borders of Soho and Greenwich Village – two neighborhoods that usually brought forth a colorful and entertaining assortment of individuals, but not tonight. Station after station, she hoped for some company, but no one else got on. Loneliness was her only companion, for even the "oddballs" of society had apparently chosen to steer clear of the subway.

She was still alone when the train reached the last stop in Manhattan – the dreaded Broadway-Nassau Station. It wasn't so much the station she dreaded, as it was the three long minutes it took to reach the next stop in Brooklyn. To pass the time, and to calm her nerves, she retrieved a pad from her bag and began reviewing notes for an upcoming test.

This was an excellent diversion – finally allowing her to take her mind off her fears. She soon started having difficulty seeing the page. The words were being partially obscured by small puffs of white vapor. She looked up and realized that she could see her own breath. That's when she felt it. The temperature in the car had dropped… drastically.

A loud clunk came from the far end of the car.

She looked in the direction of the sound. An empty soda bottle was rolling down the aisle toward her from the opposite end. Her anxiety returned.

Where the hell did that come from! She wondered.

She heard some rustling, then, a series of moans and grunts. Leaning forward, she carefully surveyed the rear of the car. To her surprise, she discovered that she, in fact, *wasn't* alone. Lying flat on a bench on her side of the car was a man… a homeless man.

Had he been there all this time?!

His prone position and location made him virtually invisible to her when she entered.

The bottle continued its journey down the aisle on a steady course in her direction. A sudden jolt of the train caused it to veer right and smash into the metal plating under the seats on the other side of the car, making a loud "clink." It spun around, then, rolled diagonally back across the aisle, coming to rest under the bench a few feet away from her feet.

She returned her attention to the homeless man. His moans and grunts got louder, and gradually developed into a prolonged, guttural sound – a sound she had never heard coming from any human *or* animal. It didn't even sound like it was coming from a single source, but rather a multitude of sources, producing a simultaneous chorus of low, mid and high tones. It was a sound that sent ice-cold chills throughout every inch of her body.

Suddenly, some type of seizure took hold of his body, causing him to twitch and jerk. His movements became frighteningly violent and erratic – as though he was being subjected to a steady stream of electrical jolts from an invisible defibrillator.

She watched in absolute terror as his entire body was repeatedly thrust up to a foot into the air, then, viciously slammed back down on the bench. Many times it looked like he was going to bounce completely off the bench. Then, as mysteriously as it began, it all came to an abrupt end. The seizure, as well as the weird sound immediately stopped. In a way, the sudden silence was even more frightening. She wondered if, perhaps, she had just witnessed a man die. After a few seconds of eerie silence, she didn't have to wonder any longer. In one smooth, fluid motion, the man quickly rose to a sitting position. She gasped, and almost lost her grip on the notebook she was holding.

She was now able to get a good look at his face. He was a white man in his fifties. Balding in the middle, he had two clumps of dirty, grayish hair on either side of his head. His face had a leathery texture, with lots of wrinkles, which over the years, had dug in and formed a virtual road map of deep-set canyons and fissures. He wore a heavy overcoat zipped all the way up, and a pair of jeans. So filth-encrusted, and caked with years of grease and grime, his clothes actually shined. His shoes – barely reserving the right to still be referred to as such – were in even worse condition than the rest of his clothes. What was once a sturdy pair of Timberland's, was now nothing more than a few pieces of lace-less leather held together with tape and string. More than half of the soles were completely worn away, leaving his dirt-blackened feet exposed. Their only protection from the elements and the harsh subway environment were two plastic bags, which he had haphazardly wrapped around each foot.

She continued to watch as the man sat motionlessly – staring vacantly ahead. He may have outwardly looked like any one of the thousands of other ordinary homeless people in the city, but she knew there was nothing ordinary about what she just witnessed. Obviously, *The Subway Slayings* flashed through her mind. She couldn't help but wonder if her luck had finally run out.

Before she could think about what to do next, the man began to drool. Beginning as a small, barely perceptible stream of saliva, it rapidly developed into a pronounced flow of thick, yellowish mucus. It oozed down the front of his overcoat and collected into a putrid pool of pus in his lap.

The sight made her nauseous. Her instincts told her to flee, but she was frozen with fear – unable to move or even look away.

Suddenly, his head began to jerk in every conceivable direction. It snapped up, down, left, right and diagonally – like he had lost all control over his motor functions. Mucus was flung everywhere as the motion intensified to a frighteningly impossible speed.

She continued to watch in abject horror and disbelief. Knowing no normal person could possibly move their head that fast; she expected his neck to snap at any second.

The man began to cry out in pain. This time, his cries sounded more like a man, and less like a creature. Attempting to quell the movement, he tightly held both sides of his head. He grabbed a handful of hair in each hand, but the speed only increased. Clearly, he had no control over his erratic movements. He held on

136

until he inadvertently ripped two sizable chunks of hair from his skull, leaving a couple of bloody wounds in their place.

She covered her mouth with her hands – shocked that anyone could withstand such pain.

Suddenly, all of the man's movements and cries came to an abrupt stop. Once again, he sat motionlessly – staring straight ahead.

A brief but intense flash of red light momentarily blinded her. Although it only lasted a split second, there was no mistaking that it came from his eyes.

Her worst fears were now confirmed. This was not a man having a seizure. This was not a drug addict going through withdrawal. This was not a run-of-the-mill crazy person in the subway. This was definitely *not* normal. She thought about what happened to her almost two weeks ago. As frightening as it was to be chased out of the subway and through the dark streets, she, at least, had *somewhere* to run… *somewhere* to escape to safety. Tonight, she was trapped in a virtual moving prison deep under the East River, with absolutely no means of escape for at least another minute and a half.

She grabbed her bag and raised herself from her seat – foolishly hoping that she might not be noticed if she moved slowly. She never took her eyes off the man. More flashes of red came from his eyes until a steady, intense beam was maintained.

A range of emotions flooded over her. She felt sick to her stomach, as though she might throw up at any minute. She was angry – angry that, for whatever reason, she was being repeatedly singled out by this insidious evil. But most of all she was terrified. It was the type of terror, one probably feels when they know they're about to die.

The man slid his legs off the bench and onto the floor. Although he immediately sprang to his feet, his entire equilibrium seemed to be off. The train was traveling on a straight stretch of track at a fairly moderate rate of speed. Yet, despite the relatively smooth ride, he was having an increasingly difficult time staying on his feet. He looked straight ahead, but never directly at her. He then started moving in her direction.

"No… NOOOOO!!" she cried.

The words barely trembled out of her mouth. Tears welled up in her eyes as she shook her head from side to side in disbelief and hopeless desperation. For every step he took towards her, she matched it with one in the opposite direction – determined to maintain the distance between them.

He continued moving towards her in the most ungainly fashion. Resembling, at first, a drunk who could hardly stand, his movements now seemed more like a robot – a robot with a bad circuit, stumbling back and forth and left to right. Suddenly, his momentum changed and he began stumbling – almost running – forward.

She let out a quick scream, then, turned and dashed toward the door at the other end of the car. In her haste to get away, she dropped her notebook directly in her path. Before it even hit the floor, she kicked it and sent it flying several feet in front of her. Stopping to pick it up was the last thing on her mind. Her only concern was getting to the door. When she reached it, she grabbed the handle and pulled.

It wouldn't budge. It was locked!

Hysterics took over. She launched into a wild tirade of screams and curses, while frantically tugging at the handle. Suddenly, it opened with such unexpected force that she almost lost her footing – nearly falling onto a nearby bench. In her desperation, she was trying to pull a door that slides open. She cursed her stupidity – a stupidity that could have gotten her killed – then ran through the door.

Outside the car was a totally different, almost alien, environment. The air had a musky quality to it, and was considerably warmer. The noise was almost deafening as the train zoomed through the tunnel, only inches away from a blackened, graffiti-covered wall. Lit primarily by the glow of the train's interior lights, the wall was her only indication of just how fast the train was actually moving. From the inside, it barely seemed to be moving at all, but now, she could see that it was moving at an almost frightening rate of speed.

Going from one car to another on a moving train wasn't something she liked to do. The flimsy safety chains on the sides offered little protection from the sizable gap between the cars. It was a dangerous maneuver that she tried to avoid at all costs – preferring to wait until the train came to a complete stop at a station. Tonight, she had no choice. She was precariously balanced between the two cars, with her right foot on the small ledge of the car in front and her left foot on the ledge of the one in the back. Feeling the gentle rise and sway of the cars as they moved independently of each other was a strange and unsettling sensation. Just before grabbing the handle to open the door to the other car, she had an awful, stomach-churning thought.

What if this door is really locked!?

It was something she hadn't even considered until that very second. She was suddenly gripped by an almost crippling fear. She was in an extremely vulnerable and dangerous position. An attack now could send her tumbling off the train, through the gap, and onto the deadly tracks below. If the deadly volts of electricity coursing through the third rail didn't get her, the train itself certainly would. The thought of being sliced to pieces by the metal wheels of several 42½-ton subway cars was almost paralyzing. She couldn't think of a worse possible way to die. But turning back now wasn't an option. She could see the red glow from the man's eyes reflecting in the window of the door in front of her, and it was getting brighter. She reached for the handle and slid it to the side. To her relief, the door opened with ease.

"HELP ME… HEEEEELP!!!" she screamed, as she dashed into the car.

But it was completely empty. Any help she had hoped to receive wasn't going to be found there.

She was about a quarter of the way into the car when she heard a loud clank behind her. She turned around and saw that the door had slammed shut – muffling the outside noise. It was the first time she had the courage to look back since she began running – a decision she immediately regretted. The man was a lot closer than she thought. He had already exited the other car, and was just seconds away from opening the other door. His red eyes seemed to glow even brighter in the small area of darkness between the cars.

She emitted a sound that was a combination of a scream of terror, and a moan of despair. She whipped around, and began tearing down the aisle of the empty car – crying and panting heavier with each step. About three-quarters of her way through the car, she heard a sudden increase in the noise level, followed by a loud crash. She looked back and saw that the man had forcibly thrown open the door and entered the car. He was still moving in a weird, uncoordinated manner – zigzagging left and right, all over the car. Strangely, he never seemed to look directly at her, but continued moving forward.

Although she had only looked back for a split-second, that momentary loss of concentration almost caused her to trip and fall. Running on solid ground was hard enough under these conditions; trying to keep her balance while being chased through a moving train was next to impossible. But it was something she had to do if she wanted to survive. At the rate the man was closing in on her, she knew one slip and fall would probably be her last. Determined not to become another gruesome headline in the morning paper, she steadied herself, and charged down the aisle to the other end of the car. She blazed through both doors with surprising speed – barely even slowing up when crossing the treacherous gap between the cars.

To her dismay, the other car was completely empty as well. *WHERE THE HELL IS EVERYBODY?!!!*

She began to wonder if she had missed an announcement calling for all passengers to exit the train. It *did* seem to be taking a lot longer than usual to get through the tunnel. A litany of sickening thoughts filtered through her mind.

What if this train isn't going to Brooklyn at all!?

What if it's just going to some underground train yard!?

What if there aren't any other passengers on-board except for me and that homeless guy!?

Sobbing and panting heavily, she continued running through the car to the other end. Tears of terror streamed down her cheeks, but were quickly whisked away by the powerful onrush of air she generated as she ran. Afraid of what she might see, she refused to turn around again, or to look even slightly to the left or right. Rows of empty seats whizzed through her peripheral vision on either side. Shades of *déjà vu* from her last harrowing experience flashed through her mind. She was lucky then, but she had a bad feeling her luck was about to run out.

She focused all of her attention straight ahead – never taking her eyes off the window of the door in front of her. She looked through it and into the next car, desperately hoping to see somebody... *anybody*. But from her vantage point, all she could see were empty seats.

No... NOOOO!!! THAT CAR CAN'T BE EMPTY TOO!!!

She reached the door and flung it open with authority. Acclimatized to the dangers, she crossed the gap without giving it much thought. She grabbed the handle of the other door and opened it just as forcefully. Before she could even fully enter into the car, a large dark figure suddenly lurched out of a blind spot a few feet in front of her – completely blocking her path!

Unable to react in time, her momentum drove her straight into its grasp. Everything went black.

She was literally in the clutches of evil. Everything she had been sensing and feeling throughout the past several weeks had finally come to pass. Knowing she was seconds away from a horrible death, she screamed like she had never screamed before. From deep within her soul, came such an ear-piercing, blood-curdling sound that actually drowned out the noise of the train.

For what seemed like an eternity, she screamed and fought like a crazed animal to free herself. Barely able to hear anything over her own screams, she began to make out a familiar voice.

"Melissa... MELISSA!!!"

Gradually, she stopped struggling, and her screams died down to a whimper.

"Melissa, baby... it's okay, you're okay now."

She raised her head slowly. Through her tears, she focused on the figure's face. It was a face she hadn't seen in over six long

141

years. Although hidden under a fairly thick beard, there was no mistaking who it was. Standing right before her, larger than life, was her father, Matthew!

"Da… daddy?" she asked, not quite sure if what she was seeing was real. For a brief moment, she wondered if perhaps she had already been killed and this meeting was taking place in Heaven.

"Yes, sweetheart… it's me. It's okay," he replied.

"Oh, my God… DADDDDY!!!" she shouted – throwing her arms around him and hugging him tightly.

She started crying again, but these were tears of joy and relief – a relief that every child feels when they're finally out of danger, and in the loving, protective arms of a parent. All of her fears melted away. As they stood hugging near the doorway time and place no longer seemed to exist.

The train suddenly lurched to the left, forcing both of them to grab onto a handle to keep from falling. The jolt snapped her back to reality. Her sense of urgency returned.

"Daddy, we gotta go!" She quickly freed herself from their embrace. "There's this guy behind me… he's trying to kill me!! He---"

She turned around but saw no one.

"Who… what?" He asked, bewildered. "I don't see anybody. Is that why you're crying?"

"Yeah, he was right behind me, and he---"

She turned around again, but still saw nothing.

"I don't know. Maybe he… maybe I wasn't really being chased after all."

She knew that wasn't true, but at the moment, she couldn't think of any other reasonable explanation. Perhaps it was the sudden appearance of her father that spooked him.

She looked behind her one last time, but the strange man was still nowhere in sight. As she calmed down, she focused her attention on her father.

"Daddy, what… how… when did you…!?"

Her mind was a jumble of thoughts. Seeing her father magically appear right in front of her after so many years of silence was absolutely the last thing she expected. It was going to take some time to properly process everything.

"I hope I didn't scare you too much," he said, apologetically.

"Well, yeah... a little, but---"

"A *little*... it looked like you were scared to death. What's all this about someone chasing you and trying to kill you? Are you all right? Are you in some kind of trouble?"

Not yet wishing to get into a detailed explanation of what had been going on in the subway for the past couple of weeks, she tried to downplay the situation.

"Yeah, I'm fine. I just saw this drunk guy acting kinda crazy, so I just wanted to move to another car."

It was probably the most pathetic lie she ever told, but he seemed to accept it without question.

"But dad... what about *you*!?" She asked, anxious to change the subject. "How long have you been in town!? Where have you been all this time!? Why did you stop answering my letters!?"

"Yeah, I'm sorry about that, sweetie. I came in a few days ago, but I wanted to surprise you."

"Mission accomplished, dad," she chuckled.

"But where have you been all these years? Why did you stop calling and writing?" she asked.

"I was going through a real tough time, Missy. Your mother's murder sent my life into a terrible downspin. I mean, I know that's not an excuse, but I just withdrew... I---"

"So, you couldn't call me, or anything... just to let me know how you were... that you were even still alive?! I mean, why couldn't you just---?"

"I was in the hospital... a mental hospital."

She was shocked, and completely at a loss for words. She had tried many times to get him to seek professional help, but he always refused – insisting that he didn't really have a problem.

"I realized that it was getting harder and harder for me to perform even the simplest of tasks," he explained. "Friends of mine could also see this, and suggested I check myself in before my condition deteriorated any further."

"But dad, *I* tried to get you to do the same thing years ago."

"I know, I know. I guess I just had to hear it from other people. Besides, honey… I was ashamed, I mean, what father wants to admit to his daughter that he's crazy?"

"Dad, I never thought you were *crazy*. I just thought it would help if you talked to someone."

"Well, you were right. They really helped me put the pieces of my life back together again."

"How long were you in the hospital?"

"Almost two years."

"And you couldn't call to let me know what was going on?"

"Honey, like I said, I was ashamed… I didn't *want* you to know."

"But what about when you got out? Couldn't you have called me then?"

"So much time had gone by, I wasn't sure if you would even take my call. I couldn't stand the possibility of you hanging up on me and permanently shutting me out of your life. So, I finally worked up the courage to come back and see you in person – hoping that we could get our relationship back on track, and that you'd, hopefully, forgive me for leaving you."

"But how did you *find* me?

"I guess it's what you might call 'pure luck,'" he laughed. "My heart sank when I went to Co-Op City and found out that you had moved. With no phone number or address, I had no idea how I was *ever* going to find you."

"But why are you on this train… going to Brooklyn?"

"I didn't want to leave New York without, at least, *trying* to find you. Since I didn't bring a lot of money with me, I looked all over for a cheap place to stay. I finally found a room in an old hotel in Fort Greene for just forty bucks a night. I was going to stay there for a few days until I could figure out my next move."

"Your next move?"

"To try and find you."

"Exactly how were you going to do that?"

"Believe me," he chuckled, "I didn't have the foggiest clue of where to begin. I was just on my way to my room when fate brought us together."

"Wow, talk about your chance meetings!"

"I'll say, but what are *you* doing on this train? Do you live in Brooklyn now?"

"Yeah," she said, nodding her head. "I moved out to East New York several years ago."

"My God, that's a pretty rough neighborhood, isn't it?"

She nodded her head again.

"It's all I could afford after you left."

"Sweetie, I'm so sorry you had to struggle like that. Back then, I was weak… I was sick… nothing made sense to me. Again, I know that's not an excuse, but I'm hoping you can find it in your heart to forgive me."

She could feel the pent up hostility she had harbored against him over the years slowly ebbing away. What happened in the past was the past. The only thing that mattered now was that she and her father were back together again.

"Oh, daddy," she said, as she gave him another hug, "You know I'll always love you."

"I love you too, Missy."

He gently stroked the side of her face.

"Hey, are you *sure* you're okay?" he asked. "You seemed pretty upset for just seeing a drunk."

"Yeah, I'm okay, I just---"

A worried look flashed across her face.

"What's wrong?"

"My book… I just remembered I dropped my notebook a few cars back!"

"Okay, let's go get it."

She hesitated. Even though there was still no sign of the man, she dreaded the idea of retracing her steps. Since they still hadn't reached the next station, she knew he was still on the train… *somewhere*.

"You okay?" he asked.

145

"I'm fine."

Leading the way, she opened the door and carefully stepped through the gap. Matthew followed closely behind. When she entered the other car, she hesitated once more. Although she could clearly see it was empty, she still felt very uneasy. She peeked around the corner of an empty conductor's cab – the only blind spot in the car. Remembering how suddenly her father appeared from a similar spot in the other car, she was determined not to be caught off guard again. Satisfied the area was clear, she cautiously moved on.

Noticing her trepidation, Matthew asked, "Sweetie, are you still worried about that drunk?"

She looked back at him, but said nothing – the tinge of fear in her eyes told him all he needed to know.

"Here, let me get in front," he moved her aside and took the lead. "Stay close behind me."

She felt like a huge burden had been lifted from her shoulders. Having endured weeks of a gauntlet of emotions encompassing everything from uneasy feelings to unbridled terror, she felt she could finally take a breather. Like a little girl whose father had just taken by the hand, she felt safe and protected from anything that might come her way.

They had only moved a few feet into the car when she noticed that her father was walking with a great degree of difficulty. She had almost forgotten that he had been partially crippled in the savage attack seven years ago. His right leg was very stiff – barely able to bend at the knee. Each step seemed laborious. He walked with a noticeable limp – supporting his right leg with his hand as it trailed, almost lifelessly, behind.

"Dad, where's your cane? Aren't you supposed to be using a cane?"

"Oh boy, here we go again," he said, as he stopped and turned toward her – feigning exasperation. "It's been years since I've heard that line."

"Seriously dad, where is it?"

"I left it in my room," he sighed. "You know I don't like using it... it makes me look old."

"So, you'd rather limp around like *that*?"

Again, he sighed.

"You're right… you're right," he said, not necessarily agreeing, but to avoid an argument. "I'll start using it tomorrow."

They continued walking through the train until they reached the car from which she had originally fled. Matthew was the first to spot her book, lying on the floor under a seat.

"Is that your book over there?" he asked, pointing to it.

"Yeah! Thank God, it's still here!"

Moments before she was able to retrieve it, the train finally exited the long tunnel and pulled into the High Street station. Before it came to a complete stop, they sat down and settled in for the remainder of the ride. Nervously, she looked at the bench where she first saw the strange man. Nothing looked out of the ordinary. There was no sign of him, and no indication that anything unusual had happened at all. When the doors opened, a passenger entered the car at the opposite end. Everything seemed to be back to normal.

She then realized that her father may have just saved her life. He may have run out on her six years ago, but he had more than made up for it tonight. Without saying a word, she smiled to herself and laid her head on his shoulder. Everything was going to be all right… her father was back in town!

The rest of the ride was spent catching up on the past six years. She had a ton of questions for him, starting with his hospital stay.

He told her that he had checked himself into the Coastal Waters Community Mental Health Center in Beaufort, South Carolina. He said the hardest part was taking that first step and admitting he had a problem. But, overall, he felt the outcome was well worth it. Indeed, she could see a marked improvement between the expressionless, virtual empty shell of a man he was back then, and the now livelier and charmingly engaging individual he was today. Aside from the permanent facial scars he had received in the beating and a slight nervousness, he seemed perfectly fine and back to his old self.

He told her that by the time he got out of the hospital, he had been evicted from his apartment for non-payment of rent. He bounced around for a while, living here and there with distant relatives and friends. Luckily, he was able to find work again as an auto mechanic, and was able to eventually afford a place of his own.

He reiterated that his foolish pride was the primary reason he allowed their relationship to deteriorate. For that, he deeply apologized.

Although part of her still wanted to be angry with him, she readily accepted his apology. She was too overcome with the joy of having him back in her life to do anything else.

She then began filling him in on the details in her life.

She told him that she had to move out of the Co-Op City apartment, and described the home and neighborhood where she now lived. She told him all about her interest in criminal justice, and the night classes she was taking at John Jay. She talked about her job, and of course, Richard.

He remained basically silent throughout her story – only offering an understanding nod and a smile every now and then. It was a smile that didn't need any words… a smile that a proud father gives a daughter for her remarkable accomplishments in the face of overwhelming odds… a smile that made her feel warm inside.

The smile faded when she started talking about *The Subway Slayings* and the *real* reason she was running hysterically through the train. She spoke of her premonitions, as well as her recent encounter on the street. She had kept all of this to herself for quite some time – reluctant to tell anyone how she felt strangely connected to the killings. Now, in the space of less than two weeks, she had bared her soul, not once, but twice. By the time the train pulled into the Van Siclen station, she was so deep into the conversation that she almost missed her stop.

"Oh, this is my stop!" she blurted out as the doors opened. He helped her gather her belongings, and they stepped off the train – just seconds before the doors closed.

"So, you've never actually been hurt by any of these people?" Matthew asked.

"No, but I really feel it's just a matter of time. I mean, it's like they're seeking me out personally, you know?"

"Oh, I don't think that's the case, sweetheart." He checked his watch. "Look, it's almost a quarter to one. I'm sure *anybody* who rides the subway at this hour is going to feel like that, especially with all of this going on."

"I don't know."

"Trust me, sweetie, it's just nerves." He put his arm around her as they walked along the platform. "You're going to be okay."

She was a little taken aback by his somewhat patronizing attitude. It almost sounded like he didn't believe her. But, then again, she figured he probably didn't want to be an alarmist by overreacting to the situation, thus, upsetting her more.

After exiting the station, the conversation during their walk to her home took on a much lighter tone.

"So how long are you gonna be in town?" she asked, as they walked along Pitkin Avenue.

"Well, I think I have enough money to stick around for about a week. After that, I…"

"Oh, dad, stop! I'm not gonna let you stay in some hotel! You're gonna stay with me!"

"With *you*?"

"Of course! It's the perfect arrangement… I'm gone most of the day, so you can be there to keep Mr. Snuggles company."

"Mr. *who*?"

"Oh, I forgot to tell you… I have a cat. I hope that won't be a problem, will it?"

"No… no, it won't be a problem, but I… you named him *Mr. Snuggles*?"

She laughed.

"Yeah, you know, because he's so soft and snuggly… like the little bear on TV."

"The *bear* on TV?"

"Yes, dad… from the *Downy* commercials."

"The *what* commercials?"

Realizing her father wasn't a big TV viewer; she gave up trying to explain.

"Let's just say he likes to be cuddled and snuggled," she said. "Anyway, whattaya think?"

"About what?"

"About living with me."

"Well, I guess it would save me a lot of money while I'm here."

"*While you're here?* Dad, I'm talking about you coming back to New York permanently. I'm talking about us living together again as a family!"

"Oh, now wait a minute, honey… my home is in Beaufort."

"I know, but there's no reason why you couldn't come back to New York, is there?"

"I didn't plan on staying up here for more than a few days. I can't just pack up and leave."

"Why not? You had no problem doing it before."

"That's not fair, Missy."

"I'm sorry; I didn't mean it that way. But from what you've told me, it doesn't exactly sound like you're livin' the Life of Riley down there. With your skills, you could easily get a job as an auto mechanic here, and probably make a lot more money."

"It's not about the money."

"Well, what is it about, dad? I thought you wanted to get our relationship back on track? It's gonna be kinda hard to do that over the phone."

"I know, I know… I just---"

"Look, don't worry… I'll light a match when I come out of the bathroom."

"Oh, baby," he laughed.

"Seriously dad, with everything that's been going on lately, it would really make me feel a lot safer if you were here. It doesn't have to be a permanent situation. Just stay with me until you can find a place of your own."

"But you only have a one-bedroom. What happens when you and Richard want to… you know… God, I can't believe I'm having this conversation with my daughter!"

She hadn't said anything to him about her sexual problems, or the fact that she and Richard had never been truly intimate. Had she been talking to her mother, it probably would have been their first topic of conversation. But, she found it very uncomfortable to talk to her father about such matters. She certainly had no intention of getting into it here.

"Trust me, dad… it won't be a problem."

"I don't know, I---"

"I'm not asking you to make a decision right now. Stay a few days and see how it goes. If you find that you just can't tear yourself away from Beaufort, well, so be it."

"Alright, fair enough," he reluctantly agreed.

Satisfied with her partial victory, she said nothing else about the matter. Just getting her father to *consider* the possibility of coming back was good enough for her.

They made a left at Bradford and crossed the street, with Melissa following a few paces behind. She was surprised at how fast he could walk on his injured leg – often finding it difficult to keep up with him.

"I see you're pretty used to walking without your cane, huh?" she asked, slightly out of breath.

"Oh, I'm sorry." Realizing he was getting a little too far ahead, he slowed down. "I find that if I walk fast, I tend not to limp as much, and don't really need the cane."

Minutes later, they arrived in front of her house.

"Well, this is it," she said, as she led him toward the entrance.

"Seems like a pretty quiet area," he remarked.

"It's a lot quieter here than it is on Pitkin, but to tell you the truth… I kinda feel a little safer there," she said, "I mean, at least there's more people. Here, anything could happen to you, and nobody would know, or care."

When they got to the door, she unlocked it and stepped inside.

"Here we are," she said, as he came in behind her.

"Very nice… very cozy." he said as he looked around at the décor, nodding his head in approval.

As usual, Mr. Snuggles was standing near the door waiting to greet Melissa.

"And this, of course, is the famous Mr. Snuggles," she said, as she bent down to pick him up. "Come here, sweetie, say hello to my fa---"

Before she could reach him, he recoiled and hunched his back. He then bared his fangs and hissed. The fur on his back stood on end. It was a shocking, and somewhat scary sight that made her jump back. Before she could say anything, he darted off like a shot – tearing down the hallway and into her bedroom.

"I don't understand," she said, stunned, "he's never done anything like that before."

"He's probably just not used to seeing new people," her father said.

"But that's just it… he usually *loves* it when company comes to the house."

"Well, I wouldn't worry about it too much. You know how temperamental cats can be sometimes. I'm sure, in time, he'll warm up to me."

"Yeah, I guess."

After giving him a brief tour of the apartment, they settled on the couch and talked some more. She was so excited to have her father back home; she soon lost all track of the time. When she glanced up at the clock on the wall, she couldn't believe how late it was.

"Oh, my God, it's already after three," she said. "I have to get up in a few hours."

"Oh, that's right, you have to go to work tomorrow, don't you?"

"Yeah, and getting to bed at this hour… I'm almost sure to be late."

"What are you so worried about?" he joked. "You're dating the boss... show up at noon!"

She laughed.

"Actually, Richard's going to be out of town until Friday, but even so, I would never take advantage of our relationship like that."

"I know, honey, I'm just kidding."

"Hey, speaking of Richard," she said, "I was thinking that maybe this Saturday we could all get together and go out to dinner, or something. It would be a good opportunity for you two to get acquainted."

"Yeah, that sounds nice, I'd like that."

"Great! I can't wait to call him tomorrow to tell him that you're here."

He smiled.

"Dad, I want you to take the bedroom. I'll sleep out here on the couch."

"No, honey, I'm not gonna put you out of your bed. I'll be fine right here."

"But, dad, you're my guest. And your leg... wouldn't you be more comfortable in the bed?"

"Sweetie, I appreciate it, I really do. But honestly, this'll be fine. It's actually a *helleva* lot better than the hotel where I was staying!"

"Alright, are you sure you won't mind sleeping under the plants?" she asked, pointing to her window garden.

"Not a problem, it'll be like camping out," he joked.

"Okay, if that's what you want."

She went to the linen closet at the rear of the hallway to get some sheets and blankets.

"Tonight's really cold," she said, as she spread the materials on the couch – turning it into a makeshift bed. "Even though this window's closed, it gets really chilly when you're this close to it at night."

"I'll be fine, honey, but you better get to bed. It's really getting late."

Regardless of his reassurances, she still felt bad about having him sleep on the couch.

"I'll see if I can get a sofa bed for you this weekend," she said.

"Don't go through all that trouble, honey," he said. "I still haven't decided if this is going to be a long term arrangement."

"I know, but you might as well be comfortable while you decide."

He smiled. She then hugged him and kissed him on the cheek.

"I'm glad you're back," she whispered.

"I am too, sweetie. I'll see you in the morning."

"Good night, daddy."

Having uttered the three words she never thought she would ever say again, she turned off the light in the living room and went down the hall to her bedroom. The room was dark, except for a pair of shiny eyes peering at her from under the bed.

"Mr. Snuggles… you're still awake? What's gotten into you?"

She turned on the light and got down on her knees next to the bed. After a little coaxing, he inched a few steps toward her, but remained under the bed. Not wanting to do anything to startle him, she continued speaking softly until he came within reach. Slowly, she reached out and gently pulled him out. He was trembling.

"Oh, sweetie, what's wrong? Why are you so upset?" She softly stroked his fur.

She then detected a faint, but familiar odor coming from under the bed. Still holding him, she grabbed a flashlight from her top dresser drawer, and shined it toward the odor. He had urinated and defecated on the floor – something he hadn't done outside of his litter box since he was a kitten.

"Oh, Mr. Snuggles… what did you *do*? You know better than that!"

By the time she cleaned it up and got to bed, it was after 3:30 a.m. Filled with so many thoughts and emotions, she found it difficult to get to sleep. She simply laid there on her back in the

154

darkness, staring straight up at the ceiling. She thought about all the years of separation from her father; the anxiety of not knowing whether or not he was dead or alive. She couldn't believe that they were actually going to be a together again. The possibilities of their new life filled her with new-found hope and joy.

Before drifting off to sleep, she looked over at Mr. Snuggles, sitting in his little bed on the other side of the room. By now, her eyes had acclimatized to the darkness, and she could clearly see that he was still awake. Except for an occasional ear twitch, he sat perfectly still, staring straight ahead.

"Snuggles, go to sleep," she whispered.

He showed no reaction whatsoever to her words. His body remained rigid with his eyes transfixed on the closed bedroom door.

CHAPTER 10

November 3rd – 2:01 p.m. Monday Afternoon

Perhaps he was coming down with a cold and losing his sense of taste. Perhaps they had been sitting in the vending machine a little too long, and had gotten stale. Whatever it was, he couldn't understand it. Ever since he was a kid, Famous Amos chocolate chip cookies were his favorite snack food. But today, they just tasted like pieces of cardboard.

Richard had been sitting alone in the office break room for almost a half-hour, trying to force down the small pack of sweets. He was just about to leave when Melissa excitedly bounded in, and took a seat on the opposite side of a small table separating them. Her cheerfulness seemed out of place for a Monday, and it slightly grated on his nerves. But he fully understood the reason. Saturday, he finally got a chance to meet her father when the three of them went out to dinner at a restaurant in Midtown Manhattan. She had been on Cloud Nine ever since.

"Hey, sweetie, whatcha, doin'?" she asked.

"Nothing much, just thinkin'"

"About what… wait, don't tell me, lemme guess… about my father, right?"

"Well, I… ah---"

"I really had a nice time at dinner the other night," she gushed. "I'm so glad you two finally got a chance to meet."

"Yeah, me too."

"We haven't had a chance to really talk since then, and I've been dying to ask you what you thought of him?"

"Well, he seemed like a nice guy. I definitely see a lot of you in him."

"You know, it's funny you should say that. I've always felt that I've taken mainly after my mother, but ever since he came back, I see a lot of myself in him as well."

"So, how do you feel he's adjusting?" he asked.

"Adjusting how?"

"Well, you know," he picked his words very carefully. "Since he got out of the... hospital?"

She smiled and chuckled a little.

"It's okay, you can say *mental* hospital."

"I know, I guess... I just didn't want to... you know---"

"He's fine." She cut him off, sparing him further embarrassment. "I mean, it's something that you probably never really get completely over. He's always gonna have to live with the trauma of that night."

He nodded his head, understandingly.

"But the treatment he got seems to have really helped," she said.

"That's good. So, he's coping with it pretty well?"

"Yeah, I guess he is," she replied, tentatively.

"What's the matter?"

"I don't know, I guess I'm just being selfish, but I was kinda hoping that we'd be spending more time together."

"Whattaya mean?"

"What I mean is that he's hardly ever home. He's been spending a lot of time visiting mom's grave and the graves of his army buddies."

"Where?"

"At the Cypress Hills Cemetery."

"I didn't know service people were buried there."

"Yeah, there's a whole bunch of cemeteries out there, and one of them is a National Cemetery. That's where the military people are buried. He goes there after he visits mom's grave."

"I see," he said, nodding his head again.

"The thing is he's gone there three or four times since he's been back, and he spends practically the entire day there."

"Well, honey… it *is* understandable. Considering everything he's been through, I'm sure it's made him more aware of his own mortality."

"Yeah, I know, that's pretty much what he said too. I guess I can understand that, but he's also hardly ever home at *night*!"

"He stays at the cemetery *that* late?"

"No, at night he goes to meetings at his old veteran's organization in downtown Manhattan… the Veteran's Action Association. He said he became a member after he got out of Vietnam and used to attend regular meetings."

"So why's he going back now after so many years?"

"Well, he says it helps him to cope with mom's murder by being with other people who've also experienced pain and tragedy in their lives. He also told me that since he's been going back, he's run into a lot of his old friends from Vietnam."

"Oh, well, that's great. They should really be able to help him get through this."

"Yeah, but the problem is that they like to hang out long after the meetings are over, chatting about old times."

"Well, that's understandable too, I guess."

"But he gets home really late at night… sometimes not until two or three o'clock in the morning."

"Well, honey, he *is* a grown man… quite an intimidating-looking one, I might add. I would think he knows how to take care of himself."

"I know, but with all these killings going on, it's just not safe to be out that late at night."

"Is he riding the subway?"

"No, he takes cabs."

"Oh, well then, whattaya so worried about?"

"Until these murders stop, I just don't think it's safe to be out alone *anywhere* that late at night. Homeless people aren't just in the subway. Besides, with his bad leg, he's not exactly in any condition to run if he has to. "

"Well, you can't just stop living your life, honey."

"Yeah, I know," she sighed, "I guess I gotta get used to it if he comes back to New York."

"Whattaya mean, *back to New York?*" he asked, trying hard not to sound too stunned.

"Oh, didn't I tell you? I asked him to move back here."

"You *what?* But what about his home in Beaufort?"

"Beaufort!?" she scoffed. "What the hell's in Beaufort? He'll have more opportunity for a better life here."

"Yeah, but that's not your choice to make, Melissa. What does *he* have to say about all of this?"

"So far, he's agreed to think about it and to take it one day at a time."

"So, just like that... he might decide to leave everything in Beaufort, and move back up here?"

"You know, it's beginning to sound like you don't want him back in my life. He's still my father, Rich."

"No, I didn't mean it like that. I just---"

"He's not gonna be living with me permanently, if that's what you're worried about. This is just a temporary arrangement, until he finds a place of his own."

"Yeah, I figured that. It's just... you know---"

"No... *what?*"

He felt a tightening in his chest. Beads of sweat began to form on his forehead.

"I don't know. I guess it's just because it all seems so sudden."

"I guess it would seem sudden from your standpoint, but I've been waiting for this for six long years. Hell... I didn't think I'd ever see him again."

"I thought you resented him for running out on you?"

"I did at first. But then I started thinking... at that time he probably needed me just as much, if not more, than I needed him since he was actually there, and saw everything with his own eyes."

159

She looked down at the table. He could see that her eyes were starting to water. Her bubbly mood was gone. She was now in a deep, somber reflection.

"I should have been more supportive and a little more understanding," she said, but her words were meant more for herself, than for Richard.

"Sweetie, you didn't do anything wrong. Don't forget, you were practically a child – a child who had just lost her mother."

"Yeah, I know, but still---"

"But still nothing, honey. It was a horrible, horrible situation, and from what you've told me, I think you handled it better than most people... including myself."

She smiled meekly, and wiped away an errant tear rolling down her cheek.

"I guess the thing that's really bothering me is the resentment and anger I felt towards him when he moved away," she said. "It really doesn't make me feel good about myself."

"What you felt was a natural reaction. It doesn't make you a bad person."

"Maybe not, but at least now, I can kinda make up for it."

A hint of cheerfulness returned to her voice.

"Helping him in his transition back to New York will be the first step."

Not knowing how to respond, he remained silent.

"Well!" she said, slapping the tabletop with her hands as she slowly stood up. "I better get back to work... my boss is a *real* bastard."

She leaned over and kissed him playfully on the forehead.

"See ya!" she said, as she exited the room.

He just sat there – not knowing what to make of his feelings. He had a lot of questions about her father. At the moment, only one thought came to his mind.

How the hell does he manage to find cabs in Brooklyn at night?

Nevertheless, he was happy to see her so excited about something. Frankly, he couldn't remember the last time he saw that much joy in her eyes.

He looked down at the pack of cookies in his hands. With a bit of trepidation, he reached in and pulled out another one and popped it in his mouth.

Cardboard!

He then realized that it wasn't just the cookies. For some reason, *everything* in his life seemed to have become stale in the past few days, and it was more than a little unsettling.

Something just wasn't right.

CHAPTER 11

November 4th – 5:58 p.m. Tuesday Afternoon

The smell of burning chicken sent Melissa dashing from the living room and into the kitchen. She grabbed a pair of tongs off the counter and frantically began turning over the assorted pieces of poultry in the large frying pan. The undersides were quite dark, but not completely black. Covered with a little gravy, she thought, the slightly charred taste might actually be a pleasant diversion from the ordinary fare. Dinner was saved.

As usual, whenever she got into a deep conversation with her father, she would lose complete track of time. Perhaps she was trying to make up for six years of lost time; or maybe she was just trying to take advantage of *any* time she could get with him. He was still spending almost every night out late with his friends. She understood how important it was to him and tried hard not to let her true feelings show. But, when he finally agreed to stay home tonight, she intended to take full advantage of the rare opportunity. She left work early and took the night off from school and hurried home to make a nice, old-fashioned home-cooked meal – one of her most cherished family activities from childhood.

"I think it'll be okay, dad. I got it just in time," she yelled from the kitchen.

"Oh, I wasn't worried, honey. I know you're a good cook. Remember all those fancy dishes you used to make?"

"Yeah, but that was a long time ago," she said, as she left the kitchen. "I think I might be a little out of practice."

"You don't cook anymore?"

"I do when I have the time, but with work and school… it's usually just fast foods and Chinese takeouts."

When she re-entered the living room, she saw just how much smoke her cooking had created in the apartment.

"My God!" she exclaimed, fanning her way toward the window through the hazy mist. "I'm surprised all this didn't set off the smoke detector."

She leaned over the couch Matthew was sitting on and opened the window several inches. A sudden blast of arctic-like wind shot through the room, blowing a bunch of brown, dried-up leaves from her plants all over the floor. She quickly lowered the window, leaving it open just a crack to allow the smoke to escape.

"Whoa! I didn't realize how cold and windy it was out there!"

Matthew laughed.

"Yeah, we hardly got weather like this in Beaufort."

"Are you gonna miss living down there?"

"Nah, I like the cold. I find it refreshing."

She shook her head when she looked at all the dead leaves scattered over the couch and floor.

"I don't know what's wrong," she said, as she picked them up. "I used to have such a green thumb, but lately, I just can't seem to stop my plants from dying."

"Are you sure you're watering them enough?"

"Yeah, I watered them just a couple of days ago, and again this morning."

"Well, maybe you're giving them too *much* water."

"No, I think I read somewhere that over-watering causes the leaves to turn yellow. All these leaves are brown, so I---"

Something small and yellow caught her eye on the floor in the center of the room.

"Wait a minute," she said, "maybe I spoke too soon."

As she walked over to it, she saw that it wasn't a leaf, but a piece of paper – a little yellow stickie, to be exact. Two words were written on it in her father's handwriting: "Lucifuge Rofocale."

"I think this belongs to you. It must have blown off the table when I opened the window," she said, as she handed him the paper. "What's *Lucifuge Rofocale*?"

"Oh, ah… that's the first and middle names of one of my friend's grand kid," he said.

He took the paper from her and promptly stuffed it in his pocket.

"You're tellin' me his parents actually named him, '*Lucifuge Rofocale*'?"

"Yeah, well," he replied, "you know… black people and their crazy names!"

"If you ask me, that's bordering on child abuse!" she joked.

He laughed in agreement.

She picked up the last of the leaves and returned to the kitchen to finish cooking the chicken. She placed it in a roasting pan and baked it in a 350 degree oven for about another half hour. During that time, she also made some rice and green peas from a box of frozen vegetables.

The conversation during dinner was quite pleasant. They sat at the dining table at the far end of the living room and reminisced about old times – reawakening happy, childhood memories she had nearly forgotten. In fact, she laughed harder that night than she had in years. After dinner, they settled back on the couch, where the conversation took on a much more serious tone.

"You know, dad, I don't mean to nag, but, I'm really not comfortable with you staying out so late at night."

"Wow," he laughed, "seems like just a few years ago, I was having this exact same conversation with you. Have I been gone so long that the child has become the parent?"

"Dad, I'm serious. It's really not safe out there at all right now. I told you all about *The Subway Slayings*. You *know* how dangerous it is, right?"

"Trust me, honey, ever since, well… *that* night, I haven't gone anywhere near the subway. It's not really a happy place for me anymore?"

"You still take a cab all the way into Manhattan?"

He nodded his head.

"And then you take *another* one back here to Brooklyn?"

"Right."

"Where the heck do you get the money to do that? I thought you said you didn't bring that much with you."

"What I don't spend on crappy hotel rooms, I spend on cabs."

"Alright," she sighed, "but even if you're not on the subway, it still isn't safe out there. No one really knows why the homeless are attacking people. Just because the murders started in the subway, doesn't mean that they *can't* happen anywhere else."

"They haven't so far, have they?"

"No, but... why tempt fate!?"

"Look, honey, I appreciate your concern, I really do, but I'm perfectly safe. I'm with a bunch of my friends, and afterwards, we go out for a few drinks. I'm never completely alone."

"Your friends don't come home with you, do they?"

"No, but unless cab drivers start flipping out... I think I'll be okay."

"Yeah, but dad, it's not even just about the danger. It's been so long since we've been together as a family, and I miss you. I just want us to spend more time together. I know you miss your friends, but I'm your daughter! Can't you spend a little more time with *me*?"

He leaned over and put his arm around her shoulder and gave her a reassuring kiss on her forehead.

"Don't worry, sweetheart," he said, soothingly, "things will get better real soon."

She wasn't exactly sure what he meant by that, but one thing was becoming crystal clear... she was wasting her time trying to convince him to stay home.

"Listen, honey," he said, changing the subject, "I've been meaning to talk to you about something."

"What's that?"

"Well, I think it's about time I start looking for a place of my own."

"Dad, we've been through this before. I told you there wouldn't be a problem with you living here."

"Right... *temporarily*."

"It's only been a *week*, for God's sake!"

"I know, I know, but---"

"Is it because I bugged you about staying out late?"

"No, no, sweetheart, you didn't bug me. I know you're just looking out for my welfare. It's just that I have a lot of stuff cluttering up your living room, and I'm sure we both could use a little more privacy."

"Look, the clutter doesn't bother me, and as far as our privacy is concerned... we hardly ever *see* each other as it is!"

"Yeah, but---"

"But nothing, dad. We've been out of each other's lives for far too long. All I'm asking is that we spend *some* time together, even if it's just for a few weeks. You can at *least* give me that, can't you?"

He sighed, heavily, in exasperation.

"You are your father's daughter, aren't you?

She gave him a somewhat puzzled look, but said nothing.

"You're just as stubborn as anything," he said. "Alright, I'll stick around a little longer."

"Thank you."

She smiled smugly – satisfied that she had, at least, won the battle, even if the war was still very much in question.

They continued talking a little more about old times, and even made a few tentative plans about things they could do together in the coming weeks. It wasn't until she looked at the clock on the wall and saw how late it was that she realized they should probably call it a night.

"Oh, man," she exclaimed, "It's a little after midnight. I can't believe we were talking so long."

"Yeah," he chuckled, "once we start going down memory lane there's no stopping us."

"I know, but I gotta get up early to go to work tomorrow. I think I should start getting ready for bed."

166

She gave him a quick peck on the cheek and started to stand up.

Clunk!

Her foot slammed into something hard and metallic under the couch. Startled, she reached down and pulled out a medium-sized, silver lockbox.

"What's *this*?" she asked.

"Oh, that's where I keep my important stuff, you know, papers and documents… things like that."

"You have to keep them locked up?"

"Well, when I was in the hospital in Beaufort, I didn't feel comfortable leaving all this stuff at home. I felt it was safer to keep it with me. Since there was no place to lock up your valuables in the hospital, I kept everything in there and placed it in a drawer in my room. I guess I haven't gotten out of the habit of locking everything up."

"Don't worry," she smiled, "I'll have you re-domesticated in no time flat."

She returned the box under the couch and gave him another kiss on the cheek. When she stood up, she noticed how cold it had gotten in the room.

"I thought I closed that window a long time ago," she said, as she leaned over the couch and reached for the window behind her plants.

"Huh, that's funny… it *is* closed," she said, surprised.

Matthew felt the radiator under the window.

"Well, the heat seems to be working fine," he said.

She too felt it, and remarked, "Yeah, you're right. It's hot, but it doesn't seem to be warming the rest of the room. All the heat seems to be concentrated just a few inches around the radiator."

"Do you think that's why your plants are dying?"

"Nah, I don't think so. I've always kept them there and it's never been a problem before."

He nodded his head understandingly, but offered no other plausible explanation for their condition.

"Anyway," she said, "If you get cold, you know where the extra blankets are."

She said 'good night' and went down the hallway toward her room. Before she even got to the door, Mr. Snuggles stuck his head out as if to greet her.

"Hey, sweetie, where have you been hiding all night?"

She bent down to pick him up before going inside. It was quite cold in the room, despite the fact that the windows were also shut tight. She felt the radiator and sharply pulled her hand away – it was boiling hot, just like the one in the living room.

"I'm gonna have to have a talk with the landlord about this," she said to herself, as she placed Mr. Snuggles in his bed. "*Something's* wrong with the heat in this place."

After a quick visit to the bathroom, she was in her bed with the lights out. She laid on her back for a while, contemplating the recent changes in her life. Having her father back home was something she never expected. She had high hopes about rekindling the magic of their former relationship. It was truly a joyous occasion, or at least, it *should* have been. Even though she never experienced the same strong bonds with her father as she did with her mother, there was always a special something between them – a kind of love that only a father and daughter can know. Although they had a very pleasant time together that night, something was definitely missing. He seemed somewhat detached and a little withdrawn. Of course, he was nowhere *near* as bad off as he was seven years ago. Nevertheless, she sensed there was a barrier, of sorts, in the way – an annoying obstacle preventing them from getting back to the way things used to be. Maybe, in light of the tragedy, that *was* as good as things were going to get. It was a sobering thought that made her sad.

She changed her position to lie on her side, with her hands tucked between her legs.

Knowing she would never have her mother back was bad enough. After tonight, it was clear that the father she once knew was also gone forever. She thought about all of the fun-filled, family vacations and wonderful holiday gatherings; the familiar faces and laughter around the dinner table – things she would never experience again. She then thought about Susan – the little sister she would have known had it not been for that terrible night. She thought of how different things would have been if only her parents had missed that train.

She felt a teardrop on the bridge of her nose. Before she could wipe it away, it dripped onto her pillow.

CHAPTER 12

November 6th – 5:38 p.m. Thursday Afternoon

The festivities had been going on for about half an hour. The staff was throwing a small retirement party for Stanley Greenberg – one of the firm's senior partners. A much more formal and elaborate affair was scheduled to be held at the Waldorf Astoria in a couple of weeks. This was merely a spontaneous celebration; pretty much thrown together at the last minute to commemorate his last day on the job. Most of the activity was taking place on the other side of the room from where Melissa sat. Aside from coming over to congratulate Stanley and to get a slice of cake, for the most part, she chose to remain at her desk catching up on work. She would have left work promptly at five o'clock had Richard not practically begged her to hang around for a little while so that he could drive her home afterwards. He and Stanley were good friends, and he really wanted to be there to see him off. But it was just as well since she wasn't in any particular hurry. She was playing hooky from school that night in an effort to spend more time with her father.

"We'll be getting out of here in just a few more minutes, I promise," Richard said, when he came over to her desk.

"Oh, take your time. This is giving me a chance to finish up a lot of reports I've been neglecting."

"You sure you don't want to come over for just a little bit?"

"Nah, that's okay, you go ahead and have fun."

Someone in the gathering called for a toast.

"Alright, well, right after this, we're outta here. Why don't you start packing up your things, okay?"

She nodded her head, then, began shutting down her computer. Richard rejoined the group. After the toast, he instinctively grabbed one of the glasses on the table and downed its contents – it was alcohol. It didn't dawn on him until afterwards what he had just done. It was the first time his body had tasted alcohol in over two years. He looked at the glass, as if hoping he only *imagined* drinking it. The glass was empty. He could feel the familiar, soothing warmth of the liquid as it slowly coated the inside of his throat – an almost forgotten sensation. He looked over at Melissa. She looked shocked. Clearly, she had seen the entire incident. They both knew the dangers recovering alcoholics face on a daily basis. The two or three ounces he just drank might be all it takes to erase years of sobriety. Ashamed, and a little embarrassed, he cast his eyes downward to avoid looking her in the eyes.

The conversation during the ride home was strained at best. Most of the time was spent simply trying to ignore the "800-lb. gorilla" in the back seat. After about fifteen minutes of mindless small talk, Richard was the first to broach the subject.

"You know, I… I didn't drink it on purpose. I didn't even know what it was."

"I know," she said, gazing aimlessly out the passenger-side window. She then turned and looked directly at him. "I just hope it doesn't reopen the floodgates, so to speak."

"Oh, I don't see how it could. I mean, it was just a drop of alcohol, basically."

"Yeah, but isn't that usually all it takes?"

"Look, honey, I'm fine… I have it under control. I have absolutely no desire to pull over and go to a bar."

"Well, maybe not right now, but---"

"Not now… not ever. Trust me, I'm okay. It's not like I was actually *craving* alcohol all day. You saw me; I was drinking soda the whole time. I picked up that glass by accident. It was a spur of the moment kind of thing."

"I hope so," she sighed.

He smiled and rubbed her thigh reassuringly. He was happy they had had a chance to discuss it. Deep down, however, he was trying hard to believe his own words. The truth of the matter was that he really *didn't* know if he was okay. The road for a recovering alcoholic was a rough one – filled with many bumps and detours. Maybe a sip *was* all it was going to take to knock him off the wagon. Only time would tell. But for now, he was just going to try to put it out of his mind. He had more important things to worry about. He still couldn't shake the funk he had been in for almost a week. It frustrated him because it was so unlike his usual, easy-going self.

As they traveled along Atlantic Avenue in Brooklyn, Melissa remarked about the heavy traffic.

"I'm not used to getting home this early," she said, "I had no idea it got this congested at this time in the evening."

"Yeah, it can get pretty backed up around this time. It's not exactly smooth sailing, like it is when you're coming home late at night after class."

She nodded her head in agreement.

"Speaking of which," he continued, "aren't you worried about missing class? I know you want to spend more time with your father, but couldn't you have waited for Thanksgiving recess?"

"That's so far away, and they *only* give you a few days off. Don't worry, I'm just taking a couple of days off, here and there – I'll be able to make it up later. My father and I still have a lot to catch up on, well… *whenever* he decides to stay home, that is."

"He's still going to the vet center at night?"

She nodded her head again.

"Not quite as often as he used to," she said, "but, yeah, he still does."

"Is he still considering moving back to New York?"

"I guess."

He gave her a puzzled look.

"I mean, we haven't really talked too much about it," she explained. "Lately, he seems to be a little distracted."

"By what?"

"I don't really know. He just seems a bit distant."

"Well, after what he's been through, I wouldn't be surprised if it's post-traumatic stress," he said.

Again, she nodded her head in agreement.

The rest of the ride was spent in relative silence. Richard soon turned off of the main roads and onto the smaller, dimly lit side streets. At a much-reduced speed, he skillfully maneuvered through a maze of double-parked cars and forgotten potholes. It was just a little after 7 p.m. when he finally pulled up in front of her house into a parking spot that seemed to be reserved just for them.

"There we go, safe and sound," he said.

She smiled and reached around to her right side to undo her seatbelt. After several seconds of struggling unsuccessfully with it, he noticed her predicament.

"Having trouble?" he asked.

"Yeah... damn thing seems to be stuck!"

"Here, let me try."

Still strapped into his own seatbelt, he leaned over to the right to offer her some assistance. Using his right hand, he reached down and grabbed the buckle. He pushed the release button with his thumb and tugged – nothing. He repeated the process several more times – meeting nothing but total resistance from the stubborn belt.

"This has never happened before," he said, growing more impatient as he continued trying to unlatch the belt. "This thing is really... starting... to piss... me... OFF!"

The belt opened with one final, tremendous tug. The unexpected release caused his arm to spring up like a slingshot – violently striking her in her right breast with his elbow.

"OW!" she cried.

Wincing in pain, she grabbed her breast through her slightly open coat and jacket.

"Oh, God, honey, I'm sorry... I'm so sorry!"

Without thinking, he reached for her breast and began firmly massaging it in a circular motion – all the while, continuing to apologize for his carelessness.

"Oh, sweetie... I am so sorry, are you okay?"

"I'm... I'm feeling much better now," she said, coyly.

Initially oblivious to the sexual connotation of his actions, he quickly realized the effect it was having on her. The incident that

173

took place a couple of weeks ago in his bedroom was still fresh in his mind. He had misread her signals… big time. Determined not to make the same mistake again, he looked deeply into her eyes. She showed no signs of fear or hesitation.

"Are you *sure* you're okay?" he asked – hardly louder than a whisper.

Knowing exactly what he meant, she nodded her head and smiled.

Although her smile was barely perceptible, the signal was clear. She was ready. After almost ten months of battling her personal demons, she was finally ready to take things to the next level!

He felt like a teenager on the verge of his first sexual experience. He could hardly contain himself as he awkwardly, unlatched his seatbelt. Now, able to face her more directly, he placed his hand on her cheek just below her ear, and pulled her close to him. With just a few inches separating them, he could feel her warm, cinnamon-scented breath on his face. To his surprise, *she* made the next move. Grabbing both sides of his face, she pulled him in and passionately kissed him. The sensation of her hot tongue purposefully twirling around inside his mouth was incredible. It was the first time he had ever experienced this type of aggressiveness from her… and he loved it. Lowering his hand, he again, reached for her breast, this time, giving it a slow, sensual caress. Even through her clothes, he could feel her already hardened nipple pressing against the center of his palm. With each squeeze, his fingers sunk deeper into her soft flesh.

"Oooh, careful," she moaned, "it's still a little tender."

"Sorry," he whispered.

Throughout it all, he sensed absolutely no fear or trepidation on her part. She seemed like a totally different woman – a woman whose long-dormant carnal desires and passions had suddenly been unleashed. With renewed, almost unbridled fervor, he began undoing the buttons on her blouse – practically ripping one off in the process. When he had undone half of them, he spread her blouse open, and exposed both breasts. For a woman who used to be so sexually repressed, he was stunned, albeit pleasantly, by her skimpy – almost sluttish – spaghetti-strap lace bra. Slightly see-through, and about two sizes too small, it barely contained her – allowing her ample breasts to seductively ooze out of the sides and bottoms of its two triangular-shaped cups which covered little more than her large, dark areolas and nipples.

The sight caused him extreme discomfort... in his pants. His manhood had been slowly swelling for quite some time. It was now reaching the painful stage, as his binding garments prohibited any further increase in size.

With an almost childlike eagerness, he cradled her breasts in both hands, and gently squeezed. His fingers practically melted into the spongy flesh. He could feel – and almost hear – his heart rate increasing. Breathing heavily, he began squeezing harder and harder. Each caress caused her breasts to bulge even further beyond the bounds of her flimsy bra. Her cleavage beckoned enticingly as it slowly opened and closed. Driven by raw, animal lust, he buried his face within it, and repeatedly ran his tongue through the sexy crevice. Squeezing her breasts together, he buried his face even deeper. It was a little difficult for him to breath, but he didn't care. When he finally came up for air, a thin trail of saliva swung between his mouth and her cleavage. The glow of a nearby streetlamp caused the moistened area between her breasts to glisten boldly in the dim lighting. He noticed that her right nipple had become dislodged from her tiny bra. Staring him straight in the face, it jutted out hard and erect – demanding attention. He was more than happy to oblige. Without hesitation – and without breaking the saliva chain – he firmly clamped his mouth around the thick protuberance. He rolled his tongue around the tiny bumps on her areola, sucking in deeply, and feverishly gnawing on her enlarged nipple.

She hadn't been touched like this in a long time, and had almost forgotten what it felt like. Grabbing his shoulder with one hand, and the door handle with the other, she closed her eyes and slowly threw her head back – moaning in ecstasy.

The excitement was almost too much for him to handle. All those months of pent up, sexual urges were finally being satisfied.

He had never seen her in such a ready and willing state. It forced him to use every ounce of his will power not to explode in his pants. As it was, he could feel trace amounts of watery semen beginning to trickle down his inner thigh.

A car suddenly passed by. It was the first vehicle to go by since they parked, and it caught both of them a little off guard – Melissa especially. Initially, she had felt comfortable making out with Richard under the cloak of darkness on the quiet and deserted street. But, now that her eyes had had a chance to adjust, it didn't seem very dark at all. Maybe it was just her imagination, but she felt the glow from the nearby street lamp was costing them in a virtual spotlight. Also, considering the murders, *and* the fact that they were parked in almost the exact spot where the mysterious figure stood just a few weeks ago… she knew it probably wasn't the safest place to be.

"Sweetie, sweetie," she said, as she gently dislodged his mouth from her breast. "Not here… let's go inside."

Reluctantly, he released her – giving her nipple one final tweak between his thumb and forefinger.

As she hurriedly tucked herself back into her bra and adjusted her clothing, she nervously looked out the windows at the area outside.

"Don't worry," he reassured her. "It's dark, and we fogged up the windows pretty good, too. Nobody can see in here."

"I hope not. I'd feel a lot better, though, if they were tinted."

"*I'd* feel a lot better if I had worn looser pants!" he remarked, as he tugged at the crotch of his snug-fitting trousers – desperately trying to find a little more breathing room for his cramped package.

She looked down at his lap.

"Oh, my," she exclaimed. Her comment was meant in admiration, but it came across more as a shock.

He shot her a look of feigned indignation.

"What?! You think only black guys have a monopoly on the big ones?"

They both laughed.

For several seconds, they stared at each other without saying a word. It was one of those times in every couple's relationship when the words were totally unnecessary. Suddenly, she leaned over in his direction. Expecting another kiss, he closed his eyes, puckered his lips, and waited. Nothing happened. He opened his eyes and saw that she had leaned completely past him, and was whipping a clear spot in the foggy, driver-side window. He felt a little foolish for jumping the gun, but was glad she didn't notice.

"Look," she said, pointing at her house. "The lights are out. My father said he wouldn't be home until sometime early this evening. Come on, let's go inside."

She unlocked the car door, but before she could open it, he gingerly grabbed her by the arm.

Looking her intensely in the eyes, he asked again, "Are you *sure* you're ready?"

She smiled and quietly nodded her head.

Placing his hand on the back of her neck, he gently pulled her close to him and kissed her delicately on the lips.

"I love you so much," he said.

"I love you too," she whispered back.

As they stepped out of the warm car, they were both surprised by the bone-numbing chill in the night air.

"Jesus Christ, was it this cold when we left Manhattan!?" he asked.

"It always seems a little colder out here," she said, coming around the front of the car and pulling her jacket together.

For Richard, the cold seemed to be centralized around his crotch and lower extremities. He looked down and was shocked – more like mortified – to see a fairly large wet spot on the front of his pants, with a thin trail running almost all the way down to his left knee. He then felt a cold sticky coating most of his upper thigh.

He silently cursed his lack of self-control.

Apparently, their little *sexcapade* was a bit more stimulating than he realized. Although not exactly reaching the point of a full ejaculation, he had released enough "pre-cum" to produce quite a sizable – and embarrassingly noticeable – wet spot. He felt like an inexperienced, adolescent schoolboy. With Melissa now just a few feet away, it was impossible to hide it from her. His only saving grace was the cover of darkness.

He wondered, though, how he would hide it once they were inside.

Maybe she'll be too pre-occupied with other matters to even notice, he hoped.

She kept coming closer until she was standing along side of him. She kissed his cheek and swung both arms around his shoulders in a loving embrace. He reciprocated by holding her tightly around her waist. After he locked the car door, they strolled up the walkway to her house. It appeared that the wet spot was going to be the farthest thing from her mind.

She quickly unlocked the door and they simultaneously bounded into the living room like a couple of mischievous school kids. The lights in the room were out, but the hallway light was on – casting semi-dark light, imperceptible from the street, throughout the apartment.

"Hi, kids," said a voice in the darkness.

Melissa turned in the direction of the voice and let out a short but sharp scream. Richard did his best to maintain his composure, but was also clearly shaken. As their eyes slowly adjusted to the dim light, they could see that Matthew was sitting near the window on the far corner of the couch.

"*Daddy*?! Wha…what are *you* doing!? Why are you sitting here in the dark!?"

"I'm sorry if I scared you, honey. I was just about to take a little nap."

"But, I thought you weren't going to be home for at least a few more hours."

"I just came back a little while ago. I hope I'm not interrupting anything."

"Oh, no no no! We were just going to… ah… watch some TV."

Richard almost laughed out loud. She never was a very good liar. Her high-pitched, rapid-fire delivery essentially came across as: *"Oh, no daddy… we were just gonna fuck like bunnies!"*

"Daddy, you remember Richard, don't you?" she asked, as she reached for the light switch on the wall.

"Yes… yes, of course! How are you, Richard?" He stood up to shake his hand.

"I'm fine, sir, how are you?"

The lights came on as the two men shook hands. Melissa was shocked, and more than a little annoyed, to see a fairly large amount of dirt in the middle of her glass-top coffee table.

"Dad, what the hell is *that*?!"

"I'm sorry about that, honey. I accidentally knocked over one of your plants. I was trying to clean it up before you got home."

"*I'll* clean it up," she said, sounding somewhat exasperated. "Let me go get a plastic garbage bag from the kitchen."

"That's okay, honey, I got it."

He sat back down on the couch, and carefully began scooping the dirt into a small felt drawstring black pouch.

"Try to be a little more careful, dad… okay?"

"I will. I'm sorry about that."

"Where's Mr. Snuggles? He usually greets me at the door."

"He's probably in your bedroom. He seems to spend most of his time in there."

"Oh well, I'm gonna go to the bathroom for a minute. In the meantime, why don't you two guys chat amongst yourselves?"

She turned to Richard, who was staring unusually hard at the dirt on the coffee table. She cleared her throat a few times to get his attention. When he finally looked at her, she discreetly mouthed the word "sorry."

He nodded, understandingly. Their long-anticipated moment would have to wait just a little bit longer. He then realized that the bright lighting in the room had revealed the still quite noticeable wet spot and the bulge in his pants. He casually clasped his hands in front of his crotch. After only the second meeting of his girlfriend's father, the *last* thing he wanted was to be perceived as some sort of pervert!

Fortunately, Matthew seemed more preoccupied with cleaning up his mess than to notice his embarrassing predicament.

"Have a seat, Richard," Matthew offered, without even looking up.

He sat down on the couch a few feet away from Matthew, and crossed his legs – effectively hiding most of his "problem."

"Melissa tells me that you're thinking about moving back to New York," said Richard.

"Yes, it's quite possible."

"Have you thought about where you might live?"

"I won't be living here, if that's what you're worried about."

"Oh, no, no… that's not what I---"

"Relax," he looked up and smiled at Richard. "I know you young people have needs."

Richard stared back stone-faced. It wasn't a smile that elicited warmth, but rather an off-putting look signifying some strange type of awareness – an awareness of what they had just done in the car, or of the erection in his pants… possibly even, an awareness of his very thoughts. Whatever it was, it made him feel extremely uncomfortable.

"So," said Matthew, breaking the tension, "what's it like at work?"

"Well, it's kind of a demanding job, but it's also very rewarding as well."

"No, I meant, what's it like working with your girlfriend?"

"Oh, well, it's interesting, but it can be a little difficult at times?"

"How so?"

"Well, I love the fact that we're able to spend so much time together, but it's hard trying to always maintain a professional relationship."

"Yes, I would imagine that could be quite difficult. Does being her boss make it any easier?"

"No, not really," he was starting to feel a little more at ease. "I have to be careful not to show her any favoritism; otherwise, it might lead to problems with the other employees."

"Oh, are they aware that you two are a couple?"

"Oh, yeah, they know, and believe me… they watch us like a hawk to make *sure* she doesn't get any special treatment."

Matthew smiled, but this time, it seemed more genuine.

"I see what you mean," he said, as he resumed scooping up the dirt. "You have to perform a very delicate balancing act."

"That's true, but I wouldn't trade our relationship for anything in the world. I'm happy we're together so often, especially now, with all this stuff going on in the subway."

"*Stuff?*" he asked, briefly looking up at Richard.

"Well, you know… the murders. It's not safe for anyone, especially a young woman, to be riding the subway late at night while these maniacs are on the loose."

Matthew nodded his head, but said nothing – returning his attention to his task.

"I mean, just last month, a girl was killed right here at the Van Siclen station at about the same time Melissa usually gets home from night school. Thank God, her train was delayed that night. A few weeks ago, she was actually followed home by some weirdo!"

"Yes, she told me about that."

"Well, I just want to assure you, sir, that that will never happen again. Until these killers are caught, I'm gonna be driving her straight home from work and school. She won't have to worry about taking the subway."

"You don't have to put yourself out like that."

"Oh, it's no bother, no bother at all. You know, it really *is* dangerous out there. If you don't mind me saying so, sir, you probably shouldn't be out so late at night yourself."

"Melissa and I will be just fine," he said, as he scooped the last of the dirt in the bag. Raising his head slowly, he looked Richard directly in the eyes. In a very low, guttural voice, he uttered, "Perhaps, you should be more concerned with *your* safety."

The unexpected statement sent goose bumps up and down Richard's arms, and cold chills through his body. Not knowing what to make of the somewhat threatening remark, he just sat there, staring speechlessly at Matthew – growing more and more uncomfortable. Before he could fully process the situation, or even think about a response, Melissa came back into the room.

"So, how are my two favorite guys getting along?"

Matthew was the first to respond.

"Oh, just fine, honey… just fine!"

The sudden jovialness in his voice rang completely hollow and fake in Richard's ears.

"Richard was just telling me how exciting things can get at your office."

"Really," she laughed, "and just what *exactly* did you tell him, Rich?"

He had momentarily tuned out the world, and was continuing to stare blankly at Matthew.

"Rich… oh, *Richieeeeee*!" she hollered.

Snapping back to reality, he looked sharply at Melissa.

"Huh… what?"

"My goodness," she said, still laughing, "was the conversation *that* riveting? Did you give away *all* my secrets?"

"Oh, no… not at all."

"Hey, I got an idea. It's still early… what don't we all go out for dinner again? Did you eat yet, dad?"

"No, and that sounds like a wonderful idea. How 'bout it, Richard?"

The last thing he wanted was to spend more time with Matthew. He felt uneasy and really wanted to leave.

"Oh, I'd like to, but I can't." He stood up from the couch. "My stomach isn't feeling too good. I think I just better go home."

"Oh, that's too bad," Melissa said.

"Yeah, too bad, Richard," said Matthew, as he too, rose from the couch. "It would've been fun."

"Maybe some other time," replied Richard.

"You sure you don't wanna hang out for just a little while?" Melissa asked.

"No, I better go."

"Alright, well, let me walk you out."

"Nice seeing you again, Richard," said Matthew, as he placed his left hand on his shoulder, and outstretched his right.

"Yeah, same here," he said, as he hesitantly shook his hand.

"I'll be back in a minute, dad," Melissa said, as she stepped outside with Richard, and escorted him back to his car.

"Listen," she said, "I'm really, really sorry about that. I had no idea he'd be home so early."

Still a bit rattled, it took him a second to realize what she was talking about.

"Huh… oh, yeah… *that*! Don't worry about it, sweetie, there'll be several other opportunities."

"You seem a little distracted. Is your stomach hurting you that much?"

"I'll be fine. You and your father go out and have a good time. I'll see you tomorrow."

"Alright."

She pulled him close and kissed him passionately. He cut it short by gently pulling away.

"Your father might be watching," he offered as an excuse.

"I don't care," she whispered.

She moved in for another kiss, but he firmly held her in place, and repeated, "I'll see you tomorrow."

"Okay." She leaned forward and snuck another kiss in anyway, and said, "Love you."

"I love you, too, sweetie."

He got in his car and started driving down the block – watching her wave goodbye in the rearview mirror. So many troubling thoughts were racing through his mind that he wondered if he was even okay to drive. Despite Matthew's ominous remark, something else was bothering him even more. While he was watching him clean up the dirt, he could have sworn he saw something moving in it. He only saw it for a second or two, but was pretty sure he did see *something*. Or did he? Although he told Melissa there was no way such a small amount of alcohol could affect him, he was starting to have serious doubts about it. Shades of his past hallucinogenic episodes came flooding back – but that was only after several bouts of manic binge drinking. He wondered if he had so badly damaged his system, that now, even just a few ounces of alcohol would cause him to start seeing things again?

A large plastic bag blew across the street a few feet in front of his car, causing him to come to a screeching stop. For a split second, he wondered if it was really just a plastic bag, or a child running across the street. He watched as it flew up into the air and got hung up on some tree branches. A shrill blast of a car horn behind him returned him to his senses. He resumed driving, but now, more slowly and cautiously than ever – carefully surveying every inch of the road ahead. Not being able to trust his eyes was a terrible and unsettling feeling. The driver behind him continued honking and flashing his lights – no doubt irritated at the 10 mph pace at which they were moving. Richard eventually pulled over into an open spot next to the curb and stopped – allowing the other car to pass. He sat there for several minutes... thinking.

I've gotta pull myself together!

His thoughts soon turned to another matter... Matthew's odd behavior. Initially, he thought he was simply overreacting. He wanted to believe that Matthew was just the ultimate overprotective father, but he felt it was deeper than that. He had met his share of overprotective fathers in his life, but *none* of them made him feel as weird and uncomfortable as Matthew just did.

He was suddenly struck with an upsetting revelation.

His feelings at that moment were a carbon copy of his feelings immediately after meeting Matthew for the first time last Saturday. In fact, *Matthew* was the reason he had been feeling so out-of-sorts ever since. There was just something about him that he didn't like.

He felt a sudden cold chill, even though the heat in the car was on full blast. Goose bumps formed on his arms. He was afraid, but didn't know why, or of what. Nervously, he checked his mirrors, then gingerly pulled back out into the street.

CHAPTER 13

November 7th – 12:30 p.m. Friday Afternoon

Melissa was relaxing in the office break room after finishing her Caesar salad. She was just about to catch up on the latest developments on *The Young and the Restless*, when a Special News Bulletin flashed on the screen of the large, wall-mounted TV in the corner of the room.

Her heart started to pound. Lately, these bulletins were becoming quite commonplace, and almost always meant one thing… another horrible murder had been committed. She braced herself for the news.

As she expected, the details of yet another gruesome slaughter that occurred late last night were described. The crime scene was the 63rd Drive/Rego Park Station on the "R" line in Queens. The victim was as a fairly heavyset man of light complexion, possibly of Latin descent, in his late fifties. His nose and eyes had been caved into the back of his skull by some tremendous blunt force. Unlike the other murders, where the causes of death were, basically, left up to wild speculation, there was a witness this time for the entire horrific event. The reporter began relating the graphic account of this witness, who chose to remain anonymous.

He said he was standing on the opposite platform – directly across from the victim. As he recalled, it was about one-thirty in the morning, and he and the victim were the only two people in the station – or so he thought. After a while, he started to hear a sort of rustling noise – like something moving, and getting closer. His first thought was that it was a *very* large rat. He looked up and down the length of his platform, but saw nothing. He then looked over at the victim, who was busy reading a newspaper. Either he didn't hear the noise, or was completely unfazed by it, because he never looked up. The witness said he scanned the length of the victim's platform as well, but also saw nothing. He didn't see anything on the four track beds separating the platforms either. He was about to shrug it off, when, out the corner of his eye, he saw movement at the front of the victim's platform – more accurately, *underneath* the platform. Crouching below the narrow overhang – completely invisible from the victim's viewpoint – was what appeared to be a woman, moving toward the victim at a fairly brisk pace. At first, he thought his eyes were playing tricks on him, but as she got closer, it was evident that the oddity he was witnessing was very real. He said he couldn't get a clear look at her face, because she never raised her head, but it was obvious she was homeless. With *The Subway Slayings* fresh on his mind, he was keenly aware of homeless people acting weird in the subway. By all accounts, this was definitely weird behavior. But, instead of running for safety, he continued to watch. He went on to describe her as a white woman, possibly in her thirties or forties, with long, stringy blond hair. She wore a filthy, full-length overcoat, and from what he could tell, not much else. Hunched over, in an apelike fashion, with her arms dangling loosely in front of her, she briskly trotted through the narrow space – never once looking up. She stopped when she reached the spot where the victim was standing. He said he had no idea how she knew exactly where to stop, because she certainly couldn't see him from her position. She stayed there for several seconds – completely still. The abrupt end of the rustling noise apparently got the victim's attention, because he stopped reading the paper, and began looking around. The witness said the man then looked straight ahead, directly at him. He said he knew the man was in danger, but was too shocked to yell. All he could do was gesture. He raised his arm and began to point at the woman under the platform. The victim – thinking the witness was pointing at him – just stared back with a bewildered look on his face. When he realized he was pointing at something *under* the platform, he looked down, and took one cautious step forward to investigate.

As if sensing his motion, the woman immediately sprang into action. In a frightening display of unnatural, almost impossible dexterity, she raised her left leg and swung it all the way up and over the top of the platform edge. The witness then realized that the woman was barefoot. He said the sudden appearance of the leg scared the hell out of the victim, who let out a sharp gasp and recoiled in horror – dropping his newspaper and slamming his back against the wall. Before he could think about what to do next, the woman raised one arm to the platform, immediately followed by the other. She then swung her right leg around in another incredible maneuver until, it too, was perched on the edge. She momentarily crouched in front of the victim like some large, grotesque spider, then, slowly righted herself into a natural standing position. She then raised her head and looked directly at the victim. The witness said that although he couldn't see her face, the look on the victim's face pretty much said it all. He said the man looked absolutely petrified. He tried to back up, but was pinned against the wall. He just shook his head from side to side, and started screaming, "NO… NO… NO!!!" The woman then rushed toward him with lightening speed, and punched him dead in the face. A sickening thud and squishing sound resonated throughout the station. The man's screams abruptly ceased. The punch she delivered was more powerful than any punch the witness had ever seen thrown by a man, let alone a middle-aged woman. It was so powerful that it appeared to actually go *through* the man's face. When she removed her fist, he saw just how accurate his assumption was. Where the man's nose and eyes used to be, was now a gaping black hole, spewing insane amounts of blood in every direction. He said the man just stood there for a second, almost like nothing had happened. He then began to fall forward, picking up speed, until crashing face-first onto the platform with an awful thud. The shock of what he had just seen caused him to cry out in horror. The woman, hearing his outburst, whirled around and glared directly at him. He said he felt like he was looking directly into the face of death. Riddled with hideous open wounds and oozing some kind of yellowish pus, she appeared to be growling at him – brandishing a menacing set of large, green-stained and sharpened teeth. He also said her eyes were blindingly red – like lasers. Even though there was a considerable distance separating them – considering the easy and *freakish* way she had pulled herself onto the platform – he wasn't about to wait around to see just how fast she could get to him. Shaking with fear, he turned and made a mad dash for the exit. He continued running until he reached the clerk in the booth, who eventually called the police. When they arrived on the scene, all that remained was the victim's mutilated body – the woman was nowhere to be found.

At the end of the report, Melissa just sat there with her mouth slightly agape, staring straight ahead at the screen. She had a headache, and felt a little nauseous. She had the same reaction after learning about each murder. Just the thought of having to ride the subway alone at night would plunge her into an almost crippling state of panic. Although Richard's nightly, door-to-door car services spared her that ordeal; it didn't exactly allay her fears. In fact, she was more afraid now than she ever was. Even though the killers were as varied as their victims and the crime scenes were scattered all over the city, she still couldn't shake the sickening feeling that she was somehow a target. This feeling used to be limited to the confines of the subway, but lately, she was beginning to feel a growing presence of evil all around her, almost all of the time.

"Hey, babe," said Richard, as he stepped into the room, "you watchin' the news?"

His sudden appearance caught her a little off guard.

"Huh?! Oh… no, it's a special report."

"Don't tell me… another murder, right?"

"Yeah," she sighed, "some guy in a Queens station. But this time there was a witness to the whole thing."

"*Really*!?"

Anxious to hear more details, he came over and sat down next to her to watch, but it was too late. The report was over, and *The Young and the Restless* was beginning.

"Damn, I missed it! So what happened? What did the witness see?"

"He said the killer was a woman… a white, middle-aged woman."

"My God," he shook his head in disbelief, "was she a homeless person, too?"

"Yeah, it appears so."

"Jesus Christ, what the hell is going on with all these crazy-ass homeless people, killin' everybody!?"

"I'm sure it's not *all* homeless people, Richard."

"Maybe not, but who's to say when, where or *how* the next one's going to snap!?"

It was the question that was always on her mind, as well. All she could do was shrug her shoulders, and shake her head.

"So, what happened… how did she kill him?" he asked, excitedly.

"It was horrible and I really don't feel like talking about it. I'm sure you can catch all the details later tonight on the news."

Seeing how distressed she was by the news, he understandingly nodded his head, and quickly changed the subject.

"So, tell me, how did it go last night?"

"Last night?"

"Yeah, at dinner… you and your father said you were going out to dinner."

"Oh!" she said, with a detectable amount of irritation in her voice. "We were all set to go, and then at the last minute, he tells me he has to go to another meeting at the vet center. *Somehow* it just slipped his mind!"

"Oh, that's too bad."

"Yeah, tell me about it."

Ever since last night, he had wanted to tell her about the weird conversation he had had with Matthew. Considering the fact that she was already annoyed with him, he figured now was as good a time as any.

"You know, last night when you went to the bathroom, your father and I had a little talk."

"Yeah, about the office, right?"

He shook his head.

"No, we weren't talking about the office. We were talking about the killings."

"Oh, really? Well, why did he say---"

"Because he probably didn't want you to know that he practically just threatened me."

"He *what*!? She said, almost shouting. "Whattaya mean, he *threatened* you!?"

"I was telling him how dangerous it is to be out so late at night. I told him that he shouldn't worry about you, because I'll be driving you home every night. I also told him that *he* should try to be a little more careful as well, considering how late he sometimes comes home at night."

She nodded her head, and gestured for him to continue.

"Well, that's when he told me that I shouldn't be concerned so much about you guys, but that I should be more worried about *my* safety."

She stared at him – expecting him to go on, but he didn't.

"What… that's *it*? That's all he said? That's what you considered to be a *threat*?"

"Melissa, you don't understand… it was the *way* he said it, and the *look* he gave me when he said it! I'm tellin' you, it was scary, and it really creeped me out. I honestly felt threatened."

"Oh, boy," she chuckled, "Here we go again!"

"What do you mean?"

"Have you forgotten? When it comes to you and the fathers of all your past girlfriends, well, you're like oil and water… you just don't get along with them."

"Yeah, I know, I thought about that, but this was different."

"Rich, honey, my father's always been very protective of me. He probably just wanted to let you know that he's still capable of taking care of his little girl without any help."

"That's what I thought at first also, but, Melissa, you weren't there… you didn't see…"

"As far as you telling *him* to be careful," she interrupted, "well, there's something you gotta understand. He's always been a very proud man… a strong man. What happened to him seven years

191

ago took a piece of him away that he'll never get back. In some ways, it probably emasculated him. So, he tends to get a little touchy whenever someone implies that he can't do something."

"Yeah, but---"

"Trust me, Richard, he didn't mean anything by it. Don't worry, in time, he'll warm up to you."

He wasn't at all satisfied with her explanation, but he let it go. There was one other matter he wanted to discuss. The issue with the moving dirt had kept him up most of the night. He decided not to say anything about it. The more he thought about it, the more he believed – or tried to convince himself – that it *probably* was just his imagination. But there was something else about it that he knew he didn't imagine, and he couldn't keep it to himself any longer.

"Melissa, do you remember the dirt he was cleaning up when we came in?"

"Yeah, from the plant he knocked over?"

"Right, he said he knocked over one of your plants, but where was it... did you see a plant on the coffee table?"

"Maybe he already put it back in the window."

"Without putting the dirt back in the pot? Does that make any sense to you?"

"Well, I don't know, Richard... maybe he was planning to do it afterwards."

"Alright, but here's another thing... how could he have knocked over a plant sitting on the window sill, without getting any dirt on the couch – which is right under the window – *or*, on the floor for that matter? The only place where there was dirt was in the center of the table... nowhere else."

"How do you know there wasn't any dirt on the couch?"

"Because, I was sitting on the couch right *next* to him. If any dirt was there, I would have seen it... I would've felt it!"

"Well, he had obviously already cleaned it up."

"With *what*? The only thing that could've gotten *every* speck of dirt off the couch and the floor would be a vacuum or a Dustbuster, and you don't have either, do you?"

192

At a loss for words, she just stared at him with an anguished look on her face.

"And if *he* had one," he continued, "where was it, and why wasn't he using it to clean up the rest of the dirt?"

The two of them just stared blankly at each. After a long pause, Melissa finally spoke.

"I can't believe you're making such a big deal over a little dirt!"

"Melissa, it's not just the dirt, it's… it's everything."

"Whattaya mean, *everything*!?"

He sighed. Seeing that she was getting upset, he was already regretting his decision to bring up the topic. But there was no turning back now.

"I didn't want to tell you this, but ever since I met your father last weekend, I haven't exactly been feeling myself."

"What are you talking about?"

"I mean, everything just seems a bit… I don't know… off."

"What does all that have to do with my father?"

"Sweetheart, don't take this the wrong way, but… I get a *really* bad feeling whenever I'm around your father. I can't explain it any better than that."

"Well, now how could I possibly take *that* the wrong way?" she asked, sarcastically. "I mean, is there a *right* way to tell me that you hate my father?"

"Now, wait a minute, I never said I *hated* him."

"You didn't have to… you pretty much said it all when you freaked out a couple of days ago, when I told you he was coming back to New York!"

"Melissa, I didn't freak out, I was just---"

"You were just *what*, Richard!?"

"Look, all I'm saying is that there's something about him that's just not right."

She glared at him. Her anger slowly ebbed away. She felt hurt more than anything else.

"You know, Richard, I never thought you'd be the type of person to prejudge someone."

"*Prejudge*... what do you mean, prejudge?"

"Ever since you found out he had spent time in a mental hospital, you've had this warped opinion of him."

"Melissa, that's not true, and you know that," he protested. "The time he spent in a mental hospital has absolutely nothing to do with it!"

"Does it really, Richard... does it really?"

"No, absolutely not!"

"So, you mean to tell me that in less than a *week's* time, and after only *two* meetings, and based on something you can't even *explain*... you're convinced that he's just *not right*?"

Hearing it phrased like that, he had to admit it sounded kind of silly – maybe even a little bit paranoid. But there was no denying how he felt. Unfortunately, he knew Melissa would never understand – she was just too close to the situation. Not only would it be pointless to continue the conversation, he realized that there was a very good chance that any further discussion might cause irreparable damage to their relationship.

"Sweetheart, I'm sorry," he said, as he placed his hands over hers, "I didn't mean to upset you... really, I didn't."

She just sat there in silence, with her eyes downcast.

"Are we okay?" he asked.

She meekly nodded her head. She looked him deeply in the eyes, she said, "You just need to give him a chance, Richard. He's been through hell."

The look on her face almost broke his heart. He could see that she was truly hurt, and almost in tears.

"I know... I'm sorry," he whispered. "Are you sure we're okay?"

"Yeah, we're okay," she nodded, and mustered half a smile.

"Alright," he said, as he stood up. "I gotta get back to work, but we'll talk later, okay?"

She nodded her head again.

He then kissed her on the cheek and left the room.

She remained in the room, staring at the images on the TV screen, but comprehending nothing. His comments had left her

194

numb. She knew his apology was merely an attempt to placate her, and changed absolutely nothing as far as his attitude toward her father. That bothered her.

How can I even think about getting serious with a guy who thinks my father's a nut job!? She wondered.

It was something that was going to require a lot of soul-searching. But before she could give it much thought she was interrupted once again.

"So, who's sleeping with who?"

"What!?" She looked toward the door, and was surprised to see Agnes Covington standing there.

"*The Young and the Restless*," said Agnes, pointing to the TV, "that *is* just about the only thing that happens on those soaps, isn't it?"

"Oh," Melissa smiled, "I don't know, I wasn't really paying attention."

"You look a little upset, are you okay?" she asked, as she came into the room and sat down at Melissa's table.

"Oh, yeah, I'm fine," she said, "It's just Richard. He and I just had a little… disagreement."

"Oh, oh, trouble in paradise?"

"No, nothing like that, we were talking about my father."

"Oh, yeah, I've been meaning to ask you how that's working out. How do you like living with him, again?"

"Well, it's okay… I guess."

"Wow, not exactly a ringing endorsement," she said, clearly detecting the disappointment in her voice. "You sounded much more excited about it last week. Has the novelty of it all worn off already?"

"I don't know," she sighed, "it's just a lot of little things, I guess."

"Like what?"

"Well, the main thing is the late hours he keeps. I'm constantly telling him how dangerous it is to be out so late at night with all that's going on, but it doesn't seem to faze him. I'm really getting worried."

"He's still hanging out with his buddies from the VAA?"

"Yeah, and I think it's starting to get to be a little on the excessive side."

"Have you spoken with his doctors at the hospital down in Beaufort?"

"No, why?"

"Well, if anything, they could probably tell you whether or not what he's doing is normal, expected behavior. At least, then, you wouldn't worry so much."

"That's not a bad idea, but---"

"But what?"

"I don't want him to think I'm checking up on him."

"You don't have to *tell* him that you called. Just call and tell them that you're his daughter, and you're concerned about his readjustment into society. They could probably give you some ideas of how you might be able to help him through this. Whatever they say… just tell him it was your idea."

Melissa quietly pondered her suggestion for a few seconds.

"Yeah, I guess I could do that," she finally said, "but, like I said… it's *more* than just that."

"Tell me," she said, turning inching her chair closer to Melissa.

"Ever since I can remember, he's always been a very neat and organized person," she explained. "Structure has always been a large part of his life."

Agnes nodded her head.

"But lately, he seems to have changed."

"Changed… like how?"

"He likes to keep the shades drawn, so the house is always dark. Also, he's really messy. He throws his things all over the floor, and just doesn't seem to care about how cluttered the place looks."

"Yeah, but he is, after all, *living* on your couch, right? There are only so many places he can put his stuff right now. As far as the shades are concerned… it's probably the only way he can get a little privacy."

Melissa nodded her head in semi-agreement.

"Sweetie," Agnes said, while reassuringly patting Melissa's hand, "you of all people know exactly what he's been through. You've told me on many occasions that he's not going to get better overnight."

Melissa listened silently to the very familiar sounding advice.

"And you also know that regardless of how much professional help he's received, there's still a good chance he'll never be one hundred percent."

"I know. I understand that, but it's almost like he's a different person at times."

"What do you mean?"

"Well, although it doesn't happen as often as before, there are still times when he gets very moody and distant."

"I'm sure that's all part of the natural healing process."

Melissa nodded her head again, but said nothing.

"Just give it some time," said Agnes, "before you know it, things should get back to *almost* normal."

"I'd like to do that… I just wish he could *find* the time."

"Why? What's the problem?"

"Well, if it's not the VAA, it's the cemeteries."

"The *cemeteries*?"

"Yeah, he goes to this nearby cemetery to visit mom's grave and the graves of many of his buddies that were killed in Vietnam," she explained.

"Oh, well, that's not so unusual."

"But, he goes just about every other *day*!"

"Every other *day*?"

"Right!"

"How often did he visit his buddies before?"

"I don't really remember, but I'm *sure* it wasn't this often. I don't know," she said, shaking her head dismissively, "I'm probably making more out of this than I should. Besides, I've got other things to worry about."

"Like what?"

"It's Richard… he kinda pissed me off a minute ago."

"I *knew* something was wrong! What did he say?"

197

"Basically, he just doesn't get along with my father."

"Well," Agnes snickered, "what else is new?"

"I know, right? When has he *not* had a problem with one of his ex's fathers? Only this time, he tries to justify it all on some dirt!"

"*Dirt*... what do you mean, dirt?"

"Last night, when Richard and I came home, my father was scooping up some dirt he had spilled after knocking over one of my plants. For some reason, he thought it was strange that he didn't see the plant, and that the dirt was only on the coffee table, and nowhere else."

A look of concern swept over her face. She remained silent as Melissa continued.

"I told him that he had probably just finished cleaning everything up. I mean, can you believe he'd make such a federal case out of something like that?"

"Did he *really* knock over a plant?"

"Well, that's what he *said*. I'm sure he wouldn't lie about something like that."

"What *exactly* was he doing with the dirt?"

"I told you... he was scooping it up."

"Where did he put it?"

"I don't know, in some bag, I think," she answered, impatiently. "Wait a minute... you too!? Please don't tell me *you're* gonna make an issue about this dirt as well!?"

Agnes' entire mood changed. No longer attempting to assuage Melissa's concerns about Matthew, her demeanor now reflected serious concern.

"Listen, Melissa, I---"

"Agnes! Agnes!"

Startled, the two women quickly looked up. Henry Coulter, one of the office administrative assistants, was standing in the doorway. The serious look on his face foretold a matter of utmost importance.

"Sorry to interrupt, but your mother's on the phone. She said something about your father being in the hospital."

"Oh, my God," Agnes gasped, as she hastily got up from the table. "Melissa, I'm sorry, but I really have to take this!"

"Yeah, of course, you go ahead… we'll talk later."

Agnes practically ran out of the room with Henry to take the call. Melissa was aware that her elderly father had been feeling poorly for the past several weeks. She hoped the matter wasn't too serious.

5:13 p.m.

Melissa had spent most of the afternoon just trying to get through the day as best she could. But it was hard keeping her mind on work. The condition of Agnes' father turned out to be considerably more serious than she thought. He had suffered a major stroke – forcing Agnes to take the rest of the day off, so that she could be by his side at the hospital. The situation made Melissa thankful that her father was, at least, in fairly good *physical* health. Hopefully, his other problems would eventually work themselves out.

Nevertheless, she was in pretty good spirits. The fact that it was the end of the day on a Friday afternoon had little to do with it. Matthew had called her a few hours earlier and apologized for the night before. He told her that he felt terrible about not spending more time with her, and vowed to make up for it tonight. He promised to give her a traditional father-and-daughter night out on the town – including a movie, and dinner at her favorite restaurant. It was a promise she had heard many times before, but this time it seemed different. This time he really seemed sincere. She wasn't too thrilled about missing another night of school, but figured she'd better take full advantage of this rare opportunity.

"All set?" asked Richard, as he approached her desk.

"Yep, just about."

As she began shutting down her computer and gathering up her things, he stood behind her; gently stroking the back of her neck.

"What are you doing?" she giggled.

"Just making sure you're not still mad at me."

199

"I told you I wasn't, silly." She stood up and turned around, then, gave him a quick peck on the lips. "Come on, let's get out of here."

During the ride home, she finally admitted that, she too, shared many of his concerns about her father. To avoid any further confrontation, he wisely stayed mostly silent throughout much of the conversation. As they neared her neighborhood, he decided to change the topic.

"So, what are you guys going to do tonight?"

"Well, I was thinking we might go to Times Square first and do a little sightseeing," she said, excitedly, "then, we'll probably catch a movie."

"Sounds like fun. What are you gonna see?"

"I've been wanting to see '*Finding Nemo*' for quite some time."

"*Really*... the fish movie?" he laughed. "I didn't know you were into cartoons."

"Hey, I happen to think that little fish is cute. Besides, I really need to see something light right now."

"Yeah, I can understand that."

"Afterwards, we'll probably go to dinner at BBQ's, and then, who knows... maybe check out a video arcade."

"Wow," he smiled, "you two should really have a nice time."

"You know, you're more than welcome to come along if you like."

"No, no... you really need this alone time with your father. You two go and enjoy yourselves."

It was just after six-thirty when they finally pulled up in front of her house.

"You want to come in for a little while?" she asked, as she undid her seatbelt.

"Nah, that's okay. You go ahead and get ready for your big night. Call me tonight, and let me know how everything went," he said.

"I will. Love you."

"Love you, too, bye."

They kissed goodbye.

She stepped out of the car and walked to her door. She then turned around and waved goodbye. As was their custom, he would wait until she got inside before driving away. It was a little gesture that gave them both peace of mind.

The inside of the house was completely dark. Unlike yesterday, there was no light coming from the hallway.

"Dad?" she called out.

No response.

Immediately, her blood started to boil.

God dammit! Don't tell me he stood me up again!! She thought.

But then she remembered that he told her he wouldn't be home until around seven o'clock. She looked across the darkened room at the time displayed on her VCR.

The red LCD displayed "6:44" in big, bold numerals.

She chuckled to herself for being so quick to jump to conclusions.

As she took a step toward the light switch, she heard a loud crunch under her right foot.

Dear God, please don't let that be a water bug! She prayed.

When the lights came on, she saw that it was just a dried, dead leaf under her foot. In fact, there were several dead leaves scattered all over the floor, couch and coffee table – blown in from the slightly opened window. For the past week or so, her lush window garden seemed to be slowly dying. Each day, more and more leaves would turn brown, wither and drop off, even though she had been watering them regularly. As she began cleaning up the mess, she saw Mr. Snuggles tentatively entering the living room.

"*There* you are, you little fuzz-bucket! So, what's the deal… you only come out of your hole when my father's not here?"

He cautiously sniffed around the edges of the room, but avoided coming anywhere near the couch. When she finished picking up the leaves, she went over and scooped him up in her arms.

"Have you been a good little boy today?" she asked, as she kissed and snuggled him. "Mommy missed you so much!"

She played with him for a few minutes, then, went to the bathroom to take a shower. It was a long, relaxing shower – a luxury in which she rarely indulged due to the late hour she usually got home. But tonight, she had the time to thoroughly enjoy it. As the hot water gently pelted her aching muscles, the rising steam opened her pores, releasing the tensions of the day. The experience was so soothing, she didn't want it to end. But she knew her father would be home soon, and she had to start getting ready. She stepped out of the shower and hurriedly toweled herself off. She then opened the bathroom door and went across the hallway to her bedroom to get dressed. The sudden drop in temperature between the steamy bathroom and the practically frigid hallway was a tremendous shock to her system. An even bigger shock was seeing her father down the hall in the living room.

"DAD!?" she shouted in surprise – quickly raising the towel to cover herself. "I didn't hear you come in!"

"Oh, yeah, I know," he said, as he rummaged through some papers – barely lifting his head to acknowledge her. "You were in the shower… I didn't want to disturb you."

"Okay, well… give me a few minutes to get dressed. I'll be out in a little while."

Holding the towel in front of her like a shield, she sidestepped across the hallway into her bedroom. She quickly got dressed and came out about ten minutes later. As she walked down the hall toward the living room, she could see that he was still thoroughly engaged with his paperwork.

"So, have you decided where you wanna go first?" she asked, as she entered the room.

"Huh… what?" he mumbled, without even bothering to raise his head.

"Tonight… where should we go first? The movies… dinner… what?"

"Wha… OH!" Snapping his head to attention, it finally dawned on him what she was talking about. "Oh, right… *tonight*!"

"Yeah, dad… *tonight*," she said, with tension growing in her voice, "what's the problem?"

"Honey, look…I'm really sorry, but something's come up, and I---"

"Don't do this dad! Do *not* do this to me, again!"

'Look, tomorrow's Saturday… we can spend the whole day together tomorrow."

"Dad, that's not the point! You promised me you could make it *tonight*! How many goddamn promises are you going to break!?"

"Honey, I---"

"So what you're tellin' me is that your friends at the VAA are more important than me, is that right!?"

"You don't understand."

"Do *you* understand that I've missed several nights of class because of you… DO YOU!?"

"I'm sorry," he said, coldly – returning his attention to his papers.

"Yeah, you sure are sorry… a sorry excuse for a father!!"

"Grow up, Melissa, will you, please!"

After collecting his papers, he stood up and began to walk away from her.

"GROW UP!? WHATTAYA MEAN, *GROW UP*!?" she screamed – following closely behind him.

"OH, THAT'S RIGHT… RUN AWAY!!" she shrieked. "IT'S SOMETHING YOU'RE AN EXPERT AT!!"

He said nothing as he continued to walk away, with Melissa right on his heels.

"HEY!! I'M TALKIN' TO YOU!!!"

She roughly grabbed him by his arm and violently spun him around, causing him to drop the papers all over the floor.

With his face contorted with anger, he raised a clenched fist, and screamed, "GET OFF ME, YOU FUCKIN' BITCH!!!"

His words cut through her like a knife. Never in his life had he ever spoken to her in that manner, and with such venom and hatred in his voice. Besides being shocked and a little frightened, she was hurt… more hurt than if he had actually hit her. Tears started welling up in her eyes.

Seeing her pained expression softened his demeanor. A wave of guilt and sorrow washed over him.

"Oh, my God…I'm sorry, sweetie," he softly said, as he embraced her in his arms. "Please forgive me."

Too stunned to speak, she began to cry.

"You know I would never hurt you, don't you?" he asked, as he held her tighter.

She nodded her head, but it was basically an empty gesture, for at that moment, she felt nothing for him. She may as well have been hugging a stranger.

"How… how could you *say* that to me?" she sobbed. "I'm your *daughter*."

"I know, honey, and I'm really, really sorry. I know it's no excuse, but, I guess, I'm still dealing with a lot of issues."

He broke the embrace, took a step back, and looked her in the eyes.

"Come on, sweetie, don't cry," he said, as he tried to wipe away her gushing tears. "It breaks my heart to see you like this."

"I can't help it," she whimpered.

"Sweetheart, listen to me," he sat her down on the couch. He placed one hand on her shoulder, and the other under her chin – gently raising her head to meet his gaze. "Things will get better very soon… I promise."

"You *really* have to go out tonight?"

"I do, but I'll try to be back soon, okay?"

"Just be careful."

"I will," he said, as he reassuringly kissed her on her forehead, "are *you* okay, though?"

She nodded her head, and whispered, "I'm fine."

He smiled and gave her another kiss on her tear-soaked cheek. He then hastily collected the papers and locked them in a small tin lockbox, which he kept in a suitcase by the couch.

As he gently stroked the side of her face, he said, "Tomorrow we'll spend the whole day together… I promise."

She smiled softly and nodded her head again. Within seconds, he was out the door and into the night.

She wiped away the last of her tears. Although she said she was fine, she was far from it. She remained on the couch for several minutes – thinking. She thought about what Richard had said earlier. The words that had so inflamed her just hours ago now seemed almost prophetic. She hated to think anything bad about her father, but she couldn't ignore what had just happened. The rage in his eyes was absolutely frightening, and something she had *never* seen in him before. For that one split-second, he truly was a different person.

Mr. Snuggles slowly ambled into the room.

"Come here, baby," she said, as she scooped him up into her lap, "everything's okay."

Stroking his plush fur usually had a calming effect on her, but this time, it did little to soothe her nerves.

10:48 p.m.

She had just breezed through two chapters of a steamy Danielle Steele romance novel, but remembered absolutely nothing. Earlier, she had watched a little TV, but was hardly entertained. She was trying to do everything she could to put what happened between her and her father out of her mind, but nothing worked. As the night wore on, thoughts of her father only grew more and more intense. Now, lying on her bed, she felt as though the weight of the world rested squarely on her shoulders.

Making matters worse, Richard's comments continued to rattle around in her mind. Although she didn't believe her father's condition was as dire as he suggested, she had to admit that *something* was definitely wrong. His uncharacteristic behavior made her wonder if he had been discharged from the hospital too soon. Perhaps it was something that could be easily fixed through medication.

She had a ton of questions that desperately needed answers. She then remembered what Agnes had earlier suggested: *Why not just call the hospital!?*

Of course… brilliant!

She tried to remember its name but kept drawing a blank.

Suddenly, it came to her that she had written the name down on a piece of paper so that she *wouldn't* forget! At the time, she really didn't know exactly why she had found it necessary to keep that bit of information, but now, she was certainly glad she had. If anyone could give her the answers she needed, they certainly could.

She rummaged through the hodgepodge of papers in her bedroom dresser drawer, but was unable to find it.

Damn! Maybe I didn't save it after all! She fretted.

She was just about to give up when she spotted the paper under a stack of old rent receipts.

In big, block letters, she had written: *The Coastal Waters Mental Health Center – Beaufort, South Carolina.*

She called 411 to get the number, then, called the facility. After being bounced around to a couple of different departments she was finally connected to a woman in Admitting. Melissa told her the name of her father, and identified herself as his daughter. After checking, and re-checking her files several times, the woman told her that no one by that name had been admitted to the facility within the past ten years. Thinking that he probably wouldn't want to use his real name, she gave her a detailed description, including his injuries and distinct facial defects. The woman said that she had only been working at the facility for about a year, and rarely came in direct contact with the patients. Sensing the despair in Melissa's voice, she decided to check with some of the other long-time employees, to see if the description rang a bell. After several long minutes, the woman came back on the line and delivered the news Melissa had feared: no one at the facility remembered treating anyone matching Matthew's description. Melissa thanked her for her efforts and hung up.

Not knowing exactly what to think, she stood in the middle of her bedroom – stunned. Were their records incorrect, or incomplete? Even if that was the case, they *certainly* should have remembered him by the description.

Perhaps she had gotten the name of the facility wrong.

Although she doubted that, there was the slight possibility that he had *intentionally* given her the wrong name to protect his privacy, and to prevent her from doing precisely what she was now trying to do. She went online and got the names and numbers of *every* mental health facility in the entire state of South Carolina. She spent the better part of an hour exhaustively calling each one, and inquiring about Matthew. Unfortunately, the results were exactly what she had expected.

No one had any record or recollection of Matthew.

She rubbed her ear. It was warm, and ached from having the phone pressed against it for so long.

Why would he lie to me about getting treatment? She wondered.

She knew getting help was something he didn't initially want to do, but she thought he eventually realized it was something he *had* to do. The fact that he actually knew the name of the facility suggested to her that, at one point, he was considering getting help, but for one reason or another, failed to go through with it.

She got angry. The more she thought about it, the angrier she got. It suddenly dawned on her that ever since the tragedy he had not received a single day of grief counseling. She had no idea what type of long-term effects this might have on a person, but she knew he *had* to be suffering from some type of serious psychological trauma – tonight's outburst clearly proved that. Her anger became over-shadowed by deep concern.

But what could she do?

If she couldn't convince him to get help before… how could she possibly convince him to get it now?

On the other hand, even if he did "agree" to it, it would almost certainly be a hollow promise.

Would she have to literally take him by the hand like a child, and personally escort him into the doctor's office?

And what about the time factor? With so much time elapsed, would psychiatric help at this point even be effective? Could it already be too late?

207

A litany of questions confronted her. Just thinking about it gave her a headache. She needed answers, and she needed them fast. But where could she go for help? Who would be able to---?

Wait a minute! She thought. *Why didn't I think of this sooner!?*

She could probably get all the answers she needed from the veteran's organization! All the members shared a common bond – a unique brotherhood forged from human tragedy. It was her hope that this connection would make them more persuasive than she could ever be in convincing him to seek help. They might even be able to provide free counseling!

She went over to her dresser to get the number to the VAA. She had asked Matthew for it out of her concern over the late hours he was keeping. He didn't feel it was necessary, but she had persisted – citing that in light of the *Subway Slayings*, if need be, she should be able to get in touch with him in an emergency. Reluctantly, he had given it to her. She wrote the number on an index card, and stuck it in the frame of her dresser mirror – where she quickly retrieved it. She thought about waiting until morning to call, but decided against it. Matthew might be home, and she certainly couldn't call then. She dialed the number, and after five rings, a male voice finally answered on the other end.

"Hello?"

"Yes, hi… I'm calling about my father, Matthew Manning. He's a member, and I was wondering if you could give me some information about something?"

"Ah… sorry lady… I think you got the wrong number."

"Oh, I'm sorry… I must have misdialed. This isn't the Veteran's Action Association?"

"Boy, I haven't heard that name in a long time."

"Excuse me?"

"I used to get calls for them all the time. The number's the same, but they moved out of New York years ago."

Melissa was silent for several seconds.

"Hello, lady… you still there?"

"Yeah, yeah… I'm sorry to have bothered you."

She hung up the phone and stared numbly into space. Her mind was in a fog.

First, he lies to me about getting treatment...now this!?

What else has he lied to me about!?

Has any goddamn word out of his mouth been the truth!!??

She felt sick to her stomach.

She hated to admit it, but Richard was right. Her father had definitely changed... and not for the better.

She then realized something – something that had been lying dormant in the back of her mind ever since he had come back into her life. It was the one thing she couldn't quite put her finger on when she was speaking with Agnes earlier in the day. But now, after being hit with such shocking revelations, it was thrust into the forefront of her consciousness. Right after the tragedy, her father had basically shut down and withdrawn into his own little world – a world filled with aimlessness, and devoid of any type of emotion or social interaction. Although still somewhat distant, "aimless" is not a word she would now use to describe him. In fact, he was just the opposite. On many occasions, she'd find him sitting quietly, apparently in deep concentration – almost calculating. When he became aware of her presence, he would suddenly "snap out of it," and act as though nothing was on his mind. It always made her feel a little uneasy, but, as usual, she'd blame his behavior on post-traumatic stress. But, after tonight, she looked at everything in a completely different light. She didn't know what was going on with her father, but was pretty much convinced it had little or nothing to do with stress. That frightened her. But there was one thing that frightened her even more – should she be more afraid for her father... or for herself?

CHAPTER 14

November 9th – 2:59 a.m. Sunday Morning

The incessant ticking of her watch pierced the thick silence like a dagger. It sat atop her dresser several feet away on the other side of the room. Normally, it was inaudible at that distance. But the night was unusually still, and amplified the meekest sounds to gargantuan proportions.

Melissa rolled on her back and looked up at the ceiling. She had been in bed for almost two and a half hours, but hadn't even gotten one minute of sleep. She never had a problem getting to sleep before, but the unsettling revelations about her father still weighed heavily on her mind.

How could he have lied to me about everything?

She had been pondering that question since Friday night. She wanted to confront him, but feared it would only drive him deeper into his unknown world. She chose to not even bring up the subject.

As promised, he spent the entire Saturday at home with her. He even suggested that they go out somewhere, but she declined his invitations. Clearly, he felt bad for standing her up the night before, and was desperately trying to make up for it. But she just wasn't in the mood. She couldn't stop thinking about how little she actually knew about him.

Putting a further damper on the day, was news of yet murder in the subway. A white woman, possibly in her thirties, was killed in the Rector Street Station on the #1 line in Lower Manhattan early Saturday morning. A witness to the crime described the killer as a middle-aged, white, homeless man. He said he had grabbed the woman by her neck with one hand, then in an incredible display of strength, picked her up and violently threw her to the tracks. Her head hit the third rail and she was instantly electrocuted. He said it had happened so quickly, she didn't even have time to scream. Realizing he was witnessing another *Subway Slaying,* and not wanting to become another statistic, he immediately fled the station and didn't stop running until he found a police car. He had no idea what became of the killer.

As usual, these kinds of stories made Melissa shiver. She was shivering now, but for a different reason. The day had been unseasonably cold, and the night even colder. The heating situation in her apartment seemed to be getting worse. Even though the radiators were cranked all the way up, they didn't seem to be making much of a difference. Her room was literally freezing. She pulled her comforter up to the bridge of her nose – trying hard not to move too much out of the warm spot in her bed.

She glanced across the room at Mr. Snuggles. She had been awake for so long that her eyes had completely adjusted to the darkness, and could clearly see him curled up in a ball, asleep in his kitty bed. She then caught sight of the display on the digital clock radio on her dresser just as the numerals changed to 3:00.

My God... am I ever going to get to sleep tonight?

She then heard a soft creak coming from her bedroom door. Quickly raising herself up, she turned and saw that the door, which had been closed, was now wide open.

"Dad?" she quietly called out.

It wasn't like him to enter her bedroom without knocking first, but then again, *nothing* he had done lately could be considered normal.

Receiving no response, she called out again, "Dad, is that you?"

Again… nothing.

She stared at the doorway for several seconds. The hallway outside was slightly darker than her room, but she could clearly see that no one was there. She figured that there must be a draft coming from the living room. In the summertime, when all the windows were open, the cross currents can sometimes turn the hallway into a virtual wind tunnel.

Hating the prospect of getting out of her warm bed to close the door, she reluctantly pulled back the covers and sat up. Even though her window was closed, the room was a lot colder than she thought. But she didn't want to waste time dwelling on it. She didn't even take the time to put on her large, fluffy bedroom slippers. She placed both of her bare feet on the icy floor, and winced from the momentary shock, then, stood up. Braving the cold, she ran across the room on her tiptoes – her thin T-shirt and sweatpants offering no protection against the biting chill. When she got to the door, she slammed it shut, then, turned around and ran straight back to bed. She practically dove in and completely covered her head under the blankets – desperately trying to warm up her feet and body by pumping her legs up and down. Eventually, her heavy comforter began to form an effective shield against the cold. She remained under the covers for several more minutes, basking in the warm coziness. Ever since she was a child, this was always one of her favorite places to be. Whereas most might feel suffocated, or even claustrophobic, she took immense pleasure in being tightly tucked in and completely nestled within her warm bed – especially on frigid nights like this.

When she had sufficiently warmed up, she gingerly peeked out from under the covers – exposing just half of her face. Still unable to sleep, she laid there for a while, staring frustratingly into space. By now, her eyes had so acclimatized to the darkness, the room seemed almost bright. The soft glow from a nearby streetlight made it look as though a bright night light was on in the room. She knew she would have an even harder time getting to sleep now. To block out the light, she decided to pull the covers back over her head. Before doing so, she took one final glance around the room. When she looked at the doorway, she did a quick double-take. The door was, once again, wide open!

She cursed her incompetence by not being able to properly close a door. Apparently, the latch didn't catch when she slammed it closed the first time.

Once again, she jumped out of bed and stormed over to the door. Her annoyance with herself filtered out the cold. She pushed the door closed, then, tugged on the handle several times to make good and sure she wouldn't have to get out of bed again. Satisfied that it was properly secured this time, she returned to bed – again, frantically pumping her legs to shake off the cold.

After settling down, she looked across the room and saw two tiny reflective eyes staring at her in the semi-darkness. Even though she was completely used to having a cat in the house, the sight of those mysterious eyes shining at her in the dark always sort of freaked her out.

"Hey, Snuggles," she whispered. "Did I wake you up, sweetie?"

Almost before she could finish her sentence, she heard another creak coming from the door. She whipped her head around just in time to see it slowly swinging open by itself, then, coming to an abrupt stop!

Her heart started to pound, and a chill ran down her spine.

She checked that door thoroughly and was positive it was securely in the latch. There was absolutely no way it could have been blown open by a draft!

Something else also struck her as odd. Aside from the minor creak, it made absolutely no other noise prior to opening. Normally, the sound of the doorknob turning and the latch releasing can clearly be heard. If someone were secretly trying to enter the room, these sounds would certainly be a dead giveaway.

She laid in bed for several seconds staring in shock at the darkened doorway – trying hard to think of a reasonable explanation for what was happening. But she knew there wasn't one. Something weird was definitely occurring – something that couldn't be ignored by simply sticking her head back under the covers. With immense trepidation, she got out of bed and put on her slippers. She went over to the other side of the room to get her robe that was lying on the back of a chair – never once taking her eyes off the door. After wrapping herself up, she started walking toward the doorway. Once there, she paused briefly to summon up the courage to take the next step. As if stepping out onto a busy street, she looked both ways before exiting the room. A few feet away to her right was an open-shelf linen closet at the rear of the hall, and to the left was the main stretch of the hall leading to the living room. She waited a bit for her eyes to adjust to the darker hallway, then, stepped out. Immediately, she felt a drop in temperature of several degrees. It felt like the living room window was wide open – so cold, in fact, that her breath was clearly visible. Pulling her robe tighter, she slowly walked down the hall.

A wave of fear suddenly surged through her body – a fear she had never before experienced in her own home.

It was here!

The evil presence she had been sensing for so long in the subway had finally breached the sanctuary of her very own home!

Despite the plunging temperatures, beads of sweat popped up all over her body. A trickle of perspiration ran down the small of her back. She felt like screaming and running away… but where could she go? Her only choice was to stand her ground and face whatever *it* was. Besides, she also had her father's safety to consider.

She continued down the hall until she reached the living room. The first thing she noticed was that the window was shut tight. She looked down and was relieved to see her father lying on the couch under a heavy comforter. At least now, she wouldn't be alone. She went over and nudged him on his shoulder… softly at first, then more vigorously, but he didn't wake up.

"Dad… dad, wake up!" she cried.

But it was no use; he was fast asleep. He had always been a heavy sleeper, but now he seemed to be in an exceptionally deep state of slumber. Several attempts to rouse him were unsuccessful. For all intents and purposes, she was alone. Realizing her efforts were futile, she gave up, and prepared to return to her room – dreading the prospect of having to make the trip by herself. She left the living room and was about to go back down the hall when she stopped dead in her tracks and gasped. Had her eyes not been so accustomed to the dark, it probably would have gone completely unnoticed… but there it was. At the end of the dark hallway, near her bedroom, was an even darker mass – a black hole of sorts. But it wasn't circular in shape. The more she stared, the clearer it got; until finally, a distinct human outline began to emerge.

She stood there motionlessly – petrified with fear. She wanted to scream. She wanted to run. She wanted to turn around and try waking her father again. But she was too terrified to do anything that would take her eyes off of the anomaly. Even though she had never actually seen a ghost, she knew several credible people who did. What stood just a few feet away from her didn't look *anything* like what they usually described.

Suddenly, it began to move! She took two quick steps backward and nearly fell– her trembling legs barely able to support her weight. But it didn't come toward her. It moved across the hall in a weird, jerky motion – like a video played in a stop - action mode. It continued moving until it disappeared into the open doorway of the bathroom on the other side of the hall.

Terrified, she stood in the living room and stared down the hall – wondering what to do next. She quickly glanced at her father, but he had rolled on his side and started to snore. She knew it would be next to impossible to wake him up now. She *had* to go down the hall to get to her bedroom, and she was going to have to do it alone.

She grabbed a heavy ashtray from the coffee table – the only weapon she could find – and began to walk forward. Just having *something* in her hands – no matter how useless it might be – served as a sort of security blanket. As she reached the entrance to the hall, she reached forward and flicked on the light switch.

POP!

FLASH!

The hall light blew out.

She let out a quick scream and jumped back – almost dropping the ashtray. The sharp pop and momentary flash of a blown bulb always startled her, but this time the shock was a thousand times greater. She clutched her chest to soothe her pounding heart. Regaining her composure, she cautiously began her journey down the dark hall. Inching along the wall, she held the ashtray out in front of her with both hands in a death grip – her heavy breathing producing large plumes of vapor in the frigid air. Never once did she take her eyes off the entrance to the bathroom. At any second, she fully expected the black mass to re-emerge. In what seemed like an eternity, she finally made it to the bathroom door. As much as she wanted to run into her bedroom, close the door and pull the covers over her head, she knew that wouldn't solve anything. She would never be able to rest easy knowing that that *thing* might still be lurking in the bathroom just across the hall. For the sake of her sanity and her own peace of mind, she *had* to check. Nervously, she peered around the door frame into the room. Although dark, it wasn't unnaturally dark. She detected no areas of "black holes." With a trembling hand, she reached inside to turn on the light – bracing for another blowout. The light worked. The room was immediately filled with the bright glow from a single 60-watt bulb. Having been in the dark for so long, the sudden illumination hurt her eyes. She raised her hand to shield herself from the harsh glare. After adjusting to the light, she went inside and inched her way over to the drawn shower curtain.

She was gripped by an intense, smothering fear. Her body was at its stress limit. Her legs were like rubber, and her knees felt as though they might buckle at any second. Tears of fear streamed down her cheeks as she struggled to control her rapid breathing. She began to feel light-headed, but knew fainting was not an option. She *had* to keep it together. Shaking uncontrollably, she raised the ashtray above her head with her right hand, and grabbed the end of the curtain with her left. With one quick swipe, she whipped it open.

The shower was clear.

She took a deep sigh of relief, and could feel the tension leaving her body. But she couldn't relax. *Something* definitely came into the bathroom – she clearly saw it with her own eyes. The fact that it wasn't there now, was, in a way, even more unsettling.

Where did it go?

Where did it come from?

Where was it *now*?

She left the bathroom and stepped out into the hall. The light from the bathroom spilled into her bedroom and as far as she could see, it too, was free of any ghostly apparitions. She looked down the hall towards the living room, but saw nothing but darkness. Once again, chills invaded her body. With her eyes now fully adjusted to the bright light, the black figure could be literally just a few feet away from her lurking in the shadows and she'd never see it. Just the thought of that tied her stomach in knots. Afraid of being plunged into pitch blackness, she turned on the light in her bedroom. The combined light from the two rooms made her feel a little safer and more at ease. She then turned off the light in the bathroom, closed the door and returned to her room – also closing that door firmly behind her. She then noticed that Mr. Snuggles wasn't in his little bed.

Her heart began to race again.

The black figure was standing right outside her bedroom door when she saw it.

What if it did something to Mr. Snuggles!?

She shuddered to even think such a thought.

She was beginning to panic when she heard a noise under her desk. She looked down and saw Mr. Snuggles curled up in a tight ball, and cowering behind a tangle of computer wires in the corner of the room.

"Hey, sweetie," she walked over to the desk and crouched down, "whatcha doin' down there? Come on out. It's okay, baby."

Obviously terrified, he refused to budge from his safety pocket.

She placed the ashtray on the desk. Getting down on her hands and knees, she crawled under the desk to get him, but he was still too far away to reach. After a couple more minutes of gentle coaxing, he finally came out far enough for her to grab hold. As she carried him out, she could feel just how scared he had been – his entire body was trembling. She had no idea what he had seen, but she knew it had to be terrifying.

"I know, sweetie... I know," she softly kissed him on the back of his head and nuzzled him under her chin. "It's all over now... you're safe."

Still holding him, she turned off the bedroom light and jumped back into bed – pulling the covers completely over both their heads. Rarely did she allow him to sleep on top of the bed, much less *in* it, but she was more than willing to make an exception tonight. She cradled him until his tremors began to subside. Even when it started to get a little too warm, she dared not stick her head out.

What if the door is open again!?

What if the black figure is actually in the room and looming over the bed this very second!!??

If she looked and saw *anything* out of the ordinary, it would be a shock that she didn't feel her heart could take. She knew it was foolish to believe that a few layers of fabric were going to protect her from anything, but at this point, that's all she had. She didn't know what it was she had seen in the hall, but she knew it was something she definitely didn't want to see again… certainly, not up close. Choosing to believe that "what you can't see can't hurt you," she remained under the covers with Mr. Snuggles until sleep eventually washed her fears away.

CHAPTER 15

November 12ᵗʰ – 10:45 p.m. Wednesday Evening

SMASH!

"Dammit!"

"You okay, honey?"

"Yeah, dad, I'm fine…I just dropped a dish."

It slipped out of Melissa's wet hands and shattered into pieces in the kitchen sink while she was washing it.

"Need any help?" asked Matthew – calling out from the living room.

"No, it's alright. Everything's under control."

That was a lie. In fact, ever since last weekend, she felt like her whole life was spiraling out of control. Things that were once certain and true, now seemed foreign and vague. Everything she thought she knew about her father had turned out to be a lie. And then, of course, there was the issue of the ghost (or whatever it was). Although she had not seen the frightening entity since it first appeared early Sunday morning, it shook her up so terribly that she wasn't able to enjoy one night of restful sleep since. Plagued by nightmares and waking up in a cold sweat each night, had her wondering if her life would ever be normal again.

Desperate for answers, she turned to her co-worker, Agnes Covington. Agnes – a product of the Deep South, and no stranger to things that go bump in the night – told her that what she had seen that night sounded very much like a "shadow ghost" or a "dark entity." She said they usually appear in misty, human forms that are often mistaken for natural shadows in still photographs. However, when witnessed live, as in Melissa's case, their independent and erratic movements will always give them away. She said the general belief is that they are demonic spirits, or more simply…the pure personification of evil.

Melissa really wasn't interested in hearing anything more after that. Instead of being comforted, her little chat with Agnes only made things worse. A little knowledge can be a dangerous thing, but in this case it was downright terrifying. Be that as it may, at the moment, she had even bigger problems to worry about.

What was going on with her father?

It wasn't like him to keep secrets; let alone to flat out lie to her about anything.

Since he obviously wasn't going to VAA meetings, just where the hell was he going at night?

When she posed this question to Richard, he suggested that a secret lady friend might be involved. That may have been a plausible explanation except for a couple of things. Matthew was an adult, and would have had absolutely no reason to hide a romantic relationship from her. Also, the fact that he was still visiting mom's grave so frequently was a strong indication that he wasn't quite ready to move on just yet.

She finished cleaning up the remains of the broken dish – placing the last jagged piece into a small plastic bag, then, dumping it in the trash. She left the kitchen and joined Matthew on the couch in the living room.

"All done," she sighed, as she sat down next to him.

"Huh… what?"

Clearly lost in thought, his mind was a million miles away. He stared straight ahead at the TV, but was completely oblivious to what was on.

"The dish… I finished cleaning up the dish."

"What dish?"

"The dish I just broke in the kitchen!" she snapped. "Dad, are you with me? What are you thinking about?"

"Oh, nothing honey, I'm sorry." He looked straight at her – finally giving her his full attention. "What were you saying?"

"Forget it. It's not important." Changing the subject, she asked, "Listen, it's not that late… how 'bout you and I play a game of cards, or something?"

"Oh, honey, I'd love to, but something's come up. I gotta go out for a little while."

"Go out!? Dad, it's almost eleven o'clock at night! Where could you possibly have to go at this hour… *to the Veteran's Action Association*? She asked, incredulously.

"Yeah, I'm really sorry, honey. They're having an emergency meeting tonight."

"An *emergency* meeting?"

"Yeah."

"Tonight?"

"Right."

"And you just found out about it, when… this *very* second? I didn't hear the phone ring."

"No, they told us about it earlier in the week. I just forgot to mention it to you."

"Yeah… I guess you did, didn't you!?"

"Honey, look, I know you're upset, but I think this is the last time I'm going to have to leave you at night. I---"

"Save it dad! I don't wanna hear it… I just don't wanna hear it anymore!!"

"Honey, I---"

"IF YOU GOTTA GO, JUST GO!! GET THE FUCK OUTTA MY SIGHT!!!"

Seething with anger, she jumped up from the couch, and stormed out of the room – turning a deaf ear to his repeated pleas to return. She continued down the hall and into her room – slamming the door behind her. The fact that he was able to so blatantly lie right to her face with such impunity filled her with unimaginable rage. She was literally shaking with anger.

There was a knock at her bedroom door.

"Honey?" he called out, quietly – almost apologetically.

Fuming, she methodically paced back and forth, but said nothing in response.

"Honey… I know you're upset, but after tonight, I promise you… we'll spend more time together, okay?"

"JUST GO, DAD… JUST GO, ALREADY!!"

"Alright, well… don't wait up, okay?" He paused a few seconds for a response that never came. Before stepping away from the door, he uttered, "I love you, sweetheart."

She listened as his footsteps gradually disappeared down the hall, followed several seconds later by the sound of the front door opening and closing.

Her anger began to subside.

Perhaps it was the comforting tone of his voice; or the fact that she couldn't remember the last time he had actually told her that he loved her. She began to feel bad about the way she had handled the situation. She wondered if she overreacted. Although he had broken many promises to her, she wasn't exactly a child anymore. She was an adult and should be able to deal with disappointments better than that.

She took a deep breath.

As her anger ebbed, her curiosity rose.

She decided to get to the bottom of it once and for all. She would follow him. He had only been gone for less than a minute, and if she hurried, she was sure she could catch up to him. With no time to think about fashion, she frantically threw on whatever clothing that was closest to her… an old pair of jeans, a light sweater, some sneakers and a waist-length leather jacket. She then grabbed her keys and headed out of the apartment.

In her haste to leave, she had forgotten her hat, scarf and gloves. The sub-freezing night air ripped through her like a bullet. She knew she was woefully underdressed for the weather, but at this point, there was nothing she could do about it. The aftermath of an earlier brief, but heavy rainfall, had left the streets icy and treacherous. When she slipped and almost fell on a patch of black ice a few feet outside the door, she considered abandoning her quest and retreating into the warmth and safety of her apartment. But when she looked down the street and caught a glimpse of him rapidly disappearing into the darkness about a block and a half away, she knew it was now or never. Her decision was clear. Despite her inadequate attire, she would brave the biting cold and continue her pursuit.

With his noticeable limp – made even more pronounced by his stubbornness not to use his cane – it wasn't very hard to keep him in sight. Even though a considerable distance separated them, she would have been easily spotted on the near deserted street if he should suddenly turn around. To avoid detection, she crossed the street, then, quickened her pace to bridge the gap. At Pitkin Avenue, he made a right and began to cross over to her side of the street! With only about a half a block separating them, she stopped abruptly and crouched down next to a parked car. She pretended to tie her shoe, but kept him in her peripheral vision the entire time. After crossing over, he continued walking straight on Pitkin until he disappeared around the corner – never once looking in her direction. She stood up and ran to the building at the end of the block – stopping just short of the corner. Using extreme caution, she inched along with her back up against the wall – ignoring the wary glances she got from a handful of passersby.

Although she had never tailed anyone before, she'd seen it done on countless TV police dramas. Inasmuch, she actually felt like a cop. She felt a combination of nervousness, excitement and reckless abandon. Strangely, she mostly felt a sense of power – a power she had never felt before in her dangerous neighborhood. Normally, being the one who's always timidly looking over her shoulder and jumping at the slightest sign of trouble, tonight, *her* odd behavior was putting others on the defensive.

She carefully peeked around the corner. He was about a block away – a solitary figure purposefully making his way down the center of the sidewalk, passing a small assembly of meandering bubble-jacketed youths. She stepped out in the open and began walking down the block – making sure to stay close to the buildings.

She continued to follow him for another block. The number of people on the street dwindled. With only two or three widely-scattered individuals now separating them, she had to be careful to maintain an even larger gap. Also, the vehicular traffic level at that time of night was light. This created an extremely quiet environment. The slightest sounds, such as her footsteps, seemed to echo sharply throughout the entire block.

Suddenly, he turned around and looked right in her direction! She froze!

Had he *actually* heard her footsteps?!

Did he *know* she was following him all along?!

Without any type of cover nearby, all she could do was stop and pretend she had just dropped something – all the while praying that she didn't look too conspicuous.

A few seconds later, he began to cross the street. She then realized that he had only turned around to check for oncoming traffic. She watched as he crossed over to the other side of Pitkin, then, continued to walk in the same direction.

Being on the opposite side of the street would make it considerably easier to follow him without risking detection. She took advantage of the situation to slightly bridge the gap between them. Breaking into a sort of half-walk, half-jog type of stride, she increased her speed until she was just a few car lengths behind. After about another block, his destination became clear – he was headed for the subway.

Damn him! She thought.

It was yet *another* lie she had caught him in. He had sworn to her that he was only using cabs and not going anywhere near the subways. But, here he was – despite all of her warnings to stay away – about to descend directly into the lions' den.

She then remembered something that put a knot in her stomach.

In her haste to leave the house, she had forgotten to grab her purse or any money! She couldn't accept the possibility that her pursuit might be forced to come to an end so soon. She pondered the consequences of jumping the turnstile. Normally, she would never even think of doing such a thing – but this wasn't a normal situation. She couldn't give up now. She *had* to know what he was up to!

She began rummaging through her pockets. Having searched through almost all of them and coming up empty, she reluctantly prepared herself to commit the first illegal act of her life. But then, one of her hands brushed across a small, thin familiar object. She pulled it out and gasped.

A MetroCard!

As Matthew began to descend the stairs, she quickly ran across the street. When he was completely out of sight, she ran to the stairway as fast as she could. She knew all her efforts, thus far, would be in vain if he managed to get on a train before her.

At the top of the stairs, she stopped… and listened.

Silence.

There were no trains entering or leaving the station.

Trying to be as quiet as she could, she started walking down the stairs, which led to the station booth on the turnstile level. Halfway down, she caught a quick glimpse of her father descending a second flight of stairs leading to the Manhattan-bound platform. She only saw him for a few seconds before he disappeared around a corner. She rushed over to the turnstile and swiped her card through the slot. After pushing through the bar she headed down the stairs. At the bottom, she stopped, and cautiously peeked around the corner in the direction he had gone. He was standing by himself at the front end of the station on the edge of the platform and looking in her direction. Fearing she may have been spotted, she quickly pulled her head back in. She waited a few more seconds, then looked again. She could see that he wasn't actually looking at her, but merely down the tracks for an oncoming train. She checked the other end of the platform. It was deserted. With her father being the only person present, there was absolutely no way she could step out onto the platform without being seen. She would have to wait in the stairway landing until the train arrived. Every once in a while she'd peer out at him to make sure that he hadn't changed his plans. If he suddenly decided to leave the station he would have to pass right by her, and a face-to-face meeting would be a *little* hard to explain.

She was startled by a shrill alarm. The electronic sign announcing the arrival of an approaching train was sounding.

Once again, she peeked around the corner. He had also heard the buzzer, and was now anxiously pacing back and forth. She soon began to hear a quiet rumble. It increased in volume until an "A" train surged into the station. It slowed to a stop with one of its doors opening almost directly across the platform from the stairway in which she hid. But she continued to hold her position. No one got off, and as far as the conductor could see, only one person was boarding. To avoid being seen by her father and to get on before the doors closed, she knew she had to act quickly and stealthily. Watching as her father entered the train and took a seat, she held her position and waited until the last possible second.

Bing... Bong.

She crouched down and made a mad dash toward the train's rapidly narrowing doorway. With just seconds to spare, she turned sideways, and managed to squeeze through just before the doors completely closed. Her sudden and unusual entrance shocked the only passenger in the car – an elderly man sitting by the door. With the current climate of fear, she realized the crazy thoughts that were probably going through his head. To put him at ease, she smiled, embarrassed, and said, "Just made it!"

She then focused her attention on the matter at hand. Being at least two cars behind her father, she knew she had to get closer if she ever stood a chance at keeping him in her sights. She walked to the front and hastily exited through the connecting doors, and entered the next car. Four out of the six people inside briefly glanced up at her, then, looked away – retreating back into their own private worlds. The other two people were asleep.

With the train now in the tunnel and running at top speed, she held onto the handrails and carefully walked to the opposite end of the car. Peeking through the glass doors, she discreetly surveyed the occupants of the next car. There were about ten to fifteen people in it, but her father wasn't one of them. She opened the doors and, once again, made her way to the opposite end – ignoring the salacious comments while passing through a gauntlet of teenagers in the center of the car. When she reached the front, she paused, and once again, peered into the next car. There were fewer people inside, and she could clearly see that her father wasn't there either.

She started to worry.

She was pretty sure he'd be in *that* car. She checked again to be absolutely certain – carefully studying each passenger. When positive he wasn't among them, she slid open the doors and entered the car.

The speed of the train began to decrease. It was rapidly approaching the next station and preparing to stop.

Panic began to set in.

She desperately needed to locate him before it came to a complete stop. If he got off the train without her knowing it, all her efforts would be for naught.

Quickening her pace to a hasty sprint, she dashed through the car and looked into the next one. As the train slowed to a stop, she breathed a sigh of relief. She finally spotted him. He was sitting in the middle of the car on the left side. She immediately stepped back to avoid being seen, and took a seat near the door.

Okay, now what? She wondered.

Since she couldn't see him from her seated position, she would have to get up periodically to keep an eye on him. The train began moving again and entered the tunnel. When it was up to speed, she checked on him one more time. She stood up and carefully peeked through the glass doors.

He was gone!

Could he have gotten off at the last stop!?

Panicked, she checked again.

This time she saw him. He hadn't gotten off, but had simply moved to the other side of the car and a little closer to the front. Satisfied, she returned to her seat. As she sat there, something odd struck her about what she had just seen. At the far end of the car, she noticed a homeless man sleeping on a bench. Although she only got a quick look, it appeared as though her father was intensely studying the man.

Once again, she stood up and looked into the car.

She couldn't believe what she saw. Not only was her father studying the man... he had changed his seat one more time, and was now sitting just a few feet away from him!

People normally tend to give the homeless a wide berth. Nowadays, most people would rather take another *train* just to be on the safe side. However, despite the abundance of empty seats, for some reason, her father had deliberately chosen to sit there.

When she returned to her seat, she was struck with a terrible thought.

My God! What if he's actually trying to "save" this man!?

As much as she talked to him about the dangers, she just couldn't believe that he would simply throw caution to the wind and revert back to his old ways.

When the train pulled into the next station, she stood up again to have another peek. Her repetitive movements were beginning to attract the attention of a couple of nearby passengers, but she ignored their curious stares. The sight she saw this time made her gasp.

The homeless man was now awake and sitting upright and her father was sitting next to him – *right* next to him! He was leaning in close with his arm around the man's shoulders and appeared to be speaking to him, as though they were old friends.

She became livid.

What the hell is he thinking!? Now is definitely not the time to be a crusader!

She had to fight the urge to run into the car and scream at him to get away from the man. But, if there was any hope of finding out what he was *truly* up to, she knew she would have to stand her ground and remain out of sight.

She looked again when the train came to the next stop. This time, she used the opportunity to get her first really good look at the other man. He appeared to be a middle-aged Hispanic man, with a matted gray beard and mustache. He was bald with a huge tattoo on the right side of his head of a 5-pointed crown atop the head of a lion. He wore a heavy black overcoat, glistening with grease and grime, and an equally filthy pair of jeans. On his feet were a rundown pair of light-brown work boots. He was definitely homeless, but as far as she could tell, he didn't exhibit any of the strange characteristics associated with the other killers. For the moment, her father appeared to be safe.

More and more people gradually got on the train as it continued traveling through Brooklyn. At first, she was thankful for the buffer they created between herself and her father. But as the train entered Manhattan, it became standing room only – making it increasingly difficult for her to constantly keep him in a clear line of sight. She briefly considered moving into the car, but she thought it would be a little too risky if the crowd should suddenly start to thin out. She decided to stay where she was, but rather than sitting, she remained standing at the side of the door in order to maintain a constant surveillance.

The interaction she witnessed between the two men grew stranger by the second. Even though the man was sitting upright, at times, he appeared to be fast asleep. Throughout it all, her father's attention on him never wavered.

As the train pulled into the West 4th Street/Washington Square Station, he began to aggressively shake the man to rouse him from his stupor. He then stood up and forcibly pulled the man to his feet and guided him toward the door.

This was it.

She also moved toward the door. She knew her next move would have to involve the timing of a military operation if she were to stand any chance of keeping him in her sight while avoiding being seen at the same time.

Fortunately, West 4th Street, located in the heart of Greenwich Village, was one of the heavier traveled stations on the line. Even at that time of night, a fairly large number of people were waiting on the platform, and almost as many were preparing to exit the train. Her plan was to mask her presence within the cloak of congestion between the two groups.

When the train came to a full stop and the doors opened, she cautiously hung back. Rather than immediately step out onto the platform, she remained on the train and watched as her father and the man got off. With his arm wrapped around his shoulder, he guided him down the platform in the opposite direction from her. Only then did she feel it was safe enough to step off.

She took cover behind a newsstand and watched as they slowly walked toward the exit at the end of the platform. Whether it was drugs or alcohol, it was obvious the man was under the influence of *something*. He stumbled and staggered and most likely would have fallen, had it not been for Matthew's support – a support which, in itself, was considerably unstable due to his pronounced limp. The pair made quite a sight as they forged their way through the thinning crowd – turning more than a few curious heads in their wake.

She continued to watch as the distance between them grew larger. When she felt that there was enough space separating them, she stepped out from behind the newsstand and began to follow. At that exact moment, the pair stopped and began to turn around.

She stopped dead in her tracks.

Unable to seek cover in time, she quickly grabbed a magazine from the rack and pretended to read – effectively blending in with the two customers already present. From the corner of her eye, she saw that they had only turned to go down a flight of stairs leading to the 6th Avenue line trains, two levels below. As they descended, she could see that her father was having an even harder time keeping the man on his feet. The man lost his footing after just a few steps, and nearly sent the both of them tumbling. Luckily, her father was able to regain his balance and avoided a nasty fall. A young man coming up the stairs rushed over to offer support, but her father shooed him away – almost angrily.

She too wanted to help, but stood her ground and watched as their heads slowly sunk below platform level, and eventually out of sight. She then replaced the magazine and quickly ran over to the staircase. Gingerly, she leaned over the railing and saw them just as they reached the mezzanine level, one flight below. They then had to walk a few more feet forward until they reached another flight of stairs leading to the 6th Avenue platform.

Instead of going straight, however, he began guiding the man to the other side of the mezzanine – toward the staircases for the trains heading in the opposite direction.

"What the *hell*?" She mumbled to herself.

Is he going back to Brooklyn?

Slowly, she started walking down the stairs one step at a time. She stopped abruptly halfway down when she unexpectedly caught sight of them. Instead of going directly across the mezzanine, they were walking *through* it, heading towards the back end.

Completely devoid of station booths, newsstands or exits, the mezzanine level was merely a sealed chamber – a virtual concrete wasteland – sandwiched between the platforms of the 8th and 6th Avenue lines. Home to just a handful of maintenance rooms accessible only to transit workers, it was a large, vacuous space that was almost always deserted. Whether passing through to make a connection between the two lines, or crossing over to catch a train in the opposite direction, the average passenger would usually only spend a few seconds in this area.

Once again, her fears mounted to see her father alone with a homeless man in such a confined and isolated environment. The train was bad enough, but this was just asking for trouble!

She realized she'd be easily spotted if he suddenly turned around. Following him on the mezzanine level was out of the question. There were hardly any objects that could be used for adequate cover, and the lack of activity made it the quietest area in the station. If she wanted to continue following them, she would have to do it from above. Several staircases ran the length of the upstairs platform; each leading down to the mezzanine. She sprinted back up the stairs, and ran a short distance down the platform to the next stairway. Again, before descending, she stopped and looked. Seeing no one passing by below, she began walking down. At the midway point, she stopped, and waited... and waited.

Something's wrong. She thought.

Even as slow as they were moving, they should have passed this point by now.

She feared she may have lost them. She went down a few more steps and peeked through the small space between the top of the handrail and the bottom of the platform floor.

She saw that they were tucked into a semi-darkened, recessed pocket behind a staircase on the other side of the mezzanine. The homeless man was sitting on the floor with his back up against the wall. With his head slumped over to one side, he appeared to be either asleep or passed out. Her father was kneeling next to him with his head down and his hands clasped in front.

To hide herself a little better, she backed up a few more steps, then, crouched down even further to see through the smaller space. With no trains coming in or out of the station on either level, the mezzanine was exceptionally quiet. Through the silence, she could hear a soft voice in the distance – it was her father's. She listened closely, but couldn't quite make out what he was saying. It looked and sounded like he was praying, but all she could decipher was an incoherent mumble. Without breaking his tempo, he reached into his coat pocket and pulled out a small black drawstring pouch. She had seen that pouch before but couldn't remember where.

She watched as he splayed open the top of the pouch and reached inside. He rummaged around for a while, then, pulled out a closed fist – completely concealing whatever he held. After returning the pouch to his pocket, he opened his fist and revealed its contents. From her distance, all she could make out was some strange black, ash-type of substance. He then moved in front of the man. Although her view was blocked, she could see that he was very close to the side of the man's head – practically whispering in his ear.

She couldn't believe that he would go to this extent to counsel a complete stranger in this setting *and* at this time of night.

His mumbling increased in volume and tempo. A few seconds later, it abruptly stopped. He then moved to the side – restoring her line of sight.

All of a sudden, the man's head snapped to attention. He looked straight ahead, but his eyes were completely closed. This unexpected movement caught her by surprise. No longer able to contain herself, she let out a short, but sharp gasp.

Her father whipped his head around and spotted her.

"MELISSA!? WHAT ARE YOU DOING HERE!!??" he screamed, quickly returning the black substance to the pouch and stuffing it back in his pocket.

"Dad...what are *you* doing!?" she asked, as she walked down the steps.

"How did you find me!?" he demanded, as he rose to his feet – clearly annoyed with her presence.

"I followed you."

"You *what*!?"

"That's right, dad... ever since you left the house I've been following you!"

"Why would you---"

"Because I wanted to find out once and for all what you were up to, dad! I knew you weren't going to the VAA, because I checked... they moved from that address years ago!"

Unable to deny it, he just stood there in silence.

"Dad, I can't believe that after everything I've told you, you still insist on trying to save the world! Don't you realize just how dangerous this is!?"

"Look, Melissa, this doesn't concern you! Get out of here... NOW!"

"I'm not going anywhere, dad, and this does concern me... you're my father!"

She looked down at the man, who still hadn't moved, and started walking towards him.

"GET BACK!!" he screamed – quickly stepping in front to block her path. In doing so, his right foot dragged along the concrete floor, producing a loud, familiar scraping noise.

That sound! It was *the* sound... the very sound that had been haunting her in the subway for the past couple of months!

She stared at him for a few seconds in disbelief.

"*You*... it was *you*!" she finally said. "It's been you all this time! Have you been *following* me!?"

"Honey, listen... I can explain."

"*Explain!?* Explain *what*, dad!? Explain how you've been spying on me!? Explain how, for the last two months, *you* were the cause of making me think I was losing my mind...of scaring me half to death!? Is *that* what you wanna explain, dad...IS IT!?"

"Honey---"

"So, that night we met on the train... that was no coincidence, you planned the whole thing, didn't you!?"

"I was just trying to protect you."

"*Protect* me!? Protect me from *what*!?"

Before he could answer, the homeless man suddenly began to move again. Although he still appeared to be incapacitated, his legs and upper body started to twitch violently. His head, while still slumped down, began snapping violently back and forth – strangely mirroring the movements of the homeless man she encountered on the train a couple of weeks ago. Then, almost as quickly as the weird gyrations started, they stopped. Suddenly, he began to raise his head and shake it from side to side. A large amount of grayish vomit began oozing out of his mouth and onto his chest.

"Oh, my God!" she whispered – taking several steps backward.

"Honey, it's okay... it's alright," said Matthew.

At that moment, he turned his head toward Melissa and seemed to stare directly at her. She couldn't tell if his eyes were open or closed in the semi-darkness. He then began to grin. It was a grin that embodied an unspeakable evil, and to some degree, a level of conscious awareness.

Even though Matthew has been just a few feet away, she was overcome with an even greater fear than she was during her prior lone encounter a few weeks ago. She emitted an ear-piercing scream that echoed throughout the empty mezzanine. Turning to run, she stumbled over her feet and almost fell.

"Careful!" shouted Matthew, rushing to her aid.

"Dad, don't you understand... he's dangerous, look at him! We gotta get the hell outta here!"

She grabbed his arm to pull him away, but he refused to budge.

"Melissa, hold on… HOLD ON!" he shouted.

"WHAT'S THE MATTER WITH YOU!? COME ON, LET'S GO! LET'S GET OUT OF HERE!! YOU CAN'T HELP HIM ANYMORE!!"

When he still refused to leave, she gave up and took off running as fast as she could in the opposite direction. She didn't turn around, but could hear his foot dragging along the concrete floor behind her. He was calling her to come back, but she was in no mood for conversation. She continued running through the mezzanine with no clear destination in mind. When she spotted one of the staircases leading to the lower level, she saw it as her best chance to get away. Throwing caution to the wind, she literally threw herself down the stairs – her feet barely making contact with every other step. She had never taken a flight of stairs that fast before, but miraculously, made it down without incident. At the bottom, she attempted to make a quick right, but slipped on a large patch of ice on the platform. Fortunately, she was still holding on to the staircase banister, and avoided falling. She continued running – not quite sure of where she was going. Blurry glimpses of a few widely scattered, bewildered-looking faces, was all she saw as she raced down the platform.

An incoming "F" train met her head on as it suddenly surged into the station. She continued running along the platform in the opposite direction of the train. At the point where they passed, a stiff breeze slapped her in the face. Seconds later, she heard an uncharacteristically loud squeal of brakes, immediately followed by a frenzy of panicked screams and shouts. Stopping dead in her tracks, she whirled around – almost throwing herself off balance. She expected to see her father following closely behind her, but he wasn't there. The train had come to a complete and abrupt stop, even though it was only halfway in the station. The commotion she heard was coming from a small, and highly agitated, group of people milling around the first car. They seemed to be looking at something on the side of the train. The crowd was quickly growing in size, *and* in hysteria. It was obvious that something had just happened… something very bad.

Slowly, she walked back toward the crowd. They were all congregating around the rear of the first car. Women were screaming and covering their mouths with their hands. Some would approach the scene, then, abruptly turn around and run away crying. The men were banging on the side of the train, and yelling, "CALL 911!! DON'T MOVE THE TRAIN!!"

As she got closer, some people in the crowd focused their attention on her.

"Do you know him!?"

"He came down the stairs right behind you!"

"I heard a scream… was he chasing you!?"

"Are *you* Melissa!?"

She ignored all the questions and continued making her way through the frenzied scene. Finally, she saw what all the commotion was about.

She let out an ear-piercing, blood-curdling scream that drowned out the din of the crowd.

"DADDYYYYYY!!"

Exclamations of shock and sorrow spewed from the crowd.

"Oh, my God, is he your father!?" one person asked.

"Miss, you probably shouldn't see this!" said another.

She continued to ignore everyone. Her focus was solely on her father.

In a hellishly, freakish accident, he had actually become *pinned* between the train and the platform! Trapped at the rear of the first car, only his torso was visible. It looked as though he was literally cut in half, but he wasn't. His once robust, 38" waist was grotesquely compacted into a space no bigger than five or six inches! The wooden platform edge pressed mercilessly into his lower abdomen, just below his belly button – compressing his midsection to dimensions the human body was never meant to reach. His right arm was also pinned below the platform. Amazingly, despite his horribly contorted state, he was still alive and conscious.

"Daddy what...what happened!?" she screamed, as she knelt down beside him.

He didn't respond. Even though he *seemed* fully conscious, he didn't appear to be able to speak, nor did he appear to be in any apparent pain. In fact, he seemed completely unaffected. Staring straight ahead, slowly turning his head from left to right, he looked dazed and confused – totally unaware of everything going on around him. Even when he looked at Melissa, he pretty much looked right through her.

Unable to get anything out of him, she turned to the swelling crowd for answers.

"WHAT HAPPENED!? DID ANYBODY SEE WHAT HAPPENED!?"

Their response was a fury of unintelligible ramblings.

"WHAT!? WAIT… I CAN'T UNDERSTAND YOU! CAN SOMEBODY PLEASE TELL ME WHAT THE FUCK HAPPENED!?" she screamed, in near hysterics.

An older, black woman stepped out of the crowd and knelt down next to her.

"It's okay, baby," she said, softly – putting her arm around her shoulders, and wiping the tears from her face. "It's okay."

"Please, tell me what happened to my father! How did he get like this!?"

"He came down the stairs right behind you, but he was really struggling with them," the woman explained, "I thought he was going to fall at any second."

Melissa nodded her head, and beckoned for her to continue.

"When he got to the bottom, he slipped on some ice and… and he just slipped right off the edge of the platform. Some people tried to grab him, but it all happened so fast."

"But, but if he fell on the tracks, how did he get like *that*?"

"Well, he didn't actually fall on the tracks. As he was slipping off the platform, the train came in and hit… well, no… it kind of *squeezed* him up against the platform and the side of the train. As it was coming to a stop, he rolled with it until he finally ended up there. It was horrible!"

Melissa reached for her father's unpinned hand and stared into his blank eyes.

"Daddy, I'm so sorry," she sobbed, "I'm so sorry I left you behind."

The other woman began to cry as well.

The sound of approaching sirens was heard far off in the distance.

"He's going to be okay, honey," said the woman. "Help is coming. They're going to get him out soon. Everything'll be alright."

Within minutes, the atmosphere in the station changed. Several sets of charging footsteps came thundering down the stairs. The random chatter of the agitated crowd was gradually overshadowed by more authoritative voices – periodically interrupted by loud, two-way radio banter.

"Alright, step back… I need everyone to STEP BACK!" shouted one of the voices.

The crowd gave way and a couple of police officers wearing blue baseball caps surged through. They were followed by a bunch of firemen carrying all sorts of unusual-looking gear. As the men fanned out around Melissa and the other woman, they seemed visibly shocked at the sight before them. One of the cops was the first to speak.

"Ladies, you're gonna have to get up from there."

"He's my father! I'm not leaving my father!" Melissa yelled – gripping Matthew's hand tighter.

"I'm sorry, miss… I didn't know," he said, as he crouched down next to her and put his hand on her shoulder.

He looked at the other woman and asked, "Are you any relation to the victim, ma'am?"

"No, officer, I'm not."

"Okay, ma'am, then I'm gonna have to ask you to step back, please."

"It'll be okay, baby," she said, reassuringly rubbing Melissa's back, "they'll get him out soon."

Melissa nodded her head, but was too much of an emotional wreck to thank her verbally. The woman stood up and rejoined the crowd – now, standing several more feet away.

"Miss, I'm Sergeant Randy Chartoff, and this is my partner, Officer Brian Friarson," he said, motioning toward the other cop. "What's your name?"

"Melissa," she answered, wiping the tears off her face.

"What's your father's name?"

"Matthew."

"Okay, Melissa… we're with the Emergency Services Unit of the NYPD. We're gonna do everything we can to get your father out of there."

"He's… he's gonna be okay, right?" she sobbed. "It's not too bad, is it?"

After a brief hesitation, he replied, "We're going to get him out."

"But---"

"Melissa, why don't I move you over here, so we can have a little more room to work?"

"I won't leave him, I---"

"No, you don't have to leave him, but we have to get in here to do our job. If I could just have you stand back over here… that would be great."

Not knowing when, or if, she would ever be able to hold her father's hand again; she was reluctant to let go. She held it tighter, and whispered, "I love you, daddy."

His expression still had not changed. He looked at her as though she were a stranger.

"He's in shock, Melissa," explained Sgt. Chartoff, as he gently pried their hands apart. "He's not able to speak, but he knows you're here."

He then helped her to her feet. When she turned around, she was stunned by the number of uniformed emergency personnel on the platform. Well over a dozen cops, firemen and paramedics were now present. Their presence, however, wasn't exactly comforting. She knew the situation was bad if so many rescuers were needed on the scene.

Sgt. Chartoff escorted her to a female police officer standing several feet away.

"This is Melissa… the victim is her father," he said to the cop, "she wants to stay here, so, could you please watch after her?"

"Sure," she replied.

"Melissa, I'm going to leave you with Officer---?"

"Parker… Leslie Parker."

"Okay, Officer Parker, here, will take care of you. Don't worry, Melissa, we'll get your father out."

Melissa nodded her head.

While Officer Parker tried to soothe her by offering calm words of reassurance, Melissa watched the operation unfold through tear-filled eyes. Sgt. Chartoff seemed to be the one in charge. After ordering the conductor to discharge all the passengers through the front of the train, he had the area cordoned off with yellow caution tape. A couple of paramedics had already begun administering aid. One placed an oxygen mask over Matthew's face, while the other cut away part of his clothing in order to take his vital signs. The firemen were using their flashlights, trying to see the exact way in which Matthew was pinned. People were running back and forth and everyone seemed to be talking at once – basically, it was a scene of organized chaos. Although mostly a blur, Melissa heard the phrase "space case" used frequently.

"What is that!? What are they talkin' about!?" she asked Officer Parker.

"It's what they call a situation where a person is trapped in a confined space," she explained.

The emergency personnel and the train crew debated several options for freeing Matthew. After what seemed like an eternity to Melissa, they finally reached a mutual decision.

"What's happening!? What are they gonna do!?" Melissa asked.

"I'm not sure, but it looks like they're planning to separate the first car from the rest of the train."

"What!? Why!? How's that gonna---"

"It's fairly common in cases like this. You see, your father is pinned right at the back of the car. By uncoupling it and moving the rest of the train *back*… it'll give them more room to work."

It made sense, but Melissa still didn't know exactly *how* they were planning to get him out.

After the motorman and conductor uncoupled the car, the motorman ran along the platform to get to the rear of the train. He ran as far as he could, then, used a key to manually unlock one of the train's car doors. He entered and continued running toward the last car – still buried in the tunnel.

During this time, Sgt. Chartoff came back over to Melissa, and basically reiterated Officer Parker's explanation of what was about to happen. She besieged him with a barrage of anxious questions about her father's condition, but was only given vague answers amounting to little more than mere pacification.

Suddenly, the rest of the train slowly began to pull away from the first car. It stopped when a gap of about ten feet was created. One of the firemen was the first to jump down onto the track bed, followed by a paramedic and Officer Friarson. They were now able to get a much better view of the extent of Matthew's injuries. After a thorough examination, a grim-faced Officer Friarson motioned to Sgt. Chartoff to come over.

"What is it... what's wrong!? You can get him out, can't you!?" Melissa asked, frantically.

"I'll be right back... I promise," the sergeant replied.

He walked over to the edge of the platform and got down on his hands and knees. After conferring with the men and closely examining Matthew, he slowly rose to his feet and began walking back to Melissa. He held his head down – seemingly afraid to look her in the eyes – but she could clearly see the look of anguish on his face.

She began to whimper and tremble.

Officer Parker gently turned her away from the scene and held her in a firm embrace. From her experience, she knew the outcome of most "space cases" wasn't very good. As Sgt. Chartoff approached, he confirmed her worst fears. While Melissa was looking the other way, he caught Officer Parker's eye and slowly shook his head from side to side. She lowered her head and discreetly wiped a tear from her face. Before she could say anything,

Melissa bolted from her grasp, whirled around and dashed toward her father. She was stopped by Sgt. Chartoff.

"WHY AREN'T YOU DOIN' ANYTHING TO GET HIM OUT!? WHY IS EVERYONE JUST STANDING AROUND!?" she screamed.

He held her back as she continued to struggle to get closer to her father.

"Melissa, calm down!" he said, grabbing her by her shoulders. "I need you to calm down and listen to me… please!"

"WHAT ARE YOU ALL WAITING FOR!? WHY AREN'T YOU HELPING HIM!?"

"Melissa, come with me over here… I have to talk to you!"

"TELL ME WHAT'S GOING ON!!"

"I will, I will, but please come with me over here… please!"

She reluctantly allowed him to take her behind a staircase – an area away from the scene, and offering some modicum of privacy from the curious eyes of the sizeable crowd which had now formed along the perimeters of the caution tape.

"Melissa, listen to me," he said, as he held her head – forcing her to look into his eyes. "There's nothing anyone can do at this point to help your father."

"What…whaddaya mean…he's---"

"He's already gone, Melissa. His insides are completely crushed. The only thing keeping him alive right now is the pressure from the train and the platform. But, once that pressure's released---"

"NO… NO… NO… NO!!" she screamed. "YOU'RE WRONG… YOU'RE WRONG!! HOW DO YOU KNOW THAT!? YOU'RE NOT A FUCKING DOCTOR!! SO, HOW DO YOU KNOW THAT!?"

Any attempts for privacy were lost. They were now the center of everyone's attention.

"Melissa, I've seen enough of these cases to---"

"You don't know my father… he's strong! Look at him! Does he look like he's about to die!?"

Indeed, Matthew's expression hadn't changed one bit. He still had a blank, expressionless look on his face – seemingly devoid of any pain whatsoever.

"He may *look* fine, Melissa, but he has extensive internal injuries... fatal injuries," he explained. "His organs are under so much pressure right now that it's put him in a, sort of, altered state. But, once we free him," he sighed, heavily, "everything in him is just going to, well... collapse."

Deep down, she had all along suspected that his injuries probably weren't survivable. But it was that one glimmer of hope that kept her going – that once-in-a-lifetime miracle of miracles that everything would turn out fine. Now that that hope was dashed, so was what was left of her spirit. Her legs went limp. She collapsed into Sgt. Chartoff's arms and began to wail. It was a sound that reverberated throughout the station – completely drowning out the clamor of the chaotic scene... a sound that brought all activity to a screeching halt, and tugged at the heartstrings of everyone present at the scene.

"Melissa... I'm so sorry... I'm so sorry," he said, as he embraced her – desperately struggling to keep her on her feet.

She was now in full hysterics – barely able to form words or to comprehend what was being said to her. Her fragile and uncertain world was crumbling around her.

"I was... I was... I want to talk to him," she sobbed.

"Yes, of course, but Melissa... listen to me," he cradled her face in his hands, "I know it's hard, but you have to try to pull yourself together. He might not be able to respond, but there's every indication that he'll understand everything you say. If you remain in control, it'll help to make his last moments, well... a little more bearable... okay?"

She nodded her head, then, turned around and began walking toward her father. For a moment, she understood what death row inmates must feel while taking that last walk to the electric chair. In a sense, it was also a walk of many "lasts" for her as well: the last time she would ever see her father alive... the last time she would ever be able to hold his hand and look into his eyes... the last time she would ever be able to tell him how much she truly loved him. As painful as it was, she realized that most people never get the chance to say goodbye. But she considered them the "lucky ones." The unimaginable anguish she was going through was something she wouldn't wish on anyone; and it certainly wasn't something that made her feel as though she was in a privileged position.

The closer she got to him, the more the atmosphere of the scene changed. The wild ruckus slowly melded into a quiet calm. As she passed by each rescue worker, he or she would stop what they were doing and stand almost at attention – sort of forming a makeshift line of procession in her wake. Sensing the poignancy of the moment, even the large crowd of onlookers behind the police tape had considerably quieted down. As she approached her father, a paramedic removed the oxygen mask from his face. The random crackle of two-way radio transmissions was the only sound that breached the silence. One by one, they too, were turned either down or off, until just the heart-rending sounds of her sobs filled the air.

"I'm here, daddy," she said, as she knelt down beside him and grabbed his hand, "I'm right here."

He slowly turned his head in her direction, but still showed no outward signs of recognition.

"It's gonna be okay, daddy. They're gonna get you out. Just hang on, okay?"

She tried to keep a brave face, but a steady stream of tears flowed down her cheeks. She wiped them away with one hand – refusing to let go of him even for a second.

"You always tried to protect me. Remember when I went on my first date?" she asked, trying to muster a smile. "We only went down the block to the movies, but you insisted on coming with us – walking a few feet behind us the whole time, and sitting in the back row...remember?"

He held his gaze, but his eyes were still blank and expressionless.

"I was so embarrassed," she laughed, "I mean... I was fifteen years old, after all."

She held his hand tighter and inched a little closer.

She recounted a few more fond memories from their past, then, paused and lowered her head for several seconds. Her entire body began to quiver. When she looked up, she was crying uncontrollably.

She slumped to a sitting position.

"When... when you go... I'll... I'll have no... nobody."

Her breathing was heavy – almost to the point of hyperventilation.

"I'll be all alone. I'll be an... an orphan. Daddy, please don't leave me all alone... please, daddy... pleeeease!"

Sgt. Chartoff came over and knelt down beside her. He put his arm around her and spoke softly.

"Melissa, I'm so sorry, but we really have to get started."

Once again, he gently pried their hands apart – both knowing it was the last time she would ever be able to touch him while he was still alive – and helped her get to her feet.

Still crying uncontrollably, and drooling a long trail of saliva, she turned around and let him take her several feet away from the scene. All activity was at a virtual standstill. All conversations had ceased. She then noticed that she wasn't the only one in tears. Every rescue worker she saw was affected in one way or another. Each one of these "battle-hardened," urban warriors were crying almost as hard. There was also hardly a dry eye among the other spectators. It was as if a collective consciousness was being shared by everyone present – a consciousness which foretold Matthew's horrible, yet inevitable fate.

As they continued walking, she suddenly realized that it was his intention to completely remove her from the scene. When he raised the yellow tape and attempted to hand her off to another officer to be escorted from the station, she vehemently protested.

"NO! I DON'T WANNA GO! I TOLD YOU, I CAN'T LEAVE MY FATHER... I CAN'T LEAVE MY FATHER!!"

She tried to break free of his grasp, but was restrained.

"Melissa... Melissa, please!" he pleaded while struggling to hold onto her. "Listen to me. You *can't* be here for this! Trust me, you don't want to see this! It's something you really *shouldn't* see!"

245

"I DON'T CARE! I DON'T CARE! HE'S MY FATHER AND I WANNA STAY BY HIS SIDE!!"

"Alright, alright... you can stay, but you're going to have to stay back here."

She calmed down a little, but continued crying.

"Look, Melissa, I gotta warn you that this is not gonna be easy to watch."

"I don't care," she sobbed, "he's my father, and I wanna be with him until... until the end."

"You're sure?"

She solemnly nodded her head.

"Alright, well... let me explain what we're going to do. Since he's so close to the back of the car, we're just going to move it forward a few feet until he's free."

"But, won't that hurt him!?"

"No, don't worry; he can't feel anything right now."

"So, what happens after that?"

"Well," he sighed, "like I said before... once we relieve the pressure... he... he won't have that much longer."

She lowered her head and began to cry harder.

"Are you going to be okay?" he asked, placing a comforting arm around her shoulder.

Again, she nodded her head.

He then turned toward Officer Frierson and discreetly nodded – initiating the start of the operation. Frierson and a fireman walked to the edge of the platform and jumped down onto the track bed in the space between the first car and the rest of the train. Placing himself almost face-to-face with Matthew, a paramedic got in a prone position on the platform, while other emergency personnel gathered closely around – effectively blocking most of Melissa's view. The motorman entered the car and stepped into his cab. The conductor, armed with a two-way radio, remained on the platform next to the huddle around Matthew. With everyone in position, he signaled the motorman over the radio to begin moving the train. As it began to inch forward, it caused Matthew's entire body to rotate counter-clockwise. As it did, a loud crunching sound could be heard.

Melissa screamed, and tried, unsuccessfully, to break free of Sgt. Chartoff's grasp.

"STOP IT!! STOP IT!! YOU'RE KILLING HIM!! STOP IT!!"

The conductor radioed the motorman to stop. A loud squeal came from the train's brakes.

"Calm down, Melissa… calm down!" said Sgt. Chartoff.

"What's that sound?! Are those his bones… are his bones being crushed?!"

"Yes… unfortunately, that's what happens in cases like this. But, please trust me, Melissa, he can't feel a thing at this point."

"But why is he twisting around like that?!"

"That, too, is something that can happen in these types of cases. He may get twisted a little more, but he's almost free – they don't have much further to go."

The movement of the train rotated Matthew's body approximately forty-five degrees – he was now facing toward the rear of the station. After Melissa composed herself somewhat, the conductor signaled the motorman to continue. He moved the train forward a couple more feet and was ordered to stop once again. Matthew's body had continued to rotate with the movement of the train. He was now facing backwards with his face almost touching the side of the car – just inches away from being free. At this point, Officer Friarson, the fireman and the paramedic, each grabbed a hold of him. After one final command, the train moved forward a little more. Matthew was free. Everyone within reach grabbed a part of his body and gently began raising him up to platform level.

When his entire body came into view, Melissa gasped, then, screamed. Cries of shock could also be heard among the gathered spectators. Matthew's once stately, 6'2" frame, had literally been stretched to an almost freakish seven feet. His pelvis was grotesquely crushed – flattening his midsection to practically non-existent dimensions. Had it not been for a pair of unidentified hands holding onto his pants, they would have fallen off. He was gently placed onto a stretcher, then, quickly covered with a white sheet – leaving just his head exposed.

Melissa felt light-headed. Her knees began to shake, then, suddenly buckled. Sgt. Chartoff caught her just before she collapsed.

"Melissa… Melissa, you okay?" he asked, while shaking her briskly to ward off unconsciousness. "This is why I didn't want you to see this. The body suffers tremendous stress in accidents like these, and these are some of the things that can happen. Are you okay?"

She nodded her head, but was too disoriented to speak.

"Would you like to speak to him for the last time?"

Again, she nodded her head.

He escorted her back over to her father.

"You understand that he could go at any time, okay?"

"Okay."

He rubbed her shoulder, then stepped away to give them some privacy. He motioned to the other rescue workers to do the same.

"Daddy?" she stroked the side of his face – almost afraid to touch him for fear of hurting him further.

Slowly – even more slowly than before – he turned his head toward her. He no longer had a blank expression on his face. He looked scared, almost childlike. A tear rolled down his cheek. He tried to speak, but no words came.

"It's okay, daddy," she sobbed, wiping the tear away, "don't try to talk."

"Daddy, I just want you to know that I… I love you. I've always loved you, despite everything I've said in the past. I know you've always done your best for me. I know… I---"

She was distracted by something dripping onto her foot. Looking underneath the stretcher, she saw a small pool of blood forming. She traced the drips – which were slowly turning into a steady stream – to the top of the stretcher. A growing red circle was beginning to form under the area of the sheet covering his midsection. He was rapidly bleeding-out. She looked back to his face, but it was too late. His eyes were now closed, and blood was starting to trickle out of his mouth. Her body began to convulse, and her knees became weak and rubbery. She felt light-headed.

Everything started to spin. She felt several sets of hands grab onto her. Within seconds, it all went black – affording her a brief, but merciful, respite for her tortured soul.

CHAPTER 16

November 23rd – 4:12 p.m. Sunday Afternoon

It wouldn't be a hard thing do to… just a handful of pills should do the trick. No pain. No blood. Just a little drowsiness…and then---

Melissa opened her bloodshot eyes and shook the awful thought out of her head. She had been crying most of the day – just like she had every day for the past week and a half. It wasn't the first time she had contemplated suicide, and she was sure it wouldn't be the last. It worried her that she could even entertain such a notion. She always believed she was stronger than that… that God doesn't give us more than He knows we can handle. But just how much more heartache could she possibly endure? She hadn't felt this despondent since her parents' tragedy seven years ago. Now, after actually *witnessing* the mutilation and agonizingly slow death of her father, old wounds, which never fully healed, were open and raw once again.

What made it even worse was that she was consumed with guilt. Despite hours of painful soul-searching and countless mental debates to convince her otherwise, she continued to blame herself for her father's death. If only she hadn't been so concerned with saving herself, she could've helped him down the stairs and made sure he didn't slip and fall to his death. If only she had stepped in and made her presence known the second she saw him with that homeless man, perhaps all of this could have been avoided in the first place. No matter how many times Richard told her that she was in no way responsible for what happened she simply couldn't change the way she felt.

It made her feel even guiltier to know that her father had died while trying to help others. Despite the obvious dangers *and* his handicap, he was still willing to put the welfare of strangers before his own. His selflessness filled her with a sense of pride. She always knew her father was a humanitarian, but had absolutely no idea just how deep his convictions really were. While most people are content to just sit back and *say* that something should be done, he actually went out there and *did* something to try and make a difference. She also felt an equal amount of shame. Although she was able to apologize to him before he died, no amount of apologies could erase the disgust she felt with herself for giving him such a hard time about his late-night jaunts. Cloaking such a noble endeavor in a shroud of secrecy proved to her that he was a real unsung hero – truly dedicated to changing the world, but seeking none of its rewards.

Thoughts like that helped her in her time of grief, but she needed more. With no immediate family members to turn to for support, she thanked God she had Richard to lean on. In fact, his face was the only thing she remembered after blacking out that night. He told her that the paramedics had rushed her to St. Vincent's Hospital after she fainted. Being unable to communicate coherently with the medical personnel, they were forced to access her cell phone – hoping to find the numbers of any friends or family. When they called Richard, he rushed over and was by her side in the hospital within the hour. He then drove her home and put her to bed. She awoke several hours later, staring into his loving eyes while he gently stroked the side of her face. She couldn't imagine what she would have done had it not been for his unwavering love and comfort throughout it all. In addition to giving her as much time off from work as she needed, he was instrumental in helping her deal with the stress of planning her father's cremation last Friday. Deeply concerned about her fragile state of mind, he was reluctant to leave her alone for too long, so he intended to spend as much time with her as possible. He had practically moved in with her – only leaving her side to go to work, or to return to his home a couple of times for a change of clothes. Today, she felt she needed some time alone to herself. After three phone calls earlier in the day – thinly disguised attempts at casual conversation, but clearly nothing more than anxious checkups – he finally decided to stop calling and give her the space she needed.

She was still lying in bed – having only left her room twice; once to go to the bathroom, and once to feed Mr. Snuggles. She figured it was about time she got up and faced what was left of the day. Reluctantly, she tossed the covers back and left the security of her bed. After getting dressed and paying another visit to the bathroom, she went to the kitchen and made herself a cup of tea. She then went into the living room and sat down in an easy chair in the corner of the room.

Something had been nagging at her ever since her father's death. A lot of things just didn't add up. Although she was relieved to finally solve the mystery of those strange scrapping sounds that had haunted her for so long, so many other questions remained.

Why did he follow her around in the subway for so long?

Why did he think he had to protect her from anything?

Why did he feel he had to hide from her in order to do it?

She tried to put it all out of her head so she could concentrate on more pragmatic matters.

What was she going to do with his belongings?

Should she keep them?

Should she give them to The Salvation Army?

Would she have to go down to Beaufort to settle his affairs?

After much mental wrangling, she decided it was a little too much for her to deal with at the moment. She felt the onset of a splitting headache.

She began to think about Thanksgiving – a mere four days away. Next to Christmas, it used to be her second favorite holiday. Now, with no living parents to share it with, she was sure it would be among one of the worst days of her life. By now, of course, she was used to spending the holidays without her parents. After her mother's murder and her father's seven year hiatus, she pretty much had no choice. But it was different back then. She, at least, had the

somewhat comforting knowledge that her father was still around...
somewhere. Now, even that minuscule morsel of solace was gone.

A tear rolled down her cheek. Once again, she thanked God
for Richard's love and support.

She turned on the TV to escape her depressing thoughts. An
uninspiring array of sports programs, old movies and infomercials
flashed across the screen as she surfed through the channels. She
paused briefly when she got to CNN. They were doing a follow-up
piece on *The Subway Slayings*; more accurately, the lack thereof.
She had been so distraught by the death of her father, everything else
had taken a backseat. It had completely slipped her mind that, for the
past several days, the city had been enjoying a much needed reprieve
from the grisly murders. In fact, just over two weeks had gone by
since the last victim had been thrown to the tracks and electrocuted
in Manhattan's Rector Street station. Some officials had even
suggested that the nightmare might be over. Even though she hadn't
set foot back in the subway since her father's death, she had her
doubts about that. However, she couldn't deny the fact that things
did *seem* to be gradually getting back to normal. The terrifying
"shadow ghost" she had seen a couple of weeks ago had not made
another appearance, and even her plants seemed to be slowly coming
back to life. But she just couldn't rid herself of the disconcerting
feeling that something evil was still at hand.

The fading, pre-dusk light cast a melancholy glow
throughout the semi-darkened apartment. Her eye caught a glimpse
of a shiny object on the other side of the room under the couch. It
was her father's lockbox. Once an item of mild curiosity, she had
since all but forgotten about it. Seeing it again aroused her interest.
She put down her cup and walked over to the couch. She sat down
and pulled it out, then, placed it on her lap and turned on a nearby
table lamp. For several seconds, she just stared at it. She wasn't in
the habit of invading someone else's privacy, but considering the
circumstances, it was probably the most logical thing to do. She
lifted the box and attempted to raise the lid. It was locked.

Damn!

She was disappointed, but not really surprised. After all, it was a *lock*box. She searched through all of Matthew's possessions but was unable to locate a key. Refusing to be stopped by a nickel and dime lock, she went into the kitchen and retrieved a large flathead screwdriver from her utility cabinet. She rushed back to the living room with an excited sense of urgency. Turning the box on its side, she forced the screwdriver into the tiny slit under the lid. She pounded it in deeper with the palm of her hand. The slit grew wider and wider with each blow until the flimsy lock finally gave way under the pressure. The lid flew open, spilling an assortment of papers into her lap and onto the couch. She stared at the mess in bewilderment. Expecting to find things like important personal and/or financial documents, she saw nothing but a bunch of loose newspaper clippings, torn out book pages, old movie stubs and notes – piles and piles of handwritten notes in her father's handwriting.

She leaned back on the couch and sighed. It appeared that her father was some type of packrat.

Who in their right mind would want to save such an unrelated hodgepodge of junk? She wondered.

But as she began sifting through the pile, it became clear that what she was looking at was not junk. The big, bold newspaper article headlines were the first things to catch her attention. Each one was about *The Subway Slayings*. She found it odd that he would take such an interest in the crimes, considering how little he talked about them. She then noticed something even more peculiar. All of the clippings were from local New York City newspapers. The earliest was dated October 15th, the day after the first murder.

She raised her head and stared off into the distance. Something seemed wrong.

She got up from the couch and went down the hallway to her bedroom. Making her way over to the large wall calendar, she flipped it back one page and gasped. Ever since she was a little girl, she had a habit of circling important dates. The day her father came back into her life certainly qualified as such. A thick red circle was drawn around October 28th, with the words, "DADDY'S HOME," written inside the box. It was the night she had run into him on the subway. She distinctly remembered him telling her that he came into town the day before – almost two weeks *after* the earliest newspaper article in his lockbox was printed. In fact, *six* of the articles in his lockbox were about murders that occurred before he arrived.

She briefly considered the possibility that he could have gotten them from a library archive, or perhaps, someone had mailed them to him. But, she didn't believe that was the case. He *must* have been in town for a much longer time than he had told her.

She rushed back to the living room and resumed rummaging through the lockbox with renewed vigor. She then turned her attention to the book excerpts. They appeared to be ripped out of a textbook – a textbook about the occult. As she flipped through the pages, she kept coming across a word she had never heard before: *Hoodoo*. She read one of the passages describing its origin:

Hoodoo is a type of folk magic based in African traditions. It originated in the southern United States during slavery; taking root mainly in Alabama, Mississippi, Georgia, Florida, North Carolina and South Carolina. Not to be confused with Voodoo, which is an established religion, Hoodoo is the magic without the religion. As such, it is very informal, and can be practiced by a variety of lay people. The goal of the "casual" Hoodoo practitioner (Hoodoo Man/Woman or Root Doctor) is to gain access to supernatural forces to influence their lives, or the lives of others. Generally, this influence is exercised in concerns pertaining to love, general health and happiness, predicting the future and blessing the home. Common items such as herbs, plants, roots, amulets and minerals, combined with a few simple chants and rituals, are the usual catalysts used to perpetuate one's desires. However, much more potent, and even malevolent results are possible when Hoodoo is combined with the practice of Nigromancy (literally, "demonic magic," that is, the summoning of the Denizens of Hell.)

Melissa's hands began to shake. She rested the papers in her lap and continued reading.

Let it be understood, that Nigromancy is not easily self-taught. It is a demanding art, requiring hundreds of hours of quiet meditation in a darkened room, knowledge of specific chants and

255

prayers, as well as knowledge of the particular demon (or demons) one wishes to summon. It takes years of dedicated study to become an accomplished Nigromancer – a requirement few people would have the time or the inclination to fulfill.

There are many reasons as to why one would wish to become a Nigromancer. Lust for power and basic curiosity are two of the most common. However, a few twisted souls look to this craft to satisfy their insatiable desire for evil, mainly, to exact revenge, i.e., a horrible death on their enemies. There are many ways to do this, but the most effective is a two-step, albeit, very dangerous process involving the powers of Hoodoo. So as not to "dirty their hands," advanced Nigromancers will need to enlist the services of a second party (a host). Since these services are rarely offered willingly, it is first necessary to "qualify" the host via a common Hoodoo item known as Graveyard Dirt. In actuality, it is the creatures living within the dirt (worms and/or bugs) that are used to place the host in a type of semi-paralytic state. The dirt is collected from the grave of a sinner, or someone who "died badly," i.e., before their time, through execution, or so forth. The general belief is that these spirits of the deceased would be inclined to perform evil deeds with little or no compunction. If a grave of this type cannot be found, similar results can also be derived by obtaining the dirt from the grave of a soldier. Because of their bravery and unique conditioning to "blind obedience," some Nigromancers consider this the best kind of dirt to use. Through a series of ritualistic chants and incantations, this dirt, as well as its inhabitants, is then "cursed" with the demonic essence of the demon specifically summoned by the Nigromancer. The dirt-dwelling creature(s) is inserted into a cranial orifice of the host. It will immediately begin burrowing its way into the brain – at which point, the host will become demonically possessed and "pre-conditioned" to carrying out the Nigromancers' wishes. If these wishes are truly evil in nature, it is imperative that the host be particularly susceptible to suggestion – an individual practically devoid of cognizant though, essentially, a "vacant vessel."

The name of the demon usually summoned for this type of endeavor is Lucifuge Rofocale – an exceptionally violent and unpredictable fiend, who takes great pleasure inflicting massive pain and deformity in his hosts. The name "Lucifuge," is derived from two Latin words: Lux (light; genitive Lucis), and Fuji (to flee), which means "he who flees the light." In essence, he hates daylight and can only possess a host at night.

Her jaw dropped open with shock. She immediately recognized the name as the one she had found on a little yellow stickie several weeks ago. She felt a little nauseous, but continued reading on.

A demonically possessed host may exhibit any one or more of a variety of physical anomalies; ranging from, but not limited to, rapidly developing and healing facial wounds, to the ability to stretch and bend body parts in unnatural ways. In some cases, hosts have even gained the power of levitation. The anomalies exhibited are unpredictable and vary greatly from one host to another. However, each host will possess the commonality of super-human strength and piercing red eyes.

It cannot be stressed enough just how dangerous this type of Hoodoo can be, especially for a novice. Even highly skilled Nigromancers with decades of experience are sometimes reluctant to open this potential Pandora's Box. Instability is the underlying problem. Once Lucifuge Rofocale is successfully summoned, an evil aura is unleashed, and can attach itself to the Nigromancer – an unpleasant side-effect that can negatively impact the behavior of animals and damage the cells of any nearby plant matter. When cast into a host, Rofocale's influence is not always limited to that particular host. Other "like-minded" individuals in the immediate vicinity of the host can also become affected. These affectations, however, are limited to an overall lethargic or trance-like appearance – a temporary condition that eventually dissipates in time. Many unsuspecting Nigromancers have been plagued by the presence of terrifying apparitions – evil entities that can manifest at will any time after the initial summoning. Also, this particular demon is as cleaver as he is evil – able to learn complicated tasks and even capable of operating independently of the Nigromancer's control.

She began to feel a little light-headed as she continued reading the next couple of paragraphs.

In order to insure the most horrendous demise of their enemies, it is believed that some Nigromancers, through a series of special incantations, have even summoned the Devil himself. A host possessed by the Devil will exhibit many of the same abilities and characteristics as one possessed by a demon, with a few markedly different anomalies. These anomalies will include, but are not limited to, enlarged pupils, aka, "black eyes," a forked tongue and a sentient intelligence. Practitioners of the Dark Arts have deemed this as the utmost dangerous type of summoning – tantamount to literally opening the Gates of Hell.

No matter which type of summoning a Nigromancer chooses to use, it is extremely imperative that once the job has been successfully completed that the host be decommissioned, and that the demon, and ESPECIALLY the Devil, be immediately sent back to Hell via one final command: "RETURN PEACEFULLY AND WITH ALL HASTE FROM WHENCE THEE CAME!"

She read the passage several times. It was like a veil of innocence (or naiveté) was gradually being lifted from her mind's eye. Things about her father she once considered trivial and benign – things she had barely given a second thought – were starting to take on a whole new significance – a sinister significance.

The six years he was away… his frequent visits to the graveyard… the weird way Mr. Snuggles acted whenever he was around… her dying plants… the Shadow Ghost… the time she and Richard caught him sitting in the dark… his uncharacteristic calmness when the homeless man began to change… the list goes on and on.

And then there was that black stuff – the strange ashy-type substance he took out of his pouch that night in the subway and cradled in his hands. She was now certain that it was dirt… possibly, *Graveyard Dirt?* From the moment she first saw it, she knew there was something strange about it – something that just didn't seem quite right.

"Oh my God!" she whispered to herself.

At the time, she could have sworn that she had seen something moving within the dirt. She had tried to rationalize it by assuming that her eyes were just playing tricks on her.

But no.

After reading the last passage, she realized that what she had seen was probably a worm. She then remembered that the man didn't actually begin to change until her father held it next to the side of his face – apparently, to allow it to enter his ear.

She felt numb. The sickeningly obvious question on her mind was whether or not her own father could have possibly been responsible for *The Subway Slayings*!

A sudden chill caused her entire body to violently twitch.

If that was indeed the case, it still didn't make any sense.

Why would he want to do this to so many homeless people?

Why would he want to turn them into raging, murderous zombies?

And, most importantly…

Why would he want to kill all those innocent people?

Her father had always been an upstanding, law-abiding citizen, with a soft spot for the less fortunate. For a moment, she wondered if she was simply letting her imagination run wild. Although everything she had just read was quite compelling, and seemed to point to one undeniable conclusion… in a court of law, a shrewd lawyer might classify it all as merely "circumstantial evidence."

Yes, yes, of course! She thought, refusing to believe the worst. *That's gotta be it… just a crazy bunch of coincidences!*

That *had* to be it! To think otherwise would be, well, unfathomable. Besides, she hadn't seen anything that would directly link him to the murders. She had no idea why he would be carrying around that type of information, but figured he must have had some secret interest in the occult. She continued reading more passages about the dangers of *Nigromancy* when she came across a small,

259

spiral-bound notebook, buried within the pile. The pages inside were well-worn – some almost falling out of the book – and covered with her father's handwriting. At first glance, it appeared to be some type of schedule – complete with dates and times. She remembered how detail-oriented he used to be – drawing up military precision-like itineraries for just about everything he did.

But when she looked at it closer, she could see that it wasn't exactly a schedule, but more like a log – a log of someone else's activities. A quick scan through some of the pages revealed that it was actually a log of the activities of *several* different people. At the top of some of the pages was a physical description, i.e., middle-aged black female, white man in his thirties, etc.; followed by a detailed, chronological account for each person. The strange notes bewildered her at first, but something about the descriptions seemed vaguely familiar. She went rummaging back in the lockbox for some of the newspaper clippings and read them again.

The hair on the back of her neck stood up.

The descriptions perfectly matched each of the victims of *The Subway Slayings*! Even more disturbing were the meticulous records he kept of their personal lives. He had literally been stalking them… weeks *before* they were murdered!

She read the first page.

Young Spanish Guy

(Watching from top of stairs)

Sept. 4th

7:28 a.m. Leaves 3505 Corlear Ave. (home) in The Bronx and walks to 238th St. subway station. Takes downtown #1 to 96th St. in Manhattan (sits in front of train). Transfers to #2 express. Gets off at Fulton St. in Manhattan. Walks toward South Street Seaport.

8:52 a.m. Arrives at Duane Reade (Fulton & Pearl). Employee... works in back room.

12:03 p.m. Leaves store with a couple of co-workers. Goes to Burger King across street for lunch.

12:41 p.m. Leaves Burger King

12:42 p.m. Returns to Duane Reade

5:01 p.m. Leaves Duane Reade. Walks up Fulton and returns to same station. Takes downtown #3 to Kingston Ave. in Bklyn. Walks down Eastern Pkwy. to Albany Ave. (1 block), makes left & goes to Lincoln Pl. (1 block), makes right.

5:54 p.m. Arrives at 1165 Lincoln Pl.

2:23 a.m. Leaves 1165 Lincoln with woman. Kisses woman in doorway and leaves – woman (girlfriend?) goes back inside. He takes same route back to Kingston Ave. station. Heads to uptown #3 platform. Takes #3 to 96th St. in Manhattan. Transfers to #1 local. Goes to 238th St. in Bronx. Takes same route as morning.

261

3:44 a.m. Arrives home (3505 Corlear Ave.)

That was the last entry for that day.

She was absolutely stunned. Obviously, her father had been in town for quite some time, but just *what* in the world was he doing? As she flipped through the pages, she could see that he had been following this guy for several days each week for over a month. Each entry was almost a carbon copy of the previous one. Apparently, he was trying to learn his daily routine… but *why*!?

The final entry was dated "Oct.13th." It followed a similar pattern as the others, up until the last few lines:

6:05 p.m. Arrives at girlfriend's house.

(Host conditioned and in place in tunnel between Kingston & Utica)

2:40 a.m. Arrives at Kingston station, seemed lost in thought.

3:20 a.m. Station clear – host summoned.

3:33 a.m. Host comes out of tunnel. Attacks subject, rips out heart and returns to tunnel.

3:36 a.m. Subject confirmed dead… good kill. Host de-commissioned.

The book slipped out of her hands and fell to the floor. Her heart began beating wildly, while goose bumps formed on her arms – contradicting the beads of sweat popping up on her forehead. Her breathing became labored, and her headache – now a migraine – was in full swing. All doubt was now gone. Any flickers of hope for a positive and reasonable explanation were completely extinguished.

She had no choice but to finally face the horrible truth...her father was single-handedly responsible for *The Subway Slayings*!

As horrible as that was, it still didn't make any sense. She couldn't understand why her father would engage in such heinous activities. She picked up the book and read the log again. She then read the other logs, hoping that they might be different – that they might, *somehow*, reveal that she had simply misinterpreted everything. Unfortunately, they too, included specific dates and times, and were just as graphically detailed as the first. Not only had he identified himself as the mastermind behind the murders, in many cases, he actually described details that were never reported in the media.

Another curious thing about the logs were the notes he put in parenthesis under each persons' description, i.e., *(watching from end of platform), (watching on downtown platform covering nose and mouth), (watching from top of stairs, etc.).*

At first, she thought they were the locations where he hid and watched as the murders took place. But when she read: *"white male conductor (watching from his cab)"*… it became clear that what he was describing was not *his* point of view, but *theirs*!

The more she thought about it, the less sense it made. She re-read the logs several more times. As detailed as they were, he never mentioned anything about these people watching anything from these locations. As she mulled over what it could all mean, she came across another log… her own. She already knew he had been following her, but to read it in black and white gave her chills. It was an invasion of her privacy and she felt violated. She then came across an entry dated "Oct. 17th" that really shocked her.

12:21 a.m. Melissa gets off train at Van Siclen. She hears me… starts to run. Hard to keep up with her. Heads down Pitkin Ave. Makes a left on Bradford. Falls… looks hurt… too far away to

help. Runs 2 more bks. to 352 Bradford Street
(home?)

She remembered that this was the night that she had been chased home by that mysterious figure. She couldn't believe her father had never told her that he was responsible for the fear she felt that night. But, as she thought back, it all started to make more sense. She reflected on their walk home on the night after their "surprise" meeting on the subway. He seemed to know exactly which way to go – sometimes even slightly leading the way. It was a subtle thing she overlooked at the time, but in hindsight, she now saw it as a glaring red flag.

She continued thumbing through the book, when a piece of paper fell out. It was a folded up – slightly yellowed with age – sheet of loose-leaf paper. When she opened it, she immediately recognized it as something she had seen before. It was the final straw that ultimately convinced her that her father needed professional help. At the time, she thought he had just scribbled a bunch of random words all over the page. Carefully reading it now for the first time, she saw that it was just *three* words written over and over:

... they did nothing... they did nothing... they did nothing...

She gasped.

She recalled how enraged he was by the fact that no one tried to intervene while he and her mother were being attacked. The media called it "bystander apathy" – a situation where a crowd of people will watch a crime being committed, but do nothing to stop it.

Watch!

"Watched from the end of the platform... Watched from the top of the stairs---!"

Like the pieces of some horrifying puzzle she never *really* wanted to solve... it was all starting to come together. The victims – the people her father methodically stalked for weeks before orchestrating their murders – *must* have been some of the actual onlookers he saw standing around and watching during the attack!

But wait a minute! She thought. *How could he have been so sure that these were the same people?*

And, mainly---

How in the world could he have possibly found them again after so many years?

This *really* didn't make any sense. It was bordering on the realm of impossibility. Even if a few random faces stood out in the crowd, he certainly didn't know their names or where they lived. There's *no* way he would have been able to track these exact same people down after seven long years.

She sat there for a long time… thinking… re-reading the logs and the newspaper clippings. Nothing she read could explain it. Perhaps her father had some more notes locked away someplace else. Maybe they weren't even in New York, but with the rest of his possessions down in Beaufort.

Her headache was turning into a migraine.

Realizing she wasn't going to get any more answers, she slowly started stuffing everything back into the lockbox. Just before closing the lid, she grabbed a handful of the loose movie stubs and tossed them on top of the thick pile.

That's odd. She thought.

It seemed strange to her that he would save things like that – even stranger that he would save them with materials of such contrasting natures. She picked one up out of curiosity and saw that it wasn't a stub from a movie, but from a *seminar*… an "RV" seminar.

Recreational vehicles!?

Yet, another side of her father she knew nothing about. He never said anything about having an interest in RV's, much less, a desire to learn more about them in a seminar.

She picked up a few other stubs and saw that "RV" actually stood for "Remote Viewing."

What the hell is that!?

The information on the back of one stub explained it all.

Learn the art of remote viewing (RV) – the skill by which a person (a viewer) can perceive objects, persons or events at a location removed from him or her by either space or time. Develop your senses to gain information about a target without the aid of conventional sources, such as television or telephones. All it takes is a sincere investment of time and energy to master the principles of this amazing technique. With practice, you will learn to locate your target – whether it is in the next room or on the other side of the planet!

She vaguely remembered hearing something about remote viewing in old, Grade-B, science-fiction movies. She never dreamed that it was something real – something that people would actually pay good money to learn how to do. Not only had her father shelled out hundreds, possibly even thousands of dollars, to learn this technique, he had traveled all over the country in the process. She saw stubs from RV seminars and workshops in Sedona, Arizona... Enid, Oklahoma... Mobile, Alabama... New York City... San Antonio, Texas... there was even one from London, England! All of them were dated between the years of 1997 and 2003 – the exact years she had lost touch with him.

It angered her to learn that he had told her more lies than she could even count. At least now she knew the whole truth. It sickened her to know that she was the daughter of a man capable of harboring such hatred and rage towards other human beings – a man so totally consumed with rage that he would devote seven years of his life to perfecting a plan – a "psychic weapon," so to speak – to assure their demise. It sickened her even more to know that he was more than willing to use the homeless – those to whom he had shown so much compassion for in the past – to carry out his twisted plan. Perhaps, it was his familiarity with them which led him to believe that they would serve as the perfect hosts.

She felt another wave of nausea.

She returned the stubs to the lockbox and quickly closed the lid, sorry that she had ever opened it in the first place. Knowing the truth was a horrible thing. The fact that her own father was the mastermind behind one of the most shocking murder sprees in the

266

city's history was a burden she would have to carry with her for the rest of her life – a secret she would take to the grave. She didn't even want to tell Richard – not because she feared he would blab it to the world, but because she was just too ashamed and embarrassed.

She then thought about the media.

If there was even the *slightest* chance that they could ever find out about the box, her life, for all intents and purposes, would be changed forever. After her parents were attacked seven years ago, her private life became a virtual open book. She was relentlessly hounded by the press, and her whole world was turned upside down. At that time, she made the news because her father was the *victim* of a terrible crime; but now, as the *perpetrator*, she knew it would be completely different. She could see the headline in the New York Post: "DIARY OF MADMAN FOUND IN DAUGHTER'S HOME." Most likely, she would be called in for questioning by the police. Even though there wasn't anything that could implicate her in any of the crimes, the stigma of being related to a killer was more than she was willing to endure. Some people – *maybe* even some of her own friends – might consider her "guilty by association."

She placed the box beside her on the couch and knew what she had to do. She got up and went to the utility closet in the kitchen, and brought back a metal pail, a can of turpentine and a small book of matches. After dumping the entire contents of the box into the pail, she doused it with a healthy amount of turpentine. She then struck a match and dropped it in. There was a muffled *whoosh*, immediately followed by an unexpectedly large plume of flame. It rose several inches above the rim of the pail – causing her to momentarily jump back to safety. As the flames subsided, the room filled with an acrid odor of smoke. She cracked open a window to air it out. Within seconds, the sizable mound of papers was reduced to a smoldering pile of ash.

The soft crackle of burning embers was suddenly drowned out by the shrill ringing of the phone. With a pretty good idea of who it was, she sat back down on the couch and answered the phone on the end table.

"Hello, Richard," she said.

"I know you don't have Caller ID," he laughed, "So how did you---"

"Who else could it *possibly* be?" She asked, sarcastically.

"Well, okay, sue me. I care about the woman I love."

"I know you do, sweetie."

"You sound a little funny… you okay?"

"Yeah, I just got up a little while ago."

"My God!" he laughed, again. "You practically slept the entire day away!"

"I know," she sighed, "I just… I---"

"I'm just messin' with ya', sweetheart. It's gonna take time… lots and lots of time before things get better."

"I just hope I don't turn into the basket-case I did seven years ago."

"Well, I wouldn't worry too much about that. Back then, you didn't have me for support, and you were younger… less able to cope."

"I wasn't *that* much younger, and now that I know my father---"

She caught herself just in time.

"Your father *what*?"

"That he, ah, well, you know… died so violently," she said, effectively masking her near slip of the tongue. "Now that I know how violently he died, and the fact that I was there to see it… well, it just makes it a little harder."

"Yeah, I know, but from what the cops told you… *hopefully*, he didn't feel much of anything. I mean, I know it's not much, but that should give you *some* piece of mind, right?"

"I guess," she whispered.

"Listen," he said, trying to change the subject, "whattya say we go into the city tonight?"

"On a *Sunday* night?"

"Sure, why not? You haven't eaten yet, have you?"

"No."

"Great! I know this new Italian restaurant in Midtown that serves better pasta than Sicily."

"I don't know, Rich, I really hadn't planned on going anywhere today."

"I promise to make it worth your while."

"I really don't have much of an appetite."

"Well, you can just have a light salad."

"I'm sorry, I just don't think I'd be very good company right now. Maybe we could do something later in the week?"

"Alright," he sighed.

"You sound really disappointed."

"No, no, I understand… it's still too soon."

They chatted a few minutes more, then, said their goodbyes. She felt a little guilty for ruining his plans. He sounded like he really had his heart set on going out. But, considering everything that was on her mind, she knew she had made the right decision.

She got up and looked into the pail. The odor was still strong and most of the smoke had all but dissipated, but the ashes were still glowing bright red in many places. She watched the embers slowly fade out and die. It was a chilling metaphor for what her father had done in his life, as well as the lives of so many other innocent people. She thought about all the families that would never again be the same… all the children that would never again see their parents… all the husbands and wives and boyfriends and girlfriends who would never again feel their partner's loving touch.

And it was all for *what*?

Within a matter of hours, her emotions had gone full circle. Her hero worship had given way to a degree of hatred and disgust she never thought she could feel for another human being. But, right now, she didn't even think of her father as a human. How could she? Anyone who could so methodically and patiently orchestrate such a heinous plan was, in her opinion, nothing short of a monster. For the first time, she realized just how accurate Richard's initial instincts of her father actually were.

The last of the ashes faded to black.

She went down the hallway to her bedroom and got back into bed, even though she didn't feel tired. Although she hadn't eaten anything all day, she didn't feel hungry, either. Except for the throbbing pain of her migraine, she really didn't feel much of anything at all.

CHAPTER 17

One Week Later – 7:08 p.m. Sunday Evening

"Donnie, go sit over there with your sisters so I can get a picture of the three of y'all," his mother said, in a thick southern accent.

"I don't wanna," he grumbled.

"Come on, son, listen to your mother," ordered his father. "Now, go over there next to your sisters."

He mumbled something incoherent, then, reluctantly got up and slowly shuffled toward his two older sisters sitting across the aisle. A sharp jolt almost threw him completely off balance. The quick reflexes of a nearby passenger, who grabbed him by the arm, prevented him from making a nasty face-to-floor encounter.

"Oh, thank you, sir! Thank you so much!" the mother said, gratefully. "He's still gettin' used to ridin'... we all are, actually."

The man politely smiled and nodded.

She picked him up and physically placed him into position on the bench.

"Okay, smile!"

She aimed the camera at the children and prepared to take a picture.

"Come on, Donnie... *smile!*"

Even though her plea was met with a scowl, she snapped the picture anyway.

It was the Claven family's first visit to New York City, as well as their first ride on the subway. Having never ventured more than about 50 miles outside of their hometown of Valdosta, GA, this trip was one of the biggest highlights of their lives. Florence Claven and her husband, Arnold, were traveling with their three kids; Cindy, 12, Regina, 9 and Donald, 7. They had spent the day visiting The Statue of Liberty, Ground Zero and Chinatown. They were now traveling uptown on the "B" train to The Empire State Building. All of their sightseeing was taking its toll on the children – especially Donald, who, by now, had grown tired and cranky, and was only interested in seeing the inside of their hotel room.

"Mommy, Donnie didn't smile!" tattled, Regina.

"Yeah, he ruined our picture," cried Cindy. "Can we take another?"

"Tell you what," suggested Arnold, "Why don't I get a shot of the four of you… squeeze in there, Flo."

"Okay," said Florence, as she joined the kids. "Try to get the subway map in the shot as well."

"It's in there. Everybody say, 'cheese'."

With the exception of Donald, they all smiled, and shouted, "CHEEEEESE!"

He took the picture holding the camera with one hand and gripping a pole with the other.

"Hey, I just realized," said Florence to her husband, "We don't have any pictures of *you* on the train."

She looked to the only other person in the car with them – the man who had just saved her son from falling.

"Sir, I hate to bother you… but would you mind taking a picture of all of us?"

"Sure, no problem," he replied.

He got up from his seat and approached the family. Arnold handed him the point-and-shoot camera, pointed to the top of it, and said, "Just press this little button, right here."

He backed up a few feet in order to get the entire family in the shot, and asked, "Everybody ready?"

"YEEEEES!" they all shouted in unison.

He held the camera about a foot away from his face and looked puzzled.

"Oh, no," explained Florence, "It's not one of those fancy digital thingies… ya' gotta look through the little window at the top."

"Oh, okay," he said, with a small chuckle.

After a click and a flash, the Clavens' adventure was recorded for posterity.

"Thank you so much," said Florence.

As she came over to retrieve the camera, the train made another violent jolt – forcing *everyone* to quickly reach for the nearest support pole.

"My *goodness*," she exclaimed, "Is it always this rough!?"

"Actually, no," the man replied, "It's usually a much smoother ride… probably the motorman's first day on the job."

They all laughed.

"Tell me," she asked, "Do you know if this train goes to The Empire State Building?"

"Yeah, that's on 34th Street… the next stop."

"Is it a long walk from the station?" asked Arnold.

"No, it's just about a half a block away. When you get out of the station, you're gonna be on 6th Avenue. The Empire State Building's between 5th and 6th, you can't miss it."

"I guess we'd be pretty *blind* if we did," joked, Florence.

They all laughed again.

"Where are you guys from?" the man asked.

"We're from Georgia… it's our first time in New York."

"Are you having a good time?"

"Oh, yeah, well… I guess most of us are, anyway," she said, pointing to Donnie.

The girls were amusing themselves by swinging around a pole. Donald, however, had returned to his seat – sulking.

"I guess he's seen enough of the city for one day," the man laughed.

"Yeah, but he'll cheer up as soon as he sees the view from the top of The Empire State Building," she said.

The man nodded his head and smiled.

It had been quite a week for Melissa. On Monday, she had won $500 from a "Scratch & Match" card she had purchased for $2.00 in a local grocery store. On Wednesday, her entire Forensics class at John Jay was treated to an on-set visit to *"Law & Order: Criminal Intent"* – one of her all-time favorite TV shows. But Thursday, Thanksgiving, was, surprisingly enough, the best day of all. It was the day she *definitely* had something to be thankful for. It was the day Richard finally proposed to her. Actually, he had been planning to do it for some time, but for obvious reasons, he hadn't felt that the moment was right. He was all set to ask her last Sunday, but she had, unknowingly, thwarted his plans. But everything finally came together Thursday night, when he took her out to a swanky Upper East Side eatery. He had the waiter place the ring atop a mound of whipped cream on her slice of pumpkin pie. He stressed that he wanted the ring to be visible and not hidden within the cream. Choking on an 18K white gold diamond engagement ring, he reasoned, just might put a *slight* damper on the evening. Through tears of joy *and* the adulation of several well-wishing patrons, she accepted his proposal.

For the past three days, Melissa's entire outlook on life changed dramatically. She approached everything with a giddy – almost childlike – enthusiasm. It was a side of her he had never seen before – a refreshing new aspect of her personality he was thrilled to bring forth. Today was the first full day they had had together since the start of their young engagement. With a wedding date set for early May of next year, she was anxious to spend the day at the Macy's Bridal Registry in Manhattan's Herald Square. Considering the fact that they hadn't even come to a decision on where they were going to live, Richard thought it was a bit premature. But, seeing the sparkle in her eyes – a sparkle he rarely saw due to so many years of heartache and tragedy – was all it took to convince him that the time was just right.

"Do you really think we need a whole new set of dishes?" he asked.

"Of course we do," she replied. "You have bits and pieces of about three mixed-matched sets, and most of them are chipped."

"Yeah, but you have a pretty nice complete set."

"I'm tired of that design. I want something new... *everything* should be new when we're just starting out."

She could see he was becoming a little overwhelmed by the process.

"I know it seems like we have a lot of stuff on our list, but it's better to have too much than not enough. Remember... there's no guarantee we're actually going to get all of this."

"I guess you're right," he said – giving her a peck on her lips.

They selected a few more items and decided to call it a day. Slowly, they walked hand-in-hand toward the elevators.

"I still can't believe it," she gushed, as they rode the elevator down to the street level, "*Mrs. Melissa Lordan.*"

"Kinda has a nice ring to it, doesn't it?" he asked.

"Oh, I dunno," she said, jokingly, "I've kinda gotten used to the double "M" sound of 'Melissa Manning.' It flows off the tongue better."

"I'll give you something to flow off your tongue."

He pulled her close to him and passionately kissed her – totally ignoring the uneasy glances from their fellow riders.

"Oh, it's okay," he said to them after the kiss, "she needs that for medical purposes."

Everyone smiled and chuckled.

When the elevator reached the first floor, they stepped out and weaved their way through the throngs of shoppers in the designer handbags department. They left the store through the revolving doors on the 34th Street side of the store closest to Broadway.

"Wow, it's already dark," she remarked, as they maneuvered toward the center of the windswept, crowded sidewalk. "I can't believe we spent the whole day in there."

"Well, you know... time really flies when you're havin' a good time."

Assuming he was being facetious, she responded, "I know this wasn't exactly your idea of a fun Sunday."

"No, I'm serious. I actually enjoyed it. I mean, I'll admit… I thought you were jumping the gun a bit when you suggested we register, but once we got into it, I thought it was a lot of fun. I can't wait to see how all that stuff is going to look in our own little love nest."

"Me too."

They stood there in silence for several seconds holding hands.

"*What*?" she coyly asked – brushing a wayward curl off her face. "Why are you staring at me like that?"

"I just love the way the night lights sparkle in your beautiful eyes."

Before she could respond, he kissed her again – much more passionately than before. They were magically transported into another dimension where only the two of them existed – a dimension completely devoid of the frenzied hustle and bustle swirling around them. For the moment, the only thing they could feel was the excited thumping of their hearts beating as one. The only things they could hear were their soft moans in between each deep kiss. Even the sting in the cold night air was tempered as their steamy breaths warmed each other's soul.

"I love you so much," he whispered in her ear.

"I love you, too."

Her eyes welled, and a tear of joy streamed down the side of her face. He gently tilted her head and sensuously licked it off as it rolled passed the curve of her mouth. They kissed again for several more seconds.

"I guess we should get going," he finally said, wishing the moment could last longer.

"Yeah, I guess we better. I wouldn't want someone to have to throw a bucket of cold water on us," she joked.

"Come on," he said, taking her by the hand, "I'll walk you over to Eighth," he said, referring to the subway she would normally catch on Eighth Avenue.

"Oh, I forgot to tell you... I'm not going straight home."

"You're not?"

"No, there's this cute little church, somewhere in the upper seventies on Central Park West that offers evening services on Sunday nights. I've been meaning to check it out, but I'm never in the area, and, well... I haven't really been in much of a mood to rejoice lately. But I think I'll give it a shot tonight."

"Oh, okay."

"Hey, why don't you come *with* me!?"

"I'd love to, sweetie, but I really gotta get home. I need to organize some notes for a big meeting tomorrow."

"Working on a Sunday night?"

"Yeah, well, you know... it's the downsides of makin' the big bucks."

"Awww... you poor baby. So, how are you getting home?"

"I guess I'll just go down here to Seventh," he said, pointing down the block toward Seventh Avenue, "I can catch the LIRR at Penn Station."

"I'll bet you're sorry you didn't drive in today, huh?"

"No, not really, parking would have been a far bigger hassle than dealing with the train."

"Well, alright," she sighed.

"But, wait a minute," he said, "What about you? How are you getting up to that church?"

"I can take the "B" train right here." She pointed to the subway entrance on the corner behind them.

"The *train*!? Oh, no, no, no... let me give you some money for a cab."

He started to reach into his pockets, but she stopped him.

"Oh, no... it's okay," she insisted, "I'll be fine."

"Honey, just because there haven't been any more murders recently doesn't mean the subways are safe. They still haven't caught---"

"Sweetie, trust me... I'll be fine."

The conviction in her voice took him somewhat aback. Realizing this, she quickly modified her remark.

"I mean, it's still early and the trains are full of people."

"Well, how long is the service? What about when church is over?"

"Service is only about forty-five minutes, so it's still going to be fairly early when it's over. I'll be okay, honey."

"Well, alright, but try to ride in cars that are full of people, okay?"

"I promise."

"Okay, well… call me tonight when you get home."

"Will do."

"Love you."

"Love you, too."

After another quick kiss, he left her and began walking down 34th Street toward Penn Station. She felt a little guilty as she watched him slowly melt into the crowd. It was just three days into their engagement and she had already lied to him. She wanted to tell him the truth about her father, but she couldn't… at least, not yet. She wondered if she would *ever* be able to reveal such a dark family secret. It wasn't going to be easy, but if they were to have any chance of a marriage built on trust, she knew that skeleton would, *one day*, have to come out of her closet. She turned around and began making her way down the stairs toward the train.

"How tall is the building, mommy?"

"Did they really make 'King Kong' there, or was it done in Hollywood?"

"Remember when we saw those people running up the stairs to the top on TV? Was that part of the New York City Marathon?"

"Will we be able to see our house in Georgia?"

"I'm hungry, is there a restaurant up there where we can have dinner?"

The questions were coming faster than they could be answered. Cindy and Regina could barely contain their excitement about visiting the Observation Deck of The Empire State Building. Donald, on the other hand, was still whining about returning to their hotel. As their train pulled into the 34th Street station, he was not shy about voicing his displeasure.

"My feet hurt... I wanna go hoooooome!"

"Look, Donnie," his father explained, "we're not gonna be there too long. When we get back to the hotel, you can have chocolate ice cream for dessert after dinner. How's that sound?"

He stubbornly nodded his head in approval. The promise of being treated to his favorite dessert was enough to temporarily stop his complaining, but it was going to take more than that to change his sour attitude.

There was a loud squeal of the brakes and the train came to a jarring stop.

"Okay, y'all," shouted Florence to her family, "this is our stop... get ready!"

The other man in the car got up and stood by the door.

"Oh, no, sir... I didn't mean you too," she joked, "you can stay on if ya' like!"

"No, no," he laughed, "I'm getting off here, too."

"You wouldn't, by any chance, be goin' to The Empire State Building, would ya'?" Arnold asked.

"No, actually I'm making a transfer to the "R" train. But don't worry, you won't get lost."

The doors opened and they all stepped out onto the platform – leaving the car completely empty.

"Thanks again for all your help," Florence said to the man.

"It was my pleasure," he said, as he made his way toward a flight of stairs at the front of the platform. "You all have fun now, okay?"

"Okay, BYE!" They all – with the exception of Donald – shouted in unison.

The train stopped twenty or thirty feet away from the front of the platform. Since they were riding in the first car, Florence saw an opportunity for another quick photo shoot.

"Hey look, y'all... let's get a shot right here in front of the train!"

"Oh, yeah, that's a good one," agreed Arnold. "Come on kids; gather 'round real quick!"

Cindy and Regina dutifully obeyed, but Donald – determined to be obstinate – lingered behind.

"Come on, Donnie… get in there before the train leaves… MOVE!" Florence shouted.

"Hurry up, Donnie!" Arnold yelled. "Get over here!"

His sisters even tried to persuade him, but it was no use… he stubbornly refused to take part.

"Forget it, Flo," said Arnold, "we don't have time… just take the picture without him!"

"Alright. Donnie, just go sit over there on the bench for a minute," she told him.

Almost in tears, he took a seat on the bench and pouted. A series of bright flashes began to pierce the semi-darkness of the station.

Melissa paused for a second to get her bearings when she reached the base of the stairs. As a regular rider of the Eighth Avenue line, she wasn't too familiar with the stations or the trains on Sixth Avenue. The 34th Street Station was a huge hub – bringing together a total of eight subway lines, as well as the PATH trains to New Jersey. She reached into her pocketbook for her MetroCard, then, worked her way through the crowds toward the turnstiles. She then followed the signs leading to the uptown "B" platform on the lower level – a convoluted journey through a confusing catacomb of ramps and stairs. When she turned a corner to descend the final flight of stairs, she could see that a "B" train was already in the station with its doors still open. She decided to run for it. She had only taken a few steps and stopped – startled by the thunderous sound of several sets of footsteps running even faster and coming up quickly behind her.

"YO… HO' DAT DO'… HO' DAT DO'!!!" A voice suddenly boomed, demanding that the train door be held open.

Before she could turn completely around, three men came charging past her. Had she not quickly dodged out of their way, they probably would have bowled her right over. Although she didn't get a clear look at their faces, it was quite obvious from their behavior *and* attire that they were no strangers to the ghetto lifestyle.

All three were wearing "bubble" jackets and oversized jeans – one with a pair so baggy, he actually had to hold them up with one hand. Another man – the shortest of the three – sported a huge, seventies-style Afro that bobbed and weaved with each step he took down the stairs. The last of the trio was downright frightening in size. He was well over 300 pounds and towered head and shoulders above his companions. Despite his size, however, he was incredibly agile – taking the stairs two at a time. As he rushed by she caught sight of a large, shiny object on his right hand. It was a ring – a large, two-finger gold ring that covered the entire upper portion of his fingers.

"HO' DAT DO'… HO' DAT DO'!!!" he shouted again, as he rudely brushed by her on the stairs.

After they passed, she was about to continue running for the train, but stopped. Something caught her eye on the ground. The one wearing the baggiest pair of jeans had apparently dropped something out of his pocket as he blazed by. From a distance, it just looked like a wadded up piece of green paper. But when she bent down for a closer look she could see that it was money. When she picked it up and unfolded it, she was surprised to see that it was actually two bills… a twenty and a ten! She thought about calling out to them, but they were making such a ruckus and were too far away to hear.

Oh, well. She thought. *That's the price they'll have to pay for scaring me half to death.*

She quickly stuffed the bills into her pocket.

When the trio reached the platform level, they had to run another twenty or thirty feet to reach the train. A family of tourists taking snapshots had to quickly move out of the way to avoid being trampled. The doors closed as soon as they ran into the empty first car.

She was a little upset that they caused her to miss the train, but considered the extra $30 in her pocket adequate compensation for the inconvenience. With no longer a need to run, she walked the rest of the way down the stairs. As she neared the family of tourists, she made a wide berth around them so as not to ruin their shots. She slowly walked down the platform alongside the still stationary train – hoping that its doors would reopen, but they never did. She continued walking until she reached a set of benches just past the escalator at the center of the platform. After moving a discarded *Daily News* newspaper to one side, she took a seat and settled in for what would undoubtedly be a lengthy wait for the next train.

"Honey, move a little to your left so I can get the "B" on the front in the shot!" Florence shouted, just before she snapped another photo.

"Ma, let me get a shot of you, dad and Regina," suggested Cindy.

The Clavens were making the most of their photo opportunity in front of the train. They took a series of individual and group shots in every conceivable combination. Throughout it all, Donald remained on the bench – no longer whining, but now quietly looking straight ahead, staring strangely into space.

From out of nowhere, a group of three African-American men came charging down the stairs headed directly toward them. Fearing the worst, Florence quickly moved behind a bench, and Arnold grabbed both of his daughters and held them close to him. But when one of the men began shouting, "HO DAT DO'… HO' DAT DO'," it was obvious that they were merely trying to catch the train before its doors closed. The trio ran pass the family and charged into the first car.

Bing… Bong.

The doors closed immediately behind them.

The Clavens quickly regrouped, and continued taking pictures – now, with an even greater sense of urgency since they knew the train would be leaving at any second.

Oddly, Donald didn't seem to be phased one bit by the disturbance. In fact, he barely flinched as the men ran by. He was still looking straight ahead – but not in space. His gaze was locked –

practically transfixed – on the motorman. Just as oddly, the motorman remained motionless in his cab – also facing straight ahead, but his eyes were closed and he appeared to be asleep.

As the family scrambled to take the last of their photos, Donald looked even *closer* at the motorman. Instead of a uniform, he was wearing a heavy black overcoat, glistening with grease and grime. He was a middle-aged Hispanic man, with a matted gray beard and mustache. He was also bald with a large tattoo on the right side of his head of a 5-pointed crown atop the head of a lion.

Suddenly, he began to turn his head slowly to the right in Donald's direction – stopping only when he was directly facing the youngster. The corners of his mouth began to arc upward – producing an expression that was neither a grin nor a smile. His mouth slowly opened to reveal a broken set of badly decayed, yellow-stained teeth. A forked, slimy black tongue oozed out of the blackness – undulating obscenely, as if molesting the air. At first, just a few inches long, it continued increasing in length to almost a foot. A revolting stream of thick, white mucus dangled from its tip. His eyes suddenly sprang open revealing a frightening blackness that seemed to go on forever.

Most likely in shock, the youngster remained completely still and silent throughout the motorman's hideous metamorphosis.

But then he found his voice.

A scream reverberated throughout the station – a blood-curdling, spine-chilling scream few would have thought could possibly emanate from such a small child. It was a scream that drowned out *everything*, including the noise of an incoming "V" train on the downtown platform.

"DONNIE!!!" his parents shouted in unison, as they rushed to his side.

"What is it, son… what's wrong!?" his father asked, nervously.

"Donnie, talk to me… what's wrong with you!?" Florence demanded.

"Mommy, why is he shaking like that?" Cindy asked. She stood off to the side, holding onto her little sister. They both had puzzled and worried looks on their faces.

A small group of onlookers began to gather. Donald continued to scream hysterically. Frantically writhing back and forth on the bench, he appeared to be trying to escape from something. The sheer look of terror on his face convinced his parents that this was much more than an ordinary tantrum thrown by a cranky child. He kept pointing forward to the train, which was now moving out of the station.

"Son, it's just a train! You were just on it!" Arnold told him. "What are you so afraid of!?"

All attempts by his family – and even a few of the onlookers – to calm him down failed. He continued to scream to the point where he was almost hoarse. When he started to hyperventilate, someone in the crowd suggested they call 911. Arnold wasn't sure medical attention was needed, but he knew he had to get his son out of the station as quickly as possible. After conferring with his wife, he scooped the child up in his arms and ran up the stairs toward the exit. Florence was right on his heels, followed closely by Cindy, who held Regina tightly by the hand. The small group of assembled onlookers made a few comments to each other, then, nonchalantly disbanded – each heading in a different direction.

"Please be careful when riding the escalator."
"Please do not sit on the steps or the handrail."
"Please watch your step while getting on and off."
"Have a nice day."

Melissa had been sitting on the bench for a couple minutes, listening to a string of recorded safety announcements looping over the PA system of the nearby escalator. She wondered if it was really necessary to constantly remind people of such basic things. She also wondered why the train was still sitting in the station. The fact that she had missed it was bad enough; having to watch it idle for so long right in front of her with its doors still closed was like rubbing salt in the wound.

Normally, she would have been highly annoyed, but today, it didn't seem to bother her much at all. The jubilation she was experiencing over her pending nuptials had a way of canceling out all of life's little negativity. All she could think about was just how wonderful life was going to be as a married woman.

A child's scream suddenly resounded throughout the station – fracturing the robotic drone of the safety announcements. Some type of commotion was going on at the front of the platform. She leaned forward to see what was happening, but too many obstacles blocked her view. At the same time, the train slowly began to leave the station.

Finally! She thought.

After a few moments, the screams gradually started to wane in the distance. The train then came to an abrupt, screeching stop.

Oh, great! Maybe they've decided to reopen the doors after all!

She quickly stood up and approached the train – elated that her wait wasn't going to be as long as she thought. When the doors still didn't open, she looked towards the front of the platform and could see that the first car was already in the tunnel. Realizing that the doors probably wouldn't open with a portion of the train already out of the station, she leaned in close to see if she could hear any announcement from the conductor explaining what was going on. She heard nothing. She was about to return to her seat when a strange sound caught her attention. Interspersed amongst the recorded safety announcements were what sounded like screams – not the sharp, pronounced screams of the child she heard moments earlier, but muffled screams of several grown men coming from somewhere inside one of the cars at the front of the train. At first, she thought it was just her imagination. But the more she listened, the more distinct the screams became. She found it odd that no one in the station seemed to be paying much attention to them, but considering the earlier outburst, she assumed everyone had simply grown accustomed to such disturbances.

Gradually, the screaming began to cease.

After a brief pause, the train lurched forward and continued its journey out of the station. She returned to her seat as the last car zoomed by. As she watched it leave, she was overcome by a strange, but very welcomed sensation. She felt a sense of peace – a peace she hadn't felt for months within the subway system, or *anywhere*, for that matter. She then turned her attention to the newspaper lying next to her on the bench. Initially catching her eye was the big, bold headline on the front page: ***STATE OF STUPIDITY*** – a story about a penny-pinching New York State official who refused a request for a free NYS flag for a Staten Island soldier stationed in Iraq. He wanted to charge him $49.95. As she shook her head in disgust, her attention was captured by something else on the page… the date at the top.

November 30, 2003

A surge of emotions washed over her – bringing a tear to her eye and a tiny smile to her face.

"Happy anniversary, mom and dad," she whispered. "Happy 30th anniversary!"